Outstanding praise for the n

A GOOD MAN

"In this deceptively light but ocean-deep sendup of dating and reality television, Murray takes a fun, reflective look at interracial relationships . . . the religious elements are always uplifting and never overbearing, and readers should brace for a three-hanky finale."
—*Publishers Weekly*

"Murray orchestrates another smart, entertaining interracial romance . . . Murray's wonderful characters, caring perspective, humor, and the story's fabulous ending make this a winning read."
—*Booklist*

"It's hard to be more surprised by a story's direction. What starts out as a retelling of finding romance through a reality show turns out to be a sweet, funny tale of people who refuse to sink to the lowest level. The fact that they find their heart's desire is the bonus. Readers will be cheering for all of Murray's characters to find their joy."
—*RT Book Reviews*

"J. J. Murray uses the reality TV show and the behind-the-scenes machinations to launch a romantic comedy between well-developed characters with a unique introspective style. The burdens of interracial love are interwoven without a squeamish approach. On the flip side, the blessings of interracial love are celebrated with a masterful touch that rings true with genuine respect and consideration. *A Good Man* earns a place at the top of the to-be-read pile."
—*USA Today*

Turn the page for more rave reviews
for the novels of J. J. Murray!

2013

OCT

CH

I'LL BE YOUR EVERYTHING

"Tart and topical commentary about a caricatured New York subculture of 20-somethings."
—*Publishers Weekly*

"Murray's heroine is sharp-tongued but totally lovable . . . fast moving, laugh-out-loud funny and smart."
—*RT Book Reviews*

"A sexy story of love, romance, and getting even."
—*Upscale Magazine*

THE REAL THING

"Murray tells a sexy story of interracial love that's long on charm, romance, and humor."
—*Booklist*

SHE'S THE ONE

"*The Taming of the Shrew* meets Hollywood in this hilarious tale about a diva dethroned the hard way. Murray's dialogue sparkles, and the characters are witty and fun, especially Bianca Baptista, the beleaguered assistant. Readers won't want to miss this clever, steamy nod to the Great Bard."
—*Booklist*

you
give
good
love

Books by J. J. Murray

RENEE AND JAY

SOMETHING REAL

ORIGINAL LOVE

I'M YOUR GIRL

CAN'T GET ENOUGH OF YOUR LOVE

TOO MUCH OF A GOOD THING

THE REAL THING

SHE'S THE ONE

I'LL BE YOUR EVERYTHING

A GOOD MAN

YOU GIVE GOOD LOVE

Published by Kensington Publishing Corporation

you
give
good
love

J.J.
Murray

KENSINGTON BOOKS
www.kensingtonbooks.com

KENSINGTON BOOKS are published by

Kensington Publishing Corp.
119 West 40th Street
New York, NY 10018

ISBN-13: 978-0-7582-7725-1
ISBN-10: 0-7582-7725-3
First Kensington Trade Paperback Printing: October 2013

eISBN-13: 978-0-7582-7727-5
eISBN-10: 0-7582-7727-X
First Kensington Electronic Edition: October 2013

10 9 8 7 6 5 4 3 2 1

Printed in the United States of America

For Amy

Acknowledgments

I'd like to thank Astrid Arzu for her excellent descriptions of life in Edmonton and what it's like to grow up as an "Island girl" in Canada—*write* your novel now. I'd also like to thank Vacirca "Vadie" Vaughn for all things West Indian, body paint, black cake, and *patois*—*finish* writing another novel . . . and start the next one.

I hear America singing, the varied carols I hear . . .

—Walt Whitman

OCTOBER 13

Only 72 more shopping days
until Christmas . . .

Chapter 1

Hope Warren was depressed because she had nothing else to be.

And her feet hurt.

Her feet were depressed, too.

"*Mes pieds font mal,*" she whispered in French, as appropriate a language as any for a depressed woman to speak. Hope had owned her depression since one cold, blustery Christmas Eve when her heart broke and refused to mend itself. Depression was simply an expected guest Hope never expected to leave.

Standing in front of a Xerox DocuTech high speed printer nine to six Monday through Friday and ten to five Saturdays didn't help Hope's *pieds*. Neither did the antifatigue safety mat that allegedly gave her feet some comfort. Hope looked down at the size-seven indentations on the mat, indentations she had earned from working for Thrifty Digital Printing on Flatbush Avenue in Brooklyn, New York, for fifty hours a week, her feet and thoughts screaming.

For eight of the last ten years.

She focused on the digital numbers, dials, and buttons and listened to Mr. Healy, a hoodie-wearing, long-haired Irishman who usually came in at 5:30 PM to get his ridiculous greeting cards printed in black and white on sixty-five-pound stock coated on both sides.

Dylan Healy, president of Odd Duck Limited Greeting Cards, usually needed his lame duck cards as soon as possible. "Have to hit the PO bright and early every Saturday morning," he said just about every time, only "early" came out as "*air*-lee," which seemed to make Dylan Healy more Irish than the Irish-American he was.

As a result, Hope rarely left at six, and Thrifty didn't pay her any overtime, an unpleasant fact that left her PO'd at the man who had to "hit the PO bright and *air*-lee."

I get the privilege of reading Mr. Healy's cards later, Hope thought, *all one hundred of the same freaking front and inside copy. If his cards were at least mildly amusing it might not be so bad, but his ideas are brutal. One of his cards read, "You had me at . . ." on the cover and "Jell-O" on the inside with a huge mound of Jell-O in a bowl. You had me at Jell-O. What? Another card had "I will always . . ." on the cover and "shove you" inside with a feminine stick figure hand pushing a long-haired stick figure man over a ledge. Brutal! He wastes his money using heavy stock paper and coating. He could get by with lighter stock and no coating at all.*

At least he has the name of his company right. Odd Duck. Check out his beak! Are those bleach spots on his jeans? No. Those are multicolored paint splotches. Long black hair over his ears, dark-brown eyes, rounded shoulders, a little over 180 centimeters—excuse me, a little over six feet tall—and definitely overly outgoing in a typical Irish-American, smiling, in-your-face way. Because we only have three major clients, however, Mr. Healy is paying a good chunk of my paycheck, so I have to tolerate him, his cards, and his accent.

"And how much does it cost to fold them again?" Mr. Healy asked.

The same cost per card as it was yesterday and the day before that and the day before that, Hope thought. *The man is only here to flirt with Kiki Clarke, who I have secretly nicknamed "Rafiki." I like Jamaicans and all "Island" people, but she is too Jamaican, if that's possible. She's too colorful! All the time! She sighs audibly as if her job is so freaking hard. All she has to do is stand there, greet customers, and smile. Instead she giggles, looks cute in her multicolored scarves, tops, and* bandeaux *that hold back a mountain of braided hair, and struts around in her tight jeans, singing and dancing to music only she can hear, and ringing up sales while bobbing her head back and forth like an old school Rastafarian. She jiggles through her shifts with too many teeth, too-wide eyes, too-long dangling earrings, and too many jingling bangles, baubles, and bracelets. The* vooman *may be curvier than a mountain road, but a speck of dust may be smarter than she is. Kiki hasn't been here long, so maybe there's more to her than meets the eye—but all she* does *is meet the eye!*

Every time I look up from this machine, it seems there's an entirely new staff here, and once again, my latest manager, Justin Tuggle, has left early to pick up "an important order" that I'll never run through a machine. Justin is almost a circle sprouting stick legs in his purple belly shirt, unkempt dusty-brown hair flying over bushy blond eyebrows, a boy's face quivering on a man's middle-aged, round body, a thin voice quavering over lips lost in the flab somewhere under his nose.

Hope looked down through her thick glasses at her old Kenetrek hiking boots. *These boots have outlasted six managers.*

Bad managers.

Good boots.

Hope tuned out Mr. Healy and worked herself into a deeper, darker level of depression. She had every right to be depressed, and not only because of her stationary, monotonous, mind-numbing job as background dancer for a singing Jamaican *ragga*.

American television, movies, magazines, her old-fashioned Bahamian parents, her Trini grandparents, and her older sister, Faith, had told Hope that she would never be beautiful. Long, brown, Medusa-like dreadlocks framed a dark-black face highlighted by a small, flat nose, somewhat smooth skin, severe cheekbones that held up her glasses, dark-brown eyes a little too wide-set and huge behind those glasses, plump brown lips pinched perpetually into a straight line, and a long tight jaw and chin. The perfect teeth behind her lips rarely emerged unless she was eating, and she worried that years of grinding her back teeth at Thrifty would cause permanent damage to her jawbone. She considered herself linear instead of flat as a board, though her sister had once told her, "Hope, you are so flat, a man will get splinters giving you a hug." Aside from a nice set of abs, a flat stomach, and long legs, Hope Warren had none of the curves she was supposed to have as an African-Bahamian-Canadian woman transplanted to Brooklyn, and she wore a plain blue work smock over baggy jeans to hide her flatness and her hardness, her heavy locks bunched with a simple white hemp string.

I will never be an American booty queen, Hope thought. *My derriere is not completely flat. It has some roundness, but I am not nor ever will be a Rastafarian.*

Hope's faculty advisor at the University of Alberta in Edmonton had told her she would never be hired anywhere in the world with only a BFA (Bachelor of Fine Arts) and a minor in French. "Get your master's in art and design, learn to speak French fluently, and doors will open anywhere you go in the art world."

So she did.

No doors opened in Edmonton, Calgary, or Vancouver. Toronto and Montreal were wasted trips.

Against the wishes of her parents, themselves emigrants from the Bahamas whose parents had emigrated to the Bahamas from Trinidad, Hope left Canada, escaping to New York, the supposed arts capital of the States, and she still couldn't find work in her field no matter how much French she spewed. She didn't want to be the assistant to the assistant curator at a minor museum, and she was too truthful to work for very long in any of the hundreds of galleries in and around New York City. "Those paintings and sculptures are brutal" or *"Ces peintures et sculptures sont brutaux,"* she would have to say eventually, and she would be out of a job. All she did artistically now was doodle on the backs of rejected and wrinkled copies and occasionally try to make sense of the modern art at the Brooklyn Museum.

Most of the art there looked *brutaux* to her, too.

Her Brooklyn-born almost-fiancé, Odell Wilson, had told her eight years ago that she would never marry, and so far he had been right. "Who would marry your plain, hard, underemployed ass anyway?" he had said in parting. "You only needed me for a green card anyway."

Odell wanted me for more than my ability to speak French, didn't he? Hope thought. *And I only wanted Odell because . . . Hmm. It wasn't the sex. It wasn't that good. I had much more fun after he left.*

When Odell had said good-bye that fateful Christmas Eve, Hope hadn't reminded him that he had once hinted at getting married and having children, that he had craved her "long, hard, muscular body," and that he loved the feel of her "solid muscles and sharp bones." She didn't remind him that he thought she was an exotic "foreigner" since she was from the rolling prairies of Canada by way of the Bahamas and Trinidad and spoke sexy French.

Instead of running back to Alberta's turquoise lakes and prairies blazing with yellows and purples, I went through the five-year hassle of becoming a naturalized U.S. citizen. Instead of returning to a province that has half the population and over five hundred times the area of New York City, I became a citizen of Brooklyn. Instead of dodging bison, moose, bull elk, mule deer, and bighorn sheep, I dodge pedestrians, taxis, motorcycles, street vendors, and buses. Now that I'm only a plain, ordinary black American woman, no man will look twice at me, even if I drop in a French phrase every now and then, tell him that I'm originally a West Indian Island girl, and shake my dreadlocks at him. A real man, American or otherwise, should know what to do with all this hair.

Hope sighed and looked up, her bunched locks swaying across her back. *Kiki gives Mr. Healy the same information every day. Is Mr. Healy brain-dead or what? Kiki and Mr. Healy would make the perfect couple. They could even make a tape of their daily conversations and play the tapes instead of talking to each other for the rest of their lives. Just press play.*

"As you know, Mr. Healy," Kiki was saying, "it takes time to fold your cards using our Baum—"

"Your what?" Mr. Healy interrupted with a smile. "Your *bomb?*"

Get me out of here! Hope moaned in her mind. *This conversation never changes! Four straight weeks of "Your bomb?" I'm about to go inhale some toner! I may paper-cut myself to death! If this machine had moving parts I could easily access, I'd stick in a dreadlock and let the machine suck me through!*

"Our Baum Eighteen Twenty-Two, Mr. Healy," Kiki said. "It is a right angle folder, and we guarantee—"

"Does it also do left angles?" Mr. Healy interrupted.

I'm sure Mr. Healy has scribbled this idea down for his next brutal card, Hope thought. *He'll probably misspell it on purpose in an attempt to provide depth to his greetings. On the cover it will say, "I'm looking for the right angel," and inside it will say, "But I'll settle*

*for the left." Or "the leftover angel." Or "the fallen angel." Something
brutally obvious like that. Some irony is just too foolish to point out,
you know.*

Hope rarely ended her sentences with "Eh?" like a normal
Canadian. Instead, she substituted "you know" to make herself feel
more like an American.

Hope ground her teeth, reached into her pocket, and felt a thin
five-dollar bill and some change, and she became even more depressed.

Hope's checkbook and bank account told her she would never
own a car, a big home, a designer wardrobe, or even a kitchen ap-
pliance from this millennium. Her retirement account, however,
was off-limits, no matter how bad life got. One day Hope planned
to retire to her own beach house somewhere, and so far, she had
pinched and saved $48,000.

In another, oh, thirty *years, I'll be able to afford the down payment for a tiny beach house looking out on the ocean somewhere. I'll
be sixty, and I probably won't be able to walk over or even see the
dunes or the shoreline clearly, but I'll finally have that blessed piece
of peace and quiet.*

Hope's smoking electric stove told her she'd never be able to
cook as well as her sister did. Her sister, Faith, was an only child
until Hope came along, and Faith played that role to the vicious
hilt, even if her soufflés sometimes resembled diarrhea.

"You will never take my place as the queen of *this* family,
Hope," Faith had told her. "I *own* Mudda and Fadda. They *never*
wanted you. You only got the leftover *specks* of their DNA. You are
a loose collection of ugly. You will *always* be the switched-at-birth
mistake child."

Hope wouldn't have been surprised to find out that she had
been switched at birth. Faith had curves in all the right places,
curves that had the Canadian boys and now her husband, Winston
Holt, the "guru of natural gas" at TransCanada Corporation, eating
out of her glands. Faith and "Winny" lived in a penthouse in the
prestigious Carlisle condominium tower in downtown Edmonton,
spent a mint on Carrara marble floors and washroom tile, spent a
bank vault on Tuscan and French window treatments, and posed
for pictures wherever they went.

Posers, Hope thought. *That's all they are. At least they don't have to worry how they'll pay their rent this month or any month of any year for that matter.*

She checked the clock. *Another hour of this monotony, and I'm still alive. Why? I'd kill for a good American drive-by right now.* She closed her eyes. *No one does drive-bys on copy shops, not even in the movies. No one even tries to rob this place.*

Hope opened her eyes and squinted at Mr. Healy flirting with Kiki. *She is gay, Mr. Healy. Can't you tell? Didn't her "Another Friend of ELLEN'S" button give you a clue? Can't you see the "I was gay before it got trendy" bumper sticker on her rainbow-colored backpack? Don't waste your breath. You should see Kiki's Hungarian lumberjack girlfriend, Angie, who could probably cut down a spruce tree one-handed with a nail file.*

"So I can pick these up tomorrow?" Mr. Healy asked.

Kiki shot a glance at Hope. "I am sure our production staff will once again make your order their top priority, Mr. Healy."

I am the production staff, Hope thought. *You shouldn't try to glorify me, you know. I doubt you even know that I have an MFA. Call me the copy girl. I know you're thinking it. You're the funny cashier girl, Mr. Yarmouth is the invisible owner, Justin is the non-managing manager, and I'm the hardworking copy girl. Know your place in the Thrifty Digital Printing pecking order.*

"Hope, do you have time to run these tonight?" Kiki asked.

Hope nodded. *Sure. I have plenty of time. I have no life, no boyfriend, no lumberjack girlfriend, and no hope, apparently, of a drive-by shooting at this copy shop this evening. I already have to lock up and turn out the lights again. What's an extra half hour of unpaid monotony anyway?*

"Great," Mr. Healy said, smiling at Hope. "Half up front, right?"

"Right, Mr. Healy," Kiki said, taking his money.

He usually pays in cash, Hope thought. *Whom is he trying to impress on Flatbush Avenue? He probably can't afford a bank account, and from the looks of his greeting cards, maybe he isn't smart enough to fill out the bank account application.*

"Um, Kiki," Mr. Healy said, "you wouldn't want to maybe get

something to eat when you get off, would you? I've always wanted to go to The Islands over on Washington Avenue, and—"

"I have a date," Kiki interrupted.

With an eight-foot-tall Hungarian woman named Angyalka, which means, ironically, "little angel," Hope thought. Where's the symmetry in that? Five-foot-nothing Jamaican Kiki and Angie, whom Kiki calls "On-Gee," the Sasquatch goulash woman. Ellen's friends are getting taller and wider. At least Kiki and "On-Gee" have something, though I'm not sure what, especially since Kiki never says "I have a girlfriend" to stop Mr. Healy's advances.

I used to be someone's girlfriend, Hope thought. I had short hair and an appetite then. Why did I ever put up with Odell saying I was the whitest black woman on earth? I'm not. Just because I don't use American slang and I carry myself with dignity at all times does not make me white. My Trinidadian-Bahamian-Canadian family raised me this way. Hope sighed again. I shouldn't miss him still, but I do. I wasn't in love with him, and he broke my heart. Maybe I miss the idea of having a boyfriend.

"Oh," Mr. Healy was saying. "Well, um, Kiki, anytime you're free, we can . . . um, go somewhere to eat, okay?"

You can't, Hope thought. You're not tall enough or feminine enough, and you don't have the right plumbing. I shouldn't be thinking about plumbing. My plumbing hasn't been flowing since the Winter Olympics. It was during the luge. Hope rolled her eyes. Odell lasted about as long as that event, too. They need to make that luge track longer.

Kiki handed Mr. Healy his change. "Have a nice evening, Mr. Healy."

As Mr. Healy strode out to Flatbush Avenue, a blast of cold October wind fluttered paper all around Hope as she drifted away from her machine and snatched up Mr. Healy's latest hand-drawn card. The outside of the card read: "The best laid plans of mice and men . . ." Hope paused, took a breath, held it, and opened the card to read "aren't really all that different, are they?" She almost smiled at a simple drawing of a stick figure man with long hair and a somewhat rodent-shaped mouse sharing a slice of cheese pizza.

Better, Hope thought. The drawings are still brutal, but . . . better. That Microsoft Paint program sure makes people think they have talent. I'll bet Mr. Healy got the inspiration for this card by looking at his computer mouse. I know I can doodle better than that with my eyes closed, and all I really have to do is take off my glasses.

The clock ticked past six.

Hope ran Mr. Healy's card through the DocuTech, then shot the copies through the Baum. She looked at the clock.

6:38 PM.

"Permettez-nous de faire la promenade à Brooklyn," she whispered, turning out the lights and locking the door behind her. "Let's go for a walk in Brooklyn."

Chapter 2

Bundled in a heavy chocolate-brown wool coat, her dreads spill-ing out of a dark-brown hemp toque, Hope weaved through heavy foot traffic down Flatbush Avenue, the lights of the Manhat-tan Bridge behind her, her stomach grumbling. A subway ride to her apartment would only take nine minutes, a bus ride slightly longer, but Hope preferred to walk because a walk gave her stom-ach aromas to hate her for.

She skirted other pedestrians past Yummy Taco, Taro Sushi, and the Burrito Bar.

No gas-inducing food tonight. I should have gone up to Court Street to Tim Hortons for some Timbits or cheese croissants. No. Too much fromage *gives me gas, too.*

Hope passed Prospect Perk Café, Tom's, Café Shane, Natural Blend, Coffee Bites, Teddy's, and The Islands.

No Drano or jerk chicken tonight.

Her stomach pouted because it missed double-doubles (coffee with two creams and two sugars), oxtail soup, curry goat, and jerk chicken.

She entered her apartment building on Washington Avenue in Prospect Heights. Once inside her "amazing newly renovated charming two-room studio near the Brooklyn Museum with bright natural sunlight for *only* $1,400 a month," Hope turned on her only overhead light and looked up at the high ceiling. Her rental agent had pointed at those ceilings and said, "Don't they have lots of character?" Hope often wondered how many characters had hanged themselves from the main beam among the cross-thatch of beams in that high ceiling.

I'm thinking . . . twenty-seven. Are those scratch marks? Someone had second thoughts? Here?

She sighed and looked out the only window not smudged with grime, a lonely one-foot-square window squeezed between two much larger windows. *God, how I miss birch and aspen trees and wild roses. I miss the River Valley, where the North Saskatchewan River divides Edmonton with a vein of pure green forest, the sky endlessly blue, golden fields rolling like the ocean in all directions. All I see outside this soiled window are cars, buses, taxis, graffiti, and the shadowed apartment building on the other side of Washington Avenue.*

Hardwood floors, harder water, and stained steel appliances greeted Hope in a kitchen where she only saw "bright natural sunlight" on Sundays, when she wasn't working. Her granite countertops looked and felt like old asphalt. Cabinets occasionally shut and stayed shut. The Formica table and chairs leaned mostly to the left, and her washroom fixtures only wept or dripped on days ending in Y. Warped shelving opposite the refrigerator held no pictures, knickknacks, or bric-a-brac, instead displaying nothing but a former moth or two.

She had few pieces of furniture. A red quilt tried to hide a secondhand gray futon that slumped under her windows, and a lamp-less thrift store lamp table hulked beside it. A thirdhand coffee table held down a dark-gray braided oval rug like a wooden skiff beached on an island. A gunmetal-gray metal wardrobe concealed her meager stock of clothes, its single drawer rusted shut years ago, a wire metal shoe caddy displaying a dozen pairs of shoes and boots in the corner beside it. A coatrack collected a maudlin, earth-tone assortment of toques, scarves, and jackets, none of which quite matched one another or anything else she wore.

Hope stood dead center in her apartment under the main beam. *I am so exposed here. I can see everything I own in this life by turning once in a circle.*

At first, Hope didn't think she'd need a bed, so she had bought the futon. After several sleepless nights of tossing, turning, the squeal of metal on metal, and a frisky metal bar digging into her back, Hope had sacrificed some of her beach house money for a wooden platform bed, an antique hurricane lamp, and a clock radio resting atop a matching nightstand.

She frowned at Whack, a stray mixed-breed cat that had adopted her a few years ago and refused to leave, now resting on her bed from whatever cats do for eleven hours at a time in a nearly empty apartment in Brooklyn.

One day, Hope thought, *that cat will greet me at the door. What does Whack do all day? She probably tries to catch all that "bright natural sunlight," gives up, and then leaves as much of her black, white, brown, orange, and gray hair on my bed as she can. I've told her hundreds of times, "The futon is all yours," and all she does is blink. I point at the braided rug and show her my claws, but she never gets the hint.*

Hope looked at her used twenty-inch television/DVD combo gathering dust. She looked at the rectangular space on the counter where her Bose Wave radio had died one morning during *The Howard Stern Show.* She didn't miss the music or the noise—or Howard Stern. Aside from a Kindle, which contained hundreds of cheap electronic novels, and a decent laptop computer, there wasn't much to see in Hope's apartment.

She had no clutter.

And no life.

She only splurged on the platform bed, the Kindle, the laptop, and the extortionate rates for high-speed Internet and satellite TV, and she often didn't even feel like sleeping, getting online, or reading.

Or thinking.

She glanced at her yellowing crème-white walls. *These walls are so thin they may as well be transparent.*

She closed her eyes and listened to the neighbors around her. "*Limpie su cuarto ahora, Juan!*" cried Mrs. Carranza, a refugee from Guatemala who had a hellion for a teenage son next door. "*Che cosa vuoi dire, si non cucinare? Ho fame!*" spat Mr. Antonelli, who lived across the hall, worked for Con Ed., drank too much, expected his wife to feed him the second he got home, and sometimes tried to open Hope's door by mistake. "*Vamos nos conservar a loja abrem-se depois amanha,*" said one Vaz twin to the other, co-owners of a struggling Brazilian bodega in Midwood, as they trudged up the stairs past Hope's door. "Where the %&#! is the %&#!-ing remote control!" yelled Mr. Marusak in his thick Ukrainian accent in the apartment below.

Hope, who rarely added French to the mix of voices because she didn't want to confuse her neighbors any more than they already were, sat on her bed and cradled Whack in her arms.

Whack didn't purr.

She rubbed behind Whack's ears.

Whack still didn't purr.

Whack had *never* purred.

I have a defective cat. She has her own tongue. There's really nothing wrong with that, but it's strange to have a cat that is as quiet as a mouse. Hope closed her eyes. *A cat as quiet as a mouse.*

I am so tired that my mixed metaphors are starting to make sense. Hope lay back, nestling her locks into a pillow. *I work, I sometimes eat, I sleep, I sometimes dream, I bathe, I feed Whack—*

I think I fed Whack today.

She left Whack on the bed and slipped into the kitchen, which smelled of Lysol, bleach, and Whack's litter box. She looked at Whack's water and food "bowls," Tupperware containers that had melted into interesting Cubist art after repeated use and misuse in the microwave.

Whack's bowls are as empty as my life has become. She sighed. *Okay, it's not true* all *the time. Just most of the time.*

Hope poured some dry cat food into one container and filled the other with water.

Whacked slipped in and began to eat.

Whack still didn't purr.

Sometimes, life is whack.

Hope rubbed Whack's back.

Whack continued eating silently.

Sometimes life is whacker than Whack.

Life is a cat that does not purr.

"I am so wise," she whispered. She shook her head. "No, I'm not wise. I actually thought Odell was giving me a present that night. I thought he was giving me an engagement ring." *Yeah, he gave me the boot instead, and he left me with an unfilled stocking.*

Hope went to her bed, pulled back a quilt, and fell onto the mattress. She put her glasses on her nightstand and stared at the ceiling, which now looked like a blurry game of giant pickup sticks. A moment later, a fuzzy ball of fur leaped onto her stomach, rolled off, and disappeared under the quilt.

"Good night, Whack," Hope whispered.

Then Hope floated off to sleep, her night as silent as her cat but as loud as her neighbors.

Will someone please *find Mr. Marusak's remote control!*

OCTOBER 14

*Only 71 more shopping days
until Christmas . . .*

Chapter 3

Early the next morning, Hope hiked north on Washington Avenue, dodging pigeons and hoping her depression would leave her alone. Her depression was as persistent as a cricket Hope could hear but not see, as constant as an atomic clock, and as rude as the average maître d'.

Hope passed Divine Connection Hair Spa.

I should go inside and sit in the waiting area one day, Hope thought. *I'm sure my presence would get their hopes up and make their scissor fingers twitch. My hair would hit the floor with a* sound. *I know I have saved thousands of dollars these last eight years by not letting anyone else touch my hair and hundreds more for doing my own nails.*

She grumbled at Love Liquors & Wines.

That's a lot of truth in advertising there. Folks around here do love their liquor and wine. I wish there was more of that kind of advertising. A cigar store could announce, "Get cancer here! Cancer on sale now! Smoke until your lips fall off!" A fast food place could advertise, "Get fat here! Hardening of the arteries on sale now! Eat until your gallbladder explodes!"

She moved west on Sterling past Beacon of Hope House and Duryea Presbyterian.

I wonder if there's truly any hope at either place. Hmm. Churches only seem to offer hope at Christmas. I wonder why.

Hope went north on Flatbush Avenue past Bikram Yoga.

Yoga: human pretzels in search of enlightenment. Given the choice between medication and meditation, I choose reality. It's cheaper. Yoga is only organized yawning and stretching anyway.

She shook her head as she passed Victoria's Secret.

Why is there a Victoria's Secret store on Flatbush Avenue? Real *women walk to work here every day and night. Those aren't real women in those windows. Those brainless models would freeze to death in Edmonton on a* normal *winter's day, when the temperature barely rises above -17°C (1°F) all day. Those so-called "angels" are already wearing Santa hats. It's freaking October! Buy these wisps of fabric, ladies, and keep Christmas and your man coming all year long. Wear these little nothings so you can keep jingling his bells throughout the holidays. Waste your money on these spandex Band-Aids so that* we *can have a merry profitable Christmas.*

They look like ho, ho, hos.

Hope marched past the U.S. Army Recruiting Station.

Where they failed me because they don't allow blind soldiers to join. Hope blew out a steamy breath. *So they* said. *I'll bet it was because I was once Canadian. Americans don't trust foreigners, especially if they speak the same language. I told them I spoke fluent French, and the recruiter said, "They don't speak French in Afghanistan, and it's highly unlikely that the French will ever be a threat to the United States."*

Hope shuddered. *That was the* last *thing I will ever do on a whim. What was I thinking? Odell dumped me, I stopped taking care of my hair, and I nearly joined the U.S. Army. I actually walked in and filled out all the forms. I could have been in Afghanistan, speaking* two *languages the Afghans don't understand while straining to see what I was shooting at.*

She stood in front of Thrifty Digital Printing, two doors down from Siri Pharmacy and the 99¢ and Up Store. *For another penny, it could have been a dollar store. Why does ninety-nine cents seem larger than a dollar?*

As she reached for the front door handle precisely at nine, Justin opened the door.

My lovely boss, Hope thought. *Misery loves company. Hmm. If misery loves company, why are so many people alone?*

"Right on time as usual," Justin said, sighing a rank breath past Hope's ducking head. "You're always on time, aren't you?"

Why does Justin make it seem as if being punctual is a problem? Hope thought. *Did I interrupt you doing something you shouldn't be doing, Justin? Like working? Please don't sigh at me with your brutal breath.* She looked at his outfit. *White boat shoes, no socks, brown khakis, and a purple polo. This is his managerial attire. This is a problem. This man is at least forty, but he dresses like a child. Balding, tubby, bad breath, stick fingers protruding out of fat hands, no fashion sense. This is what passes for a store manager in America. On top of that, he's a die-hard New York Rangers fan! I know I'm supposed to be an Edmonton Oilers fan, but the Montreal Canadiens have nicer uniforms.*

Hope moved past the self-serve copier and around the front counter to the back "paper wall," where hundreds of reams of paper rose to the ceiling. *To keep these old walls from caving in.* She draped her coat over a heavily duct-taped rolling swivel chair, donned her smock, and checked the mainframe computer for overnight Internet orders.

"Um, Hope, right?" Justin said.

Hope nodded. *I'm right on time as usual, and as usual, Justin, you don't remember my name. You've had months to learn my name, and it only has one syllable. You must be on drugs. I wonder what kind. I should ask him. I'd like to be able to forget other people's names, too.*

"Kiki called in sick," Justin said, "so you'll have to run front, um, too."

Hope blinked. *Maybe Kiki's Hungarian lumberjack smothered her, oh no. I've always been worried about the size difference. If the "On-Gee" tree falls, Kiki the braided shrub will die.*

"We shouldn't be too busy, um . . ." Justin said.

"Hope," Hope said.

"It's Wednesday, right, Hope?" Justin asked. "We're always slow on Wednesdays, aren't we?"

You're slow every day, Justin, Hope thought. *It must be part of your job description. The owner, Mr. Yarmouth, whom I have seen at most a dozen times in ten years, interviewed five people, and you were the slowest. Therefore, you were hired. Why can't you run front, Justin? There are a dozen orders back here, and all you're going to do is go into that office, get on Facebook, and look at porn. Oh, wait. That's right. You can't run front. You're in charge of the* back, *where you do the daily totals. Can* you *add? Please don't multiply. If I could subtract you, I would.*

Justin sidled up to her, looking over her shoulder at the computer screen. "Are there many overnight orders?"

Gee, they're numbered right there on the screen, Justin. The last order has a little number twelve next to it. That means there are twelve *overnight orders. Isn't counting fun?*

Hope shook her head.

"Well, uh, good," Justin said.

Though tedious, the orders aren't that complex. A couple of restaurants, a few hospitals, one from Brooklyn Borough. Maybe an hour's work here, Justin. Nothing I can't handle by hitting the commands you still *don't know like* ON, FORMAT, *and* SEND. *Luckily, these orders are all black and white on plain white paper.*

Justin started shuffling toward the back. "I'll be in the office if you need me."

I won't need you. Come to think of it, no one will need you, Justin. Isn't that why you're working here? I'd call him an imbecile, but that would be a compliment.

After filling the DocuTech to capacity with eight reams of white paper, Hope configured, ordered, and sent all twelve jobs to print. As they finished, she pulled them from the exit tray, shoved them into plain white plastic bags, attached work orders, and stacked the bags under the counter.

And now, to watch the front.

It never seems to move.

It just sits there all white, gray, and smudged.

That ficus plant on the counter is growing out of control, probably from all the "nutrients" like snot, spit, dirt, sweat, and food crumbs our customers leave behind on the counter. Kiki wipes up that daily concoction and whisks it into the dirt under the ficus.

Bored after an hour of watching nothing happen and seeing no customers, Hope counted red and yellow floor tiles. *It's the same number every time.*

She watched no one stopping to buy used DVDs and blue jeans from Mr. Al-Hamsi, a vendor on the sidewalk across the street in front of a Chase bank branch. *Really, Mr. Al-Hamsi? DVDs and jeans was the can't-miss idea to make you rich this morning? You know, whenever I buy a new previously watched and scratched DVD, I always feel the need to wear a pair of almost-new, gently stained blue jeans.* She sighed. *I'll bet he's selling Christmas DVDs already, too. What a waste. Doesn't he know there are people who hate Christmas? I know he doesn't mean to be cruel. He's just trying to make a dollar or two like everyone else.*

Hope missed seeing Dario selling oranges, apples, and bananas at his cart under his red-and-white umbrella. *Dario was colorful, despite all the fruit flies and, oh, his arrest for selling more than nectarines. No wonder his prices were as high as his regular customers were.*

The front door opened precisely at eleven, and Dylan Healy, Mr. Odd Duck himself, entered.

Hope located and picked up Mr. Healy's order, placing the bag on the counter and ringing him up.

"Hi," Mr. Healy said.

Hope nodded. *I do not say "hi," "hey," "bonjour," or "how you doin'?" In fact, I don't intend to speak to anyone today. Kiki told me there's a National Day of Silence in April. I am declaring National Shut Your Mouth Day today, and I intend to keep it holy. I don't need any unnecessary noise today. It's hard enough maintaining a good, healthy depression in silence. Conversation spoils a high-quality depression nearly every time.*

Hope pointed at Mr. Healy's balance on the register's screen.

"This is my busiest time of year," Mr. Healy said, withdrawing his wallet.

Hope blinked. *It's October, and these aren't Halloween cards, though they're scary enough. Who would ever buy these? Maybe he sells them to blind people. Oh, excuse me. Sight-challenged people. What American political correctness foolishness. Without my glasses, I'm not sight-challenged; I'm blind, and the world is a fuzzy haze of shadows.*

"I'm getting all sorts of orders for Christmas cards these days," Mr. Healy said. "That's why I'm so busy."

My least-favorite holiday lasts for three full months now. As soon as the back-to-school sales end, here comes Santa. Joy to the brutal world and merry brutal Christmas for ninety brutal days on the radio, too. How festively, brutally miserable.

Mr. Healy handed Hope the money. "Keep the change."

Twenty-seven cents? Is he kidding? I can't take his twenty-seven cents. It might break him. He may need twenty-seven cents one day. Hope made and handed him his change.

Mr. Healy shook the change in his hand. "You need a tip jar or something. You deserve a tip for your excellent service."

This isn't a bar, mainly because we have no happy hours. I suppose I could put out a "Hope's Future Beach House" jar. Justin would never notice.

Mr. Healy pocketed his change, his bag untouched.

You have your change, you have your order, and it's time for you to leave now, Mr. Healy. Now be a good American and run along as if you actually have something interesting to do on a Wednesday morning while the rest of us work. Bye. See you. Au revoir. *Have a nice day.* Adieu. *Shoo.*

Mr. Healy smiled. "I don't sell as many cards as I used to," he said. "Christmas cards, that is."

Hope nodded. *Go away. Now. Or I'll throw ficus dirt on you.*

"People send e-mails and those e-cards instead these days," Mr. Healy said. "Or they post Facebook messages. They don't send anything with permanence, you know, something that will last, something the recipient can actually feel and touch."

You're still not going away, Hope thought. *Maybe if I just nod one more time, cut my eyes to the killer ficus, raise my eyebrows in warning, turn, and go back to the—*

Mr. Healy leaned heavily on the counter, the laminate strip crackling under his elbows.

Get off my counter.

"With a real live Christmas card, you get something to hold on to, to cherish, to show off," he said. "Look what *I* got, you know? Look who took the time to think about *me* during the holidays."

I don't waste my time looking. I barely think about myself at any time, much less the holidays.

"Some people prop them up and display them on fireplace mantels and bookcases," he said. "Want to know where I put them?"

No. I want you to leave. It's October, and you're talking about my least-favorite holiday. Maybe if I widen my eyes he'll get the hint, but he's not even looking at me. He's talking to the walls and the ceiling. Maybe if I dragged the old paper cutter up here and slammed it down a few times on a pencil—

"I tape every Christmas card I get onto the back of my door in the shape of a Christmas tree," he said. "It usually goes all the way to the floor. I put up *so* many cards. If I have any leftovers, I try to make snowflakes."

Let's see, if I kept all the Christmas cards I have ever gotten since moving to the States, I could make a triangle.

"Do you hang up Christmas cards like that?" Mr. Healy asked.

I don't even hang up stockings. They tend to be empty anyway. Hope blinked.

"Oh, I'm sorry," he said. "I'm such an idiot sometimes. You must celebrate Kwanzaa instead, right?"

Hope shook her head. *Right. Because I'm black, I celebrate Kwanzaa. What, maybe two percent of all African-Americans celebrate Kwanzaa? Do I look as if I'm in the top two percent of anything? Please leave. Now. You have your order. You have paid. You have stressed out the counter. You have graciously left hoodie lint for me to scoop up to feed the ficus later. Shoo. Some of us have to work and be depressed.*

"That gives me an idea," Mr. Healy said, squinting now at the ceiling. "Maybe I should do Kwanzaa cards this year, too. I could probably have them ready by next Friday."

Hope sighed softly because it seemed to work for Kiki. *I will get to see those Kwanzaa cards if you foolishly make them, won't I? I'll have no choice. You'll be in here with a few Kwanzaa cards for me not to laugh at, and they'll all be brutal, and since you're a white American, they'll probably be racist.* She sighed softly again. *I do not want to speak to this odd duck of Odd Duck Limited Greeting Cards! Go away now!*

"Do you have a cold?" Mr. Healy asked.

He thinks I'm sick because I refuse to speak. How presumptuous of him. He's correct, though. I am sick. I am sick of hearing his voice. Hope shook her head.

"Really? I thought you might have a touch of the laryngitis." He smiled. "You are by far the quietest person I think I've ever met in my entire life."

Because it's National Shut Your Mouth Day. I should have made a quick "National Shut Your Mouth Day" poster and taped it to the counter. All I'd need would be an open-mouthed smiley face with a big X through it for the graphic. Come on, Mr. Healy. Let me fade away and get back to work doing nothing.

"Hanukkah's tricky, but I try." He smiled and shrugged. "Not many takers, but you have to try, you know? Something for everybody, right?"

Go. Away. Now. Please. Shoo.

Mr. Healy leaned over the counter and looked Hope up and down. "One . . . twenty-five," he said.

Hope squinted.

"Maybe one twenty-seven," he said.

Hope continued to squint.

"Your weight," he said.

Which is twice your IQ! Weighing me with his eyes! What kind of man does that? Is that an Irish thing, an American thing, or an Irish-American thing? How can he tell what I weigh? I'm wearing a baggy smock and baggier jeans!

"I did a little street boxing once upon a time," he said. "I used to wrestle, too."

I used to think people had intelligence and tact! Oh, right. I'm in the States, more specifically, Brooklyn. Who goes around guessing the weight of complete strangers and continues to smile? It's not a bad smile, as smiles go. It almost makes that little fingernail of a scar on his chin disappear. He has quite a few little scars on his knuckles, too. A street boxer, huh? I'll bet the street won. But really! I have to be closer to forty-eight kilograms—I mean, one hundred and five pounds—these days. The metric system is so much nicer when it comes to weight.

Hope took a deep breath and exhaled slowly. *How can I make the evil man with the nice smile go away? He obviously is an insensitive fool who prefers the taste of his own feet in his mouth.*

"What are you, five-seven, five-eight?" Mr. Healy asked. "It's hard to tell with all your pretty hair. I'm adjusting for the height of your hair."

What is his problem? Are vital statistics that important to him, and what does he mean by "all your pretty hair"?

"I used to wrestle at one twenty-five, if you can believe it, and I was about your height at the time. I was an early bloomer."

An air-*lee bloomer. Now I can believe anything! And I am one hundred and seventy-five centimeters tall, about five-nine, thank you.*

"Thanks for making such good copies for me, Hope," Mr. Healy said. "Oh, I'm Dylan, if you didn't already know. I've been coming here for about five years now. You make the best cards in Brooklyn. I mean, you copy the best cards in Brooklyn. No, that's not right. You are the best copyist in Brooklyn. There."

Because we have excellent machines, Dylan. I can't call him Mr. Healy now. He just complimented me, the first compliment I have ever gotten here, but how does he know my name? I accidentally on purpose threw my name tag away years ago in a fit of boredom. Oh yeah. Kiki said my name just last night.

"I've been selling my Odd Duck cards for five years now," Dylan said, "and I think you've done just about all of them, Hope." He looked at the ceiling. "No, I'm pretty sure you've done all of them. You do fantastic work."

I only push some buttons, and if you'll stop pushing mine, I can go back to work. She turned to glance behind her and swallowed. "I have a lot to do, Mr. Healy," she said softly, "so if you don't mind . . ."

Dylan smiled and cocked his head to the side. "Please call me Dylan," he said. "Mr. Healy is a name fit for an old man on a TV sitcom."

"Okay, Dylan," Hope said, "I really have a lot of work to do."

Dylan smiled. "I didn't know you were Canadian."

Hope blinked. *How does he know this? I have no accent now! I'm not Canadian in any way these days, and I'm Bahamian and Trini in DNA only. I am an American.*

"Where are you from exactly, Hope?" Dylan asked.

Hope turned slowly to face the counter. "Brooklyn," Hope said.

Dylan squinted. "I meant *before* you came to Brooklyn."

Do I confuse him and say Deadmonton or Edmonchuck? Or do I really confuse him and say I come from the land of Medicine Hat, Wood Buffalo, and Red Deer? Or do I seriously confuse him and tell him I'm the emigrant Canadian daughter of emigrant Bahamian parents whose parents were emigrants from Trinidad? No. I'd need a map to explain it.

Hope decided to be civil. "Edmonton."

"Cool," Dylan said. "Cold, too, huh?"

Hope nodded.

"A lot colder than Brooklyn, huh?" Dylan said.

You'd be surprised. Weather sometimes isn't the only thing that's cold about a city. There are city men like Odell who break up with women on Christmas Eve.

"You hungry?" Dylan asked.

Hope narrowed her eyes. *Do I look hungry? I must. Just because I'm five-*nine, *thank you very much, and only weigh one hundred and maybe . . . four or five pounds, that doesn't mean I'm hungry!*

Dylan tapped an old Mickey Mouse watch on his wrist, the black leather watchband grayed, fraying, and held together by gray duct tape. "It's about lunchtime, you know."

Hope looked at the watch. *It's a watch that only tells the time. How rare and old-fashioned is that? A grown man who flirts with obvious lesbians is wearing a Mickey Mouse watch and walking shoes. Dylan is so generic, aside from his long hair. Is this the kind of man I attract?*

"It'll be my treat, Hope," Dylan said. "Is Subway okay?"

"My treat." I do like the way that sounds. His treat. Subway's okay. I like their Italian B.M.T., and he's paying, and Subway is only a few doors down next to that hair-braiding place, but they look at me funny whenever I walk by. I bet they'd like to have some of my hair. I wonder how much my hair is worth. It would be so strange to see my hair walk by me on some other woman's head. It would also be so nice to have someone buy me lunch for a change so I can save some of my change. If only I felt hungry, I'd take him up on his nice offer. But I don't, and anyway, this man has been flirting unashamedly with another Island woman right in front of me for the last month. Hope nodded slightly and set her jaw. *Dylan just last night asked freaky Kiki to go out to eat with him. The potential two-timer!*

"What about Kiki?" Hope asked.

Dylan blinked. "Kiki isn't . . . She's not here today."

Obviously. "So you just ask whoever's in front of you to go out to eat with you." *That may be the longest sentence I've spoken within these crumbling walls in the past eight years. I need to rest. I feel light-headed.*

Dylan shook his head. "I don't ask just anyone."

"But I heard you ask Kiki every day for weeks," Hope said. "What were you trying to do, wear her down like water on a rock?" *Or in Dylan's case, like milk on onyx.*

"I don't like eating alone." Dylan looked at the counter. "I figured one day Kiki would get tired of me asking her and go with me." He shook his head slightly. "I guess I was wrong, huh?"

So, if I weren't here at this counter today, Dylan would have asked someone else, maybe even Justin, and here I was about to feel special.

"Do you like to eat alone, Hope?" Dylan asked.

No, but I'm used to eating alone. Hope shrugged.

"Does anyone really like to eat alone?" Dylan asked.

I'm sure it happens.

"Listen, Hope, I know very well that Kiki has a girlfriend, so I hope you don't think I was asking Kiki out on a date," Dylan said. "I was asking her out to eat. That's all. Two people eating together. I wasn't asking Kiki to procreate."

I don't even have a thought comeback for that one! "Procreate"? It almost sounds dirtier than "screw," "bang," or "get busy," some of the nicer *American idioms for having sex. But to just say it like that! I like how . . . direct he is. He doesn't waste words. Let's hear what else he has to say.*

"I prefer to have conversations with someone other than myself whenever I eat." Dylan smiled. "Right now, our conversation is a little one-sided, huh?"

Hope shrugged.

"But that's because," Dylan said, drawing in a long breath, "you're obviously shy, aren't you, Hope?"

Shy? Me? I'm closed-off, not shy. There's a difference. I'm a closed person. I have shut my doors. I am a guarded person. I only talk to my whack cat, Whack. I do not talk to men who will talk to any *woman who happens to be standing in front of them at a copy shop. So I don't speak out loud. You should hear how much conversation is going on inside my head, Dylan, and it's bilingual sometimes. You'd need subtitles.*

"Are you interested? It's just lunch, Hope. No strings attached." Dylan laughed. "No ribbons either." He frowned. " 'No ribbons attached' sounds strange." He shrugged. "Well, it's almost the holiday season, isn't it?"

The holiday season. Right. There's nothing holy about these days, but let's take stock of this situation. I am hungry, and yes, I'm not exactly rolling in the money, and yes, it wouldn't be so bad to listen to Dylan talk to himself for half an hour, and yes, "no ribbons attached" sounds completely stupide, *but . . .*

I hate being the second choice of a man who has asked a rasta lesbian co-worker to eat with him at least twenty times and listened to him ask her every time!

Hope squinted. "I don't know, Dylan." *Why did I ever call this man Mr. Healy? Dylan isn't old. What is he, thirty-five, thirty-six?*

"I promise not to talk as much," Dylan said. "I tend to . . . ramble sometimes."

Make that all *the time. Why am I not just saying no? I am obviously ambivalent about this. I want to go back to the boring machines, I really do. I miss how gloriously monotonous the rhythm is back there, but there's just something about all this that intrigues me. Is it his accent? His smile? His long hair? His ability to pay for my meal? His, well, ability to get me to talk? What?*

We'll go with his ability to pay.

"We don't have to go to Subway, Hope," Dylan said. "We could go to Popeyes or Yummy Taco . . ." He withdrew a stack of minimenus from the front pouch of his hoodie. "I think I have a six-square-block area covered." He smiled, spreading the menus on the counter. "Let's see, how about Buffalo Boss?"

Hope blinked. *He carries around menus.*

"Junior's?" Dylan said.

Hope shrugged. *He carries menus like tourists carry brochures.*

"Smashburger? What a name."

Hope shook her head. *He carries menus like lost visitors carry bus and subway schedules.*

"Rosa Delia?"

Who? I cannot believe he walks around with menus in his pouch. He is one kangourou étrange. *Maybe he's Australian instead of Irish.* Hope stared at the menus. *I have printed out most of these! I'm looking at my own work!* Her stomach chose this moment to rumble audibly. She tried to smile but only winced.

Dylan didn't seem to notice.

Now I am suddenly hungry. It sounds as if a cat is trying to claw its way out of my stomach. Am I really that hungry? Hope leaned closer to the menus and heard another howl from her stomach. *They shouldn't put pictures of the food on those menus. I know my stomach can see them.*

"Flying Saucer?" Dylan paused and held up a menu. "What's a Paddington Bear sandwich? I've never been here, have you? This might be fun."

I don't want fun. I want food to still the cat meowing in my stomach. At least it's not hissing. That would be embarrassing.

"How about Johnny's Deli?" Dylan asked. "Luv N Oven? China Star?"

The Islands is a long way from here, a few doors down from my apartment. Dylan and I have just met, and this is not an official date. This is just lunch, though I could really go for some curry goat.

Hope's stomach continued to mewl and complain. *No curry goat. The cat in my stomach would tear it to shreds. One angry animal in my stomach at a time.*

Justin burst through the office door behind her, and even Dylan jumped a little. "Um . . ."

Hope spun around. "Hope."

"Yeah, um, Hope," Justin said. "Can you work through lunch? I need to, um, go out for an, um, hour or so."

Not when I'm suddenly this hungry!

"I wouldn't ask," Justin said, "but this is an emergency."

Hope sighed and nodded. *As if I had a choice.*

"Um, thanks, Hope," Justin said, and he tore around the counter and out the front door carrying his trusty camera bag.

Dylan squinted at the door. "Was that your boss?"

Hope nodded. *He occasionally makes appearances. Oh, he doesn't really work here. He just sits in the office and looks at porn. He has a managerial degree from NYU, which qualifies him to look at porn nine hours a day.*

Dylan turned to the counter. "How long has he been working here?"

Hope shrugged. "A few months."

Dylan laughed. "I have never seen the man." He smiled. "You do all the work around here anyway."

Yes, I do. Oh! The cat in my stomach is chasing something now! Stay still!

"You could probably run this place all by yourself," Dylan said.

I already do.

Hope's stomach chose this moment to bark.

Woof? My stomach says "Woof"? Wow! Dylan had to hear that.

Dylan drummed the counter. "You know, I could go out and get us something to eat, Hope. I could bring it back here for us."

Yes. Food without the awkward silences. Lunch without the waiting. Sustenance without paying. Three good reasons to accept this man's offer. Hope nodded and sifted through the menus.

"Having trouble deciding?" Dylan asked.

Hope nodded.

Dylan gathered up the menus and fanned them out like playing cards. "Pick a menu, any menu."

Who chooses food at random? Who does anything random in life? Okay, I almost joined the U.S. Army once. Hope looked at her hand reaching across the counter. *I guess I'm feeling random today.*

"Close your eyes," Dylan said. "No peeking."

Hope closed her eyes, reached out, and plucked a menu. She opened her eyes. *Buffalo Boss. Hmm. I can smell the gas already.*

"I've never eaten there, have you?" Dylan asked.

Hope shook her head.

Dylan slipped the other menus back into his hoodie pouch, and then he opened up and flattened the Buffalo Boss menu on the counter. "Truth be told, I haven't eaten at any of these places." He looked into Hope's glasses. "I've been hoping to eat at all of them, but I haven't found anyone to eat at them with me." Dylan returned his eyes to the menu. "What looks good to you?"

Hope scanned the menu, sliding her finger down until it stopped on the twenty-four-piece hot wings sampler.

All of Brooklyn might smell the gas, Hope thought. "It says we get four sauces." She spun the menu around to Dylan. "I don't have a preference."

"Okay," Dylan said, "how about . . . teriyaki, honey mustard, OMG, and F.I.T.H."

Hope turned the menu slightly. "OMG" stood for "Oh My God" and "F.I.T.H." stood for "Fire In The Hole." She shrugged. *Those wings are going to be incendiary. We may cause a midafternoon fog and ground some flights at JFK and LaGuardia.*

"And I'll get an order of chili cheese fries, too," Dylan said.

Hope blinked.

"I like hot food," Dylan said. "I was blessed with a cast-iron stomach." He took out a cell phone and called in the order. Then he covered the mouthpiece. "What do you want to drink, Hope?"

"Ice water," Hope said.

Dylan completed the order. "They said it'd be ready in twenty minutes." He slid the menu across to Hope. "A souvenir."

Hope tried not to smile, but a tiny one escaped before she could catch it, scold it, beat it down, and send it back into her face. "But we're not even going there together."

"Maybe one day we will," Dylan said.

Hope slipped the menu into the back pocket of her jeans. *That was kind of sweet, and it was smooth, too. He actually asked me out to eat again, even before we've* not *gone out to eat today, and now I have proof that we would* have *eaten together if I wasn't stuck here running the store alone.*

Or something like that.

Dylan rapped the counter with his knuckles. "I'll be right back, Hope." Then he stood unmoving, his eyes sweeping the shop.

Oh. Right. I'm supposed to say something. "Okay. See you soon."

Dylan smiled. "I'll be back before you know it."

Hope watched him go. *He has a flat derriere, too. We have something else in common.* Hope smiled. *He has long hair, and I have long hair. He likes to eat, and I like to eat. He seems desperate, and . . . I'm not desperate. I'm about to get a free lunch. Hmm. Gas, too, but it's nice to know I can still attract a man, and I wasn't even flirting. I can't even remember how to flirt.* Hope smiled again. *I have secured a meal. I didn't eat last night, and I didn't eat this morning. Now a man is about to feed me.*

Hope sighed. *He couldn't even see much of me. I stood behind the counter the entire time, and yet he weighed me in his mind. Well. That means he . . .* Hope's hands tingled. *That means he looked at all of me, and he didn't grimace or gag. That's a good thing, isn't it? When I really think about it,* he *was the one flirting with* me, *right?*

Hope temporarily lost feeling in her hands.

Oh, wow. He was flirting with me, *for whatever strange reason.* She almost smiled yet again. *Imagine that. A man was flirting with me, right here at the counter of Thrifty Digital Printing on Flatbush Avenue in Brooklyn on a Wednesday.*

The cat in Hope's stomach continued to howl.

Chapter 4

After Dylan and his flat derriere left Thrifty Digital Printing, Hope straightened up the stacks of unpaid orders under the counter, aligning them perfectly with the edges of the shelves.

I never straighten up this place. Why am I working here at work? I really should clean off this counter. It's about to be our lunch table, right?

Hope went into the storeroom and found a bottle of all-purpose cleaner and a thin roll of paper towels. She took the bottle to the front and sprayed the counter, wiping it down in wide arcs.

When is the last time a man brought me lunch? Eight years ago.

Hope sprayed and wiped the counter again.

Odell brought us Chinese. Sesame chicken and noodles from Hunan Delight. He had the Sha Cha beef. That's all he'd ever get. I could never get him to expand his gastronomic horizons. I could never finish my entrée, but he would finish his and then mine and say, "Man, I'm still hungry. That's the problem with Chinese food." I would tell him he should have ordered some egg rolls or some shrimp dumplings, then he'd call me his little dumpling, and then we'd save our fortune cookies to open later in bed, and then—

And then he left, and I started to hate Christmas.

Hope sprayed and wiped the counter again.

What did I see in Odell? I don't remember. Maybe I don't want to remember. I wish I didn't have to remember the last time I saw him. He was carrying a large Di Fara pizza and holding the hand of an-

other woman . . . who was holding the hand of a little girl who had Odell's eyes.

Hope hunched down and squinted at the surface of the counter. *It's still smudged, but it'll have to do.* She returned the bottle and the roll of paper towels to the storeroom and stopped in front of the DocuTech to run a systems diagnostics check.

She was the most beautiful little girl I had ever seen. And though I smiled at them, and though I spoke to him as "an old friend," and though I wished them both well, I secretly wished that child was my very own.

A tear dropped to a red tile. *Come back here. I didn't give you permission to leave my eye. We've already cried for this man.*

She started a diagnostic test on the Ryobi 3404.

Was there ever a moment with Odell that didn't involve food? Odell liked to eat. I liked to eat. Once. I fell for Odell with my stomach. I didn't think with my head. If I had thought with my head, I would never have fallen for Odell. I almost fell in love with the man through food. And what did I have left after he left me? Nothing. No. He did leave me with a refrigerator full of leftovers, and I didn't eat any of them because . . . I was saving them in case he came back.

And then I stopped eating, lost what few curves I once had, and became anorexic.

I am an anorexic.

The last time I was at the doctor, I looked at that height/weight chart. I am at least thirty pounds from having a healthy body. I tell myself I'm slim and trim, that's all, and any weight I put on comes off because I walk five miles a day. Some women would kill *to have a body like mine. I can wear whatever I want. I have no trouble finding my size.*

But . . .

My bras don't fit anymore. It's almost a waste to wear them at all. My ribs stare at me in my skinny mirror every morning, and I don't wear bracelets anymore, and not just because Odell gave them to me. They don't stay on my wrists. I have hair where I did not have hair before, and I'm always cold.

And . . .

And I haven't had a period in months. It isn't so bad. Not having my "friend" arrive saves me from having to get tampons, doesn't it?

But . . .

I wouldn't be able to be with a man anyway. I have had sexual anorexia for many years. I have all the worst symptoms of meno-pause, yet I'm only thirty-three. I am starving in more ways than one. I'm obviously getting enough nourishment to get to and from work, though. I eat, and I still have desires. Sometimes. I just don't eat as much or lust as much as I used to. My libido isn't dead. It's only dor-mant and hibernating like a—

"Excuse me."

Hope looked up at a grizzly bear of a man waving a piece of paper in front of her face. *I wonder how long he's been standing there. I hope not long.* "Yes?"

"I need to make fifty copies of this as soon as possible," he said. "Do you think you can handle it?"

Hope blinked at the middle-aged black man, who wore a navy-blue suit that blocked out the front windows, his matching tie loos-ened from a starched white collar squeezing a thick dark neck, not a single hair out of place on his head.

He could play American football, Hope thought. *He could play every position at once! He is a scary man. Where'd the sun go? He could probably snap me in two.*

"Hello?" the man said. "Is anybody home?" He checked his watch. "I have to be somewhere, so let's get this done."

Hope watched her thin hand take the piece of paper, turning it around and bringing it up to her face. *Marshall Word, investment manager, seeks similar position, formerly of Universal Investment House, address in Bedford-Stuyvesant, graduate of NYU School of Business. Didn't Universal Investment go bankrupt recently?* She squinted as she scanned the page. *This résumé is brutal. What's this? Eight-point type? Too many underlined words. Oh, look. He misspelled "manager" as "manger" twice.*

He's trying to make a manger scene!

That was bad. Funny, but bad.

Should I point out these errors to him? I don't want to embarrass him. Even a former executive is still an executive in his mind. If he weren't in such a hurry, I could make this résumé sing.

"Can you make fifty copies for me *now*, please?" Mr. Word asked.

Hope nodded.

"And can you hurry it up?" Mr. Word asked. "I didn't have change for the meter. I can't afford to get a ticket today."

Hope nodded. "Would you like me to put this on résumé paper?"

Mr. Word glared at her. "Yes, of course. Put my résumé on ré-sumé paper." He shook his head and spun away from the counter, whipping out a cell phone. "Yeah, Barney? I'm stuck in some copy shop on Flatbush, no telling when I'll get there because this air-head Jamaican copy girl doesn't understand English."

I'm not Jamaican, and since you're ruining my day, I'm going to ruin yours. Hope waved her hand in the air until Mr. Word looked at her.

"Hold on a second." Mr. Word covered his phone. "What?"

"Sir," Hope said, "I'd recommend using crushed cream smooth twenty-four weight instead of standard thirty-two-pound résumé paper. It's just dark enough to stand out and not too dark to—"

"You trying to up-sell me when I'm obviously in a hurry?" Mr. Word interrupted.

Hope shook her head. "Actually, using the crushed cream smooth twenty-four weight will save you—"

Mr. Word sighed deeply and glared at Hope again. "Let's keep it simple, okay? I want you to use that parchment stuff, you know, the kinda heavy paper that has the nice feel to it. Feels like cotton. *You* know what I'm talking about. Feels like cotton. That's what I need."

You also need manners and cologne that won't wilt the ficus.

Hope nodded, turned, and went into the storeroom, returning with a box of Southworth Company linen résumé paper. *At forty dollars for two hundred sheets, the paper alone will cost him ten dollars.*

She displayed the box to Mr. Word. "Is this satisfactory, sir?"

Mr. Word sighed, his eyes blinking. "Yes, and can you move any faster? I have an interview with ABD Securities in Battery Park in less than an hour, and I can't be late. So step it up, girl."

You know, Mr. Word, I can step it up, but I have just decided to move more slowly than I've ever moved before because I am not a girl. Thank you so *much for thinking you are better than me, but guess what? I have a job. You are unemployed. I hope you* do *get a parking ticket, and you* do *need someone to teach you some manners, though that's not my job and it's obvious you wouldn't learn any manners from anyone anyway. It's not my fault you didn't have the foresight to proofread and have your résumé ready for your interview today. I do hope* someone *hires you as a* manger. *You're big enough to hold a hundred baby Jesuses.*

That was bad, too. Sorry, God.

"Mr. Word," Hope said, "fifty sheets will cost you ten dollars for the paper alone."

"Ten bucks for paper?" he asked, widening his dark eyes.

"It's fine linen paper," Hope said. "It's the best we sell."

"Whatever," Mr. Word said, twirling his index finger. "Just hurry it up."

Can't. "But there's a problem with your résumé, Mr. Word." She slid the résumé across the counter. "You misspelled the word 'manager' twice. I can fix that for you."

Mr. Word snatched at the paper and held it up to his face. "Where?"

"Third and ninth lines down," Hope said.

Mr. Word sighed, tossing the sheet back across the counter. "Sure. Get some of that Wite-Out stuff and fix it. What'll that cost me? Another quarter?" He walked to the front door to look outside at his car, a long blue Lexus.

Actually, it's another ten *dollars.* "Mr. Word?"

"What is it *now*?" Mr. Word asked, still standing at the front door.

I am going to gouge the merde *out of you now.* "I'll have to scan it first using OCR, or optical character recognition," Hope said louder, "and only then can I make the corrections. It will be an additional ten dollars for the markup and preproduction fee."

"Ten bucks for two little letters?" Mr. Word yelled.

You *misspelled what you want your future position to be,* not *me, but I expect you to be upset since you're too cheap to put some change in the parking meter.* "I could use correction fluid, Mr. Word, and I have neat handwriting, but it won't look nearly as professional to ABD Securities if I do."

Mr. Word's body shook. "Look, do what you gotta do, all right? Just move it."

What would have cost him ten cents a copy on plain paper at the machine to his right will now cost him so much more. I hope Universal Investment gave him a nice severance package.

Hope scanned in the résumé using OCR, corrected the misspellings, loaded the DocuTech with the linen paper, and ran fifty copies. She wrote up Mr. Word's work order and handed it and his copies to him as Dylan banged through the door with lunch.

Mr. Word blinked at the work order. "This is over forty bucks!" Mr. Word howled. "Are you kidding me?"

"I've made a detailed list of your costs, Mr. Word," Hope said, "and I informed you prior to each step what the costs—"

"Do I at least get matching envelopes?" Mr. Word interrupted.

"That will cost you eight dollars more," Hope said. "Plus tax."

"*Are you serious?*" Mr. Word exploded. He looked at Dylan, who began placing Buffalo Boss bags on the counter. "Can you believe this shit?"

Dylan looked at the work order. "Works out to eighty cents a copy." He peered at the résumé. "Looks good. Not bad on this nice paper for only eighty cents a copy. You'd pay much more uptown." He smiled at Mr. Word. "And you can always deduct it as a business expense, right?"

Mr. Word growled. "She's robbing me, I tell you." He pulled two twenties and two dollar bills from his wallet. "I won't need the envelopes. Keep the change."

"I can't do that," Hope said, making and putting the change into his meaty hand along with the receipt. "I hope you get the job, Mr. Word." *Not.*

Mr. Word dropped the change on the counter and stormed outside. A minute later, Hope heard him arguing with a meter maid. A few moments later, Mr. Word returned to collect his change, going outside and putting the coins in the meter. He still received a ticket.

Serves you right, Mr. Word, Hope thought. *Your résumé just got* much *more expensive.*

Dylan took several boxes from the bags and arranged them near the ficus plant. "I hope all your customers aren't like him."

"A lot of them are," Hope said. *Smells good. Smells spicy, too.*

And then they ate.

And ate.

Hope polished off twelve wings dipped in various tasty sauces in less than ten minutes, wiping her hands and lips on napkins often and sucking down most of her water.

"You were hungry," Dylan said, only six empty chicken bones in front of him.

"I skipped breakfast." *And dinner and lunch and breakfast yesterday. Did I eat dinner Monday night? I think I fell asleep as soon as I got home. When did I eat last? I had some crackers on Sunday afternoon. I need more crackers. They were going stale.*

Dylan dabbed a napkin at his lips. "Not bad, though, huh?"

Hope nodded and sipped more water through her straw, the cat in her stomach purring. *He has sauce on his cheek. Do I tell him? I barely know the man, but if he walks out of here and sees his reflection, he'll think I'm mean because I didn't tell him.* Hope sighed. "You have some sauce . . ." She pointed at her own cheek.

Dylan wiped both of his cheeks. "Sure they weren't freckles?"

"It was sauce." *Freckles don't dribble down one's face like that, and if they do, you need to see a doctor.*

"When I was a kid, they would have been freckles." He tapped a finger on his cheek. "I am Irish to the core. I used to have some red in my hair, too." He reached behind his head and flopped long shanks of hair toward his shoulders. "It may be time for a haircut."

It's actually kind of sexy. "Do you ever wear it in a ponytail?" *Lunch is officially over, but now I've gone and asked him a question. What's wrong with me?*

"Most of the time." Dylan took a sip from his Pepsi. "Forgive me, Hope. I have not properly introduced myself. My full name is Dylan Riordan Healy. Dylan means 'flash of lightning, faithful and loyal.' "

He was back in a flash, and he faithfully brought me my food. "Dylan" works.

"Riordan means 'poet of the king,' " Dylan said.

"Riordan" does not work.

"And Healy means 'ingenious and artistic.' " Dylan smiled.

Dylan Riordan Healy is the most poorly named man on planet earth, Hope thought.

Dylan picked up another wing, dipping it into the F.I.T.H. sauce. "I don't think my mother thought I'd grow up to be a faithful, loyal, ingenious, artistic poet when she named me." He took a bite, quickly washing it down with the rest of his Pepsi. "It's hot! Wow! There is a definite fire in the hole."

"I'll get you some water," Hope said, knowing it probably wouldn't help, and took his cup to the washroom. As she filled his cup, she looked in the mirror. *He's not bad looking at all.* She squinted at her face. *I wonder what he looks like under that hoodie. I also wonder where he learned to eat. His beard stubble must like hot wing sauce.*

She returned to the counter and handed the cup to Dylan.

"Thank you," Dylan said, drinking several more gulps. "I think I'll stick to the honey mustard from now on." He smiled. "What's your full name?"

More vital statistics. Maybe he works for the census bureau. "Hope Elizabeth Warren."

"Hope Elizabeth," Dylan said. "I like it. H-E-W. Hew. I always wanted a word for initials."

He's so strange and yet so familiar, Hope thought. *I must be familiar with strange.*

Dylan offered Hope some chili fries. "They're not that spicy."

"I'm okay," Hope said.

A wide gray counter between them, Hope and Dylan stood not speaking for several lonely minutes, Hope cradling her cup, Dylan munching on his fries.

What do I say? I say nothing all day and go home grumpy. A man fed me. I should at least say . . . "Thank you for lunch."

"You're very welcome, Hope." He blew out a breath behind him and fanned the air. "If mosquitoes were still flying, I would have killed a swarm just then."

Gross, and yet . . . he's . . . nice. That's what's so familiar. I used to recognize "nice." I need to keep this nice man talking. "Dylan, how exactly do you sell your greeting cards?"

Dylan smiled. "Through my website. Odd Duck dot-biz. Orders come in, I run over here—I live over in Crown Heights, by the way."

We're practically neighbors. Well, not really. He's a couple miles away from my apartment.

"You, my dear Hope, copy and fold the cards," Dylan continued, "and I go to a PO."

Hope blinked.

Dylan's eyes popped. "The post office. Yeah, they sometimes get PO'd at me. All those different zip codes give them fits, and I don't always band and stack my packages in numerical zip code order. Did you think I meant a probation officer?"

Hope shook her head.

"Well," Dylan said with a sigh, "I had one of those once. A long time ago. When I was a kid. Having that kind of PO is no fun."

He's a felon? Where are his tattoos? All American felons, rappers, and athletes are supposed to have them.

"I am not a dangerous man, Hope," Dylan said. "Really. Maybe I better explain."

Yes. Please do.

"When I was twelve, I took a cab," Dylan said.

Hope nodded.

"Um," Dylan said, "I *took* a cab."

"You . . . *stole* a cab?" Hope asked.

Dylan nodded. "It seemed a good thing to do at the time, but everything seems a good thing to do when you're twelve."

Oh.

"I saw an opportunity, and I took it," he said. "The cab driver left his cab running right in front of me while he went into a bar on Pitkin Avenue. That's down in Brownsville, where I grew up. I figured, well, I didn't want the guy driving drunk, so I got in and drove off." He shook his head. "No, that's not true. I was a bad little boy. I stole the cab so I could go for a joyride. But when a man waved me down a few blocks later, I stopped."

Is he pulling my leg? What's this called, blarney? He does know how to tell a story, I'll give him that.

"The man got in, and I decided to make some money." He smiled. "I picked up and dropped off *seven* fares that day, and I made thirty-five bucks in tips. I even put gas in the taxi. I would have been driving all night, but . . ."

You had an accident.

"The last time I have ever driven a cab was to an address . . . on Pitkin Avenue." He smiled. "The address just happened to be *right* across the street from the bar where the driver went." Dylan laughed. "That was embarrassing. A cop was standing there taking the driver's statement. Evidently the driver had been drinking a *long* time before noticing his cab was gone, and there I was about fifty feet away from him. I'll never forget the look on that cop's face as I tried to slouch down in the seat." Dylan sighed. "I knew I was caught, so I got out, crossed the street, and handed the driver the keys. I even gave him the fare money and what was left from my tips after I bought the gas. Then I told him I had gassed it up, told him it was idling rough, probably needed a new air filter, the shocks were bad—that sort of thing. I was so cocky. Then I turned to the cop and said, 'I'm in big trouble, aren't I?' The cop nodded, hand-cuffed me, and took me away." He shook his head. "It was probably the smartest dumb thing I ever did."

That made no sense.

"I was arrested and charged with grand theft auto and truancy," Dylan said. "I didn't much like school back then. I used to skip school, but then I'd show up for wrestling practice." He sighed. "The coach never knew."

"Did they take you into custody?" Hope asked.

"They did," Dylan said. "Though the judge took into account my age and seemed happy that I gave back the money, he nailed me. I already had a few other charges on my record. Trespassing, vandalism, a dozen truancy charges. Several elementary schools had already kicked me out, mainly for forging notes to get out of class. I was not a very nice lad or a very smart criminal." He nodded. "I was mean. I ended up spending all of my teenage years as property of the state of New York. Yet those were some of the best years of my life."

"How were they the best?" Hope asked.

"When I was locked up, I *had* to go to school," Dylan said. "I was a captive audience, and I found out I was smarter than I looked. I got my GED at sixteen. Then I went into independent living and started volunteering at Kinderstuff down the street from here to complete my community service."

Kinderstuff? I walk by that day care center every day.

"I liked it so much I went and got my associate's degree in early childhood education from Brooklyn College," Dylan said, "and the very same Kinderstuff hired me as a teacher. I have been there ever since. Fifteen years next May."

Mr. Odd Duck with the long sexy hair and juicy laugh plays "Duck, Duck, Goose" for a living?

"It is the *best* job in the world," Dylan said. "I love the kids, and they seem to tolerate me. I took today off so I could catch up on my card orders and pay a few bills." He shook his head. "That's not entirely true. I can always catch up on weekends." He stared into Hope's eyes. "I don't really know why I took today off, actually."

I'm glad you did. Hope blinked. *Where did* that *thought come from?*

"Now I don't plan on staying at Kinderstuff for the rest of my life, Hope," Dylan said. "One day, I plan on owning and running my own arts center just for kids, and we'll have art all day. I plan to call it 'Art for Kids' Sake.' I'll need a big space, of course, and I've been saving like crazy." He laughed. "I'm rambling again, aren't I?"

"It's okay," Hope said.

"I'm getting to be as talkative as my students," Dylan said. "I have a blast working with them, especially during art from three to five. You should take a break and come down to see us in action. Do you get breaks?"

This lunch hour is turning into one. "Not really."

"Maybe you could just sneak off then," he said.

"This place keeps me busy," Hope said. *What a boring thing to say!*

"Oh, the kids *love* doing art," Dylan said. "Their parents? Not so much. We're messy. Great art should be messy, don't you think?" He looked at his pants. "I don't own a single pair of pants that doesn't have some kind of paint or stain on it." He started bagging his leftovers. "Hope Elizabeth Warren, I would love it if you could drop in sometime and meet the kids." He smiled and sighed. "I know I have taken up too much of your time. Thank you for sharing your lunch with me."

You haven't taken up too much of my time! That's all I have! "Dylan, tell me more about the children."

Dylan held up his hands. "Do you have some hand sanitizer?"

Hope grabbed a jug of hand sanitizer from under the counter. "We go through a lot of this stuff around here."

Dylan squirted some on his hands and rubbed them together. "The kids are so much fun, and they are so little! I'm always afraid I'll step on them. And they ask the craziest questions, and so *many* questions. They're question machines."

I like how his eyes light up, and they seem to glow more whenever he talks about the children. Have my eyes ever lit up or glowed like that?

"And Ni-Ni—I mean, Aniya—that girl is the worst!" Dylan said. "She's five now and refuses to be called Ni-Ni. I swear Aniya plays twenty questions with me every day." He sighed. "And she has leukemia, yet she never stops smiling." He looked up. "She wears baseball caps. Chemo, you know. She had hair as thick as yours only a few months ago."

That's so sad! So tragique!

"But Aniya doesn't let it get her down," Dylan said. "She never complains. She's . . . she's like a sunrise, you know? She brightens everyone's day."

A child like a sunrise.

"She needs a bone marrow transplant soon. Neither of her parents matched." Dylan sighed. "I went in to the hospital to see if maybe I matched, but I'm a little too Irish for Aniya Pierre-Louis. She's Haitian."

At least he tried.

"She has the cutest accent, too," Dylan said. "I wish you could meet her."

"I will," Hope said before she could stop the words from escaping her lips. "I mean, I'd like to meet her. Sometime."

"I will tell Miss Aniya all about you tomorrow," Dylan said. "And once I do, she will ask about you until either my ears bleed from her asking or you show up." He nodded. "I hope you will show up. I happen to like my ears."

"Sometime," Hope said again.

"Maybe Aniya and I can take a field trip up here one day to

meet you," Dylan said. "We'll bring you lunch and eat it right here on the counter. She'd like that. Oh, only if it's okay with you."

Another free meal? "It's . . . it's fine," Hope said.

"Is tomorrow too soon?" Dylan asked.

Is Christmas coming too soon? "No," Hope said.

"I don't mean to rush you into meeting her," Dylan said. "It's just that Aniya spends a lot of time in hospitals. She's pretty healthy now, though."

"It's okay," Hope said. "I look forward to meeting her."

Dylan smiled. "Great." He grinned. "Great! Maybe tomorrow or Friday then. I'll have to work something out with her parents and the lead teacher, but we will make this happen."

I don't want this conversation to end. Why is that? I'm normally bored into a coma on Wednesdays, but now my heart is actually beating. It has to be his voice. It has life in it. It has laughter in it. It has music in it.

Sometimes I am too romantique for my own good.

"Dylan, how does your card company work? I mean, what do you charge? Do you break even?" *It is customary to let someone answer the first question before asking the second. Why did I ask him three?*

"I'm pretty reasonable compared to the standard Hallmark cards," Dylan said. "I charge three bucks a card plus shipping, and for ten or more cards I charge two-fifty per card and give free shipping. I make about a buck-fifty on each card when you take out all the expenses and postage. I net anywhere from fifteen bucks to seven-fifty a week."

Seven-fifty? "You make that much?"

"I only make that kind of money during the holidays," Dylan said. "The best week I ever had was mid-November a couple years ago. Fifteen hundred bucks. I sold a thousand 'Skinny Santa' cards. Do you remember that one? It's still one of my best-sellers."

Hope nodded. *How could I forget? On the front is a stick figure Santa. Inside it says, "Santa might be thin this year, but I hope your Christmas is fat." He made fifteen hundred dollars in one week from that weak card. Why?*

"It's funny what people like and don't like," Dylan said. "The ones I think people will buy like crazy sit there gathering cyberspace dust while the ones that don't even thrill *me* get snapped up. It's a funny business."

Cyberspace dust? Hope pulled a Sharpie from a drawer and started doodling on a napkin. She drew a stick figure woman with dreadlocks, adding some huge, dark glasses and a frown.

"Hey, I like that," Dylan said. "It's you, isn't it?"

Hope nodded.

"Except it's missing your eyes," Dylan said. "Why the dark glasses?"

So he has *been looking at my eyes.* "It makes her more generic," Hope said.

"*And* more universally appealing," Dylan said. "I like that."

Hope spun her doodle around. "A souvenir for you."

Dylan held up the napkin. "Thank you." He smiled. "I will put it proudly on my refrigerator." He stared at the drawing for several, long moments.

What's he doing?

He looked up. "You know, I think this is more than a souvenir, Hope. Could I make a copy of this?"

Hope shrugged, took the napkin from his hand, pulled a copy key counter from a drawer, and walked over to the self-serve copier up front. She inserted the copy key counter and made a quick copy, handing the copy and the napkin to Dylan. "I'll pay the dime," she said, leaning against the copier.

Here I am posing in front of him so he can look at the rest of me up close. I am so out of practice being a flirteur. True flirts do not pose beside copy machines, but I really don't have much of a choice.

Dylan smiled at the copy and the napkin. "Hope, I don't believe in coincidence, do you?"

Hope looked at her hands. "Oh, I don't know. Maybe."

"I believe everything happens for a reason, even the bad things," Dylan said. "I mean, I practically arrested myself to get out of my house." He leaned on the copier, his hip mere inches from Hope's. "I come from the proverbial broken home. Mother on drugs, father nowhere, one brother in jail and still in jail, one brother dead and buried. Getting myself arrested probably saved my life, you know. I took that cab for a reason even though I didn't know the reason at the time. You understand?"

"I guess." *He's practically an only child and an orphan. Kind of like me.*

"You drew this for me today," Dylan said. "Do you know why?"

I was nervous and needed something to do to keep my hands busy. "I just wanted to give you a souvenir." *Of the lunch "date" that didn't really happen.*

He turned the copy around and held it in the air. "Look at this."

Hope looked.

"This isn't a souvenir, Hope. This is a signature character. She belongs on a greeting card." He rattled the page. "Hope, I'd like to use this drawing on a few cards I'm working on, and I will give you half of whatever I make for every card sold."

I will be contributing to the beach house fund thanks to a doodle on a napkin from Buffalo Boss. Très étrange. *I guess it's no stranger than anything else in my life.*

"It's just a little doodle," Hope said. "I do them when I'm bored."

"But it's not just a little doodle," Dylan said. "I want to put her on as many cards as I can because she's unique. She's unusual. She's ethnic. She's multicultural. She catches the eye. I mean, it's not just a cute stick figure with dreads. She's saying something. She means something." He stepped closer to Hope. "We have to give her a name."

"We do?" Hope asked softly.

"A signature character needs a signature name," Dylan said. "It makes it easier to sell."

"You can call her . . ." *Oh, this will be ironic.* "Call her Noelle." Hope spelled it for him.

"Noelle," Dylan said, nodding. "And this is the first Noelle, get it?"

Hope nodded, barely successful at *not* rolling her eyes.

"Noelle is an excellent holiday name and a unique spelling." He smiled at the drawing. "Hello, Noelle. Want to help make Hope and me some money?"

I feel his warmth. I know it's just the copier, but I feel warmer.

"So, Hope, what do you say?" Dylan asked. "May I use your drawing?"

"It's not that good," Hope said, gripping the edge of the copy.

"I could dress her up a bit, maybe give her shoes, and clothes." *Aren't stick figure people essentially naked?* She tugged on the paper. "I can make it better."

Dylan pulled the copy away. "It's perfect as it is. It's simple, direct, and readily recognizable, like a symbol or a trademark. And I know just what to do with her."

He went to the counter, put another napkin in front of him, took the Sharpie, and did a rough re-creation of her stick figure as Hope drifted closer. Then he joined his long-haired signature stick figure to hers at their skinny hips. "I call him Dylan, for obvious reasons."

It's a good name. Better than Riordan.

"This drawing will be on the outside of the card," Dylan said, "and on the inside it will read, 'Siamese snow angels.' "

Hope bit her lip. *That is the most* preposterous *idea I have ever heard!* Très *bizarre, but it's funny!* A soft laugh escaped her lips. "Siamese snow angels."

"Ridiculous, isn't it?" Dylan asked.

"I like it."

Dylan smiled. "You do?"

Hope nodded. "They look like Siamese snow angels. It fits."

"So what do you say?" Dylan asked.

"About what?" Hope asked.

"About letting me use Noelle," Dylan said.

"I guess . . ." She laughed a little louder. *That is in* such *poor taste! Siamese snow angels! We're bound to offend someone.* "I guess it's okay."

"I'm going home to make this exact card right now," Dylan said. "How late are you working tonight?"

"I work every night until six." *Sometimes six-thirty when I'm running your ridiculous cards, and I might not even mind staying later tonight.*

"I'll be back well before then," Dylan said, "and if you like what you see, maybe you'll consider doing more than only giving me the use of Noelle. Maybe you'll think of joining me and my little company."

At the hip and making snow angels. "We'll see," Hope said.

"And I will see you again soon," Dylan said. He snatched up the bag containing his card order and the Buffalo Boss bags. "I am so glad I took today off." He smiled. "Thank you, Hope."

"For what?" Hope asked.

"For everything."

Hope watched him leave, enjoying the view of his paint-spattered jeans.

He will see me later, Hope thought, *but will he really see me? I'll have to let him see more of me.* Hope took off her smock and unbuttoned the top button of her shirt. *I can be a* mâtine, *a hussy, when I want to be.* Hope smiled and loosed another button. *Now he'll have plenty to see.*

Chapter 5

Justin burst through the front door a few minutes later, his camera bag swinging wildly around him.

It's a regular circus in here today. This slow Wednesday certainly isn't.

Justin rounded the counter and stopped. "I smell hot wings."

"It was my lunch," Hope said.

"Oh, right, um ..." He squinted at the floor. "Sorry for taking so long. Why don't you, um, why don't you take a break for a few minutes, maybe go outside and stretch your legs."

A break? What's that? "Okay."

Hope put on her coat and darted through the front door before Justin could change his mind. The Brooklyn air was crisp and metallic as usual, but at least she was out in the sun. *I wonder if I was a sunrise child.* She closed her eyes and let the sun warm her face. *Maybe I can get a freckle today.*

Hope crossed between several cars until she stood in front of Mr. Al-Hamsi. While he sat bundled up in a brown-and-white blanket on a green-and-white lawn chair, she browsed his DVD titles, most of them some of the newer releases with Christmas movies sprinkled here and there. She saw *Elf*, *Four Christmases*, *The Nutcracker*, *This Christmas*, *Christmas with the Kranks*, and all the *Home Alone* movies.

"Gently used," Mr. Al-Hamsi said. "You will enjoy."

Right. "How much?"

"One for ten, two for fifteen," he said. "Three for twenty."

"Even the Christmas movies?" Hope asked.

"Yes," he said.

"But you don't celebrate Christmas, do you, Mr. Al-Hamsi?" Hope asked.

"I celebrate money," he said.

"But it's the middle of October," Hope said.

"Seventy-one shopping days left until Christmas," he said with a smile. "Get them now before price increases."

She looked at the jeans, all of them *men's* jeans, most of them overly washed and faded to a robin's egg blue. *Men's jeans? Is he kidding?* "And these?"

"Gently worn," he said. "Top quality."

"How much?"

"One for twenty, two for thirty, three for forty," he said. "Top quality. No disappointments."

She checked several labels. *These are all huge, and a thirty-six is the smallest size. I could put one of me inside a single pants leg.* "Nothing smaller?"

"Baggy is still in," he said. "Top quality. No disappointments."

She held a size thirty-six to her hips. The pants legs hit her at her shins. She held up a size thirty-eight, and the pants legs barely traveled past her knees. *Where did he get these?* "I need something much longer than these." She nodded at her knees. "These are no better than shorts."

Mr. Al-Hamsi shrugged. "Wear as shorts then. Top quality. Gently worn. No disappointments."

Hope saw a man in a purple shirt waving to her from across the street. *Who is that poorly dressed man?* She shielded her eyes from the sun and squinted. *Oh. It's the boss. What was that, five minutes?* She folded and returned the jeans to the stack. "If you get any size thirty with a thirty-two inseam, let me know."

"Do they make such a size?" Mr. Al-Hamsi asked.

I am a thin woman in a baggy world. "They make," Hope said, and she weaved around a bus and two honking cars to return to Thrifty.

Justin already wore his coat. "I have to go, um, pick up a special order."

Right.

"I'll be back in half an hour at the latest," he said, and he bolted out the door.

Hope took off her coat, looked around for anything to do, found nothing, and stepped into the washroom, leaving the door open in case a rare customer or someone needing directions out of Brooklyn came in. She looked in the mirror and decided to remove the hemp string, letting her locks cascade down her back. *I look like a black-haired lioness. Roar. Grr. I'll bet the average lioness doesn't have her hair going every direction at once, though.* She looked at the dark-brown skin on her chest. *Another button? No. I don't want to scare the man away with my shiny breastbone.*

And then Hope watched the counter again.

More nothing happened. Perhaps the ficus plant grew.

At three PM, Justin returned, locking himself in the office.

At 3:39 PM, a customer made ten self-serve copies.

Hope collected a dollar and paid the tax out of her own pocket. The woman didn't thank her.

At 4:32 PM, Hope had some indigestion.

At 4:35 PM, Hope's indigestion passed.

Perhaps the ficus wilted slightly.

At a quarter to five, Justin emerged from the office, his coat already zipped up, his trusty camera bag on his shoulder. "I'm knocking off early today. Can you count down the register and put today's money and receipts on my desk? You've done it before, right?"

I hate you. Hope nodded. *Please walk into a speeding bus.*

Justin handed her a key. "Here's the key to the office. Make sure you lock everything up."

I always do. Hope took the key. "What about the deposit?"

"I'll, uh, I'll do that in the morning."

That's not the correct procedure and you know it. Are you trying to lose the job you never do anyway? "I've made night deposits before." *For other equally useless and former managers.*

"Um, well, okay," Justin said. "Just sign my name to the deposit slip."

So it will look as if you did your job and stayed until closing. "Sure."

Justin left.

Hope shook her head. *That man has either a bookie or a girl-friend somewhere who is more important than his paycheck, and why does he carry a camera everywhere?*

By five, Hope's stomach completely settled down, and Dylan breezed in waving a piece of paper. "Take a look."

Hope looked.

Well, take a look at me—I mean, Noelle. She looks like a skinny blind Medusa with no breasts. Did he do something to Noelle's lips? He turned them up. She's actually smiling a sexy, sly, Mona Lisa smile. "How did you . . ."

"Make her smile?" Dylan asked.

Hope nodded.

"Just added two little lines at the corners of her mouth," Dylan said. "I hope that's all right."

"It's fine," Hope said. *Noelle actually looks happy. The snow angel outline around the "twins" could use a little work, but there's no doubt what they're doing.*

"Turn it over," Dylan said.

Hope turned the card over and saw "Odd Ducks Limited" instead of "Odd Duck Limited." *He added an* s. "You changed your name."

"Only on the cards," Dylan said. "It'd be a big hassle changing the name of the website. Maybe I'll do that when the domain name expires in a few years."

"Why did you change your name?" Hope asked.

"I'd like us to be partners, Hope," Dylan said.

So would I! I can see his tall body wrapped around my tall body and all our hair flowing together. Hope blinked. *Where has my li-bido been? I feel like unbuttoning two more buttons and loosening my belt. No. My pants will hit the floor, and I'm wearing some old pink underwear today. Now if I were wearing some black satin underwear—*

"Hope?"

Oh. I've kept Dylan waiting while I've been mingling with his body and disrobing us in my mind. She looked up. "Are you serious? Partners?"

"Yes," Dylan said. "Business partners."

Hope pouted for a moment. *I like the sound of "partners" better.* "But on the basis of one card?"

"But what a card it is," Dylan said. "Can you get on the Internet here? I'll show you how well it's already selling."

It's already selling. Don't I need to be under contract or something before he can do that? Why am I fighting this? The card is making money.

Hope knew she could get to the Internet on the mainframe quickly, but she wanted a little more privacy. *And intimacy.* She dug out the office key. "Step into my office."

As Dylan came around the counter and followed her to the office, Hope had a momentary doubt. *Now I'm breaking procedure by letting a customer come to this side of the counter. Oh well. No one will know. Or care.*

She opened Justin's door, New York Rangers posters and player pictures assaulting her eyes. She wiggled the mouse and froze.

That's a naked black woman with very large breasts on that screen. Those can't be real, and what is she doing with those two men? Those . . . things . . . can't be real either.

"My boss, he must have . . ." Hope started to say.

"No explanation needed," Dylan said.

Hope quickly minimized the page, shrinking the threesome to a safe blue bar at the bottom of the screen. Then she opened another Internet browser.

Dylan slipped around her but not before rubbing his hip against hers. "May I?"

Yes, you may. You may rub my hip with your hip. You may even rub your hands all over my body and put me in the position that woman was just in. Where are all these thoughts coming from? I haven't had these thoughts in years. "Sure."

Dylan's fingers flew over the keyboard until the Odd Duck website appeared. "It's a rudimentary site," he said. "Nothing flashy. Easy to navigate, though."

Hope saw a series of white thumbnail pictures set against a black background. Each picture was of a different card cover, typed copy underneath.

Dylan smells nice, like incense, and he has removed the stubble from his chin. He took time to shave. He looks so . . . clean, and I'm not being racist because he's white. He looks clean. His skin looks and smells clean. He reminds me so much of that actor Colin Farrell, who had long hair in a couple movies, but why am I fixating on some distant Irish actor when a real Irishman is centimeters away?

Dylan clicked a button to open a new page, typed in a password in a white rectangle, and a page bursting with text, columns, and numbers appeared, the numbers occasionally increasing. He pointed to the word "Siamese," the last word on the screen. "One hundred and thirty-two bought and paid for already."

Is he kidding?

"And in only two hours," Dylan said, "you just made ninety-nine bucks."

Hope blinked at the screen. "Really?"

"Really." Dylan smiled. "I'm hoping 'Siamese Snow Angels' takes off like 'Skinny Santa' did."

Wow. "That's . . . amazing." Hope smiled as the number changed to 137.

"Five more while we've been watching," Dylan said. "Your character is amazing. Noelle is going to make us a *lot* of money."

I do not want to leave this office. I want to watch that number change for the rest of the night. I also want to bask in this man's warmth. He is putting off so much heat!

Hope sighed, realizing she couldn't stay forever in the tiny office. "I'm kind of running the store, so I need to be . . ."

Dylan closed the browser. "Should I . . . No."

What's he mean—oh! Oh, yes. "Yes, I think we better return things to the way they were." She reopened Justin's last web page. *Why don't the women ever smile? She looks . . . fulfilled. Twice. There's no way this is physically possible. I'll bet they used Photoshop. I like her tattoo, though. I'll bet it hurt to put it way down there.*

Hope took one more peek and followed Dylan out of the office, locking the door behind her.

Dylan returned to the front of the counter, propping his chin up on his hands. "So what do you think about us becoming partners?"

After what I just saw in the office, I like the idea very much. I would need, of course, only one of you, Dylan, and I would promise to smile. "You really want to become business partners on the basis of one drawing?"

"Yes."

He seems so sure. "Well, I guess it sounds . . . great."

"I am detecting doubt in your voice, Hope," Dylan said.

"Well . . ." *This isn't doubt. I'm feeling a chill. It was so much warmer in that office.* "May I ask you a few questions first?"

"Sure."

I have so many. Where to begin . . . "When your customers buy ten or more, you give free shipping, right?"

Dylan nodded.

"So you're only pulling in a dollar net per card because of that, right?" Hope asked.

"Right," Dylan said.

"So in order to keep at least that dollar-fifty net per card, I'd suggest making some minor changes." She smiled. "You know, to save money and increase our profit."

"*Our* profit?" Dylan said. "So we *can* become partners?"

Only ask that question of me if you truly mean it. Otherwise, stop saying that word!

"I can't say that I don't like the idea," Hope said. "I've made a hundred dollars in a few hours with a doodle."

"A great doodle," Dylan said. "What are your ideas to increase our profits?"

I have his undivided attention. When's the last time I had a man's undivided attention? I should have popped another button. No. Then he'd see my navel.

"Okay, first," Hope said, "you really don't have to use such heavyweight paper or any kind of coating. Plain thirty-two-pound paper is sturdy enough for a greeting card. That'll save you about five percent on paper costs, and it will probably save you money on bulk shipping and mailing costs, too."

"Good idea." Dylan nodded. "What else?"

I'm not sure if I can really do this, but . . . "And we could use my employee discount. That's fifteen percent off the entire order, so about twenty percent all told."

"Wow," Dylan said.

"Saving twenty percent would push our profits up to one-eighty per card." *If "Siamese Snow Angels" breaks a thousand sold, that's nine hundred dollars toward the beach house where I can one day make* sand *angels!*

"I can live with that," Dylan said. "Can you?"

Hope nodded. *I could probably live with you. In a small house. One room. No escape.* Hope blinked. *Where have these thoughts been?*

"Well," Dylan said, "we need to put all this in writing." He grabbed a little spiral memo pad from his back pocket and flipped it open, taking a pen from his hoodie pouch. "I'll type it up and make this more official looking when I get home." He began to write. " 'I, Dylan Riordan Healy, do promise that I will give Hope Elizabeth Warren of Brooklyn, New York, half of all profits and no less than ninety cents per card sold for Odd Ducks Limited Greeting Cards, as of this date.' " He signed his name, wrote down the date, and drew a line. "Sign here, please."

I'd be insane not to sign this, but this is too good to be true. But things that are too good to be true often aren't—and so are people sometimes. "Are you absolutely sure you want to do this? Before you were taking in a dollar-fifty per card, and now you're only going to get ninety cents. You're going to lose money if I become your business partner."

"I will gain so much more because of increased sales volume," Dylan said. "Please sign this, Hope."

Hope signed her name. *It's practically free money. Is that a seagull I see floating over my beach house? I think it is. Oh, look at the sunset from my deck . . .*

Dylan pocketed the memo pad. "I wish I had hooked up with you five years ago."

He said "hooked up." This is one American phrase I really like.

"With a twenty percent savings, I could have had at least another maybe ten thousand in the bank now." He flipped a dangling stray lock off his forehead and over the top of his head. "We're going to need more bandwidth for the website. I'm tired of using little thumbnails on the main page. We need to use larger graphics.

Bigger is better, and it's easier on the eyes. But I'll take care of that out of my end."

"I thought we were equal partners," Hope said. "Fifty-fifty, right?"

"It should only cost us an extra ten to twenty bucks a month, no sweat," Dylan said, "and the web host might have a better package deal. I'll check on it."

"Whatever it comes to, I should pay half," Hope said. "You should really be getting a bigger cut anyway, Dylan. You created the company. You have the website all set up and running, and I assume you have a scanner, and you're the one running to the post office. A sixty-forty split in your favor would be fairer." *That is more than I've said to another human being anywhere for the past eight years. This man has loosed my tongue!*

Dylan patted his back pocket. "We already have a signed contract, Miss Warren, so we can't change it now, and anyway, I think fifty-fifty is *less* than you deserve."

"And I think it's more than I deserve," Hope said. *Now I'm arguing with a real person. Out loud, too. This has been an exhausting day!*

"And from this moment on, I will think that I'm shortchanging you," Dylan said. "Your signature character is going to sell a ton of cards, Hope. I'll probably have to give you bonuses to keep you happy so you don't leave my company and start your own."

Bonuses. That's a B-word I like to hear, but why would I leave when I just got started? I wonder if these bonuses include up-close-and-personal time with Dylan and his flat derriere . . . "What kind of bonuses?"

Dylan flattened his hands on the counter. "Well, I could . . . take you . . . out." He looked up briefly, then smiled at his hands. "You know, to go out to eat, to see some shows, to . . . to go wherever you want to go." He looked up. "Oh, unless you want cash. I could do cash bonuses, too."

Hmm. Cash or the man? I can see this man and me making sand angels together. We will need a large front "yard." Maybe I'll take a little of both. "Whatever you think is best. My cards might not sell."

"They're already selling," Dylan said.

"It's only one card," Hope said, "and it was your funny idea that made it sell. What if I can't think up anything catchy?"

"I have no doubts in your abilities," Dylan said.

Well, that makes one of us.

"You know, I told myself just last week that this was the last Christmas I would ever do cards," Dylan said. "It takes up a lot of my free time. But now . . ." He smiled. "Hope, you've jump-started me. You've inspired me. I wish I could put a price tag on inspiration."

It goes both ways, Dylan. I wish you would touch me in some way repeatedly. I also wish I could touch you in some way. Also repeatedly. "We should shake on this contract too, don't you think? Let's make it official."

"Definitely." Dylan reached out his hand, and Hope took it. "Here's to a long, lucrative relationship."

I like this big hand holding my long skinny hand, and that word "relationship" sounds as nice as that word "partner" does. She stared at their hands. "Here's to . . ." *Warmth? Going out? Bonuses? Making sand angels? Holding hands on long moonlit walks along the beach?* "Here's to Odd Ducks."

Hope relaxed her grip, but Dylan didn't let go.

"*And* to making lots of money," Dylan said. He pulled his hand away slowly. "Speaking of money, when and how would you like to be paid?"

"Every hour on the hour," Hope said. *I can't believe I just said that! It makes me seem so greedy!*

Dylan laughed. "Me, too, but PayPal isn't that efficient. PayPal will usually deposit our money into the Odd Duck account within two to three business days. I will add your name to the account, and then you'll be able to get in there and transfer money to your account." He frowned. "Oh yeah. You'd need to be with the same bank. I use Chase."

"Me, too," *This may become a chase. He has such brown brown eyes. I know that's redundant, but they're so brown, and just saying "Dylan has brown eyes" isn't enough. Dylan has brown brown eyes.*

"That's great," Dylan said. "Yet another happy coincidence."

Hope watched Dylan's brown brown eyes move from her face all the way down to her hips. *Is he weighing me again?*

"I'm not sure what that process entails or how long it takes," Dylan said. He raised his eyes slowly to her eyes. "But once it's set up, you can go in and transfer your cut at your leisure."

He's so trusting. "You sure?"

"I trust you." Dylan stepped back from the counter. "Partners have to trust each other, right?"

"Right." *They also have to spend long nights together.* Hope blushed. *Wow. When's the last time I blushed?*

"So you'll be 'paid' about twice a week," Dylan said.

"I can live with that," Hope said. "How do I give my cards to you to put on the website?"

"You already have some ideas?" Dylan asked.

"Yes." *All I have to do is start doodling.*

"I am going to have so much trouble keeping up with you," Dylan said. "Let's see. I'll be coming in here daily—as often as I can, anyway—all the way through New Year's Day. People buy lots of cards after Christmas, too, especially since I give a fifty percent discount to get rid of my 'stock,' which really doesn't exist since we at Odd Ducks do everything made-to-order, right?"

I feel the need to smile at this man. He's so together, so there, so . . . right in front of me. I haven't smiled at him yet. I wonder if I remember how. Here goes. I hope there's no chicken fat stuck to my teeth.

Hope smiled.

Dylan took a breath and smiled back.

I have made him take a breath with my smile. I will have to smile more often. I like to hear him breathing.

"I will have to come in to pick up your originals," Dylan said. "Hmm. I'll have to bring my scanner to Kinderstuff. No. I'll just buy another one. They're not that expensive, but I'd want a better one for your drawings since they're far more intricate than mine will ever be. Yeah. I'll go over to Staples tonight and pick up a scanner."

Most people who think out loud annoy me, Hope thought. *Not him. Why? Oh yeah. I do it, too.*

"Okay, so I'll scan your cards in at Kinderstuff on a new scanner," Dylan said, "and I'll put flashing 'new' signs on them on the website. I know it's tacky, but you'd be amazed at how well that works. I could even group all the new ones on their own page. I'll have to add a button to the navigation bar. And then—"

"Dylan?" Hope interrupted.

"Hmm?" he said.

"I can scan it here and e-mail it to you, right?" *This job has several perks.* "We have a decent scanner." *Which is a million times better than any of the scanners you can get at Staples.*

"That'd be great," Dylan said. "That way you can scan and shoot your cards to my e-mail whether I'm at work or at home, I download it, post it to the website, I'll send you an e-mail confirming everything . . ." He nodded. "Can you save all our cards to a file here?"

"Sure," Hope said. "We back up all the electronic orders we get in case a customer needs more copies later. I'll just create an Odd Ducks file. No sweat."

"It's something I should have already done, huh?" Dylan said.

Hope shrugged. "Just hand me a zip drive of everything you've got, and I'll shoot it to the file."

Dylan nodded and smiled. "This is working out so well, and with our entire arsenal of cards already here in that file, you can print cards out at your leisure once I e-mail or call you with the numbers. Hope, that will save *so* much time. And ink. I go through so many ink cartridges."

"And from now on, Dylan," Hope said, "whenever you come up with a new design, you can scan it wherever and e-mail it straight to the file here."

Dylan sighed. "I've been doing everything the hard way, huh?"

"Well . . ." *He has.* "Yes."

Dylan squinted. "But that would mean . . ." His voice trailed away. "I wouldn't have to come here as often, would I? We'd be electronic files passing in the night."

That would not be good! Go back to the hard way! Hurry!

His squint vanished, his brown brown eyes whole again. "Oh, I'd still have to come by to make all the payments, pick up the orders, and get them to the post office. I'd have to do that at least once a day."

That's better. Hope smiled at the counter this time. *Oh, sure, I could explain how we can set him up with electronic billing and how he could lease a postage meter. Maybe some other time. Or never. Hmm. Probably never.*

"What am I thinking?" Dylan whipped out his memo pad. "I've given you no contact numbers." He wrote down his e-mail address and two phone numbers. "This is my cell number, and this is the number to Kinderstuff. Call me anytime you need to. I mean, in case you run into problems with anything. Sometimes I can get away for a few minutes. It's not that far from here."

Hope took a piece of scratch paper and wrote down Thrifty's phone number, her phone number, and her e-mail address, adding a miniature Noelle on the page. "I don't have a cell phone," she said. "I know that's weird." *Why own a cell phone when you have no one to call?*

"If you don't need one, why have one?" Dylan asked.

I'm glad that he's a pragmatic man, too. "And if you ever need to . . . discuss anything with me, feel free to call." She bit her lip and slid the slip of paper across the counter.

I have just given out my phone number to my partner who wants a business relationship, and I'm feeling excited and exhilarated and breathless and my mouth is completely dry and even my toes are tingling. No, they're just cold. I should wear two pairs of socks.

"So, Dylan," Hope said, "I will see you tomorrow around . . ."

"Five, unless you see me sooner with Aniya," Dylan said. "Let's run three hundred of the Siamese snow angels."

"That many?" Hope asked.

"I have a good feeling about this." He took out his wallet. "That's going to cost me . . ." He narrowed his eyes.

Hope wrote up a quick order ticket. "With my discount and the thirty-two-pound paper, that'll be two-forty, so one-twenty now."

Dylan opened his wallet, took out a check card, and handed it to Hope. "Thank you."

"I'm taking your money and you're thanking me," Hope said.

"I'm thanking you because I'm spending less money than I would have without you so *we* can make a lot more." He blinked. "Did that make sense?"

Hope nodded. She rang up fifty percent of his total order, swiped his card, and waited for his receipt to print out. When it did, she tore it off carefully. "You keep all your business records, don't you?"

"Sure," Dylan said. "Odd Ducks goes on my Schedule C."

She handed him the receipt. "And what kinds of things do you deduct as business expenses, aside from materials and costs?"

Dylan pursed his lips. "That's about it. I depreciate my equipment, but other than that . . ." He shrugged. "Why do you ask?"

"Did you save your receipt from our lunch?" Hope asked.

"Yes." Dylan's eyes popped. "That was a business lunch, wasn't it?"

Hope nodded. "In fact, any lunches we share as partners . . ."

"Or dinners . . ." Dylan smiled.

Or breakfasts . . . I can dream, can't I? "Right. So keep track of them."

"I will." He shook his head. "You're brilliant, Hope. Thank you for everything, for lunch, for the contract, for everything. It's like I've just had Christmas in October."

Don't roll your eyes, Hope.

"It will be an honor and a pleasure to be working with you, Hope." He bowed his head slightly.

I hope it's more pleasure than honor. "You, too, Dylan."

"Bye."

Hope watched him leave, hoping he would look back at least once.

Dylan looked back twice.

She held up the "Siamese Snow Angels" card. *It is so ridiculous how something so simple could do so much good, not only for my bank account but also for my self-esteem. A man walked in here today and showed me more respect in an hour than the people here have shown me in ten years. I deserve respect, and Dylan gave it to me freely.*

I wonder what else he gives away freely . . .

I have been a lonely woman for far too long.

Hope ran three hundred smiling Siamese snow angels through the DocuTech, deciding to leave them for folding in the morning. She counted down the register and made a master receipt of the day's take, putting the receipt on Justin's desk. Before she left the office, she wiggled the mouse.

That can't be ecstasy on her face, though it should be. She has two men servicing her. She tilted her head. *And they seem to be doing it well. Her smile should reach from ear to ear, though. She has two men.*

I'd settle for one.

Doing that.

And that.

She locked the office, filled out a deposit slip, put less than one hundred dollars cash into the cash bag, and secured it with a key. After shutting down all machines but the mainframe and turning out all but the purple neon light in the front window, she grabbed a ream of recycled paper and left Thrifty, locking the door behind her.

Traffic was so heavy she had to walk up to Nevins Street to use the crosswalk to get back to Chase Manhattan Bank, where she dropped the cash bag into the night deposit box.

Then she walked home with a little hop in her step.

The air doesn't smell so bad tonight.

She walked quickly until she stood under the purple awning at Kinderstuff. Through the picture window, she could see castles of every size, color, and shape made out of tongue depressors, Popsicle sticks, and toothpicks, the glue glistening.

Dylan Riordan Healy is building castles down here, too, and one day, I'll be building sand castles in my front yard because of him.

She focused on the largest castle, which seemed to be more a stadium than a castle. Instead of solid green grass inside, the artist had created a rainbow colored field.

A child's art is the purest kind of art. Straight imagination. These children haven't been sullied, influenced, or polluted by any of the other brutal art out there. These castles are dreams made visible.

After what happened today, I can actually see a few of my dreams now.

Having dreams means you have something to live for. Oh, sure, dreams can get complicated, but maybe I need complications in my life, and perhaps, maybe, hopefully, Dylan can simplify my life, too.

She smiled as she ambled off down Flatbush Avenue.

Yes, maybe Dylan can simplify my complications.

Chapter 6

Once inside her apartment, Hope put on her University of Alberta sweats, gray with green and gold lettering. Whack, as usual, ignored her in silence from the quilt on Hope's bed.

Hope was not pleased with how unflattering these sweats made her look. "*Je ressemble à un grand éléphant bouffant,*" she whispered at her reflection in the long, skinny mirror on the back of her washroom door. She looked at Whack. "Don't I look like a tall, baggy elephant?"

Whack did not reply.

Though she wished she had a proper drafting table, Hope decided her kitchen table would have to do. She set a blank piece of paper in front of her.

And drew a blank.

She drew many blanks.

In fact, she drew so many blanks that she rose, went to her nightstand, and turned on her clock radio, tuning it to WCBS to listen to some classic oldies.

She returned to the kitchen table.

She readied her pencil.

She drew in the air.

She looked down at her feet and saw Whack peering up at her. "What do you want?"

Whack licked her right paw.

Hope looked at Whack's food and water containers. "Why haven't you eaten today?"

Whack licked her left paw.

"Maybe it's all the excitement," Hope said. "You're not used to seeing me doing anything." She smiled at Whack.

Whack remained impassive.

"Please don't stare," Hope said. "I'm trying to be creative. I have plenty of ironic and twisted thoughts, but how do you illustrate irony?"

Whack didn't know, or if she did, she wasn't telling.

Hope leaned back on the chair and nearly toppled over.

She switched chairs.

That one nearly fell over.

She propped her feet on another chair.

She heard Juan cursing his mother and Mr. Marusak yelling for the remote control.

Hope closed her eyes, envisioning her stick figure girl, Noelle, looking at a calendar opened to October. *Okay, that's on the outside of the card, and inside the card . . . nothing.* She opened her eyes when she heard her pencil rolling across the table.

"Whack, leave my pencil alone."

She snatched her pencil and lifted Whack off the table, setting her onto the floor. "I could put something like 'Merry Christmas . . . Sales' on the inside."

Whack blinked.

"Yeah, that's whack. Or how about . . . 'Only two months till Christmas. Shop early, shop often. Shop now, or the world economy will suffer a gruesome death. Be a good American and spend more than you have on stuff you don't need.' "

Whack stretched her back and yawned.

"Yeah," Hope said. "That's about as exciting as *you* are."

She drew a quick calendar on the page, labeling it "October." On the back of the sheet, she wrote, "It's beginning to look a lot like Christmas."

Is this lame or what? It's just dumb enough to get someone's attention, but since October is half over, who would buy this card?

Hope heard the Vaz sisters arrive. *They're coming home later each night. Business must be getting worse.* She heard Mr. Antonelli stumbling around his apartment. *He's drunk or hungry or drunk and hungry again.*

Hope stared at Whack. "Why don't you purr? You are the only cat I have ever known not to purr. If I had any skill, I'd do a whole line of greeting cards starring you, and I'd call it 'The Silent Cat.' "

She sketched Whack quickly on a new sheet of paper. *Hmm. Maybe...* She added a little girl with a ponytail under and around Whack so that Whack appeared to be in the girl's lap. *Now what?* She "balanced" the little girl on a stick leg—

Yes!

She quickly drew her version of Dylan's Skinny Santa sitting in a throne-like chair. She created a word bubble coming from the girl's lips and wrote, "Santa, my kitty cat won't purr. Can you fix her?" She flipped the sheet and wrote, "Why?"

Oh, that's brutal. It's true in my case, but how universal is it? How many other people have mute cats? More importantly, how many cat owners wish *their cats were mute?*

She turned over the sheet and erased Whack and the words in the bubble. She tried to put herself in the average mall. *Dressed-up children and exhausted parents in line. A sign that reads, "Meet Santa Claus at noon today." An old guy with a fake beard. Overpriced "portraits." At least half a dozen children crying their guts out. Children reaching for their parents and trying to escape Santa's lap.*

"That is such a creepy tradition," Hope whispered. *Yes, please put my innocent, impressionable child on the scary, red-suited stranger's leg.*

In the word bubble, she wrote, "My mommy will be back any minute now . . ."

She flipped the sheet, erased "Why?," and wrote, "Free day care."

No. No mother would leave her child sitting on some scurvy man's leg for hours at a time. She might think *about doing it so she can actually get some shopping done without all the whining and "Mommy, can I have . . ."*

She erased the words from both sides and stared at the little girl. "What will you ask from Santa, little girl?"

Why am I not using my signature character?

She transformed the little girl into Noelle, complete with dreads and glasses.

She flexed her fingers. "Okay, now what would this *splendide*, sexy woman ask Santa?"

She smiled. " 'Santa, I want a boyfriend on the side,' and what will Santa say? ''Ho! 'Ho! 'Ho!' "

"That's funny," Hope whispered. "A bit risqué, but funny."

Hope decided that if she kept the cover concept the same and only changed the words outside and inside, she could create an entire set of cards. *A collection.*

A matched set.

She wrote down the ideas as fast as they flew into her head:

Outside: Santa, I want a faithful man . . . Inside: No! No! No!

Outside: Santa, I want a new beach house . . . Inside: Owe! Owe! Owe!

Outside: Santa, I want a new dress . . . Inside: Sew! Sew! Sew!

Outside: Santa, I want a horse . . . Inside: Whoa! Whoa! Whoa!

Outside: Santa, I want to meet a rap star . . . Inside: Yo! Yo! Yo!

Outside: Santa, I want some marijuana . . . Inside: Grow! Grow! Grow!

Outside: Santa, I want a new hairstyle . . . Inside: 'Fro! 'Fro! 'Fro!

Outside: Santa, I want to go to Europe . . . Inside: Row! Row! Row!

She counted her ideas. *Ten exactly. A ten-pack. The "Santa's Knee" collection. If we sell them as a set and give customers free shipping, however, we'll be costing ourselves five dollars on each collection, but we're going for volume, right? But there's still something missing.*

She wrote down something obvious under Santa's responses: "Merry Christmas."

She stared at the phrase. *What's truly merry about Christmas anyway? Everyone's rushing about, people seem to be in a bad mood, shopping in crowds, listening to the same carols over and over again. People who should never wear red or green or any combination of red and green are walking about acting happy when they're really tired of the whole holiday season race.*

It's a real freak show.

She added the word "freaking" between "Merry" and "Christmas." *"Merry freaking Christmas." That ought to do it.*

She redrew the cover of the first card with an empty word bubble and carefully traced nine more. Then she wrote in all ten sets of the words, centering the inside copy beside the fold and between the edges.

"There," she told Whack. "I've been successful."

Tapped out but happy, Hope flipped through the channels on her TV. *No way. They're already showing* It's a Wonderful Life. *It's October! I used to like that movie, but then I grew up eight years ago.*

She turned off the TV and her light and drifted off to sleep, dreaming of a beach house and a sunrise child, falling asleep within minutes for the first time in years.

OCTOBER 15

*Only 70 more shopping days
until Christmas . . .*

Chapter 7

Hope nearly jogged up Washington Avenue Thursday morning, her future greeting cards safely hidden in an old FedEx mailer, her shirt already unbuttoned to her bra underneath her coat. She sprinted on Sterling and even stopped at Prospect Perk Café for two House Blend double-doubles.

She had to buy a coffee for her partner, didn't she?

She slowed and only race-walked up to Kinderstuff and saw Dylan inside wearing his standard hoodie and paint-spattered jeans while working a puzzle with a little Hispanic boy, a little girl wearing a Yankees cap adding more orange paint to her stadium castle on a table nearby.

That has to be Aniya, Hope thought.

Aniya wore jeans, a flowered top, the cap, and the hugest smile, her eyes far too big for a child's face and yet fitting her. She had honey, almost golden, skin, her tiny hands covered with five kinds of colorful paint.

Dylan looked up, smiled, and came to the door. "Good morning. I didn't expect to see you so early."

Hope handed him the coffee. "I hope you like your coffee plain, strong, and sweet." *Like me. Okay, only the plain part is right.*

"Do you want to hang out for a few minutes?" Dylan asked.

"I'd love to," Hope said, "but my business partner is working me to death this morning."

Dylan smiled. "He is?"

"He is such a mean taskmaster," Hope said. "Since I have the key to the store, I decided to go in early so I could fold three hundred cards and scan in ten cards I stayed up all night to create."

"You made . . . ten." Dylan sipped his coffee. "It is sweet. Strong." He took another sip and touched the FedEx mailer. "May I see them?"

Do I want to see his reaction in person? What if he doesn't like them? What if he thinks I'm a Christmas-hating psychotic? It's true, but . . . "You will. I have to scan them first, and then I'll e-mail them to you in about half an hour."

"You're keeping me in suspense, Hope," Dylan said.

Just trying to keep you interested, Dylan.

"Could you show me just one?" he asked. "Whet my appetite."

I'd like nothing more than to whet your appetite and have you asking me for seconds, but if I show you one card, I essentially show you them all. "In half an hour."

"Thank you for the coffee," Dylan said.

Hope took a step closer to him. "Is that Aniya?" she whispered.

He nodded.

"Tell her I said hello," Hope said.

"I will. See you soon, Hope Warren."

Hope backed away, a smile escaping. "See you soon, Dylan Healy."

Hope hardly felt the sidewalk as she finished her walk up Flatbush Avenue. Once inside Thrifty, she decided not to wear her smock. She hummed to herself as she scanned and sent her cards to Dylan. She even did the unthinkable: She did a little dance while she ran an overnight Internet order, a flyer for some new show called *The Sense of Sound*, which was opening at the Brooklyn Academy of Music in the Harvey Theater Friday night.

As she was putting the Baum through its paces folding the last fifty "Siamese Snow Angels" cards, Kiki swept in at nine wearing a tie-dyed orange-and-turquoise *banduu* that matched the orange of her sweater and the turquoise of her jeans.

The girl looks like a Jamaican sunrise.

"Is Justin in yet?" Kiki asked.

Hope shook her head.

"And this means . . ." Kiki frowned. "You had to open the store this morning."

Hope nodded.

"And," Kiki said, "you also had to close up and do the deposit last night."

Hope nodded.

"We must speak to Mr. Yarmouth about this," Kiki said.

Oh no! I need Justin to be my boss. I get so much free time with him not *bossing me around or being here.*

"Were we busy yesterday?" Kiki asked.

Hope shook her head. *We weren't busy, but I was.*

Kiki pulled a high stool from under the counter and perched in front of the register. "So I did not miss anything."

"No." *Just the beginning of a new relationship and a second job, that's all.*

Two hours later at eleven AM, after no one had even lit up a cigarette outside the front door, Justin arrived, and he wore the same purple shirt and khakis he had worn the day before. "Good morning," he said, and he disappeared into the office.

Say hello to your girlfriend for me, Justin, Hope thought. *She might be stiff, though. She's been stuck on your screen all night, and her "friends" might be angry for having to keep it up all night.*

"The man is a half ee-dee-ot," Kiki whispered. "He is bay-it. *Ooman naa* like bay-it."

Women don't like bait, Hope thought. *Women don't like punks.*

"We work for bay-it," Kiki said.

True, but if Justin is an ee-dee-ot and bay-it, what does that say about us? "Kiki, forgive me for asking, but how do you turn your accent on and off so easily?"

Kiki smiled. "You are suddenly speaking to me."

I drank a lot of strong, sweet coffee this morning.

Kiki pursed her lips. "I can do the speaky-spokey. I *am* an American, you know. I was born and raised in Uniondale way out in the suburbs. Some people think I have a fake accent, but it was what I heard as a child. It is what I hear whenever I go home to visit."

A customer came in to pick up an order Hope ran three days ago.

Kiki winked at Hope. "Hello, Mr. Ernesto," she said in perfect speaky-spokey. "Are you here to pick up your order today?"

"*Sí,*" Mr. Ernesto said. "What do I owe you?"

Hope turned away from the whitest-sounding Jamaican she knew and returned to the mainframe, where she checked her e-mail. She clicked on Dylan's message ("Your Cards!"), the only message in her in-box, and read:

HAHAHAHAHAHAHAHAHAHAHAHAHAHAHAHAHAHAHAHAHA-
HAHA! I've posted your masterpieces under the "Santa's Knee" collection on the website. They look fantastic! Funny stuff! Sorry I can't get away at lunch. I will definitely be there tomorrow with Aniya. She's excited to meet you. iame $now Angel$ broke 500 $old 5 minute$ ago! Run 200 more A$AP! $ee you @ 5!

Once Hope's hands stopped shaking, she did some math in her head. *Five hundred times ninety cents. Four hundred and fifty dollars. That's a lot of money for a doodle on a napkin. I have thrown away so many doodles over the years! If I had been making cards for the last five years, I might already be living in my beach house!*

She did some more realistic math in her head. *No. I'd only be closer to the down payment. Still, closer is better than further.*

She loaded the DocuTech with thirty-two-pound paper, pulled up the "Siamese" file, and sent two hundred more to print.

"What are you so happy about?" Kiki asked, spinning idly on her stool.

Hope blinked.

"First you talk to me, and now you are dancing around the machine," Kiki said. "You must be happy."

"I didn't think I was dancing." She looked at her boots. *Were you dancing without my permission?*

"You were dancing, Hope," Kiki said. "And you were smiling until I asked if you were happy. And now you are frowning. Why were you so happy a few seconds ago?"

"I guess I just am," Hope said. *Just feeling the sand between my toes, the ocean breeze in my hair, and the salt spray stinging my face ... as the real estate agent tells me she can't sell the house with only a little money down to a woman who works in a copy shop in Brooklyn.*

Kiki smiled. "I do not think I have ever seen you smile before this moment. You have a beautiful smile."

Two compliments in two days. "Thank you."

"It is the contrast of your dark skin and your white teeth," Kiki said. "So stunning."

"Thanks."

"So, what is the real reason for this smile today?" Kiki asked.

I want to tell her so badly, but I hardly know her. I know that's my fault. I haven't said more than a few words to her daily for the last month. Of course, I hardly know Dylan either, but he has been coming into Thrifty for five years. That has to count for something. "I'm ..."

Kiki laughed. "You are back to being speechless as usual." She sighed. "You do not have to tell me. Your secrets are safe. For now. Did you run those flyers for the show?"

Hope pointed to a tall stack of copies under the counter.

"Ah," Kiki said. She picked up a copy. "They look good, do they not?"

Hope nodded.

"I do good work, yes?" Kiki said.

Kiki did those? I thought someone at the Brooklyn Academy of Music did them. "They're very good."

"And I will be paying for them." She wrote up a work order. "Ticket sales for the show are slow. The cast pitched in to pay for these, and since I work here ..." She dug out a stack of bills from her leather purse, rang the purchase into the cash register, and deposited the money. "Some of my good friends are in the show, and they all say it will be fantastic." She closed the register. "Are you going? It is only twenty-five dollars."

Hope shrugged. "I don't know. I doubt it." *I have a new business to help run.*

"You should go," Kiki said. "The price is so low for such a groundbreaking performance."

Twenty-five dollars will buy a nice welcome mat on the ground outside my beach house.

"Surely the man who has made you smile and dance like this can pay your way," Kiki said.

That was very slick. Kiki is extremely adept at prying. "How do you know I'm not happy for another reason?" Hope asked.

"Are you?" Kiki asked.

She got me. She is a master *at prying. I will do well to remain speechless around her as much as I can.* "Well, no. Not exactly."

"So there is a man in your life," Kiki said. "You should get him to take you to the show. Or *you* take him." She smiled. "He is a good man?"

"I guess." *How can anyone really know?*

"And do you . . . own him?" Kiki asked.

"Oh, I don't know if I own him," Hope said. "He's not like anyone I've ever met before."

"Ah," Kiki said. "You found him in the last place you looked. My *lala*, my grandmother, she used to ask me all the time where I found something. I would tell her where, and she would say, 'Nuh, Kiki. Yuh find in de las' place yuh look.' "

Hope took a hesitant step closer to the counter. "I wasn't really looking. He just sort of appeared."

"But now you have found him," Kiki said. "It is cause for celebration, yes?"

"I guess."

"Then you must celebrate with him at the show tomorrow night," Kiki said.

I have also underestimated Miss Kiki's sales abilities. She is relentless. "I'll think about it."

"Good."

I want Dylan to take me, *oh yes, but do I want him to take me to a show? Not really. The last show I went to with Odell, which somehow won a few awards, was so pretentious, insipid, and boring that I had to wake him up at the end, and I vowed never to see another one.*

"Kiki, I'm going down to Subway," Hope said. "Want me to get you anything?"

Kiki's eyes widened. "You are eating today?"

Hope nodded.

"I did not know that you ate," Kiki said. She pulled a ten from her purse. "Get me a B.M.T. with extra black olives and extra banana peppers, light mayo, lettuce, tomato, and red onion."

Hope took the money. "I do eat, Kiki."

"But I have not seen you eat," Kiki said. "This man must make you hungry."

Hope smiled. "He does."

"Ah, then you must go out to eat *before* the show." She winked.

"Maybe," Hope said.

Hope trotted a few doors down to Subway, stood in line listening to some seriously old sixties music, ordered two B.M.T.s the same way, added two oatmeal cookies and two Pepsis, and returned to Thrifty, setting the bags and drinks on the counter.

"I didn't know what you wanted to drink," Hope said. "I hope Pepsi is okay."

"It is." Kiki pulled her sub from the bag.

"Oh," Hope said. She handed Kiki her change.

"So who is this man, and where has he buried the old Hope?" Kiki asked.

"I'd rather . . .," Hope started to say, eating her cookie first. "I just met him, and I don't want to jinx it, you know?"

Kiki shrugged. "He still has a name."

She only knows him as Mr. Healy. I think. "His name is Dylan."

"Was that so hard to say?" Kiki asked.

No recognition. Good. "No."

"Tell me about this Dylan."

How much do you tell a coworker? Should you tell any coworker any part of your personal business? Should you ever tell an Island coworker any of your business? Hmm. I will keep it generic. "Well, he's tall, and he works with children."

"Does he . . . *move* you?" Kiki asked. "Does he . . . *make* you move?"

"Both." *I did some serious running this morning.*

Kiki swiveled on the stool to face her. "How much?"

"How much does he move me?" Hope asked.

"Yes." She smiled. "How much of a champion is he?"

"A champion?" Hope asked.

"A grindsman," Kiki said.

"A what?"

"You are not Jamaican?" Kiki asked.

Hope explained her Trini and Bahamian roots.

"You are an Island girl and do not know what a grindsman is," Kiki said. "I will rephrase. On a scale of one to ten with ten being 'Oh yes, Dylan, don't stop, Dylan, I am in *ah-go-nee*,' what is this Dylan?"

"Ah-go-nee"? Oh. Agony. So, a champion or a grindsman is a man who puts a woman in sexual agony. Why would sex give a woman agony? Well, it has been a long time for me, so I suppose it would hurt quite a bit—

"Do not think too long now," Kiki said.

"Kiki, Dylan and I just met, so . . ."

Kiki puffed out her lower lip. "So there has been no *jooking*?"

Hope squinted. *"Jooking?"*

"No *jooking*, no 'Oh yes, Dylan'?"

Oh. Jooking *is having sex. In Trinidad, to "jook" means to stab. Oh!* "Not yet," Hope said, turning and stuffing half of the second cookie into her mouth. *Didn't Americans once have places called "juke joints"? Is* that *what went on in those places?*

"Ah, but you are so ready, are you not?" Kiki asked.

My mind is ready, but I doubt my body is. "Well . . ."

"Does Miss Hope want there to be some 'Oh yes, Dylan' soon?" Kiki asked.

Kiki has me thinking about jooking *during a Subway lunch on a Thursday. Who thinks about* jooking *on a Thursday? I hope she can't tell that I am blushing fiercely. My eyebrows are even starting to sweat.* "Oh yes," Hope said, attempting a smile.

Kiki burst into laughter. " 'Oh yes,' she says! I knew there was more to you than the *maga duppy* hiding under that ugly smock back there at the machines."

"The what?"

"You are more than the *skinny ghost* who wanders back and forth making copies," Kiki said. "You are a funny, beautiful woman, Hope, and I am glad this Dylan has made you happy." She stared hard at Hope. "And *both* of you must come to see *The Sense of Sound* tomorrow night."

She is a broken record. "What's the show about?" Hope asked.

"Love, sex, pain, suffering, joy," Kiki said. "A typical day in the life of the world. It is mostly about life. I do not want to give anything more away. I have seen some rehearsals, and they have been brilliant."

Brilliant? It sounds depressing, Hope thought. *Maybe I should go. Pain and suffering are good friends of mine.*

Kiki stretched, arching her back and closing her eyes. "I could fall asleep right now." She snapped her eyes open. "On-Gee and I had a late night at the theater."

Should I ask Kiki about Angie—I mean, "On-Gee"? Is that the polite thing to do? What if Kiki starts talking more about jooking? *Do two women* jook, *or do they do something else? Maybe they "cook" or "hook."*

"So, Kiki," Hope said, "how is Angie?"

"She works too hard," Kiki said. "She is on the lighting crew for this show. She comes home so late. I cannot wait for this show to begin so she can be home at a decent hour. I get no joy from eating alone." She bit into her sub, chewing furiously. "Hope, I hate to do this to you, but it is necessary. Is it okay if I leave early today? On-Gee and I must post these flyers before the full dress rehearsal tonight."

"I don't mind." *I want to have Dylan all to myself later anyway.* She looked at the clock, willing two o'clock to become five o'clock in a hurry.

After eating half of her sub, Hope tried to find anything to do to keep herself from looking at the clock. She drifted to the mainframe to check her e-mail and found her in-box empty. She ran two hundred more "Siamese Snow Angels" cards through the Baum. She ran diagnostic tests on every machine. She cleaned and polished every bit of the self-serve copier. She straightened up the wall of paper. She did everything but take inventory.

I'm not bored and anxious enough to do that. Who is?

At 4:30 PM, Dylan entered the store, the broadest smile on his face.

Hope tried not to smile, but she couldn't help it. *He's early. Does this mean he couldn't wait to see me?* Hope watched her boots dancing on the safety mat.

Kiki perked up and smiled as Dylan approached the counter. "Hello, Mr. Healy," Kiki said. "What can we do for you today? Do you have an order to pick up?"

It's time for Kiki to leave. Hope danced her feet to Kiki's side. "If you want to go now, it's okay," she whispered. "You want to have those flyers annoying people on their way home, right?"

Kiki slid off her stool. "That is a good idea, Hope." She reached under the counter and grabbed the stack of flyers. "I will need a good stapler, some staples, and some tape, just in case." She opened a drawer, taking a stapler and a box of staples.

Hope found a roll of clear packaging tape and handed it to Kiki. "I'll cover for you if Justin asks," Hope whispered.

Kiki rolled her eyes. "Bay-it," she whispered. She squeezed the roll of tape and the box of staples into a jacket pocket. She left one flyer on the counter, tapping on it with a long fingernail. "Do not forget."

"I won't," Hope whispered.

"I will owe you for this," Kiki said.

"It's no problem," Hope said, looking up and smiling at Dylan, who smiled back.

We're two smiling people trying to get some alone time.

After stopping to tape a flyer to the front door, Kiki swept out of the store, adding a little wave.

"Hi," Dylan said.

"Hi," Hope said. *I will say "hi" today, but now I'm suddenly nervous again.* She hefted the bags containing the "Siamese Snow Angels" cards to the counter. "Adding this morning's order, *our* balance is now two-eighty. Check them out."

Dylan reached into the bag and withdrew one card. "Nice. Light and yet sturdy."

Like me. Well, sort of. "Yes," Hope said.

He slipped the card back into the bag, took out his wallet, and slapped a check card into Hope's hand. "Ring us up."

Hope looked at the card and saw "Odd Duck Ltd" instead of Dylan's name. "You didn't use this card last night," Hope said.

"Because there wasn't much in that account last night," Dylan said. "PayPal came through this morning. How does it feel to be almost five hundred dollars richer?"

Hope zipped the card through the reader. "How do you think I feel?"

"Happy?" Dylan said.

That seems to be the word of the day. "Of course I'm happy." She handed him his receipt. *What do we do now? Our transaction is over. He can take the cards and go.* "When will you mail these out?"

Dylan leaned on the counter. "Saturday. But unless I get more stamps, I can only mail out two-thirds of them. I have only run out of stamps like this once before."

"With 'Skinny Santa'?" Hope said.

"Yeah," he said. "I like how you used him on your cards. You even improved on him. Thank you."

Maybe I just wanted to sit on your knee for a while. Hope caught her breath. *Why are these thoughts assaulting me so much lately?*

Dylan sighed. "But I truly hate waiting in line at that post office. I go to the one on Fulton Street. I try to go there only on Saturday mornings, but even those lines are vicious. They rarely open a second line even when there are twenty people in line, and the workers there have daggers in their eyes and never smile."

Hope sat on Kiki's stool. "Unlike here." She smiled. "So what's your next immediate step?"

"I get the privilege of going home to print out address labels, stick those labels to envelopes and boxes, stuff envelopes, seal boxes ..." He shrugged. "My apartment becomes a miniature UPS store."

That actually sounds like fun, Hope thought. *Ask me to help you. I want you to stick to me and stuff my envelope, too.* Hope blinked. *Where has my libido been, and why can't I control it?*

"On Saturday morning, I will walk in, dump the ones I have stamps for, and then wait in line for an hour to get more stamps." He shook his head. "It's not as bad as it sounds."

"I could . . ." Hope said, looking at the counter. "I could help you, you know."

Dylan shrugged. "I don't mind doing it, and I've got nothing better to do on Saturdays. It's become part of my routine."

"But I'm your partner," Hope said.

"And you work, what, fifty hours a week, including Saturdays?" Dylan said. "Don't you need any downtime you can get?"

*I've had almost eight years of downtime. I couldn't stand another minute more. I need up*time.

"I can ask off," Hope said. "I have plenty of sick days saved up."

Dylan leaned forward. "Then who will run the store?"

Good question. Hope sighed. "No one, I guess." *I need to train Kiki and Justin on these machines soon.* "You will ask me if you need help, won't you?"

"I will," Dylan said. He gathered the bags of cards.

No! Don't leave yet! "How long does it take for an order to get across the country?"

"It depends," Dylan said. "Three to five days, I guess. I've only had a few complaints, mostly from Canadian customers."

"Only a few?" Hope asked. "How many do you send to Canada?"

"Roughly ten percent of my—I mean, our—sales," Dylan said. "It may increase once I post your biography on the site."

"My biography?" Hope said. "Is your biography on the web-site?"

"No, but I really didn't need it before now, right?" Dylan asked. "Anonymity has its privileges. Now that I have you as a partner, however, I want to put our pictures on a 'Meet the Odd Ducks' page. I'll put you on top, of course, since you're the real artist."

I like to be on top. Or the bottom. Standing is fine, too, and you're tall enough to grab my legs and—Hope blushed. *I have to stop doing that to myself.*

"I'm even going to put our signature characters next to our pictures," Dylan said, interrupting Hope's thoughts of *jooking.* "Our characters do look a lot like us." He pulled out his trusty memo pad and a pen. "So, Hope Warren, who are you?"

What a question. What if I don't freaking know? "Do you really need a picture of me?"

Dylan slid a thin camera from his hoodie pocket and turned it on. "You look really nice today."

Hope turned away slightly. "I don't want my—" Hope saw a flash. She turned fully to him. "Really, Dylan, I don't look—"

Dylan took another picture. "I like candid shots best, don't you?" He snapped another one, checking the result on the little screen. "Hope, let's go for happy and fun on this one. Smile!"

Hope smiled.

Dylan turned around the camera. "There's a keeper."

Hope squinted at the little screen and saw herself smiling. *Hey there, smiling woman. You look happy, and look at all that skin showing. I wish there wasn't such a glare from your chest, though.*

Dylan pulled back the camera and returned it to his hoodie pocket. He readied his pen, waving it in the air. "So, Miss Warren, when did you know you were an artistic genius?"

"I am not an artistic genius," Hope said. "Are you really going to put my picture on the website?"

"Yes." He pressed his pen to the paper. "Give me something good to go with it."

"I don't know if it's going to be good," Hope said. "Let's see. I have a master's of fine arts in art and design from the University of Alberta."

Dylan wrote it down. "I knew there was a reason for your talent. What else?"

"There isn't much else," Hope said. "I work here, but you know that. I became an American citizen five years ago. My parents live in Canada now but were originally from the Bahamas. My grandparents are from Trinidad. I've been living in Brooklyn for about ten years. Oh, I have a cat named Whack."

Dylan smiled and wrote furiously. "You named your cat Whack?"

"Yes," Hope said.

Dylan smiled. "That's good."

"What's good?" Hope asked.

"All of this is good," Dylan said. "Keep going."

Let's see. Do I tell him that I'm probably anorexic? That I miss being in Canada? That I hate Christmas with a passion? That my sister thinks I was switched at birth? That I haven't had sex in eight years? That my period is hiding from me? "What else do you need for the biography?"

Dylan tapped his pen on the page. "What are your hopes and dreams, Hope?"

Hope sighed. "I don't know. I hope one day to own my own beach house." *Oh, why did I say that? It makes me sound so materialistic.*

Dylan wrote it down. "What do you do in your spare time?"

Nothing! "Mainly I read." *Oh, I practice being depressed. I occasionally sleep. Oh, and now I'm pursuing the nicest man and fantasizing about what I want to do with him. Oh, if you like to get a little crazy, Dylan, I know I can accommodate your every desire. Why, if you want to reach out those big hands of yours—*

"What kinds of books do you read?" Dylan asked.

He was just about to pull on my hair! "I don't know," Hope said, "I guess I prefer anything satirical and strange."

Dylan nodded. "Let me read this back to you. 'Hope Elizabeth Warren, who has a master's of fine arts in art and design from the University of Alberta, is a gorgeous Canadian-American with deep West Indian roots living and doodling in Brooklyn with her cat, Whack. This talented artist enjoys reading satire and dreams of one day owning her own beach house.' "

Well, when you put it that way, I'm slightly interesting. "I'm not gorgeous."

Dylan closed the memo pad. "Too late. It's already written down."

"But I'm not." *There's not enough of me to be gorgeous. I vanish when I turn sideways.*

"I'm entitled to my opinion," Dylan said. "Want to know how your 'Santa's Knee' cards are selling?" He raised his eyebrows.

"You already know?" Hope asked.

"Yep." Dylan smiled. "All told, you've sold ten full sets among two *hundred* total."

Wow.

"Added to the four-fifty you've already made," Dylan said, "I owe you a total of six hundred and thirty bucks."

"Wow," Hope whispered.

"I've already added your name to the Odd Duck account and am having the bank send your check card to me," Dylan said. "They said it would take a week to ten days. I hope that's all right."

"It's fine." *Wow!*

"At this rate, Miss Hope, who doesn't think she's gorgeous but is actually more than gorgeous to me," Dylan said, "you may have an extra twenty to twenty-five *thousand* bucks in your bank account by Christmas."

"Wow," Hope whispered.

"It might even be more," Dylan said.

I like the sound of that word. "More." "But I might make much less, right?"

Dylan shook his head, and then he whipped up the camera and snapped another picture. "I like this one, too. It has wonder in it. Your eyes are sparkling, too. I think I'll title this one 'Wow.' "

She reached across the counter to grab his wrist. "Please, no more pictures."

Dylan shook his head, lining up another shot, Hope's arm stretched to the limit. "This one I'd call . . . 'Yearning.' " He snapped the picture. "Or 'Cold Hands, Warm Heart.' Or 'Dylan, Please Stop Taking My Picture.' "

Hope let go of his wrist. "You're wasting pictures."

Dylan scrolled through the pictures. "These pictures don't do you justice." He put the camera in his pocket. "You look much better in person."

What do you reply to that? Do you say anything at all?

Dylan checked his Mickey Mouse watch. "Are you doing anything for dinner? We need to celebrate. My treat. Consider it a bonus."

Wow again! "Do you still have those menus?" Hope asked. *I'm not hesitating at all this time. Why am I not hesitating? I must want to eat.*

Dylan pulled the menus from his hoodie pocket.

This man is ever ready to feed me. Hope took the menus. "I'll hold them, and you choose this time."

Dylan reached out and pulled. "Taro Sushi." He grimaced slightly. "I've only had sushi once."

"Me, too," Hope said. "I had a little trouble with that green stuff."

"The wasabi," Dylan said. "Spicy stuff."

She handed back the menus. "I guess I could be running my cards now. How many should I run?"

"Thirty each," Dylan said. "Just to be on the safe side."

Three hundred more! This is amazing! She wrote up a work order.

"I'll pay in full this time," Dylan asked, again taking out his check card. "Two-forty, right?"

"Right," Hope said, taking the card and zipping it through. She checked the clock. "I better get started on these. Can you tear off the receipt when it prints out?"

Dylan nodded. "I'll be watching you work."

Then I'll just have to give him something more to see.

Hope swayed a little in front of the mainframe, throwing out a little hip. She bent down slowly as she added paper to the Docu-Tech, her hair reaching out for the floor. She wiggled as she removed the cards, arching her back as she fed the cards into the Baum. She smiled slyly as she bagged the order and set it on the counter.

Dylan didn't say anything or even look at her, gathering up the new bags with the others and moving toward the front door.

Did I do something wrong? Did I overdo it? How would I know? I've never posed and shown off like that before! What did he see that has shut him down?

"It's six o'clock," she said softly. "I'll get my coat." She put on her coat and knocked on the office door.

The door opened a crack, Justin's nose and half his chubby face visible. "Quitting time?" he asked.

Hope nodded, handing him his keys.

"Oh, yes," Justin said. "I might need those. Thanks." The door shut.

Hope moved slowly around the counter and stood beside Dylan. "I can carry some of those bags."

Dylan shook his head and held them up with one hand. "It's all right." He looked away. "Ready?"

"Yes." *What did I do?*

Dylan held the door open for Hope, she stepped through, and as they turned south on Flatbush, Hope felt a warm hand take hers.

"Is this okay?" Dylan asked.

I must have done something right.

Hope squeezed his hand and smiled at the sidewalk. "Yes."

"Good," Dylan said. "This is good."

I am never letting go of this hand.

Chapter 8

They walked leisurely hand in hand down Flatbush to Taro Sushi, finding seats at a wooden counter in front of four Japanese men wearing white paper chef's hats. Dylan set the bags on the chair next to him, his hand leaving hers as he opened a menu.

I wish we were still walking, Hope thought. *It was an effortless walk. I didn't have to stretch my hand down to him, as I had to do with Odell. I may even get to wear heels again, not that I ever would. Not in Brooklyn, anyway. Sidewalks steal heels in Brooklyn.*

Dylan stared at the menu. "I have no idea what to order. Do you?"

"No," Hope said, looking at the pictures. *That one looks especially evil. Is that a squid? Do they remove the ink first?*

"You need more time?" one of the sushi chefs asked.

"We need help," Dylan said. "This is our first visit."

Which means this may not be our last visit. She reached under the little counter and squeezed Dylan's leg. *Nice and solid and here.*

"What do you recommend?" Dylan asked.

The chef smiled. "I hook you up."

In a matter of minutes, the chef hooked them up. Dylan stared down at something called "Spider," a fried soft shell crab covered in lettuce and smothered with spicy mayonnaise. Hope admired a dish appropriately called "Mountain," which was a mountain of sushi made out of tuna, avocado, and yellowtail.

"Where does one begin?" Dylan whispered.

Where, indeed? Hope thought. *His whisper just gave me goose bumps.*

Hope picked up a piece of sushi wrapped in green seaweed and took a bite. *This is nice.* "Try this." She held it up to his lips.

Dylan took a small bite. "Mmm."

Hope eyed the crab on Dylan's plate. "Are you supposed to eat the whole thing?" she whispered.

Dylan leaned close to her ear and whispered, "I don't know."

"Should we ask?" Hope whispered.

"Let's just . . . explore," Dylan said.

And explore they did, finishing most of both plates but leaving part of the crab untouched on the plate.

After Dylan paid and gathered all the bags, they left Taro Sushi, standing just outside. "Where to?" he asked.

"I live . . ." She pointed down Flatbush. "Not too far from here."

"May I walk you home?" Dylan asked.

Hope nodded. She held out her hand.

Dylan took it.

Hope smiled at the sidewalk again.

They walked.

"Hope," Dylan said, "where do you see yourself in ten years?"

I can only see myself walking down this street. This is a moment, and I'm living in it. "I don't know, hopefully not at Thrifty."

"Why not work at a gallery or a museum?" Dylan said.

"I looked into that possibility ten years ago, but . . ." *I'm too critical. Everything is brutal.*

"What about starting your own gallery or selling your own art?" Dylan asked. "You are certainly talented enough."

"I'd rather eat," Hope said. *Wasn't that an ironic thing to say?*

He tugged her hand and pulled her closer to him. "I can see you at an archaeological dig somewhere, like in a rain forest down in South America."

Where my hair will become a frizzy collection of spiders' nests.

"And I see you uncovering an unknown civilization's artwork," Dylan said.

"Really?" *I'm only seeing lots of mud and giant mosquitoes for some reason.*

"Really," Dylan said. "And there I am taking pictures of you for *National Geographic.*"

"Without my permission," Hope said.

"Right," Dylan said. "You'll have mud up to your knees, your hair will go in every direction at once, and—"

"My glasses will be completely fogged up," Hope interrupted. "I'll have to get windshield wipers for them." *That almost made sense.*

"Could you ever live where it didn't snow?" Dylan asked.

Hope shrugged. "When I get my beach house, I hope it never snows."

Hope steered them east on Sterling and pulled Dylan to a halt in front of Prospect Perk Café.

"Coffee?" Hope said. "My treat."

"Sure," Dylan said.

They stood under two gargantuan, grimacing red tomatoes hanging from the ceiling and ordered two House Blend double-doubles. They then sat outside on a little wooden bench under an orange awning as workers removed chalkboards advertising the day's specials. Art, mostly photographs by local artists, watched them from the other side of the window.

"Have you ever thought about teaching art?" Dylan asked.

"No," Hope said. "I'm too shy, remember?"

"But isn't art much more about doing than talking?" Dylan asked. "I'd like to see you in action."

I'd like to see me in action, too. I'd put a couple mirrors around us, and then we'd do a lot more doing than talking. "I'd be so nervous."

"You weren't nervous when you did your drawing for me yesterday," Dylan said.

"It was just a doodle," Hope said.

"But that's what kids love doodling—I mean, doing," Dylan said. "I will have you teaching in front of them one day."

"Don't hold your breath," Hope said.

The lights inside Prospect Perk Café winked out.

Dylan stood. "Guess it means it's time to go."

They continued east on Sterling.

"Where do *you* see yourself in ten years, Dylan?" Hope asked.

Dylan looked at their hands for a moment.

He's looking at our hands. Does this mean he sees us like this *in ten years?* Hope smiled at the sidewalk, and the sidewalk seemed to smile back. This, however, was Brooklyn, where nearly ever sidewalk cracked a smile.

"You know I want to open a children's arts center," Dylan said.

"Art for Kids' Sake," Hope said. "You told me about some of the costs. Do you have an official business plan?"

"I do," he said. "Art for Kids' Sake will be a preschool devoted to the arts. Art all day for active minds with active hearts. Sculpture in the morning. Woodcrafts before lunch. Drawing after lunch. Painting until we close. We can do our own art shows, have guest artists come in, especially that famous Island woman artist from Canada, Hope Warren. Ever hear of her?"

Hope squeezed his hand.

"At Art for Kids' Sake, the kids would travel the city learning everything there is to know about art," Dylan continued. "But whatever the kids do, they'll be learning by playing and creating, not stuck with their noses in some book. I only need a space I can afford."

"How much money do you need to get started?" Hope asked.

Dylan's shoulders slumped. "Much more than I have. Much more than I may ever have. Counting taxes, utilities, insurance, staff, benefits, and then all the equipment and supplies I'll need, I'll need at least fifty grand just to get into the building, and this assumes that I can tear parents away from their current day care centers. People get comfortable, you know. They get attached. I don't blame them. If you have a good thing, stick to it, right?"

It's why I'm holding your hand, Dylan Healy. "What would you charge?"

Dylan sighed. "And that's the big question, one I don't have a good answer for. I want to provide quality care at an affordable price. Did you know that some people in this city are paying as much as twelve hundred a month for day care?"

"That's insane," Hope said. *They could easily rent a cheap apartment and lock their children inside.* Hope shook her head. *I'm sure many people do exactly that anyway, and they call these apartments "home."*

"It is past insane," Dylan said. "It borders on psychosis. I want to charge only *half* that a month, but I'd need at least fifty kids to break even, and with fifty or more kids, I'd need seven or more staff, which adds payroll, benefits, and I'd want to pay them well enough to live in this city..." He sighed. "I need to gross at *least* fifty grand a month."

"Why so much?" Hope asked.

"Well, I wouldn't need so much if I didn't want such a big space," Dylan said. "That's my problem. I won't settle for a cramped space. Kids need lots of room to create."

Hope pulled Dylan south on Washington Avenue.

"I don't plan on taking a salary," Dylan said. "You don't need to get paid for your dreams to enjoy them, right?"

"I guess not," Hope said. *It certainly doesn't hurt, though.* "Dylan, I'm not quite grasping your math. You're planning to charge six hundred dollars a month. Why not eight hundred? With fifty kids, that's a gross of forty thousand, right?"

Dylan sighed. "Yeah. Maybe two hundred a week will do it, but I don't want to price anyone out. A person working forty hours a week making only minimum wage would have to work over a hundred hours in a month just to pay for day care at that price, and whatever's left would have to cover rent, food, clothes, emergencies..."

So Dylan isn't going for an upscale clientele. He wants to help ordinary people. She squeezed his hand more tightly.

"If I charge too much, Hope," Dylan said, "I won't be able to help the kids who most need it, kids like I was. I want to bring in enough so that I can even provide scholarships for those who can't pay. I looked into going completely nonprofit so I could get in on some government grant money, but there's so much red tape and an endless number of regulations, all of them designed to cost more money than if I stay for-profit."

He's really getting worked up. His hand is so hot! "You could open a card shop on the side, say, in the reception area of the arts center."

"I could do that," Dylan said.

"It wouldn't need much space," Hope said. "Our cards would be there. Any cards the children make would be there. You are going to have computers so the children can do graphic design, aren't you?"

Dylan stopped walking, leaning against a dim streetlamp. "But who would run the card shop and teach graphic design?"

I talked myself into that one. "I . . . *might* be persuaded to leave my lucrative, fulfilling, and exciting copy shop job if the salary and benefits package were right."

He pulled her close. "I won't forget you said that."

Hope looked down Washington Avenue. "It's just a little farther."

They continued to walk.

"So," Hope said, "how much space do you really need?"

"The space I want has five stories and nearly seven thousand square feet," Dylan said. "You look at it every day. It's right across from Thrifty near the subway entrance."

He wants that *massive space?* "That's been vacant for a long time."

"I know," Dylan said. "Going on two years. What a waste of space. Get this: They want twenty grand a month."

Ouch. "Maybe you can talk them down." *To reality. Twenty thousand dollars? They have to be off their medication.*

"I've tried," Dylan said. "But they won't budge. They told me, 'The economy is coming back.' "

"When?" Hope asked.

"Right, *when*," Dylan said. "I looked at a few other spaces on Flatbush, but they all want too much for narrow rooms with few, if any, windows. The space has to have lots of natural sunlight."

"Why Flatbush Avenue?" Hope asked.

"Flatbush has the highest visibility and traffic flow in Brooklyn," Dylan said. "I've done the research. I need a prime spot that will eventually advertise itself." He shook his head. "I'm boring you, aren't I?"

"No." She pulled his hand, and she turned him to look in the window at The Islands. "This is an excellent restaurant."

"You've eaten here?" Dylan asked.

Hope nodded. *Another time, another place, another person, who rarely if ever held my hand.*

"What's good here?" Dylan asked.

"Everything," Hope said.

Dylan smiled. "I think I'll get us a menu." He looked at her hand. "If it's all right."

"It is, but hurry. My hands get cold quickly." She let go of his hand.

Dylan went in and returned a few seconds later with a menu. "I'll add it to our stack."

Our stack. I like the sound of that. "I live just around the corner from here."

Dylan held out his hand.

Hope took it.

They walked half a block more and stood at the entrance to her apartment building, a blue butterfly mural on the wall behind them.

"This is nice," Dylan said, touching the butterfly, "and I noticed murals all around the building. Did kids do them?"

"I'm sure they did," Hope said.

"Well," Dylan said. "I don't want this good-bye to be awkward, do you?"

I don't want this to be good-bye.

"I enjoyed most of what I could identify at dinner," Dylan said. "I may never eat crab again, though."

Me either.

"And I truly enjoy your company." He looked at the door. "I hope you had a good time."

"I did." *Don't let go of my hand.*

"I'm no good at games, Hope," Dylan said.

"Games?" *What games?*

Dylan set down the bags and took her other hand in his. "The game where I ask you if I can come in, you get all shy and defensive and say something like 'Oh, Dylan, we've only just met, let's take it slow,' and I hesitate but then grudgingly agree it would be best and tell you I'll see you tomorrow as I walk slowly and sadly away into the cold, dark night."

"Is that the way you want this night to end?" Hope asked.

"Honestly, no," Dylan said. "But I have to be up before the sun rises, and I do believe that if I accompanied you to your apartment, we would not get any sleep."

"Oh," Hope said. *He's right. We'd be up all night talking.*

"I mean this as a compliment, Hope." He squeezed her hands.

"I took it as one." *Though it makes me sad. How can a compliment make you feel sad?*

"I don't want to leave you because you're amazing," Dylan whispered. "These last two days have been amazing. Our conversation isn't finished, right?"

Hope nodded. "Right."

"And I don't want to do anything that might interrupt or change that," Dylan said.

Hope looked at the ground. "Neither do I."

"I like you, Hope," Dylan said. "I never thought I'd meet someone who could . . ."

She looked up. "Who could what?"

"Who could help me dream again."

Oh, that is so sweet.

Dylan took a deep breath. "Now is this where we hug or . . . kiss . . . or should we just . . . squeeze hands, smile, and walk away?"

Hope stepped in and hugged him, burrowing her face into his shoulder as his arms pressed her close.

"That answers my question," Dylan whispered. "This is where we hug. I will dream of you tonight."

I will dream of you, too. Hope stepped back, reached into her coat pocket for her keys, found them, and stepped over to the entrance. "See you tomorrow."

"For lunch," Dylan said.

I'm already missing you. "Good night."

"Good night."

She turned the key, opened the door, and ran up her steps. She turned and saw Dylan peering up at her through the entrance window.

I will see you tomorrow.

"Tomorrow" is an excellent word, too.

Chapter 9

I must be getting soft, Hope thought. I let him walk me all this way and didn't invite him in. I know he didn't want to spoil anything. Nothing wrong with that. He told me if he did come up, we'd be up all night. We would have talked some more, and I would have listened some more, and then . . .

And then . . .

She sighed. *I have no idea what would have happened.*

Hope fed Whack and looked at her soft bed. *I am too tired to create, but I'm too wired to sleep.*

She microwaved a mug of water, found a stray Red Rose tea bag hiding in a box in the cupboard, dunked it until the water turned brown, added five teaspoons of sugar, and began writing:

Outside: Woman with a bandaged toe . . . Inside: Miss Ill Toe
Outside: Woman with missiles <u>for</u> toes . . . Inside: Missile Toes
Outside: Goat with a bow on . . . Inside: Season's Bleatings
Outside: Fist w/Xmas tree tattoo hitting a face . . . Inside:
　　Season's Beatings
Outside: Vampire w/ long hair biting elf . . . Inside: Season's
　　Bleedings
Outside: Christmas office party, drunks . . . Inside: Season's
　　Meetings
Outside: Dreadlocked woman with hair to the floor . . . Inside:
　　Hairy Christmas

Outside: Man shoveling dirt over tree and presents ... Inside:
   Bury Christmas
Outside: Elf milking cow ... Inside: Dairy Christmas
Outside: Santa, reindeer, sleigh, Santa passes gas; word bubble:
   "Oh, excuse me"; reindeer grimacing ... Inside: Airy
   Christmas

"*Déplaisant!*" Hope said to Whack.

Whack only blinked.

"That means 'nasty' or 'unpleasant,' Whack, old girl," Hope
said. "I am a stinker just like you."

Hope worked long into the night drawing each cover as simply
as possible with bold lines. She gave big bug eyes to the animals.
She decided against using any stick figures and made Santa extremely large, his flab leaking out over the edges of his sleigh.

*Now what can I do about poinsettias? If I'm going to trash Christ-
mas, I have to trash it all. Why would a mostly poisonous plant be
the traditional "flower" for this preposterous holiday?*

She went online and looked up the poinsettia legend. In Mexico
in the 1500s, Hope learned, a poor little girl wanted to give a gift to
celebrate Christ's birth, but she had nothing to give. An angel appeared and told the little girl to gather weeds and put them in front
of the altar at her church. Red, leafy "blossoms" grew out of the
weeds, and poinsettias were born.

*The story, while a little peculiar, is too beautiful to ruin. Give
what you can, and beauty will follow. Hmm. Maybe I can do a "real"
card with that thought one day.*

Just not tonight.

She slid her latest "masterpieces" inside the FedEx mailer and
then slid herself under her soft covers.

Give what you can.

Beauty will follow.

Maybe I am getting soft.

She shrugged and turned off her light.

Soft sure does beat hard and bony, though.

OCTOBER 16

*Only 69 more shopping days
until Christmas . . .*

Chapter 10

Washington Avenue jarred Hope's knees and bones as she *ran* to work on Friday, her FedEx mailer securely under her arm. After she picked up Dylan's coffee from Prospect Perk Café, however, she slowed to a fast walk as she turned up Flatbush Avenue.

You should never spill your partner's coffee. She noticed light-brown coffee bubbling through the top. *I suppose it's okay to shake his coffee, though. Otherwise, his last sips will be straight sugar.*

Under the purple awning at Kinderstuff, Hope waved at Dylan through the window. Dylan came to the door, took his coffee, handed her a zip disk, and pulled a folded piece of paper from his back pocket.

Hope blinked. "Good morning."

"Oh, sorry," Dylan said. "Good morning, Hope, and thank you for the coffee. It's been a crazy morning." He looked inside. "I was on my own until half an hour ago."

"Yikes." *I was on my own until I met you, Dylan. Yikes!*

Dylan unfolded the paper. "This is a printout of all the orders that need to be made today. Name of card, number of copies. All of Odd Ducks' cards are on the disk."

Hope scanned the list and saw more than twenty new orders for her "Santa's Knee" cards. *Yes!*

"Did you sleep well?" Dylan asked.

"Yes." *The three hours I got.*

"That coffee kept me up all night," Dylan said. "You were right about it being strong." He took a sip. "I'll need it even more today."

At least something kept you up all night, Hope thought. *It should have been me.* "Did you make any new cards?"

Dylan shook his head. "I had a lot of labeling and packaging to do, so I only made one. You have some more for me?"

Hope patted her mailer. "Only ten."

Dylan smiled. "Another collection?"

"You could call it 'The Pun Before Christmas,' " Hope said. "Or 'O Christmas Pun.' "

"I like that," Dylan said. "Ten. Wow. Make two more and we can do 'The Twelve Puns of Christmas.' " He narrowed his eyes. "And you said the coffee didn't keep you awake."

It wasn't just the coffee. "I felt inspired." *By you.*

"I may never catch up to you," Dylan said. "But that's fine with me. As soon as you e-mail them to me, I'll put them online and watch the numbers when I can. Don't be surprised if I e-mail you with more orders. Can I take a peek?"

At what, you naughty boy? You couldn't see much today. I'm wearing a loose sweater. Hope held the mailer tightly to her side. "It's a surprise."

Dylan sighed. "See you at lunch then. Aniya and I will be preparing it shortly."

"What's on the menu?" Hope asked.

"It's a surprise." Dylan winked. "I'd hug you, but then you might, you know, drop your work, and then I'd have to pick it up and accidentally look at it."

Hope wrapped her free arm around Dylan's neck, Dylan's arms wrapping around her waist. "You'll see them soon enough." She stepped back. "See you at lunch."

She turned, straightened her shoulders, and strode up Flatbush. After half a block, she peeked behind her. *He's still watching me go. I have to wear some tighter jeans.*

When she arrived at Thrifty, the door was locked, the store dark. She looked through the window at the clock inside. *I'm right on time. Where's Justin?* She glanced up and down Flatbush until she saw Justin waddling away from the subway entrance.

"Bay-it," she whispered.

"Sorry I'm late," Justin said as he unlocked the door two minutes later. "The train was crowded today."

Take an earlier train, Hope thought.

Once Justin had safely locked himself behind the office door, Hope got to work, scanning her drawings, saving them as jpegs, and attaching them to an e-mail to Dylan with the message:

I hope you like these, my silent knight. Get it? :) I'll try to think up two more. Hope

After sending the e-mail, Hope hurriedly doodled an obese knight in shining armor with his lips stapled together. On the inside she wrote, "Silent knight, roly-poly knight."

That makes eleven. Just one more. What's another Christmas carol I can ruin?

She smiled, quickly sketching a little circular town surrounded by word bubbles. In half of the word bubbles, she wrote "Beth?" or "Beth!" In the remaining bubbles she wrote "Ahem!" On the inside, she wrote "O Little Town of Beth Ahem."

Oh, these are brutal.

She scanned them in, saved them as jpegs, and attached them to another e-mail to Dylan with the message:

Two more to make a dozen. Why'd I do them? Be
Claus . . .
Hope

After sending that message, she checked out Dylan's new drawing called "Found." It featured a simple drawing of a black hand holding a white hand, and on the inside, Dylan had handwritten this line: "Love what you do, and love will find you."

That's so unexpected and sweet, and I inspired it. At least I hope I inspired it. I don't know if I agree with the sentiment, though. I always thought that you had to go out and find love, but here's a man who believes that love will find you if you're doing what you love to do.

She printed out a copy of "Found" and posted it on the bulletin board near the phone. *That really should go up on my refrigerator.*

Hope had barely started sending the new order of cards to print when an e-mail flashed into her in-box:

Where do you get these insanely funny ideas? No. Don't tell me. It will ruin the SURPRISE. :~) They're sensational! But you already knew that. I'll have them up and running now under "The 12 Puns of Christmas" in an hour. See you at lunch. Aniya says hi. Oh, and plea$e run more copie$ of the following card$ . . .

Hope crossed out half the old numbers on the printout, adding at least three to each order. She looked out into the store as Kiki arrived. *I'm glad she's here. I couldn't do any of this if I were juggling real customers.*

Hope spun in her chair, rolled to the counter with one kick, pulled a stack of work orders from under the counter, and walked her chair back to the mainframe. Then she started writing work orders for more than two dozen separate cards. She was halfway through the first one and stopped writing.

This is silly. These should all go on one work order. One customer, one work order. There's not enough room on this sheet for all of these, though. Maybe I'll use two or three and simply number them as I go. It would be easier to create a larger document for larger orders.

Hope was on a third page when Kiki asked, "What are you writing, Hope?"

Hope smiled. *I'm writing hope, Kiki. I hope the money I make from these cards will get me into my beach house before I'm old and wrinkly.* "Some work orders." She rose and began shooting finished cards through the Baum.

"Did they all come in overnight?" Kiki asked.

Hope nodded. *Well, they did.*

"And they are all half-paid or paid in full?" Kiki asked.

Hope hesitated before nodding again. *Sort of.*

Kiki looked through some of the folded cards. "But are not these Mr. Healy's orders? He usually comes in to pay for them in the evening. Unless he has already been here, he could not have paid."

What's the American expression? Oh, yes. I'm busted. "They're actually Mr. Healy's and mine. We've gone into business together." *I'm an Odd Duck now.* "And they'll all be paid in full by closing, I promise." *I hope.*

Kiki laughed. "This one is good. 'I want a boyfriend on the side. Ho! Ho! Ho!' " She smiled. "These drawings are so much better." She read another. "And so is the humor. *You* did these."

"Yes."

Kiki nodded. "You have talent, too much talent to work here." She read several others. "They are obviously selling."

"Yes."

Kiki dragged her stool closer to Hope. "Good. So how did you and Mr. Healy become partners?"

I can't say, "He saw a doodle I made," though it's true. "He liked a drawing I did, the stick figure girl with dreads."

"Oh, I like her," Kiki said. "She looks like you, so skinny."

I'm not skinny. I'm slim. "And after that, he made me an offer I could not refuse."

"The money is good?" Kiki asked.

"Isn't all money essentially good?" Hope said.

"Of course." Kiki laughed. "Do you need any help?"

"I'm okay," Hope said, moving from the DocuTech to the Baum and back.

"What is Mr. Healy like?" Kiki asked.

"He's easy to work with," Hope said, smiling at Kiki.

"Yes, I imagine he would be," Kiki said. "He is, as they say, easy on the eyes. So handsome. Such long hair. So tall."

Uh-oh.

"And I know that his first name is Dylan, Hope." Kiki crossed her arms. "You thought your secret was safe. Mr. Healy is *Dylan*, and yesterday you kicked me out of the store so you two could be alone."

Hope sighed. "Sorry about that."

"Do not be," Kiki said. "He is very cute."

Hope squinted.

"Oh, do not squint so much," Kiki said. "I have been with men, and I have enjoyed being with men. I like to think they enjoyed being with me." She shrugged. "This Dylan is a cute, handsome, sexy man." She hopped off her stool and looked over the work orders. "Your discount saves you a great deal of money."

"To increase our profits." The last cards popped out of the DocuTech, and Hope fed them into the Baum.

Kiki shook her head. "I am wondering if Mr. Healy is not taking advantage of you to get this discount."

I want him to take advantage of me! "He's not taking advantage of me. I am doing this of my own free will because the money is outstanding, and I get other kinds of compensation, too."

Kiki smiled. "You must tell me."

Hope started separating and bagging the cards. "I get bonuses. Lunch and dinner so far. We went out to Taro Sushi last night." She frowned. "We probably won't do sushi again."

"And *then* what did you two do?" Kiki asked.

"He walked me home." *He touched my fingertips, and gave me a hug, and let me go up into my apartment alone . . .*

"And *then* . . ." Kiki nodded. "Did you two . . ."

Hope shook her head, but she kept a smile on her face. "He went to his place, and I went to mine, but I'm okay with it because we are taking it slowly."

Kiki sighed. "*Or* he is taking advantage of you. He takes you out to eat, and your discount saves him enough money to more than pay for dinner."

Why does she doubt Dylan's motives so much? "It's not like that, Kiki. I *do* get paid. I get half of everything. It's in our contract."

"And you have this contract in writing?" Kiki asked.

Hmm. Not yet. "He said he would type it up."

"And the government says it is here to help you," Kiki said. "You had better straighten that out now." She pointed to the phone on the wall. "Call him."

Hope stood, took the phone, and dialed Kinderstuff. "Dylan Healy, please."

After a few minutes, with joyous laughter in the background, Dylan said, "Dylan Healy at your service."

What a strange greeting. "Dylan, I know you've been busy, but have you typed up our contract yet?"

"Yes," Dylan said, "but my ink ran out last night before I could print it out. All those labels sucked the cartridge dry, and it's your fault. Let me e-mail it to you so you can print it out there. Give me a sec."

"Okay." She covered the mouthpiece. "He's e-mailing it to me now."

Kiki blinked.

"Sending it now," Dylan said. "See you in about ninety minutes."

"Can't wait," Hope said.

"Bye."

Hope hung up the receiver, went to the mainframe, clicked on a new e-mail, and downloaded and printed the attachment. She held it in front of Kiki. "He even scanned in our signatures."

"Okay, okay," Kiki said. "I am not one to trust a man, okay? He is doing right by you so far, but why are you taking it slow?"

"I'm older and wiser now," Hope said. "I'm in no hurry to repeat my mistakes."

Kiki waved her hand at Hope. "You two are not old. Going slow is for the old. Who decided not to continue the night, you or Dylan?"

"He did."

Kiki's eyes widened. "And you agreed?"

Hope nodded.

"I do not understand you, Hope," Kiki said. "You want him, yes?"

"Yes," Hope said. "Eventually."

"Hmm," Kiki said. "If you want him, you *take* him."

Hope sat in her chair, swiveling back and forth. "It's not that simple. I have some . . . baggage."

"We all have baggage," Kiki said. "Take *him* and throw the baggage *out*."

Hope laughed. "Just throw it out?"

"Yes, like the trash," Kiki said. "Take him and maybe the baggage will disappear."

Or maybe it will multiply. "I will try again soon to *take* him."

"Tonight?" Kiki said. "After the show?"

She really *wants me to go to this show!* "Maybe." Hope sighed. "Will you be leaving early again?"

"So you two can be alone?" Kiki said. "I think I will stay."

Hope frowned.

Kiki laughed. "I can see from your long face that you do not want me around, but that is okay. I will be leaving much earlier today anyway."

"How much earlier?" Hope asked.

"I think . . . now." Kiki pushed her stool to the counter. "I did not finish posting the flyers. On-Gee could not help. Problems with the stage lights and only On-Gee can fix the stage lights. She will be able to help me today. She can put the flyers up much higher than I can." Kiki nodded to the office door. "You will cover for me?"

"He is bay-it," Hope said. "He will not even notice you are gone."

Kiki started for the front door. "I will see you and Mr. Healy tonight."

"I don't know," Hope called after her. "Maybe."

Kiki stopped and walked back to the counter. "No. There is too much 'maybe' in your life, Hope. You will come, and you will bring your business partner who you want to be your partner in ah-go-nee. Agreed? I will not leave until you say, 'Okay, Kiki, you know best.' "

Kiki is a trip. "I will try."

Kiki shook her head. "Say 'Kiki, you know best.' "

"Okay," Hope said. "Kiki, you know best."

Kiki waved a finger. "And do not ever forget this."

Chapter 11

At noon, Hope saw Dylan pushing Aniya in a wheelchair to the front door.

I didn't know Aniya was so weak. The poor girl!

Hope ran around the counter to open the door, and as soon as Dylan lined up the wheels in the doorway, Aniya threw off her coat, leaped off the wheelchair, and ran inside.

Hope looked at Dylan.

Dylan shrugged. "She likes to go fast."

"So she doesn't need . . ." Hope whispered.

Dylan shook his head. "She has never needed it. I thought it would be fun to take her for a ride."

While Dylan folded up the wheelchair, Hope watched Aniya wandering the store in jeans, a rose-colored shirt, and an oversized Yankees cap. Aniya also had an intricately painted pink-and-red rose on her forearm.

"Hope, meet Aniya," Dylan said. "Aniya, this is Hope."

Hope went around the counter and returned with Kiki's stool. Aniya climbed onto the stool, and it was just tall enough that Aniya could rest her elbows on the counter.

"Is anybody hungry?" Dylan asked.

Aniya rolled her eyes.

Hope rolled her eyes.

Aniya smiled.

"I'll just get the food ready then." Dylan pulled the food out of a little purple cooler: peanut-butter-and-jelly sandwiches, grapes, sliced oranges and cantaloupe, and three wild-berry juice boxes.

"Hello, Hope," Aniya said in a tiny voice.

Oh, my heart! Such a sweet, soft voice, and her accent is so lilting, so sugary.

Aniya turned to Dylan. "Does she talk?"

"I'm sorry," Hope said. "I was admiring your flower. Hello, Aniya."

Aniya looked up at Hope. "I love your hair."

"Thank you," Hope said. *I wish she had some! I'm sure it was long and beautiful, too.*

"I will have hair that long one day," Aniya said, grasping half a sandwich and taking a bite.

"Dig in," Dylan said, taking a slice of cantaloupe and holding it up to his mouth like a smile.

Hope smiled. "I'd like to see you put that entire thing in your mouth."

"Gross," Aniya said.

Dylan took a little bite.

Hope popped a few grapes into her mouth. "Long hair is no fun to take care of, though." *As if I ever do anything to my hair.*

Aniya pointed at her shiny brown head. "It's more fun than this."

Whoops. Let's avoid talking about hair. "I wish I had your pretty name."

" 'Hope' is a pretty good name, too," Aniya said, grabbing a grape.

"Thank you." Hope touched the rose on Aniya's arm. "Did you do this flower?"

"No," Aniya said, sipping from a juice box. "My Tatie Vadie did. She's my crazy aunt. I have a lot of crazy aunts, but she's the craziest. She paints herself all the time to match her dresses."

A thrifty way to accessorize. "I'll bet it saves her money," Hope said.

Aniya shrugged her little shoulders. "She could just get a tattoo, right? She'd save all sorts of money. She thought I'd look cute."

"You do look cute," Dylan said.

"With this hat?" Aniya said. "I don't think so. You never see any of the Yankees with flowers on their arms."

"No," Dylan said, "I suppose not." He grabbed for a slice of orange, but Aniya swatted his hand away.

"*My* oranges," Aniya said. She looked at Hope. "He does very weird things with orange peels. Dylan should not be allowed to eat in public."

She is so cute and precocious!

Aniya finished her half sandwich. "Dylan says you used to be Canadian."

Used to be? "I'm still Canadian in my heart, but I'm now an American citizen."

"Do you speak French?" Aniya asked.

"*Oui.*"

Aniya turned to Dylan. "You didn't tell me she spoke French, Dylan."

"I thought she might," Dylan said. "I haven't heard her speak it. Not all Canadians speak French, you know."

Aniya rolled her eyes. "I know." She smiled at Hope. "Say something to me in French."

"*Je suis si heureux de manger le déjeuner avec vous, Aniya,*" Hope said. "*C'est le rehaut de mon jour.*"

"That's pretty," Aniya said. "What did you say?"

"I said that I am so happy to eat lunch with you, Aniya, and that this is the highlight of my day," Hope said.

"How do you say 'I am happy'?" Aniya asked.

"*Je suis heureux,*" Hope said.

"*Je suis heureux,*" Aniya said perfectly.

"*Très bon, Aniya,*" Hope said. "Very good." *She's quick.*

"Not *that* good," Aniya said. "My parents speak Kreyòl. It sounds a little like French, but it's got other languages mixed with it. I hear '*Tout bagay anfòm?*' and '*Ou byen*' a lot. Are you okay? Are you okay? They ask me that to death."

I will never ask this child if she is okay. She is obviously okay.

Aniya ate a grape. "If I say '*Mwen malad toudi cho,*' they come running. That means 'I'm sick, dizzy, and hot.' I sometimes say it when I can't sleep. I even say it just to get some attention."

"I respect your honesty, Miss Aniya," Hope said.

"Thank you, Miss Hope," Aniya said, smiling. "So did you have fun on your date with Dylan last night?"

Hope looked straight at Dylan, who turned away, his eyes searching the ceiling. "Did Dylan tell you that we had a date?"

Aniya nodded.

"Well," Hope said, "it wasn't really a date. It was more like a business dinner. Dylan and I are business partners, and business partners have business dinners."

Aniya looked at Dylan.

Dylan shrugged.

"That's *not* what you told *me*, Dylan," Aniya said. She turned to Hope. "He said that you two had a *date* last night. He didn't say *anything* about business."

"Well, we are business partners," Hope said. "We make greeting cards together. I'll show you." Hope pulled an assortment of cards from the bags under the counter and placed them near Aniya.

Aniya looked at each card, giggling occasionally, but she mostly wrinkled up her tiny lips. She looked at Dylan. "These are Christmas cards?"

"Yes," Dylan said.

"Are they all supposed to be funny or something?" Aniya asked.

"Yes," Dylan said.

Aniya closed several cards. "Well, they're not."

"Good thing she's not in our target audience," Dylan said. He pulled out a Ziploc bag filled with pill bottles. "Time for your meds."

"Yuck," Aniya said.

So many! Too many!

After Aniya took and swallowed seven different pills, she sucked on an orange slice. "I need lots of Vitamin C. I can't get an infection." She set the orange slice aside and yanked on Dylan's sleeve. "Dylan, why did you tell me you had a date with Hope when you didn't have a date with Hope?"

I like this girl! Yes, she asks many questions, but she's asking the right ones.

"But it *was* a date, Aniya," Dylan said. "I took Miss Hope out to dinner, then we had coffee, and then I walked her to her door. We held hands almost the entire time."

Aniya shrugged. "I hold your hand nearly every day, and we're not dating." She blinked her eyes slowly.

This child is an actress. I cannot believe she's five.

"Did you kiss her, Dylan?" Aniya asked.

"Well, no," Dylan said. "You see, we—"

"Then it wasn't a date," Aniya interrupted.

I agree.

"We did share a nice, long hug, though," Dylan said. "The hug was nice, wasn't it, Hope?"

It was, but I'm not getting in the middle of this fascinating argument.

"It's still not a date," Aniya said. "I hug you before I leave every day."

Every day? That's so unfair. Wait. I got a hug this morning. But I have a long way to go to catch up with Aniya.

Dylan waved a crust of bread at Aniya. "Let me get this straight, Miss Aniya. Are you telling me that for a date to be a date there *has* to be a kiss?"

Aniya nodded. "*Everybody* knows that."

Dylan put his face next to hers. "What if I kissed Miss Hope right now?" he whispered. "What if I walked around that counter and laid one on her?"

I would probably cry!

"Why would you kiss Hope *now*?" Aniya asked. "You have crumbs on your lips."

Dylan brushed crumbs from his lips with his napkin. "How about now?"

I'm waiting! Me! Over here!

"But why would you kiss her *now*?" Aniya asked, this time with a little whine.

Oh no, child. Don't get in the way of my first kiss in eight years!

Dylan leaned closer to Aniya's face. "I would kiss her right now to test your theory about dates. You say a kiss makes a date. Therefore, if I kiss her right now, it's a date. Right?"

"But this is where she works," Aniya said.

It's also where she generally hates life. Let him kiss me, Aniya, so I'll at least have one good memory of this place!

Dylan rested his elbows on the counter. "Oh? So the *location* of the kiss matters."

Aniya nodded. "And it's not nighttime. A date is *supposed* to happen at night. *Everybody* knows that."

Dylan nodded. "So the *timing* of the kiss matters, too. You have so many rules for dating, Aniya. I mean, according to your rules, if I laid a fat, juicy kiss on Hope right now, it wouldn't count as a date."

Aniya shook her head vigorously. "Nope."

Dylan sighed and closed his eyes. "Then I guess I had better not waste a kiss if it doesn't count."

It would too count! Look at my eyes, Dylan. My eyes are saying yes.

"Tell you what," Dylan said. "What if I took Miss Hope to a show called *The Sense of Sound* tonight and gave her a kiss afterwards?"

I am going to the show. Kiki does know best.

"Well . . ." Aniya looked at Hope. "*Where* are you going to kiss her?"

"Does it matter?" Dylan asked.

Of course it doesn't matter! As long as it's everywhere!

"If you only kiss her on the cheek, it doesn't count," Aniya said. "If you kiss her hand, it doesn't count. You have to kiss her on the lips for it to count."

"I do?" Dylan asked.

"You do," Aniya said.

He does. But if he wants to kiss anything else between my toes and my forehead, he is certainly welcome to do so.

Dylan sighed and turned away. "But alas, dear Aniya," he said sadly, "there is a problem."

There is? No problem. I'll go. We don't even have to go to the show. He can just kiss me and save twenty-five dollars!

"You see, I am not sure if Miss Hope will go with me to the show," Dylan said. "She may have other plans."

My only plan is to get a kiss.

Aniya turned her too-big eyes toward Hope. "Do you have other plans?"

"No, Aniya," Hope said. "I am free for the entire evening." *And for the rest of the night, and tomorrow morning, and Sunday, oh, and next week . . .*

Aniya scrunched up her nose. "They why won't you go with Dylan to the show?"

I didn't see that *question coming.* "Because Dylan hasn't asked me yet."

"Oh." Aniya's nose relaxed. She looked up at Dylan. "Well? Go ahead and ask her already."

Dylan smiled.

Hope smiled.

Dylan's eyes twinkled. "Hope, will you go with me to see *The Sense of Sound* and then have dinner at The Islands afterwards?"

She looked into Dylan's eyes. "Why, I'd be delighted to go with you, kind sir."

Aniya smiled.

"So, Hope," Dylan said, leaning heavily on the counter, "is it a date?"

Which is another way of saying . . . "Will you allow me to kiss you tonight?"! What a sneaky man! There is only one answer. "Yes. It will be a date."

"I'll need proof," Aniya said. "I will need proof of the kiss."

Wow. This girl is tough!

"Isn't my word of honor enough?" Dylan asked.

"Nope." Aniya shook her head. "I need a picture."

Dylan laughed. "What if, in all the excitement, I forget to take the picture?"

Hope cleared her throat. "I won't let him forget, Aniya. I'll remember."

Dylan smiled broadly.

What did I say? Oh! I have just said I want to kiss him, too! She munched on some cantaloupe. *I just walked into a kissing trap! Time to bring some reality to this situation.* "But Dylan, I won't have time to change. The show starts at seven."

Dylan scooped up the leftovers and put them in the cooler. "So we don't change. We go to the show as we are."

"Gross," Aniya said.

I agree, but what can I do?

"Dylan is taking me to see *The Nutcracker* in December," Aniya said.

"He is?" Hope said. "That's wonderful."

"And you have to come, too," Aniya said.

Here we go again. "But he hasn't asked me yet, Aniya."

Aniya threw up her hands. "Don't you two *ever* talk?"

Dylan turned away, laughing.

It is kind of funny. "We talk. A lot." *Tonight, however, we might not talk as much.*

"Well," Aniya said, "talk *more*."

"We will, Aniya," Dylan said, "and I will get Miss Hope a ticket to *The Nutcracker*." He rubbed Aniya's shoulders. "Ready for another wild ride?"

"I guess," Aniya said. "He nearly ran over someone on the way here."

"*You* were navigating," Dylan said, helping her off the stool.

"Yeah, I was," Aniya said, "but I said 'Go right' and you went left." She shook her head. "He doesn't know his left from his right." She reached up and took Dylan's hand.

"It was very nice to meet you, Aniya," Hope said.

Aniya turned. "When my hair comes back, you have to make my hair look like yours, okay?"

"I will," Hope said. *Though your mother might object.*

Dylan opened up the wheelchair and set the brake. "Your chariot awaits, good Princess Aniya."

"I am not a princess," Aniya said, putting on her coat and climbing in. "I'm going to play for the Yankees when I grow up. *Geez.*" She flashed a smile at Hope. "Good-bye, Hope." She pantomimed taking a picture.

"*Au revoir, Aniya.*" She shook her head at Dylan. "And bye to you, too."

"Bye." Dylan released the brake. "A little help here."

Hope walked to the door, opened it, and stood to the side. Dylan squeezed by her and pushed Aniya out onto the sidewalk.

"Wheelies!" Aniya cried.

"Oh, my back," Dylan said with a wink, and off they went, Dylan leaning hard on the handles and Aniya holding on tight.

Save something for me!

Hope watched until she couldn't see them anymore. Then she closed the door, returned the stool to the other side of the counter, and sat.

I must do lunch with that child often. That girl is a gift to this world. She's young, naive, funny, and shrewd. She's all the things a child should be.

She's also a decent little matchmaker.

I'm getting a kiss tonight because of a future professional baseball player named Aniya.

Chapter 12

Two hours later, after Hope had successfully juggled several customers and more orders via e-mail from Dylan, Justin came out of his man cave, his purple shirt untucked and his eyes bleary.

"Where's Kiki?" he asked.

"She took off a little early today," Hope said.

"Oh." He scratched at a reddish fledgling goatee. "Did we have a good week?"

He has no clue. I could tell him the building burned down and we rebuilt it around his office. "Yes. Better than usual."

He nodded his head. "Good. That's good."

He returned to his man cave.

Yet another of life's ironies: That *man makes more money than I do.*

While Hope finished ringing up a woman making flyers for Georgie, a lost miniature schnauzer, Dylan threw open the door precisely at five and stepped inside. He pretended to browse a rack of dust-encrusted stationery that had been there for years.

After the woman took her copies and left, Hope moved around the counter and stood beside him.

Look at those bristles. "You need to shave again," she whispered.

"I'm going for a new look," Dylan said, not looking at her. "It's the can't-get-a-shave-because-I'm-going-to-the-show look."

"I don't want you to scratch my tender skin," Hope said.

He smiled. "I won't." He turned to her. "Hi, Hope."

She looked into his brown brown eyes. "Hi." *Oh, now I'm shy. What is this madness? I was fine when Aniya was here. Now that I'm inches away from him, I freeze up.*

Backing away to the register side of the counter, she asked, "Do you want to know the damage?"

"Not really," Dylan said.

She put a stack of work orders onto the counter, spreading them out. "I haven't had to work this much in years."

"And we're not really busy yet," Dylan said.

Hope blinked. "You're kidding."

"As soon as November begins, people start thinking about Christmas cards," Dylan said. "Including yesterday, we have to have broken a thousand, right?"

Hope began pulling bags and bags of cards from under the counter. "At least."

Dylan pulled out his wallet. "Good thing I was paid today." He took out and held up a check card. "This is the one." He handed the card to Hope.

Hope looked at the card, "Odd Duck Ltd" staring back at her. "Is this our corporate card?"

"Yes," Dylan said, "and I'd like you to hold onto it from now on. This way you can ring us up whenever you need to."

"Are you sure?" Hope asked.

"Yes," Dylan said. "This will save us time, and we're going to be busy."

Hope totaled the order and punched the numbers into the register. "You are one trusting man."

"I'm a pretty good judge of character," Dylan said.

"I might just empty the account and buy a beach house," Hope said, swiping the card.

"It would have to be a very small beach house," Dylan said. "A one-room shack on some backwater cove on Long Island Sound."

Hope smiled. "It's a start."

Dylan gathered the bags of folded cards into a large pile. "You know, I think we'll travel in style tonight. We're going to take a cab to the show."

She handed him the receipt. "The theater is only ten blocks from here."

Dylan signed the receipt. "Well, I need to drop all these off at my place first."

Where we can get out, go in, lose track of the time . . . "You could pick them up here in the morning," Hope said. "We open at ten." *That way I can see you tomorrow, that wonderful word.*

"But then they won't be ready to mail," Dylan said. "We are going to get slammed with orders in November, Hope. Trust me. If we fall behind now, we'll be way behind in November."

"It's such a short walk to the theater from here," Hope said.

Dylan reached across the counter and took her hand. "Don't you want to see where I live? I've seen your place. I want to show you mine."

I'll show you my body if you show me yours. Hope squeezed his hand. "Okay."

"Can you get off a little early?" Dylan asked. "You don't look that busy."

"I'll try."

While Dylan called a cab, Hope went to the office door, knocking loudly. *I hope I interrupted something.* She winced. *On second thought* . . .

Justin opened the door a crack. "Yes?"

"I'm taking off early," Hope said. *For the first time ever.* "All orders have been completed, and there are only two orders that may or may not be picked up before six."

"Okay." Justin closed the door.

Hope knocked again.

Justin opened the door a little wider. "Yes?"

"Kiki's already gone, so you'll have to run front."

"Oh." Justin stepped through the door, shutting it quickly behind him. "I'll, um, just run front then."

Hope nodded. *Your brilliance is going to waste here, Justin. You need to work for the government.*

After putting on her coat, Hope joined Dylan on the sidewalk, the air cold, the sun beginning to set. "It's going to be a beautiful night," Dylan said.

Yes. Any night that involves kissing is a beautiful night.

When the cab arrived minutes later, Dylan opened the door and stepped aside. "After you."

"Thank you, kind sir," Hope said.

Once she slid across the seat, Dylan handed the bags to her.

"Where to?" the driver asked.

"The two thousand block of Pacific Street in Crown Heights," Dylan said.

Hope looked at all the bags. *It's as if we've been shopping, only we're selling everything inside the bags.* She took Dylan's hand. "I haven't ridden in a cab in years."

"Me neither," he said.

They rode through thick traffic up Flatbush and turned onto Atlantic Avenue.

I like the sound of these street names, Hope thought. *We're riding on Atlantic and we're going to Pacific.* "How long of a walk is it to work for you?"

"About three miles," Dylan said. "Takes me about an hour, and I am definitely awake by the time I get to work. Never liked the subway or the bus."

She saw flecks of white paint on his knuckles. "Did you do some painting today?"

"The young artists and I," Dylan said in a deep voice, "painted haunted houses today. I suggested that they paint some ghosts in the windows. I tried to impress upon them that ghosts didn't have to be white, but they persisted." He flexed his fingers. "We nearly ran out of white paint."

The cab swung right on Ralph and took a quick right on Pacific.

"Can you wait for me?" Dylan said to the driver. "I'll only be a minute."

The driver shrugged.

Hope handed the bags out to Dylan, and he went through a white wrought-iron gate into a tan stone apartment building older than hers, with King's, a chicken-and-pizza place, anchoring the corner. She stared at an ad on a billboard to her left hyping some new sitcom she'd never watch and a radio ad featuring a scantily dressed black woman.

Do they think her attire will sell music? She squinted. *No. Her lack of attire will sell music. I'll bet they fixed all her blemishes with a computer. No one is the same dusky color from head to toe.*

"Where are you going next?" the driver asked.

"Brooklyn Academy of Music, the Harvey," Hope said.

"We were practically just there," the driver said with a scowl.

"So we're disorganized," Hope said. "It's our first date."

The driver didn't respond.

I'll bet he's just a lonely man on a Friday night.

The cab door opened, and Dylan slid in wearing a jean jacket. "To—"

"She told me," the driver interrupted, pulling away from the curb.

Hope held onto the door handle. *Maybe the driver has a date. Whoa, slow down.*

Dylan put his arm around Hope's shoulders. "Miss me?"

"Yes," she said, "but you changed."

"I only put on this jacket," Dylan said. He poked out his chin. "And I didn't shave. You wouldn't want to be seen at a show with a man wearing a hoodie, would you?"

"I might." She smiled. "That was quick. Do you live on the first floor?"

"The fourth, actually," Dylan said. "Great view of Mount Sion Baptist Church. I'm three floors up from King's. Everything smells like chicken and pizza."

Hope's stomach rumbled. *I'm hungry already?* "I hope I'm dressed up enough."

"You look *splendide, beau, sexy, et délicieux*," he whispered.

Hope's mouth dropped, her eyes searching his.

"Did I say it right?" he asked.

"*Oui*," Hope said. "*Vous semblez élégants et délicieux vous-même.*"

"Uh, I only caught 'delicious,' " Dylan said. "The rest? Not a clue, but thank you. I think."

"I said you were handsome," Hope said. "You said the words perfectly."

"I did? Okay." He smiled. "I looked up some French words on-line when I got back to Kinderstuff. I hit the "listen to the word" button so often the rest of the kids were yelling, '*Splendide!*' I think it's cool that the word 'sexy' is the same in both languages, don't you? It sounds so much better with a French accent, though."

It does.

Dylan turned slightly. "Hope, I am going to be nervous all night thinking about kissing you. Would you mind if I kissed you and took the picture now?"

"A staged kiss before a show on a stage." *That's not very spontaneous.*

"Right," Dylan said. "I want to enjoy the show without worrying about the kiss. It's been a while since I've kissed anyone, and I'm worried I'll botch it up."

I wait eight years, and this is the kind of kiss I get? In the back of a cab in Brooklyn? Where's the romance? Hope smiled. *Ah, whom am I kidding? Lay one on me, Mr. Healy.* "I suppose it would be okay."

Dylan turned his head, moved in, and met her lips with a firm, soft kiss.

That was sweet. Lasted about two seconds, but as first kisses go, not bad.

"Oh," Dylan said. "I forgot to take the picture." He pulled his camera from a jacket pocket.

Hope bit her lip. *He forgot. I'm glad he has a faulty memory.* "Do you really need to take the picture?"

Dylan nodded enthusiastically. "Miss Aniya expects it."

Hope nestled her head on his shoulder. "I'll bet you forgot to take the picture on purpose."

"You have figured me out," Dylan said. "Take two?"

Their second kiss was much longer, much sweeter, and ended with a flash. Dylan showed Hope the screen on the back of the camera. "Looks like I missed."

He got a nice shot of the cars behind us.

"Oops," Dylan said. "What *shall* we do?"

The cab swung to a curb with a screech, jerking Hope into the door.

"Gimme the camera," the driver said. "The flash is distracting me."

Dylan laughed and handed the camera up to the driver.

"Go ahead," the driver said.

Hope Elizabeth Warren and Dylan Riordan Healy kissed for a good thirty seconds this time, the driver snapping five pictures.

The driver handed back the camera. "No more flashes."

The cab pulled away from the curb.

Hope looked at the pictures and noticed that her eyes were closed but Dylan's eyes were open.

"Why do you keep your eyes open?" Hope asked.

"I don't want to miss," Dylan said.

"My lips aren't that small," Hope said. "I have full lips."

"Then I just want to make sure I have full coverage on your full lips." He kissed her cheek. He looked out his window. "I think we're here."

After paying the driver and tipping him a twenty for taking their picture, Dylan took Hope's hand and helped her out of the cab. They stood in front of the Harvey Theater and its Greek columns, "*Carpe Diem*" and "*Fugit Hora*" carved into the stone on the side of the building.

"Seize the day" and "The hour flies," Hope thought. *I'd rather seize the night and have time stand still.*

Once inside, they found their seats five rows back in the center of the auditorium, gold leaf columns and box seats above them on either side.

"These are great seats," Hope said, looking at the stage. *Why does that stage look like a big, black tongue? And why am I thinking about tongues? Oh, yes. I got a little tongue on the third kiss.* "When's the last time you went to a show?"

"Almost . . . six years ago. *The Nutcracker.*"

The lights began to dim, and once the auditorium was bathed completely in darkness, Hope could see the actors scurrying to take their places on that tongue of a stage as a curtain parted upstage to reveal a rust-colored wall that seemed to glow brighter and brighter until the backlights illuminated the actors standing or sitting in various poses holding musical instruments.

This is a musical. Hmm. Do I even like musicals? I hope they don't do any Christmas music.

A spotlight roamed the stage until it found a gray-haired man downstage center on the tip of the "tongue" dressed like an orchestra conductor. Once the spotlight framed him, he "thawed" and flipped out the tails of his tuxedo behind him. He tapped a baton on an imaginary music stand, raised both arms, and pointed to his left.

A bass drum played like the sound of a heartbeat as the conductor's spotlight traveled the stage to "find" the location of the drum. The spotlight stopped, changed from bright white to a soft blue, and circled a massive black man kneeling next to a bass drum.

Hope grabbed Dylan's hand. *That is so cool.*

A dimmer, smaller blue spotlight lit up the conductor, who pointed his baton at a tall, leggy Latino girl in heels and a long flowing white dress upstage left. When a spotlight bathed her in amber light, she flicked out castanets and held them high above her head, adding a complementary rhythm to the drum, her arms whirling as she danced and spun around other "frozen" actors. Her castanets and heels rattling, she danced over to the drummer.

She smiled.

He smiled.

Then they both turned away as if they were shy.

That reminds me of two people I know. I wonder who has smiled at the sidewalk more, Dylan or me. Probably me.

The drummer thumped the bass drum faster, and she danced faster. When he slowed the beat, she slowed her feet and the castanets, becoming a graceful, leaping ballerina with only an occasional click in the air. After a pause, he grabbed another drum mallet, leaped to his feet, and pounded on that drum with both hands for all he was worth until the girl ran over and straddled his drum, swaying wildly to his rhythm, her back to the audience, the blue and amber lights becoming green. She shot out her arms and played the castanets so fast it sounded as if something was being ripped.

Wow! It honestly sounds as if her dress is ripping apart!

Then they played off each other, two *poom*s followed by two clicks, three *poom*s, three clicks, until he dropped one of his drum mallets, and she dropped one of her castanets. One final click, one final *poom*, and they froze in the sweetest, shyest kiss.

That got my heart beating. Wow! But how long will they have to hold that kiss?

"Amazing," Dylan said as applause broke out.

The conductor pointed his baton at a young gangster wearing an orange bandana, a tight green T-shirt, ripped jeans, and boots. The gangster spun a snare drum in the air, light flashing off the silver. Then he stalked the stage as an orange spotlight followed him, "shooting" his drum, menacing the frozen actors, the conductor, and even the front rows of the audience with staccato bursts that made Hope jump repeatedly.

That boy can play! I wish his face wasn't so mean, though. Oh, and I like his earrings.

As the gangster neared the kissing couple with an evil sneer on his face, the conductor pointed at an old man with a harmonica sitting downstage left, a pool of purple light enveloping him as he added a lazy, mournful ballad to the sound of *rat-a-tat, rat-a-tat-tat.*

Hope gripped Dylan's hand.

The gangster acted as if he "heard" the harmonica and raced over to the old man, trying to *rat-a-tat* him into silence. The old man didn't even look up, playing his song more mournfully than before. The gangster played as fast as he could, sweat flying, his arms straining, veins sprouting in his forehead—and still the old man played his sad, sad song. Exhausted, the gangster sat shaking out his arms and panting. The old man lowered his harmonica and smiled at the audience.

The old man wore that gangster out! Slow songs win every time. Slow songs last the test of time.

The old man smiled at the gangster, but the gangster only scowled. The old man shrugged, lifted his harmonica, and played a livelier tune until it sounded like the chugging of an old steam train. The gangster reluctantly joined in, adding a rudimentary beat, and then the two played together until the end of the song, their spotlights fusing to a rich brown. After one more beat of the snare drum, the two clasped hands and froze.

More applause.

"This is so good," Hope said as the ovation subsided.

Dylan squeezed her hand. "So is this." He pulled up her hand and kissed it.

I may begin to like musicals now.

The conductor turned and faced the audience, smiled, sighed deeply, and shook his head. After giving an exaggerated shrug, he turned and pointed his baton at a tall, sexy black man in an old-fashioned three-piece suit and feathered hat playing the saxophone dead center in a growing blood-red spotlight.

There's no doubt what this *song will be about.* "This is going to be *sexy,*" Hope whispered in Dylan's ear.

Dylan turned and kissed her lips. "You're *sexy.*"

Hope finally took off her coat. *It's getting warm in here.*

As the saxophonist began, Hope could almost see his notes. She heard flesh and skin, sweat and sighs.

I hope they make a CD of this performance. What he's playing is perfect music for playing around.

The conductor motioned to a white woman playing a black clarinet in a circle of pink light.

Uh-huh. Okay. I see ruby-red lips sucking on a long black instrument. A bit obvious, isn't it? She shot a glance to Dylan. *His mouth is open, too. That's good. It's shocking him, too. Kiki said some of the show would be about sex. She wasn't lying.*

The sexy saxophonist and lily-white clarinetist played together immediately in beautifully blended harmony and got as close to each other as was legally allowed in public in the state of New York, his saxophone sneaking under her tight miniskirt and popping out in front of the audience.

The conductor waved both his arms, the music stopped, and the lovers froze. He turned to face the audience, his hands grasped together at his chest. "I am so sorry," he mouthed.

Lots of laughter.

The conductor shook his head, smiled, and mouthed, "Oh well." He turned and pointed at the woodwind lovers, and they continued to play. She danced back and forth over the bell of his saxophone, his head thrown back in ecstasy.

Then suddenly, she squeaked.

He squeaked.

A count of four later, her clarinet shrieked, and his saxophone shrieked.

That was the first musical orgasm I have ever heard. Wow.

Then the two lovers laid back on the stage with their instruments high in the air playing the first few notes of "That Old Black Magic" as the red and pink spots shrunk to dots and winked out.

Applause and laughter.

Dylan let go of Hope's hand and rubbed her leg.

Very nice. If he keeps that up, I may squeak and shriek.

The conductor pointed his baton toward a black woman Hope's age upstage center in turquoise light. She rolled her neck and pulled out . . . a kazoo.

Now there's an instrument I can play.

She started humming a slow blues melody through the kazoo as she walked to the edge of the stage beside the conductor, who nodded behind him at another black woman, this one younger and dressed colorfully, who rose from the first row in yellow light and played her kazoo in short, jazzy bursts. Each woman held her kazoo in her teeth, which made them look as if they were smoking cigars. The younger woman slunk up a set of stairs downstage left, weaved around the woodwind lovers, and approached the older woman with her hands on her hips, that kazoo still blowing those staccato notes. The two women began circling each other, and then they started to "argue," and it was the funniest unspoken, hummed argument Hope had ever heard.

Hilarious! I can actually see the story. The younger woman cheated on the older woman, and the older woman is letting her have it! The younger woman doesn't seem to care a bit, however, shrugging, laughing, and pointing at the older woman's body. That's some cruel foolishness there.

The women eventually stood back-to-back, calming down somewhat, and blended into one steady hum as their lights blended to teal green. Using only their teeth to hold their kazoos, they turned to each other and embraced—until the younger woman put both her hands on the older woman's derriere and gave a firm squeeze.

More applause.

Hope leaned over to Dylan. "Did you think that was hot?" she whispered.

"I cannot answer that," Dylan whispered.

Hope let go of Dylan's hand and rubbed his leg.

"Okay, it was hot," he whispered.

The conductor tapped his imaginary music stand again and pointed to an old woman playing a violin down right in dark-blue light, her music so desolate that Hope felt tears forming.

I've heard that sound before. That's the sound of grief, anguish, heartache, misery, and pain. I hope this part doesn't last too long.

An obviously pregnant young girl approached the old woman

from down left in sky-blue light, playing an oboe, and they had a musical conversation full of fierce, strident violin and pleading, weeping oboe. Abruptly, the old woman turned her back on the young girl and resumed her first, sad song while the young girl's oboe wept her completely off the stage.

There was only a smattering of applause this time, but there was no scarcity of men clearing their throats or women sniffling.

"You okay?" Dylan whispered.

"I'm okay," Hope whispered. *I could be an oboe in another life.*

The conductor turned to the audience and waved his baton to the right. He pointed at a section. He pointed again, lifting his left hand. A few people stood. The conductor crossed his arms and tapped his foot. The entire section stood, laughter rippling through the auditorium. The conductor nodded. He turned to the center section and pointed. The center section, including Dylan and Hope, stood immediately. Once he had the entire audience standing, the conductor smiled. Then the conductor frowned. He held his left hand to his ear.

"He wants *us* to make some music," Dylan said.

I didn't know this show would require audience participation! I don't have a musical bone in my body.

"I'm waiting," the conductor mouthed.

In moments, hundreds of people started singing random songs while hundreds more drummed or tapped on the seats in front of them.

Dylan tried to sing the Canadian national anthem.

Hope made him stop.

The conductor waved both arms until the audience quieted. As soon as the laughter died down, the conductor stuck his baton under one arm and clapped his hands once.

Dylan and a scattering of others echoed him.

The conductor nodded and clapped again.

More people echoed him, including Hope.

Okay, okay, I get it, Hope thought. *What a cheap way to get an audience to give a standing ovation.*

In moments, the entire audience clapped in a slow, steady beat. The conductor made the okay sign, winked, turned, and pointed left at the bass drummer, who pounded the drum in time with the audience. The conductor pointed at the Spanish girl, who began clicking away, and at the gangster, who rat-a-tatted. It wasn't long before the audience had to applaud faster to keep up with the increasing tempo of the percussion as a rainbow of spotlights crisscrossed the stage.

The conductor turned to the audience and bobbed his head to the beat. "Not bad," he mouthed. He then did an extremely funky monkey before spinning completely around once, twice, and then faced the stage, pointing at each musician and "unfreezing" him or her.

He's an overgrown, dancing Tinker Bell, and this is incredible!

While harmonica, saxophone, and clarinet formed a lilting, almost calypso melody, the two kazoo players did arpeggios up and down the scale while the violin and the oboe harmonized—

I have never heard such a sound! This is the music of the spheres! I have goose bumps on my arms! I wish the conductor would slow this down! I don't want this song to end!

With the song at its highest crescendo, every light in the theater winked out one by one until only a single green spot washed over the conductor.

The audience was already clapping wildly and continued to applaud as the footlights came up.

"Encore!" Dylan yelled loudly.

"Dylan, shh," Hope said.

"Encore!" Dylan yelled again. "Encore!"

In seconds, cries of "encore" rang all around the theater.

The conductor held up a finger, and the cast formed a huddle.

"See what you've done," Hope said.

"You know they've got something more," Dylan said.

The cast seemed to argue for several moments before slinking away to various spots on the stage. Most of the actors-musicians looked glum. Only the conductor and the oboe player seemed happy.

The conductor tapped his invisible music stand, and the "band" played a sluggish, dirge-like song featuring a gloomy solo by the oboe player under gloomy gray lights. None of the musicians seemed to be enjoying life, frowns in abundance, and all but the oboe player turned their backs on the audience. The conductor stopped the music, mouthed "I'm so sorry" to the audience, "screamed" at the musicians, nearly came to blows with the gangster, and had to be restrained by the violinist. He turned to the audience, mouthed "I'm *really* sorry," and waved his baton again. This time the band played an up-tempo, jazzy version of "Downtown," the old Petula Clark classic, while the two kazoo players belted out the melody.

All right, Hope thought. *Hey, look at me! I'm dancing in the theater.*

When the singers arrived at the chorus, Dylan tried to sing along. "*Down*town, things'll be something something when you're *down*town."

Even Hope tried to sing, but not very loudly.

At the conclusion of the song and after the bows, the house lights came up and Hope put on her coat.

"That was incredible," she said, "and I didn't know you could sing."

"There's just so much we don't know about each other," Dylan said, following her out of the row. "Perhaps we could take the rest of the evening to become better acquainted." He hooked a finger around one of her belt loops and pulled her hip to his as they moved up the aisle to the lobby. "Now would be a good time to start. Are you free for the rest of the evening?"

She kissed his cheek. "Yes." *I'm actually free for the rest of my life.*

They were almost through the lobby when Kiki and Angie leaped out in front of them. "Mr. Healy?" Kiki said. "Hope? What are *you* two doing here?"

Hope rolled her eyes. "As if you didn't know."

Wow, On-Gee—I mean, Angie—is taller than I remembered. I only got a glimpse of her outside Thrifty once or twice before. She's at least three inches taller than Dylan, and she's gorgeous, with long dark hair, blue eyes, and legs for days but in proportion to the rest of her body. I was expecting her to have arms to the floor and the wide face of a giant, but it's a cute face without a shred of makeup.

Dylan stepped behind Hope, resting his hands on Hope's hips. "Hi, Kiki, Angie."

How does he know On-Gee? "You two have met?" Hope asked.

"Of course I know Angie," Dylan said. "She was a volunteer

during my . . . fifth year, I believe, at Kinderstuff. She helped us out in art for four years before she disappeared on us."

"I had to go to college, Dylan," Angie said with no trace of a Hungarian accent.

Even her voice is cute, a lilting alto.

"I made a bigger mess than the kids did, Hope, and I had the biggest crush on Dylan back then, mainly because of his hair," Angie said. "I was barely fourteen when I started volunteering."

I'm so glad Angie's not heterosexual. She could steal my tall Irishman in a second if she wanted to.

"Did I say 'encore' loud enough, Angie?" Dylan asked.

Angie laughed. "You said it *way* too soon! You should have let the applause go at least thirty seconds longer. You know musicians. They love to hear applause."

Hope turned her head and stared into Dylan's eyes. "You were actually *part* of the performance?"

He raised his eyebrows.

"Only for tonight," Angie said. "We'll find somebody else we know tomorrow night, and whoever it is will let the applause build for at least a minute."

"I was feeling the moment," Dylan said. "Couldn't help it."

"You two make such a nice couple," Kiki said.

"You do," Angie said.

"Thank you," Dylan said. "Angie, are you doing what you love?"

Angie nodded. "And love has found me." She kissed Kiki on top of her head.

He must say that phrase to all of "his kids." Love what you do, and love will find you. So simple and yet so profound.

Kiki smiled broadly at Hope. "So I was right about this show, and you are glad you came."

"You were right," Hope said. "But it needs a much bigger stage."

"The producers are thinking of expanding it with a few horns, a piano, and a xylophone, if you can believe it," Angie said.

"They should add a *fundeh* to the bass drum and castanets," Kiki said.

"A percussion threesome?" Angie said.

"I have told you the drum and castanets are not enough," Kiki said. "The *fundeh* would keep the tempo steady. Your castanet player is still too fast."

Angie squeezed Kiki's shoulders with two delicate hands. "We can argue about it later. I gotta go. Some of the colors still didn't blend right, and the backlights aren't bright enough at the beginning."

"Can you not do them tomorrow, On-Gee?" Kiki asked. "We must go celebrate."

Angie sighed. "I want to adjust them while they're still fresh in my mind."

"*I* should be fresh in your mind," Kiki said.

"You are," Angie said, "and if you help me, we can go celebrate sooner."

Kiki sighed. "I go to work, I go to a show, and I go back to work. It is always work."

Dylan stepped away from Hope and gave Angie a big hug. "It is really good to see you again. Let me know when they add the marching band."

"I am not lighting a marching band," Angie said.

Kiki grabbed Angie's hand. "Let us go finish so we can begin." She dragged Angie back into the auditorium.

Dylan took Hope's hand. "Having fun?"

"Yes." She leaned into him as they followed the crowd outside. "When did Angie recruit you to yell 'encore'?"

"About three weeks ago, I think," Dylan said. "She still stops by Kinderstuff occasionally to say hello."

Because she still has a crush on you. "So you were going to the show whether I was with you or not, huh?"

"Well . . ." Dylan nodded. "Yeah. But I wouldn't have had a good time without you."

"Right."

"It's a long walk to The Islands," Dylan said. "We could get another cab."

"I am starving," Hope said, "and I need another kiss, and you only seem to be able to kiss me in a cab, so . . ."

Dylan faced Hope, took her face in his hands, and kissed the enamel off her teeth while hundreds of people streamed out of the theater around them.

Hope had to catch her breath.

"Yes," Hope said, "I think we'll need a cab." *I'm feeling weak in the knees.*

On the ride to The Islands, heavy traffic allowed Hope and Dylan to share several long kisses interrupted sporadically by car horns and curses from the driver.

After a particularly passionate kiss involving a mutual trading of hands, Dylan caressed the back of Hope's neck. "What instrument best portrays *your* voice?"

"A French horn," Hope said. "No. Too obvious. What's the quietest instrument? A flute. I'd be a flute."

"But a single flute can often be heard over the entire orchestra," Dylan said.

I can't be a flute then. I don't really want anyone to hear me. "Maybe I'm a . . . tambourine."

"Why a tambourine?" Dylan asked.

"Because you have to shake or hit me to make me talk," Hope said.

Dylan squeezed the back of her neck gently. "I would never do either."

Hope rested her head on Dylan's shoulder. "I know you wouldn't. What instrument would you be?"

"I'd have to be a trumpet," Dylan said. "I talk too much. That means we'd be a trumpet and a tambourine."

That's only slightly phallic.

"You know, I think we'd make a good piano," Dylan said, "and not just because of the color of the keys. I think we'd strike some nice chords."

"You have strange thoughts, Dylan Healy," Hope said.

"And the black keys are on *top* of the white keys," Dylan said.

I like it on top. "But there are more white keys," Hope said.

Dylan smiled. "But the black keys are more fun to play." He slid his hand off Hope's shoulder and slipped it down Hope's side, pulling up her coat and tickling her ribs.

She swiveled away from his hand and moved toward the door. "Is that all you want to do with me? Play?"

Dylan nodded. "I want to run my fingers through your hair and all over your body. I want to see what kinds of sounds you make."

I cannot wait for this man to play me. She slid back to him. "Just kiss me until we get there, okay?"

"May I continue to tickle you as we do?" Dylan asked.

"Just tickle my ivories when you kiss me," Hope said, pulling his face to hers.

Chapter 13

The Islands, boasting "Exotic Caribbean Cuisine," was as crowded as it always was, no matter the day of the week or the time of night. At least a dozen people milled around the front door, and twice as many packed the small first-floor interior around the counter.

"We may be getting it to go," Hope said.

"Is it always crowded like this?" Dylan asked. "It's nine o'clock."

"It's a happening place," Hope said, "and it *is* Friday night. We could place to-go orders, and then we could eat at my apartment. If you want to."

"You know I want to," Dylan said, smiling at everyone around him. "But how much would we eat when we got there?"

He has a point. We might not be eating much.

"I love this place," Dylan said. "The aromas are amazing. I don't mind waiting."

"We may be waiting a long time," Hope said. "Once I was second in line, and one of the owners made the woman in front of me wait ten minutes while she prepared a take-out order in front of us."

Dylan shrugged. "So we wait. This time last week, I was warming up some leftover spaghetti in the microwave."

This time last week, I was asleep.

"Tonight I am out with a beautiful lady," Dylan said. "There isn't anywhere I'd rather be."

"It might be a *very* long wait," Hope said.

"The night is still young, isn't it?" Dylan asked.

"Yes, but . . ."

"And it's going to be a long night, right?" Dylan asked.

So long I hope it doesn't end. Hope nodded.

"Then we'll wait." He kissed her cheek. "I want to drink this place in."

Hope hated to wait for a table in any restaurant, but she especially hated waiting for one of the few tables in the upstairs loft at the Island.

This was Odell's favorite place to eat, and we never took anything to go. We could have brought our own drinks, picked up the order, and eaten in Prospect Park or on the steps of the Brooklyn Museum like most people do, but Odell didn't like eating in the park, even on a nice day, because he said it was what "the common folks did." He seemed to enjoy standing shoulder-to-shoulder and hip-to-hip in a crowd, and the whole time he'd complain about the wait. I once suggested we get it to go and eat it at my apartment, and he said, "This place has more ambiance *than your apartment ever will." That word, "ambiance," was one of the few French words Odell knew.*

"Can we at least find out how long it will be to get a table?" Hope asked.

"Sure," Dylan said.

Dylan and Hope weaved and twisted their way through the crowd to the wooden counter, where a large, smiling Jamaican woman shook her head often at the people around the counter asking her if their orders were ready while she chopped green peppers and onions.

"Excuse me," Dylan said to the woman.

The woman cocked her head toward him. "What?" she shouted, waving her knife.

I'd be testy, too, if this many people were yelling at me in my kitchen, Hope thought. *I wouldn't want to get her mad. That woman is at least three of me. One swipe of her meaty arm and she'd clear the restaurant.*

"How long is the wait for a table?" Dylan asked.

The woman smiled suddenly. "You want a table?"

Dylan nodded. "A table for two."

The woman dropped her knife, grabbed two menus, flipped up

the counter, pushed through the complaining crowd, and started up an extremely narrow set of stairs.

"Follow her?" Dylan asked.

"Follow her," Hope said, holding onto Dylan's jacket as he parted the swarm. At the top of the stairs, Dylan ducked his head because the ceiling was barely seven feet high. The woman handed Dylan two menus, pointed to an empty circular table to the right, and returned to the noise below. Dylan and Hope squeezed between couples at two nearby tables and sat at the small table, a flowery tablecloth atop it and a vase of fragrant flowers on a side table nearby, glowing candles giving off fitful light.

Odell and I once sat at this very table, Hope thought. *I hope the man across from me can erase those sad, old memories and replace them with happy, new memories tonight.* She glanced under the table at their knees touching. *That's a new thing already. Odell hated when I tried to get frisky with his legs, but are Dylan and I getting frisky now? This* is *a small table.*

Dylan looked at the menu for several minutes before announcing, "Since this is my first visit, and since you've been here before, I want you to order for me."

Hope smiled at her menu. *That is certainly another new thing. Odell ordered for himself or for both of us. He never let me make any culinary decisions or suggestions because he thought he knew food better than I did because of his size. He didn't. The only thing smart about Odell was his smartphone, and even that had its limitations.*

When a waiter appeared at the table with a notepad, Hope closed her menu.

"You have it memorized?" Dylan asked.

Hope nodded.

"We'll have one order of curry goat, two orders of oxtail soup, one order of jerk chicken, two orders of red beans and rice, two sides of cabbage, and two salads." *Am I forgetting anything? Oh.* "And keep the ice water coming."

After the waiter left with their menus, Dylan laughed. "Hope, that sounds like a *lot* of food."

"It *is* a lot of food," Hope said. "I'm hungry."

"Are you that . . . ravenous?" Dylan whispered.

"Yes." *And not just for food.*

While they waited, Dylan took Hope's hand and held it on top of the table, his thumb gently moving over her knuckles while his eyes roamed the cramped dining loft, prints of parrots and seashells on the walls.

Here's another new thing, Hope thought. *Odell rarely even held my hand, even when we were alone. I had to clutch his elbow if I wanted any contact with him in public. Dylan obviously wants to be seen with me. He even kissed my cheek out there on Washington Avenue in front of all those people. Odell hardly ever smiled, especially at The Islands. He was too busy saying "They need to expand this place if they want more business" and "How long have we been waiting?" and "The jerk chicken is dry tonight" and "This dining loft is definitely not up to code." Not Dylan. This man is content to be wherever he is, and I am content to be wherever he is.*

Dylan leaned in, whispering, "What instrument would the man in the far-right corner be?"

Hope laughed. "I thought you were going to say something romantic to me."

"Later." Dylan's eyes traveled to the man in the corner. "What instrument?"

What instrument has a big head, a rotund body, and two stubby arms? "Definitely a tuba. What about his date?"

"She looks like . . . a cello," he whispered.

"A . . . cello."

"Her color and shape," Dylan whispered. "She's brown and kind of thin up top and rounded at the bottom."

Oh, I get it, Hope thought. *But what is Dylan doing looking at her derriere?* Hope stared openly at the woman. *Okay, so her derriere is round and curvy. Mine used to look like that. At least it might mean Dylan is more interested in derrieres than breasts, both of which I have in short supply.*

When the food arrived, they dug in, sampling from each other's plates and generally gorging themselves while their feet and knees played tag under the table.

"You let a man eat from your plate on the first date," Dylan said.

I am so shameless. "What do you think so far?"

He pointed his fork at the curry goat. "This is so good." He chewed furiously. "Spicy, hot, and delicious." He took a gulp of ice water. "However, I don't feel my tongue. Wow! That's some fiery stuff."

I don't want to tell him it's not the spiciest curry goat I've ever had or that some types of roti *could put his tongue in a coma.* "I didn't know you could be so voracious," Hope said.

"Neither did I," Dylan said, finishing his third glass of water and leaning back from the table. "I have to stop. I want to save some room for dessert."

"You have room for dessert?" Hope asked.

He puffed out his cheeks and exhaled softly. "I was hoping that *you* would be my dessert."

Hope blushed. *There's not enough of me to be anything but an appetizer or an after-dinner toothpick.* "I'm sure the banana dumplings will taste better." *If they have them ready. They run out of things without notice here. I have yet to eat their bread pudding, which I hear is the best on earth.* "You'll really like the dumplings."

"I'll bet that you taste just as sweet," Dylan said.

I like a salty man who thinks I'm sweet.

While they waited on the banana dumplings to arrive, Dylan asked, "What about the couple over there? What instruments would they be?"

My opinions and ideas actually matter to this man. Odell rarely asked what I thought about anything. She glanced at the couple. *Are they Dominican? Colombian? Brazilian? I can never tell. He has a smooth chest and silver chains, and she wears a shimmering silver dress, a slit all the way to her thong. I wish I had shapely legs like hers.* "She's a shiny silver steel drum, and he's a golden trombone." *He does have many teeth. Hmm.* "Or he's a xylophone and she's a flute."

Dylan wiped his forehead with his napkin. "Put those four instruments together and you'll have a unique sound."

"What instrument do you think I am?" Hope asked.

Dylan reached out and took her hand. "You, my dear, are a *djembe* drum," he said. "You are tall and slender, you have very nice rhythm, and yet I know you could make a big noise if you wanted to."

Hope pouted. "But the *djembe* has a large, round derriere. I don't."

"I like your *djembe*," he said, smiling. "It's cute. I wonder how I would play you."

He wants to play my djembe. *I want him to play with my* djembe *very much. Just one of his hands could make my* djembe *jump.*

"I wouldn't beat you, though," he said softly. "I might . . . spank you, though."

Hope blushed, and sweat formed on her nose. *I have been very naughty.*

"And then I'd caress you," he whispered. "Softly. Tap-tap, tap-tap. I would probably rub your *djembe* until I heard your soft, sexy sound."

It wouldn't be a soft sound. I'd make a loud, sexy sound. At least I hope I would. No one has hit my djembe *in so long.*

"What instrument do you think I'd be?" Dylan asked.

What instruments aren't phallic in some way? I already said trombone for someone else. Trombones have slides that go in and out, up and down . . .

"Hope?"

"Hmm? Oh." *Just dreaming of things sliding in and out.* "You are a . . . guitar." *Why'd I say guitar? What's sexy about a guitar? They have G-strings, don't they? But Dylan's neck isn't that long.*

"Am I that high-strung?" Dylan asked.

"Well, you certainly like strumming my heartstrings," Hope said.

"I do," Dylan said. "What if I go out of tune?"

"Then I'll tune you up," Hope said, "and then I will pluck you."

Dylan's eyes popped while he laughed.

What did I say? Oh, wow. I just said I wanted to pluck him. Well, I do. I'm feeling plucky. I love all this sexy talk! Odell never said anything like this! He only "talked shop" and hardly ever gave me a compliment. Dylan and I are actually talking about things that matter to me.

"So we're a guitar and a *djembe* drum," Hope said. "That would be an interesting combination, what with all that plucking and tapping going on."

"And at the same time," Dylan added. "Tap-tap . . . pluck."

Hope nodded and shakily drank her water. *We might not sound that good, but we would definitely be loud.*

The banana dumplings arrived in a covered aluminum pie pan.

"Let's take these to go," Dylan said.

"Why?" Hope asked.

"I'm feeling out of tune." Dylan picked up the pie pan. "I need a tune-up."

And I need to do some plucking. We are going to have a jam session at my apartment. It's payback time for my neighbors.

When they finished their short walk to her apartment entrance, however, neither Hope nor Dylan rushed to open the door.

"Before we go in, Hope," Dylan said, "I want to know what you're thinking."

You mean besides the plucking, the tapping, and the tuning?

"Last night I heard myself saying right here in front of this blue butterfly that we should take it slow," he said, "and here I am tonight wanting to go much faster. I want to make sure we're on the same page."

Dylan has much better brakes than I do. I would have started tuning him up right here. "Well, I feel full." She smiled. "I may not have to eat at all tomorrow or even Sunday."

"Yeah," Dylan said. "What else are you thinking about?"

"I feel comfortable with you, Dylan. I'm thinking about how peaceful this is, how calm I am." *Most of me. My lips, however, are buzzing.*

"You aren't normally calm?" Dylan asked.

"I'm normally so calm I'm comatose." She pulled him close. "I had a wonderful time tonight with a wonderful man, and I don't want this wonderful night to end out here with the wonderful man walking away again. That's what's running through my head."

"You have such wonderful thoughts," he said. "Ask me in."

"Dylan, will you join me for banana dumplings and . . ." *I have nothing in the apartment to drink!* "Will you join me for some dumplings and some tap water?"

Dylan laughed loudly. "I would love to join you for some tap water. I am so parched."

Hope opened the entrance door, and they climbed one flight of stairs and walked down the shadowy hallway to Hope's door.

"I must warn you," Hope said, holding her keys. "Whack is an unusual cat."

"How unusual?" Dylan asked.

"You'll see."

Hope unlocked and opened her door.

Dylan stepped inside.

Hope closed the door behind them.

Whack jumped off Hope's bed and trotted over to Dylan, rubbing against his leg.

Whack purred.

What? Hope screamed in her mind. *I take care of you for* three *years, and you* purr *at the* first *man who comes through the door?*

Whack continued to purr.

Vixen!

Hmm.

I'm purring over this man, too.

That makes me a vixen, too.

Chapter 14

Dylan bent down and let Whack sniff his hand. "Hello, Whack. I'm Dylan. It is a pleasure to meet you."

I can't believe this! "Give me your jacket," Hope said.

Dylan rose and removed his jacket. "Is something wrong?"

"No."

Hope took his jacket to the kitchen and hung it on the back of a chair. *The nerve of that* stupide *cat! I feed her and give her a safe place to stay, I clean and keep her nasty litter box smelling fresh, and she* never *purrs for me, not even once! The second Dylan walks in, she purrs like a* prostituée*! Ooh!*

"I will prepare the tap water, sir," Hope said. "Is there any special way you want your tap water prepared?"

"On the rocks," Dylan said.

He's still standing by the door. Where do I want him to sit? On a kitchen chair that might tip over? On my bed where I might hurt him? Or on the futon that might not hold him? "Please make yourself comfortable on the futon."

"As you wish," Dylan said, moving to the futon carefully as Whack circled his legs. As soon as he sat and set the pie pan on the coffee table, the futon creaked loudly and Whack leaped into his lap.

Such an ungrateful gigolette*! Get off his lap! That's where I want to be sitting.*

Hope opened the freezer section of her refrigerator and saw two empty ice cube trays. *Figures. My life has been as empty as two ice cube trays.* "We are all out of ice, *monsieur.* Would you prefer your tap water neat?"

"Are you trying to get me drunk?" Dylan asked.

"*Oui,*" Hope said.

"That's fine," Dylan said.

I'm about to serve room temperature tap water to the first man to visit my apartment in eight years. I am a horrible hostess. She snatched her only two glasses from a cupboard. *At least the glasses are clean.* She ran water for a full minute before filling them, but the water temperature never changed.

She approached the futon and handed a glass to Dylan. "Brooklyn's finest, tapped at the peak of perfection."

Dylan took a sip. "Ah, this was a good month." He set his glass on the coffee table. "Your cat won't stop purring. She sounds like a chain saw."

She used to be mute! "Yes. Doesn't she?" Hope sat next to Dylan, the futon complaining, Whack purring louder. *Oh, shut up.* "Sorry about the futon."

"I like it," Dylan said, looking directly across the room at Hope's bed. "You have such a . . . small place. Don't you get claustrophobic sometimes?"

Hope sipped her water. "Sometimes. I don't need much. Is your place bigger?"

"I have a two-bedroom with four total rooms," Dylan said, picking up and putting Whack on the floor.

His apartment is easily twice as big as this place, but why does a single man need two bedrooms?

"I use the smaller bedroom for the international headquarters of Odd Ducks Limited Greeting Cards," Dylan said. "I wish my apartment was this clean."

The word is "empty," not "clean." "How long have you lived there?"

"Twelve years now," Dylan said, "and I have accumulated a great deal of clutter." He turned to Hope. "You don't believe in clutter, do you?"

"I like to live simply," Hope said. *Translation: I'm too cheap to buy things.* "I could never have a roommate." *What a stupid thing to say! Why not announce you never want to get married!* She stared at Whack. *It's your fault I can't say the right thing tonight. All your purring is confusing my thoughts.* "I mean, I'm very particular about how things are organized. Have you ever had a roommate?"

Dylan nodded, shifting slightly. "Yeah. Once. About five years ago."

Where did my smiling man go? Why are his eyes so sad? But more importantly, what happened to his roommate?

"Hope, before we go any further," Dylan said, shifting and leaning against the black metal armrest, "there are some things I need to tell you."

Hope nodded. "I have a few things I need to tell you, too." *I might be talking until the first Tuesday in November.* Hope took another sip and set down her glass. *Do I want to spill it all? Will he want me to spill it all? Can I spill it all?*

"The best way to begin is to begin," Dylan said. "It's probably obvious to you that I'm a bit out of practice when it comes to dating."

He's a bit out of practice? *If that's true, I've never practiced at all.* "You could have fooled me. You have been the perfect gentleman. You're playing me like a *djembe*."

Dylan smiled. "You're fun to play with. That didn't come out right."

Yes, it did, and I am fun. I had just forgotten how fun I am.

"What I meant to say is that you're easy to play." Dylan grimaced. "That's not what I meant either."

Well, once you warm me up, I'm easy to play.

"What I'm trying desperately to say, Hope," Dylan said, "is that you're *forgiving* of my social clumsiness and ineptitude."

Hope reached across the futon and held his right hand. "Your hands seem to know exactly what they're doing."

"My hands must have a better memory than I do." He sighed. "Hope, I've been out of commission for a long time. I have not been out with anyone in five years."

Hope blinked. *Five years.*

"I know," he said. "That's a long time to be out of action."

Hope squinted. "It's not quite as long as eight years, though. I haven't been out with anyone in eight years."

Dylan seemed to stop breathing.

I've killed him. Please breathe.

"Eight years," Dylan said softly.

Hope nodded. *Okay. He's not dead. I'm sure he thinks I'm pathetic.*

Dylan blinked rapidly, his hand becoming stiff to Hope's touch. "Why? Were you sick or in a coma?"

"No." *Actually yes, though I've recently come out of a coma thanks to you.*

"So you weren't in the hospital," he said.

"No." *I probably should have been.*

Dylan's hand flinched, but Hope held on to it. "Were you in jail?"

"No." *Well, sort of. I made my own cell, and I am sick, I should be in the hospital, and at the rate I'm going, I could be in a sugar coma from the addictive banana dumplings sitting on the coffee table in front of me.* "I've been in kind of a voluntary solitary confinement. Right here in *l'appartement de claustrophobie.*"

Dylan closed his eyes, opening them slowly. "I never would have guessed that about you. You're so wonderful. Why did you put yourself in solitary confinement?"

Hope sighed. *Life is so strange. He was about to tell me some deep, dark secrets about himself, and here I am spilling some of my pathetic little life to him.* "I had a bad breakup." She let go of Dylan's hand and wiped her hands on her jeans. *I haven't had sweaty palms in such a long time.* "I thought he was the love of my life. I was dead wrong, but that was eight years ago and I'm over it now." *That wasn't so bad. I feel some relief.* "Why have you been alone for so long?"

Dylan's eyes seemed to focus on nothing in particular, not that there was anything in particular in Hope's apartment to focus on.

Am I losing him already? Hope nudged his thigh with her knee. "You were about to tell me something."

He nodded. "Yeah. I was. It doesn't seem that important now."

"Tell me," Hope said.

He looked at the ceiling. "Eight years," he whispered.

"Yes," Hope said.

"I can't imagine that," he said. "I thought five years was bad, but eight is . . ." He sighed. "Hope, I wish I had met you sooner."

"Me, too." *Now it's time to talk about you.* "So, what happened to you five years ago?"

Dylan sighed. "It's really not that important, Hope. Do you want to eat some dumplings now?"

"I don't have room," Hope said. "I *do* want you to tell me what happened to you."

His hand went limp. "I broke one heart too many."

I can see him doing that, hopefully never with me. "So you've left a trail of broken hearts."

Dylan shook his head. "No." He leaned forward, picked up his glass, and took a sip. "The only heart I broke was my own."

I know that feeling. "How did it happen?"

"I loved two people at the same time," he said, "and I ended up alone."

He . . . cheated? This nice man was unfaithful? "You had . . . an affair?"

He set his glass on the table. "Oh no, nothing like that, though it seemed that way to Marie."

"Who's Marie?" Hope asked quickly. *Too quickly! Just let the man talk!*

"Marie was my girlfriend at the time."

And?

"It's really not important, Hope," he said. "I don't want to ruin our first date."

"You're not ruining it," Hope said. "What was Marie like? How long were you two together?" *And who was the* other *woman you loved?*

"Marie was . . ." He sighed. "I'll use your phrase. She was the love of my life. She came here from Bermuda when she was a child. We met at Brooklyn College and dated for five years before she moved in with me."

Five years. They were practically married, and she was from Bermuda. She had to be pretty. "What happened?"

"A tiny little girl named Shayna," Dylan said, shaking his head slowly. "She happened." He gripped the armrest with his left hand.

So it wasn't another woman. I shouldn't feel relieved, but I do.

"I'm sure you've noticed that I become attached to the kids I work with."

Hope nodded.

"I love each of them. I even miss them when they're not there. I'm with them up to twelve hours a day, and sometimes I think I know them better than their parents do." He closed his eyes. "I gave my heart to Shayna. I couldn't help it. She had such a big smile, and she was so tiny."

Like Aniya.

"Shayna came to us when she was three," Dylan said. "She was dying of NCL, neuronal ceroid lipofuscinoses. NCL is extremely rare, and kids with NCL rarely live past the age of five."

That's so sad! Now I see why he doesn't want to talk about her. Something similar is happening to him with Aniya.

Dylan cleared his throat. "And along the way, kids with NCL lose their sight and have endless seizures. Shayna could barely see me when we met." He smiled. "She liked listening to my watch and holding onto my nose."

"I like your nose, too." *It's not really a beak.*

"Thank you."

I shouldn't have pried so hard. I don't like seeing him so sad. This apartment has seen enough sadness.

"I held Shayna through *so* many seizures," he said. "They weren't all grand mal seizures. Sometimes only her eyes would move back and forth. She couldn't even speak. She barely made a sound. I like to think that she knew I was there, but I'll never know. We were inseparable from the day she arrived." He finished his water, his hand shaking slightly.

"Do you want some more water?" Hope asked.

"I'm all right," Dylan said, sighing. "And that brings us back to Marie. I had been asking Marie to marry me for years, but her momma and deddy kept getting in the way. They kept her close to them, what they called 'under heavy manners,' and they said they didn't come across the 'pawn' from 'de rock' to have some 'pawn dog' like me 'put the munch on' their daughter."

I can hear Marie's parents speaking. They almost sound like my own.

"So I had finally gotten Marie to entertain the idea of getting married when . . . when Shayna was nearing the end. Marie couldn't understand why I worried so much about Shayna. 'She gon' die,

Dylan,' she said. 'It is *word* yuh care so much for dis *garrl*.' Marie said '*word*' instead of 'weird.' " He smiled and shook his head. "But I couldn't help caring for Shayna. I wanted Shayna's last days to be her best days, even though I knew she couldn't see or hear any of those days. I talked to Shayna nonstop, though I knew she probably couldn't hear me. We went on walks, we went to the zoo, we fed the ducks..." He sighed. "We were two odd ducks, a grown white man and a little brown girl bundled up in a wheelchair. That's where I got the original name for my—I mean, our—company. I named it 'Odd Duck' because only I was left in the end."

Hope felt a lump forming in her throat. *I should have kept my mouth shut and eaten some banana dumplings. This is tearing him apart.*

"I truly loved that little girl," Dylan continued, "but Marie couldn't accept that. When Shayna lay in the hospital taking her last breaths, I was there with Shayna's family. I asked Marie to meet me at the hospital, to meet Shayna for the first and last time, so she could see why I had to be in Shayna's life. To see why I loved her so much." He bowed his head. "Marie never showed up. Shayna died a day later with the tiniest little sigh. When I got back to our apartment, Marie was gone, and everything that was hers was gone. Everything, even the wooden napkin rings and the plastic corncob holders, and all I had for company after that was my grief."

They were together a long time. He had to try to get her back. "Did you..." *I don't have a right to ask this.*

"Did I what?" Dylan asked.

"Did you try to get Marie back?" Hope asked.

"Yeah," Dylan said. "I practically stalked her. I'm surprised she didn't get a restraining order on me. I went to her job, her parents' house, her new apartment. I left notes everywhere, called her..."

"She must have been beautiful," Hope said.

He nodded. "On the surface, yes, she was beautiful." He stood and walked to a window, resting his hands on the windowsill. "But she wouldn't have me back. The last time we spoke, she told me, 'Yuh should love the livin', not the dyin'. Yuh waste yuh love on a little *garrl* who could never love yuh back.' All my life I've believed in loving the living *until* they die. I loved my mother that way, all the way to the end."

I thought I had baggage.

He turned from the window. "But even after Shayna died, I still loved her. I couldn't remove that little girl from my mind, and that made me useless for anyone else for the last five years."

"Did you date?" Hope asked.

"I went on a few dates, but I wasn't really there, you know? I was just going through the motions." He laughed. "I was the one-date wonder."

"You don't have to answer," Hope said. *But I* need *you to answer!* "But what kinds of women did you date?"

He returned to the futon. "All these questions. You used to be so shy."

"I don't think I'll ever be shy around you from now on," Hope said. "I want to know you better." *Now answer my question.*

"I guess I dated the rainbow, so to speak," he said. "I have always been attracted to contrasts. Growing up in Brownsville, I didn't see many girls my color. Not many Irish girls in Brownsville. I've dated girls and women from Guyana, the Bahamas, Jamaica, Haiti."

More Island girls. "Is that . . ." *Don't ask!*

"Is that why I'm attracted to you?" Dylan asked.

"You don't have to answer that," Hope said.

"But it's what you want to know, right?" Dylan asked.

Hope nodded. "I'm just a little insecure." *Which is like saying the Sahara Desert is only a little hot.*

"Hope," Dylan said, "I've seen you at Thrifty for five years, and I've only really known you for a few days, but I already care so much for you, and not just because you're helping me make more money. I like you."

He doesn't even really know me yet. Should I tell him anything more?

"I like being with you, I like eating with you, I like myself when I'm with you," he said. "I also like what I see. I love your eyes. They're dark and mysterious and I want to explore their mysteries."

Why can't I feel my hands? My legs are shaking.

"I want to caress your hair."

Now my scalp is tingling. Keep talking!

"Your smile is so bright, and your skin is flawless."

My skin is starting to glow. I may have to turn the thermostat down even further.

"You have long legs." He winked. "I have a thing for long legs." He took her hand. "And you have long, delicate fingers." He kissed each one. "You are dangerously beautiful."

I'm not a danger, am I? If he keeps talking like this, he's *in danger.*

"But . . ." Dylan said, sighing. "But I'm not entirely yours because of what's happening to Aniya. Do you understand?"

"Your heart belongs to Aniya," Hope said.

"Not 'belongs,' exactly, but pretty close," Dylan said. "I'm holding back a little better this time, trying to be careful. Aniya gives me so much joy, and there are days I wish I could *be* her. I wish I had her positive outlook on everything. I know that even if she gets a bone marrow transplant, she'll still only have a fifty-fifty chance, but at least she has a chance, and now that you're in my life, and I want you to *stay* in my life, I'm afraid you'll think I'm wasting my time with Aniya."

"You're not wasting your time, Dylan," Hope said. "You have a big heart. I really like that about you. You've opened your heart to me."

He nodded.

"And you're reopening mine. From what I saw of Aniya today, I feel for her, too. Aniya does more living while she's dying than most healthy people ever will." *Including me.* "So, what's her prognosis? What are the doctors saying?"

Dylan smiled, slid closer to Hope, and kissed her cheek. "Thank you for asking. Marie never asked about Shayna, as if not asking about her would make Shayna go away. You have a big heart, too." He kissed her lips lightly. "And I love your lips."

He said the L-word.

He sat back. "The doctors originally gave Aniya a one-in-ten chance of surviving, and you know what she said? 'That's a *terrible* batting average, Dylan. I'm a better hitter than that.' You should see her hit a Wiffle ball. She's deadly. I've been praying for another miracle." He took Hope's hands in both of his. "I didn't want to tell you any of this after you said you'd been alone for eight years. It didn't seem right. I've never told anyone about all this, and here I am dumping it on you on our first real date."

"Second," Hope said. "The other one counts. We held hands and we hugged. That constitutes a date." Hope took a deep breath and exhaled. "I'm glad you told me all that, though it had to hurt you to tell it. Do you want to hear about my eight-year drought?"

"Only if you want to tell it," Dylan said.

"I think I need to." *I know I need to.* "My boyfriend, Odell, broke up with me on Christmas Eve."

Dylan blinked. "On Christmas Eve?"

Hope nodded. "It's one reason Christmas and I don't get along."

"I don't know the guy," Dylan said, "but what an ass."

Odell had a big one, too. Why did I ever think he was handsome? "That *ass* broke up with me right here in this apartment. Well, not *in* the apartment. He didn't have the decency to come inside the apartment. He stood in that doorway." She pointed at the door. "And he told me things from there, like 'Who would marry your plain, hard, underemployed ass anyway?' He also called me the whitest black woman he ever knew."

"He's not an ass anymore," Dylan said. "He's a punk."

Odell was bay-it. Why did I ruin my life for the last eight years over bay-it? "A month later, Odell was engaged to another woman, who, honestly, wasn't much prettier than me." *That might have hurt the most. She was plain like me, and here it is hurting me again.* "A few months after that they got married, and a year later they had a daughter. I only know that because I bumped into them one day after work a few years ago. Have you ever bumped into Marie?"

"No," Dylan said. "I don't know where she is now. I had heard she and her parents had moved back to Bermuda"

Good, and she had better stay there. "I know it's wrong, but since that rotten Christmas Eve, I have hated Christmas. I know I shouldn't, but I do." *I don't want to say this next part, but Dylan has to know.* "Dylan, I have been severely, desperately depressed ever since." Tears welled in her eyes. "I am a certified mess." *Please, God, don't let Dylan think I'm incurably insane! I need this man! I need him to help me heal! Please don't run away, Dylan. I'm only a* little *crazy. You're making me less crazy.* Hope squeezed his hands tightly, and more tears spilled from her eyes. *He's still here!*

"Why are you crying?" Dylan asked.

"You didn't run away," Hope said, wiping tears away with the back of her hand. "Well, you haven't run away yet."

"Why would I do that?" He pulled Hope close to him. "I ran *to* you. I'm not running anywhere from now on unless it's *with* you."

Hope clung to Dylan. "Thank you." She looked into his eyes. "Thank you."

He kissed her tenderly. "Are you over your depression now?"

I can't lie to this man. "No. Not yet. I don't think my depression is going to go away without a fight. You make me so happy, Dylan, but when you're not around . . ."

"I'll have to be around more often then."

Hope smiled.

He pulled Hope onto his lap, her back resting against his chest, his hands resting on her stomach. "You're sexy."

"Thank you." *I only wish I looked sexy again.*

"Have you ever seen somebody about your depression?" Dylan asked.

"No. I know I should have gotten some professional help, gone on some medication, or at least gotten some counseling, but I didn't. I don't like to spend money on myself, and I definitely don't like paying medical co-payments." She grabbed his arms and pulled them tightly around her. "But I know I am sick, Dylan. I don't eat for days at a time." She picked up his right hand and wrapped his thumb and index finger around her left wrist. "I'm not just thin. I'm skin and bones."

"I hadn't noticed," Dylan said, sliding his hand up her arm and leaving a trail of goose bumps.

"Trust me, you'd notice if you saw the rest of me. I can see my ribs clearly. Anatomy classes could use me for demonstrations. It's why I wear baggy clothes so no one will notice. I'm cold all the time." She pointed to her bed. "It's why I have a blanket, a comforter, and a quilt, and I still shiver."

Dylan nosed through her hair and kissed her left ear. "Are you warm enough now?"

"Yes, very," she said. "Thank you." She took another deep breath and exhaled. "I'm going to tell you something extremely personal now. No one on earth knows this."

"Your secrets are safe with me."

I feel safe with you. Please don't ever leave! "I'm not quite a complete woman. I haven't had a period in over a year. I'm about twelve months late, and that's not good. It's called amenorrhea, and it's one of the signs of anorexia nervosa." *For such a light woman, I am laying it on heavy tonight.* "I don't look into a mirror and see myself as fat or anything like that. I see bony me just fine. When I'm wearing my glasses. If I take them off, I'm just tall, black, medium-size fuzz. The funny thing is, I like to eat. I *love* to eat. You've seen me eat. I just don't *feel* like eating most of the time because . . . because I don't feel like living most of the time." She held his arms more tightly around her. "Until now." She pointed up at the main beam. "I look up there sometimes and see a way out, but I'm too cheap to buy the rope. I don't even know how to tie a noose."

"You've been suicidal?" Dylan asked.

"I've thought about it, yes, but I'm too squeamish to go through with it. But by not eating, I'm essentially committing suicide slowly. But not this week. You've been feeding me. Everything I've eaten with you has been delicious, even the peanut-butter-and-jelly sandwiches. I just know I wouldn't have eaten anything but maybe a few crackers this week if you hadn't come along."

"I'm glad I came along," Dylan whispered. "Not only are you my business partner, you're my meal partner. I eat so much better when I'm with you" He slid his hands up her arms, his hands warming her skin. "Have you ever seen a specialist about any of this?"

My hairy arms are goose bumps. "I've *almost* been to the doctor on numerous occasions, but as I said, I'm cheap. I hate paying someone to tell me what I already know. I wear clothes and shoes until they fall off me. I rarely buy anything new. These are the only two drinking glasses I own."

"Why are you so thrifty?" Dylan asked.

He was nice enough not to call me cheap. "I have a crazy dream about a beach house. It's completely ridiculous, actually, because a girl who grew up in frigid, snow-swept Canada should *not* want to live in a beach house. It's absurd."

"Ah, but you are still an Island girl," he said. "That beach house is hardwired to your DNA."

"Yes, but I'm more Canadian than anything else," Hope said. "I was born in Canada. I lived most of my life there."

"Well, you know about my dream to run a day care center for the arts," Dylan said, his hands massaging her shoulders gently, "and just about everyone I've told about this dream, especially the banks, thinks this idea is absurd."

"It's not," Hope said.

"Thank you," Dylan said. He walked his fingers from her shoulders to her neck, massaging as he went. "You have a wonderful dream, Hope. There's nothing wrong with wanting to own your own place in the sun." He worked his fingers through her hair to her scalp. "You know, I can see you in a beach house. You're out on your deck, sipping your strong, sweet morning coffee and watching the sunrise. I can even see you outside walking in the sand, exploring the dunes, your skin turning darker and your hair flying in the breeze. You belong on the beach."

Keep working on my head. That feels so good. "You see me turning darker than I already am?" Hope softly asked. *Dig those fingers into my roots. Yes. Right there.*

"Yes. Except for your ears." He pulled her hair away from her left ear and nibbled on it. "Your hair covers them. You would have caramel ears on a chocolate body. You'd be like a candy bar. I like caramel."

I like to have my ears nibbled. "Do you see me making sand angels?"

"Actually, yes," Dylan said. "Am I making them with you?"

I hope so. "Yes. You have to brush the sand off me when I'm done." She reached behind her and held his arms, turning into and wrapping her legs around him as far as the futon would allow. She pulled his face to hers and kissed him. "I will have sand in *so* many intimate places."

He placed his hands in the small of her back. "I will sunburn badly at your beach house."

She kissed his chin. "I will take care of you. We will plant aloe all around the house." She kissed his neck. "I wouldn't let you out of the house very often anyway," she whispered.

Dylan's lips met hers, and his hands slipped under her jeans, his hands so hot that Hope could feel heat on her derriere.

Oh, yes. Keep squeezing. Pull me closer to you. What's this growing under me? Oh, that's a nice rhythm and your tongue is as hot as your hands—but hey!

Why isn't this feeling good?

I'm grinding on my grindsman, and nothing is happening where it definitely should be happening!

Hope grabbed Dylan's hands and held them in front of her. "Dylan, I have to tell you one more thing I've noticed about my body, just now as a matter of fact, and you're probably not going to like it. When you were working me back there, and you worked it very well, by the way, I should have felt something, you know? After eight years, I should have screamed and squeaked like that clarinetist, right? But I didn't. I wanted to. I tried to. You felt so... ready. You *feel* ready. It's definitely not you. It's me. Your hands are huge and hot, your body feels so very nice, and I should be *juteux*, *mouillé*, at least a little *moite*. This is so embarrassing."

Dylan smiled. "I'm assuming those words have something to do with ... wetness?"

Hope nodded. "Right. I wasn't juicy, wet, or even moist. I'm *aride* as a bone." She felt more tears coming. *Oh, sure. I'm wet in my head and not in my pants. I have messed up my body so badly.* "My mind is *on*, Dylan. You are making a river in my mind, a real waterfall, but my body is like a desert. My hormones are so messed up because I haven't been eating. My brain says, 'Go, go, go!' and 'Tear his clothes off!' "

"I like your brain," Dylan whispered. "It agrees with my brain."

"Thank you," Hope said, "but while my brain wants you in the worst way, my body says, 'What was that?' " Hope sighed. *And now, to complete my embarrassment.* "I've even tried ... *le fait de masturber*, and nothing happens."

Dylan's mouth became a little O. "You've tried ... oh. Oh. I have to say this. While it's awful that nothing happens when you ... do *that*, it's exciting to know that you *do* ... do that." He shifted his weight under her. "It is exciting me very much right now to think of you doing that."

I feel his excitement. Wow. "Don't you . . . do that?"

Dylan's face flushed. "Well, yes."

"And don't you . . . finish the job?" Hope asked.

He looked away. "Yes."

"Every time?" Hope asked.

He laughed. "Yes, and you're the first person I've ever admitted this to." He sighed. "Is there anything we can't talk about?"

"I hope not," Hope said. "How often do you do it?"

Dylan laughed louder. "It's not as if I keep count. Enough. That's all I'll say."

Hope ran her fingers though his silky hair. "I used to . . . *try* all the time, but once nothing happened for a while, I gave up."

"It must be awful for you."

Hope sighed deeply. "It's not really awful. It's mostly frustrating. I know if I gain back the weight I've lost, I'll be ready to get juicy again. I read every study on anorexia in black women, and there aren't many studies, mainly because the world sees anorexia as a white women's disease. One study said less than one percent of black women worldwide had *any* type of eating disorder and no study reported any black woman having anorexia for her lifetime."

"So there's hope for Hope," Dylan said. "If there's anything I can do to help you, please let me know."

She held him close. "You already have. You already are." *That mound of flesh below me that I'm riding on does a world of good for my sexual self-esteem.* "I wish I wasn't telling all this to you after such a perfect evening."

"I'm glad you're comfortable enough to share it with me," Dylan said. "Especially about *le fait de masturber.* I will not be able to sleep tonight or for many nights thinking about that."

"I just want you to know that I *do* work down there," Hope said. "Just not tonight."

Dylan bit his lip. "I can imagine you working down there. In fact, I imagine you work very well."

"I do," Hope said softly. "I have *orgasmes* quite easily."

"How easily?" Dylan asked.

"Well, if the wind blows just right . . ."

"Really?"

Hope nodded. "I'm usually really sensitive down there. It doesn't take much to set me off."

Dylan smiled. "This is very good to know."

Hope bounced her forehead on Dylan's chest. "But that's what makes all this so frustrating. I *know* I have a hair-trigger down there. I want it to work so badly!" She leaned back. "The first time I didn't have an *orgasme* when I was . . ." *I have never said this word to anyone in my life.* "When I was *masturbating*—and believe me, I tried for hours—I wept. Once I finished weeping, I went online to see what was wrong with me and found out I had all the symptoms of menopause and something called sexual anorexia. I went immediately to The Islands and ordered a ton of food. I ate and ate . . . and still nothing happened. I have screwed up my body so badly by not eating that I'm afraid my plumbing *can't* work until I'm eating regularly and eating right again, and that might take months, even years." *Here come the tears again.* "I'm so sorry, Dylan. I do want to respond to you whenever you touch me."

He kissed her tenderly. "And I will continue to touch you until you do. My fingers can't help touching you. They want to touch you all over right now." He slid his hands to her waist. "I plan on putting some meat on your bones."

Hope laughed.

"That didn't come out the way I intended it to. Of course, saying 'Hope, I want to fatten you up' isn't that much better. Also saying I want you to gain lots of weight so you can have hair-trigger *orgasmes* . . ." He smiled and squeezed her hips. "The French know how to make sexual words more sexual, don't they? *Orgasme.* Have you gained any weight this week?"

"I should have," Hope said. "I don't know for sure. I don't have a scale."

"I will get you a scale," Dylan said. "How far off was I when I tried to guess your weight?"

"About twenty pounds off, maybe more," Hope said. "I haven't eaten breakfast regularly since . . . since Odell stood at that door."

"I have a cure for that," Dylan said. "We serve breakfast at Kinderstuff. When you hand me my coffee, I can hand you a couple pieces of toast and jam every weekday as you go by."

"As long as you kiss me, too."

"Coffee, toast, jam, and a kiss," Dylan said. "An excellent way to start the day."

"The best." She moved his hands back to her derriere. "I don't want you to get frustrated sexually. I want you to feel pleasure."

Dylan pulled her closer. "Even if you don't? That's not fair. Don't worry about me, Hope. I'll be fine. Really. Kissing and hugging and holding hands are about all I thought I could handle anyway. Believe me. I can wait, and I *can't* wait, you know?"

Hope draped her arms around his neck. *I have found a good, unselfish man.* "What if I don't let you wait?"

He blinked. "I will not stop you."

"Good." Hope laughed. "I can't believe our first kiss was in the back of a cab."

"It's not a kiss I will ever forget," Dylan said. "You seemed calmer afterwards."

"I was. Some. I was still nervous about where we might end up at the end of the date. I was nervous how you'd react when I didn't react."

"There is no rush. In fact, that calms me down even more." He rubbed her back. "I was so worried I wouldn't be able to please you."

This bulge under me says otherwise. "Really?"

"It's been a long time," Dylan said. "If we were making love right now, I would be trying for a full-length movie, but my body would most likely give you a coming attraction."

Hope laughed so loudly that Whack leaped off the bed and hid under the kitchen table. "That's . . . nasty!"

"Are you sure you're not an American woman in disguise?" Dylan asked.

"I *am* an American woman," Hope said. "I'm just extremely hyphenated. Am I really that . . . sexy?"

"Yes. I am constantly aroused around you. I try not to stare at any part of you for too long. I wore underwear three sizes too small tonight to keep myself in check."

"You did?"

"I should have." He looked down. "You are still arousing me."

"I thought it was the futon," Hope said. "Just kidding. I feel you." She ground her hips into him. "I like how you feel, and it makes me feel happy to know that I can arouse you." She stopped grinding. "But it makes me feel sad that I am not aroused."

He kissed her, sucking gently on her lower lip. "In time."

Wow. My lower lip is quivering. "What arouses you most about me?"

"Everything I see works on me, especially your eyes." He pushed some hair back from her face. "I love your eyes."

"What else?"

"When we were in the office, and you were in front of me swaying back and forth . . . Not fair. I love your . . ." He shook his head. "There has to be a better word for this part of a woman's anatomy. There are so many words, and none of them sound very nice. Booty. Ass. Money-maker."

"Money-maker?" Hope said. "You like my money-maker?"

"Yes, I love your buns, your cheeks, your fanny, your heinie, your sexy derriere. From now on, I will refer to your behind as your sexy derriere." He moved his hands up her shirt and popped another button. "And right now you have delicious dark skin asking me to kiss and touch it." He drifted a finger from her chin to her breastbone. "Do you mind if I do?"

He doesn't have to ask. "Let me make it easier for you." She extricated her legs from behind him, turned, and sat her sexy derriere squarely onto his lap, wiggling once and leaning back on his chest. "Just don't cut yourself on my sharp bones."

Dylan unbuttoned the rest of Hope's shirt.

Hope watched his hot hands move down her sides to her thighs where he squeezed them forcefully. He then slid his hands slowly up her hips to her stomach, where his fingers gently pressed her skin. She moved her locks to the side and exposed her neck, and Dylan kissed it, his fingers slipping under her belt line.

"You're teasing me," Hope whispered. "I like to be teased."

Dylan's fingers explored lower, sliding under the elastic band of her underwear, moving back and forth over her soft hair.

"That's nice," she whispered.

She felt his hands move up her stomach to her bra, lightly brushing it before squeezing tenderly, her nipples rising to the occasion.

"Do you feel anything, Hope?" he whispered.

She opened her eyes and watched his fingers tracing the fabric around her nipples. "Normally I'd be close to orgasm," Hope whispered, sighing. "I do feel peace, though. It's nice to be touched again."

He worked his tongue around her ear as his hands moved down to her stomach. "Your skin is so soft and warm."

"Your tongue is so hot," she whispered.

"You have the flattest stomach on earth," he whispered. "I could put a level on it and the bubble would be perfectly centered. A marble would stay perfectly balanced."

"That's not my stomach," Hope whispered. "You're feeling the other side of my backbone."

"Your backbone has a belly button?" Dylan said, tracing her navel with a finger.

"I'm a stick figure girl," Hope said.

"Do you mind if I strum you a little?" Dylan asked.

She reached up behind her with both arms, latching them behind his neck. "You're supposed to be the guitar, and I'm supposed to strum you. You're supposed to be tap-tapping my *djembe*." She arched her back and closed her eyes. "Oh, I *suppose* you can strum me."

Hope felt Dylan's hands moving up and down her body, caressing her breasts, teasing her nipples, digging and exploring under her belt line, thrusting into her pockets.

"How does this feel?" Dylan whispered.

"Like heaven," Hope said. "It feels like heaven." *But I know I'd enjoy it more if we were under the covers of my bed.* She let go of his neck and sat up. "Let's get more horizontal."

Hope stood, took Dylan's hand, and led him to the bed. She removed her boots but not her socks, and loosened her belt, her pants dropping to the floor. She stepped out of her pants and slid under her covers. She was about to take off her glasses when she realized something. *I want to see this man's body.*

Dylan removed his boots and socks.

"Sexy," Hope said.

He turned away from her to unzip his pants.

"Hey," Hope said. "What kind of a show is this? All I see is a sexy derriere."

Dylan turned only his head. "I'm still . . . you know."

Hope smiled. "Oh? You still have *une énorme érection*?"

Dylan shook his head. "Yes, and now that you've said that, it's bigger."

"Turn around, turn around," Hope said. *Let me see what I've been missing.*

Dylan turned to face her, letting his jeans slide down his legs.

"*C'est la plus grande érection que je voyais jamai! Cette chose est énorme!*" *That thing is huge. Length* and *girth. His poor underwear!*

He stepped out of his pants. "I hope what you said is a good thing."

Hope bit her lip and nodded. "*C'est la plus grande.*"

"My shirt, too?" Dylan asked.

Hope nodded.

Dylan removed his shirt.

"*Je vois des muscles, une caisse lisse, et un estomac ride,*" Hope said. *I am going to explore this man.* She put her glasses on the nightstand. "Get into this bed right now so I can give you the translation."

Dylan slid next to her, and Hope rolled on top of him, kissing and caressing his chest. "*Une caisse lisse*, a smooth chest," she whispered. She moved down to his stomach and kissed it. "*Estomac ride*, a flat stomach."

She kissed her way back to his lips, feeling his bulge firmly between her legs. "This is not going to sound like a compliment, but it really is."

"Okay."

"You're really big, Dylan, maybe too big for me now," she said. "I mean, wow." She eased back and bounced her sexy derriere against it. "Seriously." She thrust back more forcefully. "You could hold me in the air with that thing."

Dylan gripped Hope's hair. "If you keep doing that . . ."

"Doing what?" *Uh, take that. Oh, I'm going to bruise.*

"If you don't stop, I'll . . ."

"You'll what?" *If I back up my sexy derriere and hold it there a little longer, he might . . .*

Dylan threw his head back into the pillow. "Hope, I am very close..."

She reached behind her and gave a single squeeze.

This was the first time Hope had ever heard Dylan Healy curse.

Hope's neighbors probably heard it.

People still waiting for their take-out orders from The Islands probably heard it.

Hope smiled as she continued to bump her sexy derriere against him.

He pulled her face to his and kissed her, sucking her tongue deep into his mouth. When his spasms subsided, he turned her over. "It's my turn," he breathed.

"You can try," Hope said.

"I will enjoy the challenge," he said, and he pulled the covers over his head and disappeared.

Okay, body, we have a hot man kissing, tasting, and feeling on us. I know it's been a long time, but try to remember what to do. Think wet thoughts, think juicy thoughts...

She felt his long hair tickling her ribs as he kissed and sucked on each nipple before trailing his tongue to her stomach, where he lingered for several minutes, his hands removing her underwear and feeling on her calves, thighs, and sexy derriere.

Come on, body, work! He should be driving you wild by now!

She felt his nose moving through her pubic hair and his tongue finding the right spot. She reached under the covers and grabbed his hair.

"*S'il vous plaît, le corps, soyez excités!*" Hope whispered. "*Je veux faire l'amour à cet homme!*"

Dylan quickly popped his head out of the covers. "What was *that?*"

"I thought if I spoke French I might warm up quicker," Hope said.

"What were you saying?" Dylan asked, his fingers kneading her sexy derriere.

"I was yelling at my body to get excited because I want to make love to you." She tried to focus on his eyes, but his face was a fuzzy blur.

"Did it work?" he asked.

"Not yet," she said.

"It worked on me," Dylan said. "Until I brushed against one of your feet."

"Was my foot that cold?"

The fuzzy face nodded. "The iceberg that sank the *Titanic* was warmer. Antarctica is balmy compared to your toes. The Yukon is positively tropical—"

Hope laughed. "I get the picture."

"I am really enjoying your body." He kissed both nipples. "Do you mind if I continue my enjoyment?"

"Not at all." *I may be a little crazy, but I'm not that crazy.*

"And, feel free to . . . talk *sexy*."

Hope felt a long, hot, wet tongue sliding between her breasts, past her stomach, to the place that used to work. *Put that big tongue—Oh, yes, that's the place, now work it, keep working it . . .*

"*Sa langue est si chaude!*" Hope cried. "*Je veux qu'il aille plus bas! Réveillez-vous, là-bas!*"

Dylan's head shot out of the covers. "Did you . . ."

Hope felt him readier than ready, his penis all lined up and ready for entry, but she felt nothing, even when she wrapped her legs around his hips and grabbed *his* sexy derriere. "No, not yet. I'm so sorry. You don't know how sorry I am." *More freaking tears! Maybe if I transplant my tear ducts down there!*

Dylan spun to his left and pulled Hope on top of him, rubbing her back. "Shh, shh, it's okay, shh, Hope." He kissed her forehead and nosed through her hair. "I was only supposed to warm you up anyway, right?"

"But you were right there, and I wanted you inside me, and . . ."

"Shh, Hope, it's okay," Dylan whispered, holding her close. "I'll be fine. I'm excited because it's been a while for me, but I can wait a while more, and I'm not amazed that I'm ready again. Your body is amazing."

Hope dried her tears on his chest. "I hope I didn't give you frostbite."

"You didn't." He flattened his hands on her back. "You're starting to feel hot."

"It's just your warmth reflecting off me." *And my frustration boiling to the surface.*

"No, it's not," Dylan said. "Your back is hot, and your stomach was so warm. It was even smoking when I was strumming it."

"It was probably the curry goat."

"I don't think so," he said. "I felt your heat all over, from your stomach to your long, smooth legs to your sexy derriere. I could explore you all night." He caressed her hair. "Are you sleepy?"

"A little."

"Then sleep." He kissed her forehead. "Keep me warm."

Right. My frigid body keeping his steaming-hot body warm. He was nice to say so, though. "Dylan?"

"Yes, Hope?"

"Don't leave me." Hope felt strong arms pressing her close. "Please stay."

"I won't leave you. Sleep, Hope. Dream about your beach house."

Hope closed her eyes and snuggled her head into Dylan's chest. "*Merci beaucoup, mon homme le plus patient.* Thank you for being so patient with me."

"And you are my patient," Dylan whispered, "and as your doctor, I order you to sleep and dream."

"I'll try."

"Are you on the beach?" he whispered.

"Yes."

"Are you wearing a skimpy bikini?"

I shouldn't be doing this, but . . . "I'm not wearing anything at all . . ." She felt something stirring under her.

"Hope, please put something on."

"It's *my* dream." She slid a hand lower until she found what was stirring, and it grew harder in her hand. "Shall I continue my dream?"

"It will be a short one," Dylan whispered.

She squeezed him gently and heard Dylan sigh. "I'm sweating in the sunlight, and we're the only two people on the beach."

Dylan groaned.

"Are you going to curse again?" Hope asked.

"Probably," Dylan said.

She kissed his nipples and gripped him tightly. "Go right ahead. I owe my neighbors some noise. My hand isn't too rough, is it?"

"No. Tell me more about the beach . . ."

I love a man who loves fantasies. She moved down his chest to his stomach, working him with both of her hands. "You see me standing in the water. You come up behind me. I back my sexy derriere into you, and we begin to—"

Dylan Healy cursed paint off the small apartment's walls, and for a moment, the only sounds Hope heard were his.

She crawled up his body. "You didn't let me finish my dream."

"You can continue it tomorrow night, right?" he asked.

More tears. These are okay. He's staying another night. "It's going to be a long dream."

"Maybe you'll never finish it."

She buried her head of hair into his neck. "*Merci, mon chevalier doux.*"

Thank you, my gentle knight.

Hope glided off to sleep, holding a man who found her sexy just as she was, and the two of them strolled hand in hand in the sun on the beach in her dreams until dawn.

OCTOBER 17

Only 68 more shopping days
until Christmas . . .

Chapter 15

Hope rolled over and looked at the clock.

The fuzzy red numbers told her it was either eight-something or three-something, and the lack of heat beside told her she was alone.

She scrambled to her nightstand and found her glasses, putting them on and looking at the washroom door. It was open, and no one was in the shower trying to sing the Canadian national anthem or "Downtown."

The kitchen was empty.

There was no tall Irishman anywhere.

She only saw Whack on the futon licking a paw.

"Where'd he go?" she whispered.

Whack blinked at her.

"Where did Dylan go?" she asked.

Whack purred.

Vixen!

Dylan's gone? He said he wouldn't leave. Why didn't I feel the bed move when he got up? I know I was tired, but . . .

She squinted and saw a piece of paper stuck in the crack of the door.

He left me a note. Okay, right. He had to go. He had to mail all those cards. The post office closes at noon on Saturdays. That's where he is. He's working. He's working for me. He's making money for my beach house. Okay, calm down.

She pulled back the covers and looked at her mostly naked

body. *I don't even remember losing my bra and shirt. I'm glad he left me with my socks.* She shivered and sat up, clutching the quilt to her chest. She drew it off the bed in front of her and wrapped it around her shoulders, and then she stepped out of bed onto the cold floor. She took two steps and felt the quilt pulling at one of her fingers. She peered at her hand and saw four decent fingernails and one broken, jagged one.

When did that happen? I must have broken it on his back. That's never happened before. I hope I didn't cut him.

She shuffled to the door, the cold air biting at her toes, and tugged at the piece of paper near the doorknob. Opening it, she read:

Off to get groceries. Stay warm! PS: You purr when you sleep. :~) D.

He's . . . Yes. That makes sense. I need groceries. I haven't bought them in weeks.

He's going to feed me.

Again.

She slid to her wardrobe and put on her University of Alberta sweatpants, a clean T-shirt, and a black knit toque before brushing her teeth and washing her face, the icy water chilling her nose and cheeks.

I need to wash my hair, but it's so cold! She checked her stock of DreadHead Dread Soap and found she had four bottles left. *Maybe tonight, and maybe I can get Dylan to help me, but right now . . .*

Back to bed.

Once under the covers, she stared at the ceiling. *It's just a beam today. What do you know about that?*

She looked at the light streaming in through her windows. *More beams. Sunbeams are the best beams.*

She closed her eyes.

I hope he doesn't go to Key Food. It's right around the corner, but that place is a mess. The cleanup on aisle three I tripped over four weeks ago getting Whack her food was still there two weeks later, and some of the stock boys and managers are freaks, sexually harassing customers and the cashiers. Hmm. They never harassed me. Maybe I'm just jealous. If he did shop there, I am checking every label for an expiration date.

She shivered, and goose bumps appeared on her arms as she re-played the night before. *I still should be basking in his warmth. He stayed all night. Odell never did that, and Dylan didn't get as frus-trated as I was. He responded when I wanted him to, unlike someone else I used to know who didn't* care *that I wasn't* there *yet. So pa-tient, so tender. He likes my stomach, and he's going to fill my stom-ach. I hope my libido wakes up soon. I miss that wild, careless, aching feeling.*

She glanced at the clock. *Nine something. Hmm. I don't nor-mally sleep this late on a Saturday. This is actually kind of nice. Snug-gly warm in the bed on a Saturday morning. This is—*

She sat up and threw the covers away from her. "I have to be at work by ten!"

Goose bumps sneaked up her legs.

She yanked the covers back over her. *I am not leaving this nice, toasty warm bed. I'm going to call in sick. I am sick. I just have never seen a doctor to get the diagnosis.*

She reached for the phone, the only phone she had, the one at-tached to the kitchen wall twenty feet away. *This is silly. I have long arms, but seriously . . .* "Whack, bring me the phone."

Whack didn't move.

Hope shook her head, kicked her legs out from under the cov-ers, and ran to the kitchen, dialing Thrifty. *I hope Kiki didn't stay out too late last night. I'm sure she and On-Gee had a long night, too. Justin will be useless.* After ten rings, she heard a beep: "Justin, this is Hope. I will not be coming in today. I have a bad . . . stom-achache. I will see you all Monday morning. Bye." She returned the receiver to its cradle and tore back to the bed, pulling the covers over her head. *Well, I do have a stomachache, but it's not from food. It's from lack of food.*

Why am I so freaking cold? Dylan said I was hot last night. Maybe too much of me evaporated into the night air or something.

She heard a buzz.

I am never going to get warm today.

She again wore the quilt over her shoulders and went to her in-tercom box. "Yes?"

"Yeah, I got a delivery of calories for Miss Warren," Dylan said. "Can you buzz me in?"

Hope smiled. "How many calories?"

"A gazillion."

That's a lot. "Can you break a twenty?"

"Come on, Hope. It's cold out here."

She buzzed him in and then checked the thermostat. *Why's it set on sixty-six?* She turned it up. *I never change the thermostat. Maybe Dylan did.*

After a single knock, Hope opened the door and watched Dylan carry six bags and a huge box of groceries from St. John's Marketplace to the kitchen table.

"Good morning," Dylan said, kissing her cheek and pointing to the bed. "Go back to bed."

"You need help putting all this away." *And I won't have to check any expiration dates.*

Dylan swept her off her feet and carried her back to the bed. "I'll figure it out. Get under the covers."

Hope propped up her pillow first, then got in. "Did you turn down the thermostat?"

He nodded, settling the covers on her. "It was too hot. You put off a lot of heat."

She grabbed his elbow. "It wasn't my heat."

He winked. "Yes, it was."

"Can I at least help you cook?" Hope asked, tugging on his elbow.

"Not today," Dylan said. "Let me spoil you."

Hope pulled him down and kissed his nose. "You already have."

"Get used to it," he said, and he returned to the kitchen.

Hope watched Dylan putting away the groceries, most of them filling previously empty cupboards. She salivated at the big bags of potato chips. *Mmm, grease.* She smiled at the ice cream going into her freezer. *Yes!* She sighed at the Pop-Tarts. *Eh. Butter tarts would be better.* She marveled at all the different kinds of cheese and deli meat, the two loaves of bread, eggs, bacon, ground beef, pork chops, real butter, sour cream, potatoes, green peppers, onions, oranges, apples—*and a ten-pack of Twix candy bars! Oh, my sweet tooth is dancing!*

Hope turned on some music, the festive notes of "Let It Snow" crackling from the clock radio's little speaker. "We haven't even had Halloween yet!"

Dylan located a large frying pan in the metal drawer under the stove. "Oh, the spirit of Christmas never really ends. It's always there, just under the surface, waiting to rear its red-and-green face." He put the pan on the largest eye. "And it's cold enough to snow outside. I'll bet someone called in a request."

Who requests snow in Brooklyn in October? Hope switched to another station and heard a commercial for a "two-day half-off pre-Halloween Christmas sales extravaganza!" *Are they kidding?* She snapped off the radio. "Bah, humbug."

"You're no Scrooge," Dylan said. "Not with a name like 'Hope.'" He smiled. "It's beginning to look a lot like Christmas," he sang.

"Stop, please stop!"

"Come on," Dylan said. "This is breakfast and a show."

"Then sing a Halloween song at least," Hope said.

Dylan's rendition of "Thriller," complete with some horrible dancing, had Hope nearly on the floor laughing.

Whack said nothing.

"Just cook for me, okay?" Hope asked.

Dylan raised his eyebrows. "That's what I'm trying to do."

Hope watched half a stick of butter go into the pan followed by six eggs, each cracked perfectly. *This man is a pro.* While the eggs cooked, Dylan chopped up green peppers and onions and opened a pack of sharp cheddar cheese. *Ah, the fabled western omelet.* "Where's the ham?"

Dylan pointed to himself and added the peppers, onions, and cheese to the pan, expertly folding the congealing egg mixture in half.

"When are you going to cook *yours*?" Hope asked.

He picked up the pan and slid the omelet onto a plate. Grabbing a fork from a drawer and a napkin from a cupboard, he carried the plate to Hope. He put the plate in her lap, slipped the fork into her hand, and tucked the napkin into the collar of her T-shirt. "Enjoy." He turned to go.

"We're splitting this, right?" Hope asked.

"No," Dylan said, and he returned to the stove.

Hope looked at the mound of yellow, cheesy goodness staring up at her. "I can't possibly finish this."

Dylan cracked some more eggs. "You'll hurt Chef Dylan's feelings if you don't."

She took a bite. *This is good.* She took a bigger bite. *Just what I need. Fat and cholesterol.* She took an even bigger bite. *I can't believe I'm this hungry.*

Dylan brought his omelet to the bed and sat.

"Hey, your omelet is smaller than mine," Hope said.

"Only three eggs," he said, taking a healthy bite. "I have to watch my weight while I'm watching yours."

Hope dropped her fork on the plate. "I'm full."

Dylan looked at her nearly empty plate. "Really?"

She picked up her fork. "No. It's a skinny joke."

"Sounds like a line of cards," he said.

"It will be a thin line," Hope said, "but it will bring us fat profits." She shoveled the last bite into her mouth. "I am *really* full this time."

Dylan set his plate on the nightstand and pulled back the covers. He lifted her T-shirt and began massaging her stomach with his fingers. "I think we can make a little more room."

Hope writhed. "Stop, it tickles."

Dylan shook his head. "Then I shall use my tongue."

"What?"

In moments, Dylan was back under the covers, and Hope felt the drawstring loosen on her sweatpants.

Breakfast and a workout. That *doesn't tickle. It tingles, but that's all it's doing. I should be swimming down there. Come on, body. Wake up down there! We should be rolling around on this bed with Dylan. There should be omelet stains on the walls. I should be paying back my neighbors with some freaky French shouting.*

Hope stared across the room at Whack. *Nothing. I feel the pressure, feel the motion, feel a tiny little tingle, but nothing else. You have* got *to be kidding! I should be* juteux *just from thinking about a man doing this to me. I should be screaming loud enough to break the windows.*

Dylan came up for air. "Anything?"

"A tingle," Hope said.

"A tingle is good, isn't it?" he asked.

Hope nodded.

"Not a jingle?" he asked.

"A tingle, not a jingle." She sighed. "You might as well finish your omelet." *Since you're not going to finish me.*

He squeezed her hands. "We're making progress, though, right?"

Hope nodded. *You are. I'm not.*

He looked at the clock. "Don't you usually work on Saturdays?"

"I called in sick." *I'm only heartsick now.* "Shouldn't you be at the post office? Don't they close at noon?"

"Are you kicking me out?" Dylan asked.

I need a good, long cry, and I don't want an audience. I may even put Whack out in the hallway. "You have business to attend to, partner."

"I suppose." He stood. "Before I go, I want you to promise me something."

"Okay."

"Promise that you will rest and burn no calories," he said.

Does weeping burn calories? It probably does. "I promise."

"Good." Dylan yawned and stretched his back. "You are an extremely entertaining sleeper."

Hope propped her pillow on the headboard. "I am?"

"In addition to purring, you whisper in your sleep."

She scooted back to the pillow. "In French or in English?"

"A little of both," he said. "It's quite sexy. You said something like '*donnez-moi plus.*' What's that mean?"

Even my dream self is horny. "It means 'give me more.' I was probably eating something."

Dylan flopped onto the floor and put on his shoes. "I will return with lunch. If you get hungry, eat ice cream, and I expect you to eat out of the carton. No portion control for you at any time from now on."

"How long will you be gone?" *I am already missing him, and my heart hurts. I know he'll be back, but it still hurts.*

"I have to get another ink cartridge, print out more labels, stuff a bunch of envelopes, and then stand in line to buy more stamps . . ."

He put on his jacket. "I'll be back as soon as I can." He bent down. "I expect you to be well rested. Do not do the dishes or clean up the mess in the kitchen. I'll do that when I get back."

I hadn't planned to. "I won't, but you'll need dish soap."

He kissed her. "Dish soap."

"I haven't done dishes in a while."

He nodded. "I'll get you the biggest bottle they have. You're going to need it."

Hope watched him go first to the futon, where he petted Whack.

Whack became a chain saw.

He opened the door. "Remember: Do as much nothing as you can."

"Bye."

He closed the door.

Hope wept.

I know I did this to myself, I know that, but there has to be a mistake! I'm putting on weight. I'm fattening up again. I want this man so badly. I had a healthy sexual appetite before. Where did it go? Why is it hiding? I have a man who should send me into sheer ecstasy with a single kiss. I want my plumbing to work now. I don't care if I have an orgasm. I only want to feel him inside me and not have it hurt either of us.

I want to be a whole person again.

Hope dried her eyes on the quilt and left her bed, the apartment noticeably warmer. She went into the kitchen and looked in the freezer. *Ah. Here's some antidepression medication.* Ben & Jerry's Chunky Monkey, Dublin Mudslide, Karamel Sutra, and New York Super Fudge Chunk. *Dylan said no portion control, so . . .*

She opened all four containers and set them in a row on the kitchen table. She took out a spoon and sampled from each one. *Karamel Sutra is extremely naughty. Chunky Monkey makes me want to do the funky monkey. I want to smear Dublin Mudslide all over Dylan and lick it off. If I ate anymore of this Super Fudge Chunk, I'd dream in four dimensions. I'm eating booty food. Wait. Dylan said I had a sexy derriere. I'm eating sexy derriere food.*

I am officially high on sugar.

She returned the ice cream to the freezer and stood in front of her TV. *Here's more nothing waiting to happen.* She wiped the dust off the screen with a paper towel and tuned in to a Lifetime Movie Network movie called *Dark and Deadly,* the promo hyping: "A successful stockbroker meets the woman of his dreams . . . and his nightmares." *Oh good. A stockbroker is going to die. Maybe the economy will improve.*

She snuggled under her covers and waited for the suspense to kill her.

It didn't.

Where's the dark and deadly woman? That woman is white, and how deadly can she be? She's short and tiny. Oh, the acting is atrocious, and the plot is laughable. The commercials have better acting in them. Where's the suspense? Oh, right. The cops will never know it was you because you're so innocent looking with your makeup perfect all the time. You have evil eyes, vooman. The stockbroker isn't even cute. He sighs too much, he wears the same suit in every scene, and he has to be the dumbest man on the planet. She just shot at you "on accident" and you forgive her? They should have called this Blanc et Stupide.

Hope rubbed her stomach. *I'm stuffed. I won't be able to eat lunch when Dylan comes back.* She yawned. *Why am I so drowsy? I shouldn't be. I just ate four times the daily requirement of sugar. I should be wired enough to run the New York marathon.* She took off her glasses and laid them on top of her clock radio. *I'll just rest my eyes for a little while . . .*

Hope's lower lip was buzzing in her dream. It was as if a piece of sandpaper were tapping it again and again . . .

Hope woke to see Whack pawing at her face, the buzzer sounding from near the door. She found her glasses. *One-thirty? I've been out for three hours.*

She stumbled out of bed and stood at the intercom. "Sorry, Dylan, I was asleep."

"Delivery from Basil Pizza."

Hope didn't recognize the voice. "I didn't order a pizza."

"Hope, buzz me in."

It still didn't sound like Dylan. "Who are you?"

"It's Dylan," he said. "I'm holding a couple bags in my teeth."

"Oh." She buzzed him in.

Hope had the door open when Dylan came up the steps wearing a large backpack. He balanced the pizza and two other boxes with his hands, two plastic bags dangling from his mouth.

"Do you want me to take the bags?" she asked.

"Take the boxes," he mumbled.

Hope took the boxes, and Dylan grabbed the bags. "Whew," he said. "That was a workout." He kissed her cheek. "Sleep well?"

Hope thought about setting the boxes on the kitchen table but turned and took them to the bed. "Are you going on a hike?"

Dylan took a large bottle of dish soap from one of the bags and set it on the counter, immediately running water in the sink. "Sort of." He took a scale from the other bag and headed to the washroom as the sink filled. "Let's see what you weigh."

Let's not.

Hope walked into the washroom and pushed Dylan out. "I'd rather you didn't know." She closed the door and stood on the scale. *One-oh . . . two. That can't be right.* She stepped off the scale until the needle returned to zero. *It's a new scale. Maybe it needs to loosen up.* She stepped onto the scale. *One-oh-two again. That can't be! I know I've gained some weight this week. I gained at least a pound today alone.* She bounced up and down on the scale, the needle twitching. *Still one-oh-two.*

She sat on the edge of the tub. *That means I . . . I might have been less than one hundred pounds last week.* She put her head in her hands. *I could have died walking to or from work. My heart could have given out.* She blinked several tears away. *Dylan came along at the exact right moment, but I'm still in danger.* She looked up at the ceiling. *There's a pizza outside with my name on it.* She wiped her eyes with a towel. *Thank You, God. Please bless all food I eat from now on and make it stick to my bones. Amen.*

She opened the door and ran to the bed, sliding under the covers. She flipped open the pizza box first. "What kind is it?"

Dylan was in the kitchen washing the frying pan. "Wild mushroom with goat cheese."

That wouldn't have been my first choice, but . . . She opened the next, smaller box. *French fries? From a pizza place? Funny.* She dipped one in a plastic container of white sauce. *Oh, that's sinful.* "What kind of fries are these?"

"Basil fries," he said, drying a plate. "The sauce is garlic truffle mayo and parmesan."

I may lick the little container. She opened the last box and found a clear plastic container holding a Caesar salad drenched in dressing.

Whack jumped onto the bed.

"You smell the anchovies in the dressing, too, don't you?" she whispered, shooing her away.

Dylan kicked off his shoes as he came to the bed. "I hope this lunch is satisfactory." He pulled a slice of pizza from the box, folded it, and took a huge bite. "Mmm. The crust is excellent."

Hope dipped a fry in the sauce and held it up to his lips. "Try this."

Dylan inhaled the entire fry. "Tasty." He chewed for a moment. "Everything okay?"

Hope dipped two fries in the sauce. "Yes." *No. I'm lucky to be alive. I just had a brush with death in my washroom.* "Are the cards in the mail?"

He nodded. "And I checked the sales numbers, too. You're going to be busy Monday."

"Good."

He finished his slice and opened the salad container, unwrapping a spork. "How'd the weigh-in go?"

"It went." *Not now! Tears have to be the worst uninvited guests.* "It went badly."

Dylan massaged her leg. "It'll get better. Eat some pizza." He stabbed the spork into the salad. "What have you been doing?" He stuck a huge leafy bite into his mouth.

It'll get better, eat some pizza. "I start crying, I tell you my weigh-in went badly, and all you can do is say, 'Eat some pizza'?"

He nodded. "I also said it'll get better. Eat some pizza and some fries and some salad. Did you have some ice cream while I was gone?"

"Yes, I did, but listen, Dylan," Hope said. "I was probably *under* one hundred pounds the day you met me."

"Wow," he said. "I was over twenty-five pounds off. I need to get my eyes checked. I should have swept you off your feet to weigh you then. I still might have been off by a couple pounds."

She picked up and threw a basil fry, hitting him on the chest. "Dylan, do you know how serious that is? I am five-nine, and I weighed less than one hundred pounds that day. I could be dead."

Dylan picked the fry off his shirt and ate it. "Needs more basil, and could you dip it deeper in the sauce next time? I paid extra for a double portion."

She soaked a fry in the sauce and drew it back, the sauce dripping onto the quilt. "Dylan, you're not hearing me. I could be dead."

Dylan opened his mouth. "Ahh."

She flicked the fry forward but held onto it, the sauce striping Dylan's shirt. "Are you even listening to me?"

He dabbed at a glob of sauce and sucked his finger. "That *is* good sauce. Save some for me. Eat your fry."

Hope dipped the fry in the sauce. "Dylan, you're really starting to—"

"You're here *now*, Hope," Dylan interrupted. "You're here now." He took another slice of pizza and folded it. "And I'm here with you."

"But Dylan . . ."

"Eat your fry."

Hope ate her fry.

"And try some of this salad," he said. "The romaine is fresh, and the croutons are homemade."

I'm here now. More tears fell. *I'm here now.* "Don't eat it all," she said.

He slid the salad to her. "So what have you been doing?"

Oh, just having a pity party. "Nothing," Hope said, wiping her eyes with a napkin. "I ate some ice cream, watched the worst movie ever made, and fell asleep." She pulled up her shirt and looked at her stomach. "Still flat."

"It'll get better," Dylan said.

"I will have a funny shape. I'll look like a lowercase D." She ate several bites of the salad. "I can't eat another bite."

"But I need to fatten you up, Mrs. Claus."

Hope picked up the rest of the fries. "Don't tempt me."

He spread out his arms. "Free shot, Mrs. Claus."

She threw the fries, most sailing over his head and into the waiting paws of Whack.

"I'll never understand that one," Hope said. "Why does Santa have to be fat? What kind of a message are we sending our children? That it's okay to become obese in time for Christmas? The reindeer have to get hernias flying his fatness around."

Dylan ate the fries around him. "A fat Santa is a jolly Santa."

"All fat people aren't jolly."

"True." He waved the last fry in the air. "I think it's all because of Santa's suit. It only comes in one size. He has to fill it or it will cause too much wind resistance when he's flying."

Hope smiled. "That is a seriously *word* theory."

"It's not a *word* theory," he said, sliding closer. "It's scientific law." He rubbed her stomach. "You can rest from eating now. By Thanksgiving, I want to be able to pinch an inch down here. Have you always been slender and svelte?"

"For the most part," Hope said, pulling her shirt higher. "I had a little baby fat when I went to college."

"Where?" Dylan asked.

"Where you're rubbing."

"I will stop rubbing then." He lifted his hands.

"No," Hope said. "Don't stop. It feels good."

Dylan rubbed slowly, barely touching her. "You have sexy little hairs down here. They all stand up when my hand goes by."

She yanked her shirt down. "I'm glad my little hairs are so entertaining." She pushed his hand away. "What will we do all day that doesn't involve analyzing my physical defects?"

"What defects?" He kissed her. "You're perfect."

Hardly.

"Now, Miss Hope, it is important that you do nothing and do it well, and you have to do it while burning as few calories as possible." He took out a memo pad. "I did some research on this."

"You're kidding."

"I'm not." He flipped a few pages. "Did you know that at your weight you burn forty-five calories an hour sleeping? How long did you sleep?"

"About ninety minutes."

"That's sixty-seven calories," Dylan said. "How much TV did you watch?"

"About two hours."

He frowned. "Watching TV burns seventy-two calories an hour, which, by the way, is the same number of calories burned while kissing for an hour."

Who figures this stuff out? "Where did you get these numbers?"

"From Discovery Health, a very reputable website," he said. "How long is your walk to work, and how long does it normally take you?"

"About two and a half miles in just under forty minutes. Why?"

Dylan did some figuring on his pad. "You burn over three hundred calories every day walking."

"That's all? You would think it would be more." *Five hours of watching TV burns more calories than walking five miles?*

"Work is what really knocks you back," he said. "You're on your feet all day, walking back and forth between machines, rarely sitting. You burn about one *thousand* calories there. Add it up and you need at least seventeen hundred calories just to maintain your weight from walking, working, and sleeping for eight hours."

"So what you're saying is . . . *what* exactly?"

"You want to put on weight gradually, right?" Dylan asked.

Hope nodded.

"In order to do that, you have to eat more calories than your body burns. A pound of fat is equal to thirty-five hundred calories."

That's a lot of calories.

"To gain, say, two pounds a week, you need to eat an extra seven thousand calories a week above what you burn off. If you burn off, say, two thousand calories a day, you need to eat three thousand calories of food. Every day."

"Wow."

"Another key is to do only those things that burn the fewest number of calories," Dylan said. "Sleeping is your number one priority. After that comes watching TV, sketching new cards, and kissing me. You must become an artistic, kissing couch potato to gain weight."

"When did you research all this?" Hope asked.

"Today after the post office," Dylan said, "and after I took a vigorous ten-minute shower, which for me burned sixty-eight calories."

Hope blinked. "You're really into this."

"I'm really into you," Dylan said.

I want him in *me.* "What if our kissing leads to more? How many calories did we burn last night?"

He flipped several pages. "Let's see, fifteen minutes of foreplay followed by fifteen minutes of sex will cost you . . . only sixty-four calories. Foreplay alone will cost you roughly a calorie a minute."

We hardly burned any calories at all last night. We will have lots of foreplay and sex when I'm able to! The "Get Busy and Gain Weight Diet" can work for me!

She picked up the remote and scrolled through the listings.

Dylan slid in beside her. "Find another awful movie, one that will put you to sleep."

Is he kidding? I'm looking for something steamy and sexy. . . . What's this? Are you kidding? Again? "I can't believe *It's a Wonderful Life* is already showing."

"But it's a classic," Dylan said, moving the Basil boxes to the other side of the bed. "It's not all about Christmas."

"Halloween is next week," Hope said. "This should not be on."

She scrolled some more and found nothing steamy or sexy. *Those kinds of movies don't come on until later tonight.* She settled for a college football game. "Perhaps you can explain American football to me. Odell tried, but he had no patience with me." She eased between his legs and leaned back. "You're my back rest."

"As long as you *rest* in this position and make no attempts to grind your sexy derriere on me," Dylan said.

"You're no fun."

"I'm only thinking of your health," Dylan said.

Hope sighed. "You're the doctor." She pointed at the screen. "Explain this game to me."

"American football is like Canadian football only with one fewer player a side and a smaller field," Dylan said. "Oh, and a million silly rules designed to protect the quarterback."

My TV is too small to see these athletes' sexy derrieres. This is getting me nowhere. She turned off the TV. "I'll never understand it. I'll just sit here then."

"We could talk."

Hope sighed. "How many calories will that burn?"

"A small amount," Dylan said. "Can you take off early anytime next week, say around three?"

I've only taken off early once, and that was Friday. I figure if I've walked all that way, I had better stay and be fully paid for it. "I can."

"We'll be doing lots of Halloween projects this week in art," Dylan said. "I'd love it if you could join us. You don't have to demonstrate or teach. Just sit and create with us. Every day from three to five."

I have accumulated more than one hundred paid vacation and sick days. "I'll think about it."

"And afterward, I will take you out to eat," Dylan said.

"Don't talk about eating."

Dylan kissed her cheek. "It's for a good cause."

Yes, it is.

"What are you doing tomorrow?" Dylan asked.

"More nothing," Hope said. "I usually nap off and on all day on Sundays, maybe do some reading. I'm really pretty boring, Dylan. I have no life. What do you do on Sundays?"

"I go back to my old neighborhood," he said. "To the Brownsville Recreation Center."

"To work out?"

"Something like that. Want to join me?"

In the worst way. "Sure, but we're not walking, are we? We wouldn't want to burn any calories."

"We'll take the train most of the way there."

Hope checked the clock. "What are we going to do? It's only two-thirty."

Dylan removed her glasses. "It's naptime."

"I've already had a nap," Hope said.

"Shh."

"I'm not sleepy."

"Shh."

Hope closed her eyes. "I don't want to take a nap."

Dylan was silent.

"Dylan?"

She heard him snoring. *That was quick. I must have kept him up last night with my purring. He deserves a rest.*

Hope yawned and rested her head on Dylan's chest. *I'll rest my eyes for a little while and then maybe do some sketching. That can't burn too many calories. Maybe I'll start that line of skinny cards. You're so skinny that your fingers fall through the cracks next to the keys when you type. Now that's skinny. You're so skinny, you cut people in two when you walk sideways. You're so skinny . . . you . . . can fold yourself . . . seven times . . . like a piece . . . of paper . . .*

Hope woke alone to the sound of water running. The room was dark save the red glow from the clock and light sneaking out from under the washroom door. She searched the nightstand until she found her glasses. "Dylan?"

The washroom door opened, and Dylan padded across the floor to her side. "I'm drawing you a bath."

She looked at the clock. "It's after eleven?"

He nodded and held out his hand. "Come on."

She took his hand and pulled herself to her feet. "It's really late."

"I know," he whispered, leading her into the washroom, where steam was rising from the bathtub and fogging the mirror and her glasses. "I thought you'd like to soak for a while."

I haven't had a bath in years. "But I'm still sleepy."

He shut off the water. "Once you're in, you just soak. I'll do the rest."

"But I don't want you to see me," Hope whined. "I'm a living skeleton, and just in time for Halloween."

"Close your eyes then," he whispered.

"I don't want to scare you away."

"Close your eyes, Hope."

She closed her eyes and felt her glasses leave her face, her T-shirt slide over her head, and her sweats drop to the floor. "I'm embarrassed."

"Don't be," he whispered. "You're beautiful. Every square inch. I'm going to lift you up now."

Hope felt herself go completely weightless, her feet dipping first into the water.

"Not too hot?" he asked.

"No." Warm water enveloped the rest of her. "Don't stare at me."

"I like everything that I see," he whispered. "Just relax."

Hope held the sides of the tub as Dylan used a soapy washcloth on her arms, neck, and chest. She felt a slight tug on her left elbow and leaned forward, feeling the washcloth circling her back. A single finger pushed her back. The washcloth traveled down her stomach, lingered there, went lower, lingered *much* longer there, and then moved unhurriedly down one leg and up the other. She felt his grip on her ankles as he washed her feet, massaging them before settling them back into the water. She heard water dripping, and a moment later, the washcloth was in her hand.

"I'll let you wash your face," he whispered.

Hope washed and rinsed her face.

"Let's wash your hair," Dylan said.

Hope opened her eyes and saw Dylan's fuzzy face. "I'll wash it."

"Lean up a little," Dylan said. "I've done this before."

With Marie.

"I'll try not to pull or twist when I rinse," he said.

Hope leaned forward and tried to focus on Dylan as he squirted the DreadHead soap into his hands. "You've really done this before?"

"Like washing a sponge, right?" he said. "Work it in, squeeze, and rinse until I see no soap." He rubbed his hands together and went to work. "I really like your hair."

"Thank you."

This is unbelievable. I'm never had any other hands on my dreads, and whoa, he's making my scalp tingle. Firm but gentle, soap, squeeze, rinse with fresh water from the tub faucet cupped in his hands. "You do this well."

"Thank you."

"How often did you . . . I'm assuming you washed Marie's hair."

His fuzzy face nodded. "Often. It sometimes put her to sleep."

"It feels too good for me to sleep," Hope said. "My arms get so tired, and I never washed my hair in the tub."

"Over the sink?" Dylan asked.

"Yeah."

"That's how Marie preferred to wash, too." He laughed. "But she kept clogging up the kitchen sink, so I suggested the tub. The tub drain is much easier to unclog. Have you ever used Dread Butta?"

It is so weird to hear a man say "Dread Butta." Marie must have used it. Her dreadlocks must have been shiny. Hope reached up and squeezed several locks, finding them only a little wet. "No."

He rinsed his hands in the tub. "Yeah, I wouldn't want you to be more stunning than you already are. You'd stop traffic on your walk to work."

I need some Dread Butta.

He stood. "Take your time soaking. I'll go warm up the bed."

"Thank you." She closed her eyes.

She felt a soft kiss on her cheek.

She heard the door close.

I'm clean and weightless. My hair is clean, and my arms and fingers don't hurt. A man so strong, so caring, and yet so gentle is in my bed waiting for me.

She shivered.

This water is getting cold.

She stood, stepped out of the tub, and dried off. She used a smaller towel to squeeze her locks. After putting on her glasses, she lotioned her body from head to toe and then turned out the light. She left the washroom, put her glasses on the nightstand, and slipped under the covers, her cool skin contacting Dylan's hot skin, his arm pulling her close.

"You're naked, Miss Warren," Dylan whispered.

"So are you."

"I got too hot last night and couldn't sleep," he whispered. "I hope you don't mind."

Do I mind a steaming hot man sleeping au naturel *next to me?* "I don't mind at all." She kissed his chest. "Thank you for my bath."

"It was my pleasure."

Mine, too. "My hair isn't quite dry. I hope it's not too cold on you."

"It's fine." He rubbed her back. "Warming up?"

"Yes." *Steaming up is more like it. Dylan is a woodstove loaded with kindling.* She wandered her hand across his chest and down to his stomach. "Are you sleepy?" she whispered.

"Very," he sighed.

Guess we're not burning a calorie a minute then, but I'm sleepy, too. I could have dozed off in that tub if the water had stayed warm. "Then let's sleep." She kissed him on the neck and wrapped her arm around him. "Marie was a fool to leave you."

"Thank you." He nuzzled her hair. "I needed to hear that."

"Bonne nuit, Dylan," Hope whispered.

"Good night, Hope."

Good night, you sweet, sweet man.

OCTOBER 18

Only 67 more shopping days until Christmas . . .

Chapter 16

While Dylan showered and Whack chased and danced with the dust floating in the sunbeams streaming through the windows, Hope analyzed the back of the Pop-Tart Frosted S'Mores box.

I'd have to eat ten of these a day to hit two thousand calories. That's a lot of sugar. She bit into one. *Not bad. I'm sure they'd taste better toasted.* She toasted the other one. *Pretty good, but I will not eat ten of these every day. I'll eat two of these, drink my coffee, and eat the toast and jam Dylan gives me, so roughly . . . eight hundred calories for breakfast, which is eight hundred more calories than I've been eating every morning for the last eight years. I've missed eating nearly three thousand breakfasts! I'd need about a thousand more calories for the next two meals just to maintain my weight, and then a thousand more after that so I can start putting on weight.*

I don't know if I can do that, but I have to gain weight to give myself more time on this earth and more of me for Dylan to love. He was so interested in my body last night! He bathed me, washed my hair, and held me all night long. He was just too tired to get frisky, that's all. I was so relaxed, and he was so hot. Yes, I wanted him. I still do. And it doesn't really matter if Marie was gorgeous. She left him. *I'm* here with him. *He's getting out of* my *shower. He has spent the last two nights in* my *bed, and when I get back to what I should weigh, I will be* la plus belle femme sur la terre, *and we will be getting frisky every night.*

But what if Marie comes back? What then? I hope she doesn't.

Five years is a long time to be gone. He has to be over her by now. I know Dylan loved her, but that's in the past, and I know firsthand that "loves of a lifetime" go away. If she were truly the love of his life, she wouldn't have left. Therefore, because she left, Dylan has yet to meet his love of a lifetime, and I plan to be her.

I want to be the love of his life. I want to be his love.

Hope rubbed her eyes under her glasses. *I'll say one thing for severe depression. It really makes you zero in on what you want.*

I want Dylan.

It's obvious that I need him.

It's becoming obvious that he needs me.

I want him, and as soon as I admit that, my depression takes a break.

I want Dylan.

I also want to know what's in that backpack.

She tried but failed to keep her eyes from darting to the long backpack on the floor by the door. *I saw him take out some clothes and a shave kit, but what else could be in there? It's such a big backpack, the kind mountain climbers use. If I could somehow get Whack "stuck" in there, I could rescue her and take a peek.*

Dylan walked out of the washroom shirtless and sock-less, his long hair slick and shiny. "We need to leave soon. Did you eat?"

Hope waved the last half of her second Pop-Tart. "What's in the backpack?"

He smiled. "You shall see."

"You could tell me," she said.

"And ruin the surprise?" He winked. "I like surprising you."

Hope finished her Pop-Tart. "Do I need to bring anything besides my curiosity?"

"Just your creativity and imagination." He looked out at the coffee table. "And some paper and pencils. You might get an idea while we ride . . ."

They walked to the subway station at the Brooklyn Museum, rode the 3 train to the New Lots station, and began a half-mile hike to the Brownsville Recreation Center on Linden Boulevard.

They had no shortage of people staring.

I'm holding hands and walking in Brownsville with a long-haired, smiling Irishman wearing a backpack that makes him look eight feet tall, and he is the only white man I can see. These people driving by might get in a wreck if they don't stop staring at us.

"Why are they staring so hard?" Hope whispered.

"They've never seen such a beautiful woman before," Dylan said.

"Right."

"I understand, Hope," Dylan said. "I felt the same way when I was a kid. I kind of stuck out."

"Really? No. You? I can't imagine why. Did you wear the backpack then, too?"

"I love your sarcasm," Dylan said. "I grew up in the Tilden Houses, about a mile or so from here. That was a wild place. Eight buildings sixteen stories high. Noise. Crime. Violence. But what I learned there helped me survive. I knew never to walk on Pitkin or Sutter after dark, to keep from making eye contact with anyone, and to avoid walking by the seventy-third police precinct at any time, especially on a day I was skipping school."

"It's so hard to believe that you grew up in a place like this," Hope said. "You're so . . . gentle and kind."

"Most people from Brownsville are good people, Hope," Dylan said. "Larry King and Al Sharpton are from here. U-God of Wu-Tang Clan is from here. Mike Tyson lived here."

"But Mike Tyson is a thug," Hope said. "Isn't he?"

"I prefer to think of Mike Tyson as misunderstood," Dylan said, "and if anyone around Brownsville asks you, you tell them Mike Tyson is the greatest boxer and gentleman who ever lived."

He guided her west on New Lots Avenue. "You hungry?"

"I just ate some Pop-Tarts," Hope said.

"Not enough," Dylan said. "We have to compensate for this walk. Let's go eat some grease."

Crown Fried Chicken provided them with five delicious, salty, oily pieces of chicken and two spinach-and-cheese rolls. Hope surprised herself by eating a wing, a thigh, and half a breast.

"I shouldn't be hungry at all," Hope said, finishing her roll.

"It's the fresh October air," Dylan said.

Or the fresh-faced man in front of me. She looked across the street at a wide expanse of fields, tennis courts, and open space. "Is that the recreation center?"

Dylan nodded. "Beautiful, isn't it? Like an oasis on Linden Boulevard." He picked up his backpack. "Come on. There are some artists I want you to meet."

He led Hope through several ball fields to a playground swarming with children, and when they saw him approach, Hope heard "It's Dill Pickle!" and "Hey, D-Funny!"

"Dill Pickle?" Hope whispered.

"So I'm Irish."

Dylan swept into the enclosed playground and set his backpack down near a park bench as a dozen brown and black children danced around him. "How are my young artists today?"

"Ready! . . . You're late! . . . Who dis?"

"Ladies and gentleman," Dylan said, putting his arm around Hope, "this is my girlfriend, Hope Warren. She is an artist."

His girlfriend. I wondered what he'd call me. I'm okay with that, but calling me an artist?

"She came all the way down from Canada to be with you today," Dylan said.

"Yeah right," one boy said. "She from Jamaica, yo. Look at them dreads."

"Okay, okay, Devon," Dylan said, "she's from Prospect Heights, but she grew up in Canada, and her parents are from the Bahamas."

Devon, who might have been eleven, smiled. "I got to get me to Canada, yo."

They sure grow up fast in Brownsville.

A little girl looked up at Hope. "Can you paint a butterfly on my face?"

"I'll try." She looked over at Dylan getting hugs and handshakes from children no taller than his hip.

The little girl yanked on Hope's coat sleeve, and Hope squatted. "He's not very good at butterflies," the little girl said.

Dylan then pulled three small fold-up easels from the backpack and set them up in front of the bench. He clipped a large piece of paper to each easel and then took out what looked like a skinny camping table, setting it up close to the easels. He pulled ten different jars of paint from the backpack, placed them on the table, and handed out brushes to six children, who immediately opened jars and started painting, two artists to an easel, their legs dangling off the end of the bench.

He has organized this chaos in two minutes! Hope smiled at the little girl. "What's your name?"

"Deja."

"Well, Deja, let's make you a butterfly."

Deja took Hope's hand. "A green-and-orange one."

"Okay."

For the rest of the afternoon, Hope and Dylan painted dragons, butterflies, caterpillars, initials, cartoon characters, and even a few Nike swoosh symbols on faces and arms while six small artists painted sheet after sheet of buildings, people, fields, and animals. As soon as one "canvas" was "finished," Dylan would clip it to the chain-link fence to dry and attach another for two new artists to attack.

As the sun started to set and children ran home waving their masterpieces, Dylan pulled out a sketchbook and a pencil and handed them to Hope. "You do caricatures, don't you?" He stood sideways and struck up a heroic pose.

"I'll need a bigger piece of paper," Hope said.

"My nose isn't that big," Dylan said.

How do you fit a hero onto a single piece of paper? "For all your muscles."

Deja watched Hope sketch Dylan, overemphasizing his hair, his nose, and his chest. "He doesn't look like that," Deja said.

"I know," Hope said. "This is called a caricature. When you create a caricature, you make things bigger than they really are to make a funny picture."

"It's funny, all right." Deja pointed at Dylan's nose. "He looks like an elephant."

That wasn't what I was going for, but ... "He does. Would you like me to draw you?"

Deja nodded rapidly.

Hope flipped the page and sketched Deja's eyes. "You have very big, brown eyes, so I will make them huge."

Deja giggled.

"And then I'll add the rest of you." She drew Deja's tiny nose and gave her a smile as wide as her face.

"I don't smile like that!" Deja yelled.

"You have a beautiful smile," Hope said. "And now let's add all your pretty hair."

While Dylan packed up and waved good-bye to the last group of artists, Hope made Deja into a princess complete with a crown on her cornrows, a paintbrush and a palette in her hand. She handed it to Deja and watched Deja's eyes.

"This isn't really me," she said.

But your eyes tell me that you wish it were you, Miss Deja.

"Sign it," Deja said. "Dill Pickle says artists should always sign their work."

Hope wrote her name under the caricature.

"Hope," Deja said.

Hope. That's what Dylan's selling here. Lots and lots of hope.

On the train ride back to Hope's apartment, she rested her head on Dylan's shoulder, his backpack bag of artistic tricks on the seat in front of them. "You really love children, don't you?" she asked.

"Yes." He put his arm around her. "And one day, I want eight or nine of my own."

Eight or nine? Is he kidding? "Really?"

"Or ten," Dylan said. "I haven't decided. How many do you want?"

This has to be a test. "I'll start with one."

"You have too much love in you to have only one child, Hope," Dylan said. "I watched you with those kids, Deja especially. You weren't just painting faces today. You were sharing love, and I believe that you have an infinite amount of love inside you. You just need someone to draw it out of you."

I have to ask. "Did Marie want eight or nine or ten children?"

"No," Dylan said. "She was too proud of her figure. She was extremely vain. Working out all the time, fixing her hair and makeup for hours, and she really didn't like kids at all. Not like you do."

Hope traced a heart on the back of his hand. "Am I anything like her?"

He shook his head. "No." He smiled. "Not at all, and that's what I'm learning to love about you. You're like no one else in the world."

Neither are you, Dylan. "You didn't have any ulterior motives for taking me to the playground today, did you?"

"Of course not," he said.

"Right," Hope said. "You wanted to see me in action."

"Okay, you have figured me out," Dylan said. "I had a feeling you would be good with children, but you amazed me. You are a *natural* with children. They are drawn to you, pun intended. You had Deja talking up a storm."

"She's not usually talkative?"

"No," Dylan said. "I couldn't get anything but the word 'butterfly' out of her, and I've been coming here and knowing her for over a year."

"She said you weren't very good at butterflies."

"See why I need you?" He squeezed her shoulder. "Without you, there will be no recognizable butterflies in Brownsville. Please consider joining us this week at Kinderstuff. We'd make a good team there, too."

He wants more of me in his life, and this scares and excites me. Seeing him every morning, maybe sometimes at lunch, finishing the day with him covered in paint or glue or chalk. I've never felt more needed and wanted. "I will be there."

"What day?" Dylan asked.

"I don't know," Hope said. *Maybe every day. I figure I could get off three hours early six hundred times and still have vacation days left over.* She drifted her fingers over his leg. "You'll probably get sick of me."

"Not a chance." He kissed her. "Thank you."

"For what?"

"For everything." He looked out the window as they came to another stop. He jumped to his feet. "Let's get off here."

"This isn't our stop, is it?"

He shook his head and grabbed the backpack. "It's dinnertime. I know you're hungry."

For more than food. "I suppose I could eat."

He took her hand and led her off the train. "I know a place where we can increase our bad cholesterol . . ."

They went to Dutch Boy Burger on Franklin, where they inhaled Dutch burgers with mushrooms and onions, Abita root beer, and toasted-marshmallow milkshakes.

There had to be at least one thousand calories in the milkshake alone.

"Aren't you gaining weight, too?" Hope asked as they took a leisurely stroll to her apartment.

"I'm actually losing weight," he said.

"That can't be true," Hope said.

"There is more than one kind of weight," he said softly.

True.

"When I get back to my place tonight and take off this back-pack, I will feel much lighter," Dylan said. "That's how the last few days with you have made me feel. I'm losing the weight of regret, you know?"

Hope nodded. *I know exactly how you feel.*

"You've made me feel lighter, and I'm not making a skinny joke," he said. "You were appropriately named. The hope you're giving me is lightening my load. Thank you, Hope."

"And you're making me *fat* with hope," Hope said. "I suppose it's an even trade."

So he's not planning to stay with me tonight. That's okay. That makes sense. We work different hours, and we're only boyfriend and girlfriend. I have a boyfriend! I want more than a boyfriend, of course, but it's not as if he's going to move in with me after only a few days.

Though I really want him to. Small apartment, big him, nowhere to hide. That would be paradise.

"You okay?" Dylan asked.

I can't ask him upstairs. I know I will make a scene and cling to him, begging him to stay. "I'm just a little tired," Hope said. "I'm sure you are, too."

"Yeah, but it's a good kind of tired."

They stopped at the entrance, the blue butterfly peering over their shoulders.

Dylan set down the backpack and hugged Hope tightly, then held her at arm's length. "I'm sorry I called you my girlfriend at the playground. 'Lady friend' sounds ridiculous, and only calling you my friend wasn't enough."

"It's okay," Hope said. "It made me feel younger."

"How old are you? Twenty-five?" Dylan asked.

Wow. He doesn't know weights or ages. "I'm thirty-three."

Dylan's eyes widened, and his mouth dropped open. "No way." He held her face in his hands. "You can't be."

"I am."

"You *really* look younger, Hope."

Such a nice compliment. She dropped her chin.

"I wasn't saying that to flatter you," Dylan said.

"Thank you." She kissed his chin. "And what are you, thirty-six?"

"Is that what you really think?" he asked.

"You're not?" Hope asked. *Oops. I hope he's not younger.*

"I just turned thirty-six," Dylan said, frowning. "I thought I looked younger than thirty-six." He sighed. "So I *look* my age."

"As long as you don't act it," Hope said, "and you don't."

"So it's okay if I tell people that you're my girlfriend?" Dylan asked.

Hope nodded. "Yes, but I wish . . ." *I were more.* She hugged him. "I'll see you tomorrow."

"For breakfast?"

Hope nodded against his shoulder.

"What kind of jelly or jam do you like?" he asked, stepping back.

"Surprise me." She forced a smile.

"I will," Dylan said. He kissed her tenderly.

Hope took out her keys.

"And Hope?"

She turned back.

"I wish . . . too." He hoisted the backpack onto his shoulders. "And I will wish . . . all the way home. Good night, Hope."

"Good night."

Hope trudged up the stairs, entered her apartment, and sniffed the air. "Whack?"

The cat shot out of the kitchen to the bed.

Those fries must not have agreed with her, and if I don't deal with it now . . .

She raked and double-bagged Whack's *merde*, setting the bag in the trash can. Then she disrobed as she walked into the washroom, turning the hot water tap of the tub. *I may never take a shower again. Besides, taking a shower burns calories.* As the tub filled and the room filled with steam, she looked at her face in the mirror.

This is a happy face. It isn't a content face yet. Dylan should be behind me in here or waiting for me out there in my bed. I guess this is the face of a woman—

A pattern of lines appeared on the mirror, and as the steam billowed around her, the lines became words:

I
miss
you.
:)
D

"I miss you, too," she whispered, tears forming behind her eyes.

He wrote that before we left for the recreation center this morning. He was thinking that far ahead, and if I don't wipe it off, I can see him missing me anytime I steam up this room.

I now see the face of a woman who likes to be surprised by hidden messages.

This man surprises me all the time.

It's almost like Christmas every day with him.

OCTOBER 19

Only 66 more shopping days
until Christmas . . .

Chapter 17

Hope leaped out of bed with gusto the next morning.
Then she remembered to take it slow.

"I mustn't burn calories" became a whispered mantra as she *languidly* brushed her teeth, *lazily* dressed, and *lethargically* fed Whack. She *leisurely* left her apartment at 7:45 AM instead of 8:10 AM, *gradually* snacking on two toasted Pop-Tarts by the time she *sluggishly* arrived at Prospect Perk Café and *unhurriedly* ordered two triple-triples instead of her usual double-doubles.

She even sipped her coffee, now fortified with more fattening milk, *slothfully*.

Once she slowed to a snail's pace and stood under the multicolored Kinderstuff awning, she realized she hadn't broken a sweat.

Dylan opened the door. "Good morning."

"Good morning," Hope said, kissing him dreamily, then handing him his coffee. "I missed you, too."

"You got my message," he said, and he handed her two pieces of paper. "The one on top is a breakdown of your earnings. The one on the bottom is a list of orders you need to do today."

Is this right? Twenty-four hundred dollars? Look at all these orders! I'll be busy all morning! "Wow. I better get going then."

"Not before your toast and jam," Dylan said. He stepped aside to reveal Aniya holding a paper plate. On it were two pieces of brown toast slathered in red jam resting on a paper towel.

"Thank you, Aniya," Hope said, picking up the toast. "Strawberry?"

Aniya nodded. "It's a special kind from Canada."

"Crofter's," Dylan said. "It wasn't easy to find."

She took a bite. *Wow. It's a taste of home.* "Delicious."

"Dylan showed me the picture of the kiss," Aniya said. "You had your eyes closed."

"Yes, I did," Hope said.

"Was it a good kiss?" Aniya whispered.

"The best." She smiled at Dylan.

"It looked like a good kiss," Aniya said, and she carried the empty plate inside.

"Send me the kiss," Hope said. "I need a new screensaver."

"I will," Dylan said. "Take your time getting to work."

"I have been," Hope said. "I know I'll be late."

Dylan hugged her, careful to avoid her toast. "So be late. Bye."

She nibbled both pieces of toast and barely made it across several crosswalks before the lights changed, arriving at Thrifty at 9:05 AM. *I am late for the first time in ten years. I wonder if anything will change.*

More truthfully, I wonder if anyone will notice.

She breezed up to Kiki at the counter, wiping her lips with the paper towel. "How was Saturday?"

"I do not know," Kiki said. "I did not come in. I was busy, as I am sure you were."

"I was." Hope raised her eyebrows, eased around the counter, and took off her coat, laying it over her chair by the mainframe. *So Justin ran the store by his own little self? Highly unlikely.*

"On-Gee and I had the whole theater to ourselves," Kiki said.

No chance of claustrophobia there. I wonder what that would have been like, to have your pick of places to be intimate.

Hope squinted as she looked around the store. *Was Justin even here Saturday? The store looks the same way I left it on Friday.*

"We found that one of the box seats had an old-fashioned fainting couch," Kiki said. "I am so glad I was small enough to use it. I wanted her to put a red spotlight for us on the stage, but she is so shy sometimes."

The office door opened, Justin striding to the counter. "From now on," he said, addressing the red and yellow tiles on the floor, "you both can't be sick on the same day."

Kiki stared at Hope. "We did not plan to be sick on the same day."

"Well," Justin said, now addressing the ficus plant, "don't let it happen again. I was so busy."

He has to be lying. He probably came in Saturday morning, found out we were both "sick," and immediately closed the store.

"Just be here from now on, all right?" Justin glanced at Hope and walked back to the office, shutting the door behind him.

Kiki smirked. "That may have been the first day that man actually had to work here. Is this the moment we ask for a raise?"

Hope shook her head slowly. She checked the mainframe and found orders that came in Friday night that Justin hadn't accessed on Saturday. "He didn't check for Friday's overnight orders, Kiki. They're still here. Including one for the House of the Lord Pentecostal Church."

"Oh no!" Kiki cried. "They didn't get their Sunday service programs. They must be so angry."

"I'll bet they are," Hope said. "I've been doing those programs for years. Have you checked the copy key counters?"

Kiki nodded. "The count is the same as the count for Friday. We usually have a minimum of one hundred a day." She pointed under the counter. "Orders you did Friday to be picked up Saturday are still here."

"I don't think he opened the store, Kiki." *The man is useless and should be fired.*

Kiki smiled. "This *is* the day we ask for a raise."

"I doubt there's any money available for a raise," Hope said, "and Justin will never admit he closed the store. He might have been here all day in his office." *With his girls.* "You may have a few upset customers today. Let's call House of the Lord right now and get ready to apologize." Hope called out the number from the work order, and Kiki dialed it.

"Hello, this is Kiki Clarke from Thrifty Digital Printing." Kiki held the phone far from her ear, wincing. "Yes, ma'am, I know there was a serious problem on Saturday, and I would like to help you . . ." She covered the mouthpiece. "These Pentecostals are always so loud." She uncovered the mouthpiece. "When did you come to the store, ma'am? . . . I see . . ." She wrote a number on a scratch piece of paper and showed it to Hope.

Eleven. If Justin was even here, he probably heard the knocking and hid in his office until they left. What a coward and a fool! All he had to do was collect some money.

"We are so terribly sorry we let you down," Kiki said. "What can we do to earn back your trust?"

"Make their next two orders free," Hope said.

Kiki nodded. "We would like to do right by you and give you your next two orders free . . . Yes, ma'am . . . No, ma'am. It will not happen again." Kiki hung up. "We *really* cannot be sick together. This place will lose all customers and go out of business. As low-paying as it is, I need this job. On-Gee only makes money when a show is in production, and some of the shows she works on are so bad they last only a few days." She ground her hands together. "We *must* bust Justin out. We *must* let Mr. Yarmouth know what kind of bay-it he has managing his store."

Should we cause some drama? I'm not supposed to work too hard today. "Let's just keep this to ourselves for now. It might be more to our advantage to leave it hanging over Justin's head."

"I want to bust some bay-it today," Kiki said. "But I understand. We can bring it up whenever we want to get away early from now on."

Hope nodded. "Or when we want to take another day off."

Now I will take a load off, Hope thought. *I will sit as much as I can today. I will become one with this padded, duct-taped, rolling swivel chair.* She sat in her chair and spun to face Kiki. "After this weekend, I could have used another two days off."

"So the rest of your date went well?" Kiki asked.

"It went . . . so peacefully." Hope smiled and sighed.

Kiki dragged her stool to within inches of Hope's chair. "You must tell me everything."

Should I? I have to tell someone. "It was . . . nice."

"He became your champion?"

Why not? He will be. Soon. He's already my hero. "Yes."

Kiki grabbed Hope's arm. "And is he . . ." She widened her eyes.

I'm not lying here. "He's . . . abundant."

Kiki shook Hope's arm and laughed. "He is abundant! I knew it."

I shouldn't have told her. Kiki will stare at Dylan's "abundance" every time he comes into the store now. "But more importantly, Dylan is officially my boyfriend as of yesterday."

"That's wonderful!" Kiki let go of Hope's arm. "Yesterday? Your date was Friday."

"He stayed," Hope said. "*Both* nights."

Kiki leaned back and sighed. "That is the problem with abundance. So you may be 'sick' again next Saturday."

"I might." *That gives me another idea.*

Kiki frowned, picked up her stool, and returned it to the counter. "Just give me ample warning so I can get as much *abundance* as I can from On-Gee Friday night."

"She'll understand, won't she?" Hope asked.

Kiki rolled her shoulders forward. "She has never understood why I have to work on Saturdays."

"Doesn't it make the reunion Saturday night sweeter?" Hope asked.

"Sometimes she is too tired from doing nothing all day without me," Kiki said. "Sometimes she is tired from working a Saturday night show." She sighed. "But I will manage without you." She shook her head at the office door. "It is him I am angry with. If he could do any part of our jobs . . ."

That confirms another idea. I can't share these ideas now, though. The timing has to be right.

Hope worked at a steady, measured pace completing Friday's unprinted Internet orders, several flyers for upcoming Halloween parties, and all the Odd Ducks cards by eleven while Kiki fended off two more fuming customers. A teacher collecting 150 "Reading is Fun!" bookmarks that she had "planned on giving out *today* as a *reward* to my *deserving* students" eventually relented and thanked Kiki for a generous twenty percent discount.

The owner of Party City on nearby Atlantic Avenue wouldn't shut up, however, ranting, "The lights were on, but no one was home! My time is valuable! I should not waste any more of my business on you!" He tossed his "30% OFF!" sale flyers into the air, many of them spilling off the counter. "What good are these now? My three-day sale is two days old!"

"We can change the dates, sir," Kiki said.

"And run a three-day sale starting tomorrow?" he howled. "No one runs three-day sales in the middle of the week."

Kiki smiled. "So you will be the *only* one running that sale during the middle of the week."

The man swallowed his next outburst. "Okay," he said.

Hope reprinted the flyers, changing the sale dates.

Kiki did not give this man a discount.

"He was bay-it," she said.

Hope felt her stomach grumble precisely at noon. *Now that I'm eating again, my stomach has become a clock.* "Kiki," she said, "I'm hungry. It's your turn to feed us." She handed Kiki a ten.

Kiki threw on her coat. "I will do anything to leave this place and get some fresh air. Where should I go?"

"I want..." She tried to remember some of Dylan's menus. "Yummy Taco."

Kiki grabbed her throat. "You want to eat burritos made by Chinese people? Why not get the jerk chicken combo from Golden Krust?"

Hope sighed. She knew from a visit to Yummy Taco years ago that Chinese people did run the Tex-Mex restaurant down the street. "Americans make all kinds of ethnic food, Kiki. The man who started Taco Bell was a white man. So what if the Chinese in Brooklyn are moving in on the Mexicans? Food has no nationality when you're hungry." *That sounds like a slogan. I may get that one trademarked.*

"I have never eaten at Yummy Taco or even *thought* of eating there." Kiki said. "But I will try it since I am hungry. What is good there?"

Hope told her.

Kiki brought back two chorizo burritos, two orders of guacamole nachos, and two sodas, and they dug in.

"Not bad," Kiki said. "But if Mexicans start making Chinese food, On-Gee and I are moving to Jamaica." She smiled. "If Mexicans made *Chinese* food, would the fortune cookies be written in Spanish?"

When Hope finally had a chance to check her e-mail, she found an untitled message from Dylan, opened the attachment, and stared at "the kiss." *Too much glare from the left lens of my glasses, and the driver cut off the tops of both of our heads. Look at his eyes staring longingly at my thick glasses. It's not very romantic. Still, it's—*

"What is that picture?" Kiki asked, having left her stool to stand behind Hope.

"Our third kiss," Hope said.

"You took a picture of your third kiss?" Kiki asked. "Who does such a thing?"

It does sound odd. "The first two were practice."

"Did you practice all weekend?" Kiki asked.

Hope smiled, exposing all her teeth. "Yes. My tongue is tired, and my teeth are crooked."

"Is that all that is crooked?" Kiki asked. "Does his . . ."

That is a bit too personal. "Why are you so interested in my sex life, Kiki?"

"I am curious," Kiki said. "I had wonderful times with white boys when I was young, and sometimes they were curved to the right, sometimes to the left, sometimes over the top like a finger." She sighed. "They came at me from all directions."

Hope laughed. "You're nasty!"

"I am not nasty," Kiki said. "I am an open book. I say what I think. Life is too short not to say what you really think."

I wish I could speak with such abandon. "So you won't mind if I ask why you are now with a woman."

"I was wondering when you would get to that question," Kiki said, "and I have an answer. I am beautiful, no?"

"*Oui.*" Very. *She has more curves per square centimeter than ten women have and lets many of her curves spill out of her clothes.*

"I am attracted to beauty in all forms," Kiki said. "On-Gee is the most beautiful person I have ever known. Therefore, I *must* be with her."

That was logically illogical. "You two are really cute together," Hope said. "I can tell she loves you very much."

"And I love her very much." Kiki's eyes narrowed. "Go ahead and ask the question you *really* want to ask."

I don't have a question I really *want to ask.* "What if a more beautiful *man* should come your way?"

"I like how you phrased that."

What did I say? Oh. "What if a beautiful man *appeared* in your life?"

"That phrasing was not as fun," Kiki said. "On-Gee and I have discussed this often. Men instantly fall in love with her every day. She is a tall dream for any man, and she has a body . . ." Kiki sighed. "She is a goddess, agreed?"

"I agree." *It is the truth. Angie should be a model.*

"Men only sometimes fall in love with me," Kiki said. "What can I say? I am an acquired taste."

I wish I had half of Kiki's curves. "You know you're gorgeous, Kiki."

Kiki smiled. "So you have noticed? I flirted briefly with you when I first started working here."

She did? "You . . . did?"

"I have a thing for tall women," Kiki said. "But when you would not speak to me, I stopped flirting." She smiled. "With *you.* I *did* flirt with Dylan, and now that I know he is truly abundant . . ."

Hope frowned and stared.

"I am kidding," Kiki said. "But I must admit that for a moment, I considered Dylan very seriously."

Excuse me?

"Do not stare so hard, Hope, or you will hurt your eyes." Kiki smiled. "He was so persistent in asking me out, and he is very handsome and abundant."

"He was only asking you out to eat, Kiki," Hope said.

"Ah, but was he only asking me out for food?" she asked. "Food always leads to sex."

"No, it doesn't," Hope said.

"It does with me," Kiki said.

It sort of does with me, too. Hmm.

"And I even told On-Gee about Dylan," Kiki said. "I said, 'Perhaps he can join us some evening, On-Gee. We will have so much fun together.' "

Hope blinked. *Kiki is a predator!*

"And when On-Gee told me she knew Dylan and had this crush on him years ago, I thought maybe he was the one for us," Kiki said. "But On-Gee said it would be strange to be with him. She has the greatest respect for Dylan. Her own father died when she was young, and Dylan became in many ways her father. Did you know that Dylan helped her with her English?"

"She barely has an accent at all," Hope said.

"Dylan is a good teacher," Kiki said. "He also wrote her recommendations to help her get into college. So we decided not to pursue Dylan. In the meantime, we wait."

"For what?" Hope asked.

"For *whom*," Kiki said. "One day we will find a man on whom we can *both* agree, and then the three of us will be beautiful together."

This is beyond my experience. I have enough trouble caring about myself, much less one or two other people.

"And when we find this man, he will be paid very well so neither On-Gee nor I has to work ever again." Kiki laughed. "I do not know if such a man exists, but until then, we wait and we search."

"So you're not strictly, um . . ."

"I am open and I am loving," Kiki said. "Homosexuality, bisexuality, heterosexuality, they are only labels. I do not like labels."

"Wouldn't you be worried, um . . ." *Suddenly I feel curious.* "I'm trying to understand this possible situation, Kiki."

"It is an interesting possibility, is it not?" Kiki asked.

Hope shrugged.

"I did not expect you to understand," Kiki said. "Yes, I would be worried, perhaps even jealous, of a man taking On-Gee's attention from me, but as long as he loves me, too, I will be content. I would also *never* let the two of them out of my sight." She leaned close to Hope's ear. "You have not had such a fantasy?"

Hope shook her head. "No." *One person at a time exclusively for me.*

Kiki spun Hope's chair around. "Ask Dylan if he has this fantasy."

"I can't do that," Hope said. "That's his business."

Kiki shook her head. "It is your business to know your lover's fantasies. Otherwise, how will you help your lover fulfill them?"

Well, we're not exactly lovers yet . . . "I hope his only fantasy is me," Hope said.

Kiki spun Hope's chair back to the mainframe. "Deep in your heart you know this is not true about *any* man, but I hope you are right about Dylan. If it is true, Dylan is a rare man, indeed." She returned to her stool. "If I were you, though, I would ask, just to be sure."

Right. She wants me to ask him, "So, Dylan, did you ever want to be with two women at the same time?" What kind of question is that for any woman to ask any man? That's like telling him that I don't think I'm enough for him, that I know he needs more than I can give him. I am more than enough for him, thank you very much, and as soon as I gain some weight, I'll be twice the woman he'll ever need.

I hope.

Hope checked the clock. *It's two, and I have to be at Kinderstuff at three. Now is the time to share my ideas.* She stood, stretching her legs. "Kiki, I need to speak to you and Justin about my future plans."

"You are not quitting this job, are you?" Kiki asked.

"No," Hope said. "Please go rouse Justin."

Kiki went over and pounded on the office door. "Hope wants to speak to us!" She returned to her stool muttering "bay-it" repeatedly.

Justin came out, his face red and sweaty. "What's wrong?"

"Nothing." *Yet.* Hope hopped up onto the counter. "Kiki, Justin, I will be leaving at three o'clock until further notice. My new hours will be nine to three, Monday through Friday and—"

"You can't!" Justin interrupted. "We can't run the store—"

"I'm not finished, Justin," Hope interrupted. "I will also not be working on Saturdays at least through Christmas."

"That's . . ." Justin nearly doubled over. "That's not possible."

"Sure it is," Hope said. "I have worked here ten years, and until this past Saturday, I hadn't taken a single vacation or sick day. I have over one hundred days saved up, Justin. According to the employee handbook, I am entitled to take them whenever and however I please."

"Not at the expense of this store," Justin said, shaking his head. "This store works most efficiently when you're here."

And when you're not *here.* "We'll discuss all that in a minute. I know I don't need to give you a reason for these absences, but because I care, here's the reason. I will be down the street at Kinderstuff doing and maybe even teaching art to the children there with my boyfriend, Dylan."

"That is wonderful, Hope," Kiki said. "I know you will be good at it."

Justin started to speak.

Hope glared at him.

Justin kept his mouth shut.

"As for Saturdays, I want to sleep in," Hope said. "I have given up over five *hundred* Saturdays for this store. I intend to find out what I've been missing. I live in Brooklyn, but I don't really know Brooklyn. So much happens in Brooklyn on Saturdays, and I want to be a part of it."

"But what will *we* do?" Justin whined. "Neither one of us knows the machines like you do."

"You have all the manuals in your office, Justin," Hope said.

"I know I do," Justin said, scratching at his hair, "but it's not the same as actually running them."

It does *help if you actually* read *those manuals.* "For the rest of this week and probably some of next, I will train each of you on every machine in the store. Is that okay, Kiki?"

"Yes," Kiki said. "I have wanted to learn how to run them."

"You can't do this, um . . ." Justin sighed. "You *can't* do this!"

For the last time! "Justin, my name is Hope. Why can't you remember that? Hope. My name is Hope. Rhymes with 'dope.' "

"I know your name, um, Hope," Justin said, "and you just *can't* do this."

"I *am* doing this, Justin," Hope said, sliding off the counter, "and there's nothing you can do about it."

"I haven't done your year-end evaluation yet, Hope," Justin said.

Now he's threatening me? Bay-it! Hope took several deep breaths to keep from wasting any angry calories. "It's October, Justin. You do those evaluations in December."

"Then I'll start taking notes now," he said, crossing his arms. "I'll write, 'Refuses to work during normal store hours.' "

Hope decided to expend a few calories. She stepped within a foot of Justin's rank, sweaty, red-faced space. "I could say the same thing about *you*, Justin. Don't be threatening me about *my* job. I have so much to tell Mr. Yarmouth about your management style and how often you leave for parts unknown and disappear during normal business hours and *hand* me *your* store keys and the deposit only *you* are *ever* supposed to make."

Justin leaned away from her waving hands. "You can't prove—"

"Can't prove I didn't make deposits?" Hope interrupted. "Yes, I signed your name, but I have great handwriting. Your handwriting is *la merde, l'excrément, et le pus.*"

Justin turned away. "But it's still my signature."

"I can also prove you didn't open the store on Saturday," Hope said, moving closer to Justin's odor before stepping back. *Ew.*

"No, you can't," Justin said. "I was here."

"Friday night's Internet orders are still in the mainframe," Hope said. "Did you check those? No. They're supposed to be our first priority when we open. Saturday pickups are still under the counter. Were you here to sell those? No. The numbers for the copy key counters are the same as they were on Friday. That's not normal for any copy shop, even on a slow day. Three customers, including a longtime customer from a church, told us they came to the store Saturday to find the door locked between eleven and two. You couldn't have taken a three-hour lunch. What'd you do, come in, get our messages, flip the sign, and lock yourself in your office?"

Justin backed away from Hope's shadow. "I was here the entire time."

"I'm sure you were on the computer in your office the entire time," Hope said, "and you were locked in with your girls."

Justin blinked and blushed, his lower lip trembling.

You are busted, bay-it. "You should always close your browser, Justin. You never know who might see where you've been and what you like to look at."

Justin seemed to be looking for a place to hide, ducking and bobbing his head. "You, you can't prove any of it."

"Don't *bay-it* me, Justin," Hope said.

Kiki laughed.

"Who will Mr. Yarmouth believe?" Hope asked. "I have been here ten years and you've been here a few months. I'm sure he'll listen to everything I have to say." *It is time to go.* "Do you have any questions, Kiki?"

Kiki shook her head.

"Good," Hope said. "I am leaving now. Tomorrow, you two will learn everything there is to know about the Xerox DocuTech high speed printer. Bye."

Hope put on her coat, winked at Kiki, and headed for the door.

Kiki caught up to Hope as she stepped outside. "Justin has had girls in his office?"

"No," Hope said, buttoning up and shivering at the thought. "He looks at porn."

"Oh," Kiki said. "No wonder he is so sweaty all the time."

Hope shivered again.

"And who would have him?" Kiki asked. "What has he been looking at?"

"Interracial threesomes."

Kiki's eyes grew wide. "Him?"

Hope nodded.

"Kinky. Two women and one man, huh?"

Hope shook her head. "Two white men and one black woman."

Kiki's jaw dropped. "What did this girl look like?"

Hope exhaled sharply. "What?"

Kiki rolled her eyes. "I am kidding. I would not do such a thing." She shrugged. "Unless the men were abundant." She laughed. "Go. Do your art."

She said she was kidding, but I wouldn't put it past her. Sometimes I wish I could be that free with my body. Of course, you have to have a body before you can be free with it.

Hope slowed her walk almost to a shuffle as she moved down Flatbush. *I need to go slow, calm down, and bring a smile to my first day of school.*

Hope opened the door at Kinderstuff and approached an older Asian woman, who wore a gray sweater and black slacks.

"Hello," Hope said. "I'm here to help with art today."

"You must be Hope," the woman said. "I'm Mrs. Sun, but please call me Mei."

Mei Sun. What a beautiful name.

"They are in the back preparing the room to make *papier-mâché* masks while I straighten up," Mei said. "Do you have a smock?"

Oops. "I left mine where I work," Hope said.

"And we don't have one your size." She shrugged. "Dylan never wears one, and whatever he gets on his clothes washes out. Eventually. Give me your coat. I will put it in my office."

Hope handed her coat to Mei.

"Go on back," Mei said, "and thank you for coming, Hope."

Hope moved through a primary-color heaven of posters, shelves, tiny desks, and tinier chairs to a back room where cribs lined one wall and eight little rainbow children wearing rainbow smocks jumped up and down on a plastic tarp covering most of the floor. Dylan stood over a small table nearby mixing goopy white *papier-mâché* paste in a large bucket.

"There she is," Aniya said. "Hi, Hope."

"Hi, Aniya." *I love how this child always smiles! Aniya is light itself.*

"Aniya," Dylan said, "why don't you introduce our guest artist today?"

"Okay." Aniya took Hope's hand. "This is Hope. She is my friend."

For life, Aniya. "I'm very happy to be here." She raised her eyebrows to Dylan. "What do you need me to do?"

"Shred paper," Dylan said. He nodded at a stack of newspapers under the table. "Don't worry if my young artists don't make long strips. Their masks won't be that wide." He pointed at a dozen small red helium balloons bobbing on the ceiling, their short strings dangling down. "We'll be covering those today and painting them tomorrow."

She looked at the balloons. "Why the balloons?"

"Oh," Dylan said. "I have found that if I blow up regular balloons, my young artists would rather play with them than do art."

"He's right," Aniya said. "We play football and soccer with them."

"And once I do pull down the balloons and weight them with these"—Dylan pointed to a pile of heavy fishing weights—"they become much easier for them to work with."

Good idea. "I smell cinnamon," Hope said. "Have you all been baking cookies?"

"No," Aniya said. "Dylan puts cinnamon in the bucket. Otherwise, it stinks real bad."

"Have you done papier-mâché before, Aniya?" Hope asked.

She nodded. "I made a baseball bat, ball, and glove last time. They're hanging up in my room."

"I also add salt to the paste so it doesn't mold," Dylan said, "and this is liquid starch instead of flour and water. It leaves a nice, shiny glaze, and with liquid starch, the bugs don't eat the art as fast." He pointed at a stack of white paper. "That's for the last layer. We might get there today if we're lucky. We're shooting for two layers of newspaper followed by one layer of white paper."

This man knows his stuff, and he's so organized. Why did I think he wouldn't be? Oh, yes. He's still a man.

"Okay, my young artists," Dylan said, "my able assistant Hope is going to tell you everything there is to know about papier-mâché. Are you ready?"

"Yes!"

Wow, they're loud!

"Take it away, Hope." Dylan smiled.

No . . . way. Oh, right, I'll only be doing *art with them. He now expects me to* teach *them, and on my first day.*

Hope slid the newspapers onto the tarp, knelt down, and sat back on her heels. Eight sets of blinking eyes, busy feet, and busier hands surrounded her, one little boy reaching for her hair. *They are all so cute!* "Today, we're going to make papier-mâché. Does anyone know what 'papier-mâché' means?"

Eight cute shrugs.

"It means 'chewed paper' in French," Hope said.

"Eww!"

They all use one voice. Good. I won't have to call on anyone. I wish they had name tags. "But it's not good to chew on paper, is it?"

"No!"

"Doing *papier-mâché* is very, very messy," Hope said. *I am going to miss my smock.* "Are you all ready to make a mess?"

"Yes!"

I love this audience! "We first need to tear these newspapers into strips." She opened a newspaper and pulled out a single large page. "Watch." She tore several long, vertical strips and set them in a pile on the tarp. "Do you think you can do that?"

"Yes!"

Of course you can! "I'm going to hand each of you a newspaper." She did. "Now, pull out the big pages, and tear them up!"

While the children essentially made newsprint confetti and Dylan continued to stir his concoction, Hope helped the younger children tear their newspapers while they sat on her lap. Once the children had created a pile threatening to bury Hope, Dylan pulled down balloons and attached the fishing weights to them, spacing them out and physically positioning each child in front of each balloon. He took one more balloon down and set it in front of Hope.

"*Pour vous, mon amour,*" he said.

Not in front of the children. Hope smiled. "And now, for the *really* messy part."

"Yay!"

Dylan dunked handfuls of newspaper into the *papier-mâché* paste.

"Eww!"

"Oh, but it smells so good!" Dylan shouted. "I smell like cinnamon rolls." He removed one hand and smelled his finger.

"Eww!"

He brought his finger close to his mouth. "But I'm so hungry," he said.

"Eww!"

"But I will *not* eat the paste," Dylan said. "Do *not* eat the paste. Okay?"

"Okay!"

"I am going to hand the chewed paper to Hope," Dylan said, "and Hope will show you what to do." He handed a particularly slimy strip to Hope.

Despite the texture, this is really fun and cinnamony. Is that a word? "First stretch out the paper *very* gently. You don't want to tear it. And then place it on the balloon." She wrapped the strip around the center of her balloon. "Smooth it down with your fingers until it sticks." *Wow, that stuck fast.* "And then add another strip. We are going to make your balloon disappear."

A little boy started to whimper.

Oops. "The balloon will still be there," she told him.

"It will just be hiding, Ramón," Dylan said.

Ramón nodded and sighed.

Ramón likes his balloons.

Then Dylan, Hope, and the children became papier-mâché machines. Dylan handed a dripping strip to Hope, Hope handed it to a child, and the child slapped it on the balloon. In less than an hour, each balloon hovered lower, covered by two layers of newspaper and one layer of white paper.

Because they're floating, Hope thought, *they'll dry quicker overnight and they won't stick to anything. Dylan is a genius.*

But I have goo under every one of my nails. And in my hair. And on my cheek. She looked down. *And on my shirt, and on my pants, and on my stomach. How'd that get there?*

While Mei corralled the children so they could clean up in their washroom, Dylan wrote the children's initials on their balloons with a Sharpie and then rinsed out the paste bucket in a janitor's closet.

Aniya returned wearing a puffy blue coat. "I'm leaving, Dylan." She looked up at him. "You're a mess." She hugged his leg. She approached Hope. "You're not as bad." She gave Hope a proper hug. "Dylan says we're going to make two masks. What kind of masks will you make, Hope?"

I don't want Dylan to know I'm coming back tomorrow yet. "I won't know until I start to play with it tomorrow," Hope whispered. She twisted her own balloon slowly. "Tomorrow I will see two faces staring out at me."

"You will?" Aniya whispered.

"Yes," Hope whispered. "I hope they're not too scary. What are you going to make?"

"I don't know," Aniya whispered, "but whatever they are, they are going to have lots of hair. Bye!" She trotted off.

Dylan pulled Hope to her feet and directed her to the janitor's closet. "What were you two whispering about?"

"Girl talk," Hope said.

"You were sensational," he whispered. "They were so quiet today."

They were quiet? I'd hate to hear what a loud day sounds like. "I will smell like salty cinnamon for days," she said, running hot water over her hands and picking dried paste from her nails. "Don't take this the wrong way, but I expected chaos in there today."

"We have controlled chaos here," Dylan said. "Wait a minute. You thought that I would let them run amok?"

"I didn't know what to expect," she said, flicking some paste off her forearm. "You looked like a mad scientist when I walked in. The helium balloon trick was clutch, though. It's such a pain to lay the strips and hold onto the balloon at the same time."

"And they were all red balloons," he said. "Did you notice? I made the mistake of using a number of different colored balloons my first year. They literally *fought* for the only purple balloon. Very ugly."

"What kind of masks are you going to make?" Hope asked.

"I think one will be . . . a mad scientist." He smiled and reached his hands into the stream of hot water. "You're taking too long."

"I'm not done." She felt his hip pressing into her sexy derriere. "And I won't be done if you do that."

"Maybe I don't want you to be done," he said, scrubbing the backs of his hands.

"What about the other mask?" Hope asked.

"It will be a surprise," he said. He stared at his hands. "I should really use sandpaper." He kissed her neck. "Did you have fun?"

"Yes." *Please do that again.*

"I had fun watching you," he said, "and I'm going to have even more fun watching you eat some hot dogs. Let's go!"

A few blocks away on Bergen Street, they sat on metal stools at a long wooden table drinking butterscotch milkshakes and eating two Bark Dogs, hot dogs basted with homemade smoked lard butter and smothered with sweet pepper relish, mustard, and onions.

"Don't stare," Hope said.

"I can't help it," Dylan said.

"I'm *not* that kind of *garrl*," Hope said.

"You don't have to be," Dylan said.

"I could be." She took another sensuous bite. "Is it a fantasy of yours?"

"You're my fantasy," Dylan said.

That's sweet, but I don't believe it. "Uh-huh," Hope said. "I'll bet you have all sorts of fantasies."

"No more than the average guy," he said. "You could say I have a healthy appetite."

I'm glad he does. Do I ask Kiki's question now? Not yet. "Tell me one of your fantasies."

"Only if you promise to tell me one of yours," Dylan said.

Hmm. I still have a few of those. I'll have to pick the safest. "You go first."

Dylan looked around and leaned closer. "You promise not to think I'm a freak?"

"I make no promises." *How freaky is this going to be? Is anyone listening in?*

"Well, it involves you," he whispered. "Obviously. And we're walking back to your place, and when we get to a dark alley, I take you into the alley and take you."

Wow. "In public?"

"Standing up against the wall, yes," Dylan whispered. "My back will be against the wall, of course, and you'll be facing me."

Wow. "And then we just continue home?"

"I haven't gotten that far in the fantasy yet," Dylan said. "I guess so. We may be in that alley for a long time."

His back is going to have brick dust on it.

"Your turn," he said.

I doubt if I can top that one. Should I even try? "I've always had this fantasy of making love in the ocean."

"Am I there?" he asked.

"Oh, of course," Hope said.

"And are we alone?" he whispered.

"Yes."

"And is the water warm?"

Hope nodded.

"And are the stars out?"

"Yes, there's a gazillion stars in the sky." *He is improving so much on my fantasy!*

"And is there a full moon?" he asked.

Hope bit her lip. "There are two. Yours and mine."

Dylan smiled. "And then we just continue home?"

Hope sighed. "Yes, we continue home to my beach house."

Dylan collected his trash. "Sounds doable." He checked his watch. "We have to hustle if we're going to get to Thrifty before they close."

Oh yeah. We have to pay for and pick up the orders. "But I'm not allowed to run, right?"

"We'll walk fast," Dylan said. "Come on."

They arrived at Thrifty at 5:58 PM, and Kiki already had her coat on, Justin waiting at the door with the deposit bag.

"Was it fun?" Kiki asked.

"Very," Hope said, showing Kiki her nails.

"You were doing sculpture?" Kiki asked.

"Chewed paper," Dylan said.

"I'll explain later," Hope said.

After Dylan paid for and collected nine bags of cards, Hope smiled at Justin. *Oh, you poor man. You're going to have to stay late to revise your numbers, aren't you? It's about time you had to stay late.*

Then Dylan and Hope sauntered to Hope's apartment, Hope eyeing every alley and Dylan saying, "That one looks sufficiently dark and mysterious."

"Stop it," Hope said, but in her mind, she saw them moving as one in the darkness against every alley wall. "What are we doing in art tomorrow?"

"We? You can be there?" Dylan asked.

"I will be there every day until my vacation and sick days run out," Hope said.

"How long will that be?" Dylan asked.

"Until I run out," Hope said. "At least through Christmas."

"That's wonderful," Dylan said. "That's ..." He stopped and hugged her. "Thank you."

"You need the help," Hope said. "You needed my expertise today. So, what's the next step? Besides popping the balloons."

"That's the best part!" he yelled.

Hope blinked.

"Well, it is." He laughed. "You and I will cut the 'eggs' in half to give them two masks to make, we'll line up their eyes, noses, and mouths as best we can and cut holes, and then we'll start painting them."

"How long will that take?" Hope asked.

"Two or three days. We will then be sewing simple costumes to go with them."

"Making the whole ensemble," Hope said. "Clever."

"And thrifty," Dylan said. "You know what Halloween costumes cost these days? They all look the same, too. These kids will be like no other kid on their blocks."

They reached her apartment entrance. "So you're going to be seeing me every day, but I'm worried that you'll get tired of seeing me."

"I will never get tired of seeing you," Dylan said. "I see you in an alley right now. I even see your full moon."

She grabbed his arm. "What about the ocean?"

"Oh, we'll have to go to the ocean after the alley to cool off," he said.

"Was that your freakiest fantasy?" Hope asked.

"No," Dylan said. "But I don't want to tell you about it. I want to do it."

"Now?" *Please? Upstairs?*

He sighed. "We can't. I don't have all the props."

"Props?" *How involved is this fantasy?*

"See, I've already told you more than I should have." He kissed her quickly. "I am so happy that I get to see you every day."

"And all day Saturdays," Hope said, "all the way through Christmas."

"Really?"

Hope nodded.

Dylan lifted her into the air. "*Fantastique! Surprenant! Magnifique!*"

"You have been learning more French," Hope said. *I like the view up here.*

He eased her to the ground. "There is so much we can do."

"Involving . . . props?" she asked.

He laughed. "I never should have used that word. Is my French improving?"

"*Oui,*" Hope said. "Can you teach me any Irish words?"

"A few," Dylan said. "I didn't hear many growing up in Brownsville. Not ones you can repeat anyway."

Hope pulled him closer. "Could you teach me upstairs? I'm cold." She looked at the door.

He took her hands. "Hope, I would love to. Really. But I have to prep these orders, print labels, stuff envelopes, get up at five to make an updated printout for you to run—"

Hope put a finger to his lips. "I get it. It's okay. You're a busy man." She sighed. "I could help you do all that, you know. We're partners. We could work on them here."

"Ah, but if we worked on them here, my *álainn milis cailín,* I would give you no time to be creative," Dylan said. "I would also keep you up all night, and you need to rest and sleep."

"What did you call me?" Hope asked.

"I called you my beautiful girl who is sweet to the taste," Dylan said. "You're my *cailín,* my colleen, my girl."

Colleen. Such a pretty name. "Am I really sweet to the taste?" Hope asked.

"Every morsel of your body is delicious, some morsels tastier than others," he said. He lifted her chin with his hand. "And I intend to taste every square inch of you this weekend."

"Every square millimeter," Hope said.

He laughed. "Every square millimeter. If you'll have me."

"I'll have you," Hope said, "provided you let me help you at the post office on Saturday morning."

"But you can't," Dylan said. "You will burn off too many calories."

She pushed him away, or at least she tried to push him. Dylan didn't move, and Hope fell back two steps. *I am such a lightweight.* "So I have to say good-bye to you like this five days a week."

"Hey now," he said. "I have to say good-bye to you like this, too. This isn't easy for me either."

Hope shuffled back into his arms. "You're right. I'm sorry. This weekend was so . . ." *There are too many words to describe it.*

"Magical?" he said.

"Yes. *Très magique*. And I'm going through withdrawal."

"So am I." He kissed her forehead, her nose, and her lips. "And this coming weekend will be *très magique*, and we will both get our fix."

She hugged him tightly. "I'm missing you already." She turned toward the door.

Dylan swatted her gently on her sexy derriere. "Go eat some ice cream."

Hope stopped. "You just spanked me, Mr. Healy."

"It felt nice, Miss Warren," Dylan said, "and I didn't really spank you. It was a love tap."

A love tap. "Do it again."

Dylan stepped close and tapped her sexy derriere again.

I like love taps. "Good night, Dylan."

"Good night, my *álainn milis cailín*."

Hope ran up the stairs to the second-floor landing and looked out the window, watching a man walking up Washington Avenue carrying nine bags of greeting cards.

And her heart.

OCTOBER 20

*Only 65 more shopping days
until Christmas . . .*

Chapter 18

Hope fell with Dylan into a comfortable but passionately frustrating weekday routine of Frosted S'Mores Pop-Tarts, Prospect Perk Café coffee, toast smothered with Crofter's strawberry jam, and kisses; of working fast-food lunches with Kiki and art with the children; of dinners with Dylan, collecting bags of cards, and long walks to her apartment that ended with sighs, a cold platform bed covered with cat hair, and at least half a pint of Ben & Jerry's ice cream.

Hope continued to gain weight while she waited. She conserved her calories and ambled more than walked to work each day. She did as much nothing as possible every evening, sometimes reading, sometimes sketching, but always falling asleep to the droning of the TV after a healthy ice cream high. She also ate well as she and Dylan branched out to other restaurants around Flatbush Avenue for dinner. They went to Sugarcane for jerk chicken wings and Flatbush Farm for chipotle cheddar grits and pastrami sandwiches. They ate *poulet à l'estragon*—smoked jerk chicken breast with goat cheese, tarragon, and honey sauce—and coconut rice and sautéed vegetables at Kaz An Nou, and gorgonzola walnut ravioli with wilted arugula in brown butter sage sauce at Alchemy.

Hope was still hungry, however, for more than food.

She was hungry for *nuits humide passionnées,* passionate steamy nights.

Being immersed in *art d'enfant* at Kinderstuff relieved some but not all of Hope's yearnings. Hope helped the children make their

236 • J. J. Murray

masks, some scary, some fanciful, and several unintelligible animals from the land of make-believe. Aniya made two complementary masks, what Dylan called "smiling Medusas," every snaky lock of hair on each mask a different vibrant color. Dylan finished his evil scientist by adding a huge nose, pale-green face, and short, spiked hair, and then he created his "surprise": a fat, cheeky, winking Santa with a long flowing beard.

The Santa mask scared Hope more than the mad scientist mask did.

Because being without Dylan at night during the week made her feel exceptionally *grincheux* and crabby, Hope created her version of Dr. Seuss's Grinch who stole Christmas, adding long black hair to the Grinch's light-green, dill-pickle-like face.

This fact was not lost on Dylan once Hope nicknamed it "The Dill Pickle Who Stole Christmas."

She then fashioned her stick figure girl complete with dreadlocks, dark glasses, and a wide frown. She named this one "Noelle."

The resemblance to Hope in her current state of longing for Dylan was unmistakable.

This fact was also not lost on Dylan, who did his best to kiss these frowns away as often as he could.

Hope's longings eventually led to creativity of a different sort, and she started creating Valentine's Day and "Stick Figures" cards to give her Dylan-starved hands something constructive to do.

She found she could do many romantic things with her stick figures. She drew Dread Head Girl ("Noelle") kissing Long-Haired Boy ("Dylan") on the cover and wrote "Smooches" on the inside. She joined their hands on the cover and put "We stick together," "I will stick with you through thick and thin," and "Stick to me, kid" inside. Having them hug presented special challenges since their lines blended so perfectly together. "I love you so much I don't know where I leave off and you begin," "Let's be two-dimensional together," and "I feel you in my bones" finished these particularly linear cards.

Her thoughts often waxed ironic. On one intricately busy cover, she drew disconnected pieces of "Noelle" and "Dylan," their heads facing opposite directions, a word bubble from "Dylan" asking, "Do you want to go out?" Inside, she wrote, "Pick-up stick figures." She sketched "Noelle" sinking into a puddle of mud, "Stick figure in the mud" inside. She drew the top half of "Dylan" on the left side of the cover and his bottom half on the right, writing "Stick figure shift" inside. To illustrate "The wrong end of the stick," she sketched a large, fanged cobra slithering out of the stick, "Dylan" screaming, his hair leaping in all directions. On her most "punny" card, "Noelle" held two rocks on the cover. Inside, she wrote: "Stick figure and stones will break your bones."

Naturally, Hope's designs grew more risqué the longer she pined for Dylan's physique, his touch, warmth, hands, lips, and the rest of his sexy body. She drew "Noelle" and "Dylan" in various positions of the *Kama Sutra*, "Stick it to me, baby," "I like your stick," "Get on the stick, "This is a stick-up," and "Walk softly but carry a big stick" completing her lusty thoughts.

Within hours of posting these cards to the Odd Ducks website, customers were already ordering them.

In hearty *droves.*

"I guess every day can be Valentine's Day, too," Dylan commented.

Hope did not agree. *Valentine's Days only come on weekends for me,* she thought.

On the Friday before Halloween, Hope received three pieces of great news. Her weight had climbed to 109, a gain of seven pounds in ten days, and her ribs didn't look as sharp. She even had to loosen her belt a notch. She also finally had online access to the Odd Ducks account. She gazed longingly at her share of their earnings so far, a handsome sum of $5,600, and she promptly transferred it to her beach house savings account. Most importantly, Dylan would indeed spend the weekend, and she vowed to lock him inside her apartment and keep him there for all eternity whether he liked it or not.

That night, Dylan brought his backpack, and he had packed it much more fully than before.

Hope hoped he had brought his props.

Hope's man was finally in her claustrophobic apartment, he was hers for the taking, and as soon as he set down his backpack, she pounced on him while Whack purred at their feet. She pinned him to the wall next to the windows, grinding her hips into him.

"I have this fantasy," she whispered hoarsely, "involving me grinding on a long-haired man up against my wall right next to all these windows."

"You do, do you?" Dylan said. He grabbed her sexy derriere, lifted her off the floor, and spun her around, stepping over to one of the large windows. "The world sees your sexy derriere now."

Hope wrapped her legs around his back. "Hey, this is *my* fantasy, not yours. We're not in your alley." She glanced outside. *Do I care if anyone sees us? No.*

"Then let's go to a place where I can explore your alley," Dylan whispered.

Hope liked this idea very much.

Dylan first carried her to his backpack and pulled a DVD and two packages of extra-butter microwave popcorn from the top compartment. "A snack and a movie," he said.

"You're supposed to be my snack," Hope whispered.

He carried her into the kitchen, setting her on the counter next to the sink. "I'm more than a snack, aren't I?"

Hope nodded. "You're a ten-course meal." She nibbled on his right ear and then his left. "Your ears are just the appetizer."

Dylan toyed with Hope's pants zipper while Hope ran her hands through his hair as the popcorn exploded in the microwave. Then Hope held the steaming popcorn bags and Dylan held Hope, who was also steaming, as they raced to and fell onto her bed, where they generally ignored the world and Hope's loud neighbors for a few moments, letting their hands roam wild and free.

Dylan broke contact first, though Hope fought valiantly to stop him, and put *An American Werewolf in London* in her DVD player. "Whenever David—oh, he's the werewolf, by the way—"

"Oh, ruin it for me," Hope said dreamily.

"Whenever David turns into the werewolf," he said, "we will each remove one item of clothing."

"How often does he sprout hair and claws?" Hope asked.

"Three times."

Hope counted her clothes and then removed her socks and bra. "I am only wearing three items of clothing now." She yanked off Dylan's socks and shirt.

"That only gives me two pieces of clothing," he said.

"Your apartment, your rules," she said. "My apartment, *my* rules, and anyway, when am I going to see your apartment?"

"Soon," Dylan said. "Oh, you'll love the first scene. 'Stay on the road. Stay off the moors.' "

After twenty minutes of eating buttery popcorn and laughing at creepy humor, Hope asked, "He does change into a werewolf eventually, doesn't he?"

"Yes. This is just the setup."

"Skip ahead."

Dylan skipped ahead.

David transformed into a werewolf.

Two pairs of jeans littered the floor.

Hope skipped ahead again.

Dylan's boxers joined his pants and Hope's shirt somewhere in the kitchen.

When David made love to an English nurse in the movie, Hope removed her glasses, and she and Dylan forgot the rules of their game, instead clawing at each other under the covers.

Had there been a moon, they might have howled.

Hope came up for air just as the movie ended. "What can we *not* watch next?"

Dylan put in *The Thing*, a grisly, modern remake of the original sci-fi classic.

"Any rules with this movie?" Hope asked.

"No."

"Good," Hope said. "I want to thoroughly enjoy your thing."

While Hope kept Dylan's attention and kept *him* at attention, she thought back to her Bark Dogs dinner and decided to devour Dylan with relish.

Soon Dylan was back for seconds. He ripped back the covers and sat against the headboard, sweat streaming down his chest. Hope straddled him, toying with him, teasing him, watching him rise again to the occasion.

"I want to try," she whispered.

"Please do," he groaned.

She positioned his abundance beneath her.

Ow. That's not going to fit.

She tried again and felt him barely enter her.

Ow! Ow! Shoot! Get juteux down there! How can I still be so dry? He has pushed all the right buttons for the past hour!

"Dylan, I don't think . . ." She sighed. "I've been tingling down there a lot more this time, but I'm . . . I guess I'm not ready. I'm so sorry." *I feel so stupid, and now come the tears.*

Dylan shook his head, smiling. "Backpack, right side, zipper pocket."

"What is it?" Hope asked.

"Help," he said.

She slipped out of bed, unzipped the pocket, and took out a bottle of K-Y Jelly, holding it close to her eyes. *He thinks of everything. I should have thought of using this gelée. I've just never needed it before.* She read the label as she returned to the bed. *"Recommended by gynecologists."* She shuddered. *By my gynecologist? Ew. She's at least seventy.*

"Hope?" Dylan asked.

"In a minute," Hope said. *"Eases the discomfort of dryness." I hope it eases my suffering, too.*

"You're losing me over here," Dylan said.

She glanced over at Dylan, and even without her glasses, she could see that wasn't true. "It doesn't look that way." *"Apply desired amount to your intimate areas." How much? I have a lot of desire.* She popped the cap. "I can't believe you walked into a store and bought this."

"Yeah, that was a first."

So this is about to be a first for both of us. "How much do you think I should use?"

"I don't know," Dylan said. "It's my first time."

"Mine, too," Hope said. "So be gentle."

It's not exactly the natural way, but I'm willing to try anything to satisfy this man fully. Now do I put it only on me, only on him, or on both of us? Quite a few intimate areas in this bed need dousing.

"It's getting cold," Dylan said.

But you're still at attention. That makes no sense. When I get cold down there, I usually shut down. She squeezed some *gelée* into her hand. *On me and him. I'm trying to fit something big into something small and arid, and I'll need all the help I can get.*

"Here," she said. "Put out your hand."

Dylan reached out his hand.

Big hand, big gland. She gave him an abundant amount. "Go ahead, soak that thing."

After liberally lubing themselves, Hope climbed up Dylan's legs. *Let's do this.* She grimaced. *Let's do this carefully.* She eased down on him millimeter by millimeter, her mouth opening centimeter by centimeter as she did.

"Don't move," she breathed. *Oh . . . my . . . goodness. Eight years is a long freaking time to be closed for business! I was never this small down there before, was I?*

Dylan reached out his hands and squeezed her hips.

"Don't push," Hope whispered tersely. "Don't do . . . anything. Let me . . . just . . . rest a minute." She smiled. *He's in me. This is good. He can't move at all, and if he does I'll break his nose, but he's inside me. I am going to pay for this tomorrow.*

"I'm going to . . ." *What am I going to do? What can I do? If I go up, I might lose him. If I sit here, I'll dry up. If I go any lower, I'll bleed internally.*

"Do you have any suggestions?" Hope asked. "I'm afraid to move."

He sat up.

Ow! "I told you not to move."

"I want to kiss you," he said. "That's what I was going to suggest. It won't take much more than a kiss. You feel so . . . good."

Tight. He means I feel tight, which normally would be a good thing, but I want to grind on him! "Okay, but as little movement as possible. I'm stretched to the limit here." She leaned forward, leading with her lips and pressing hard on his shoulders with her palms. *Ow. Kiss me quick!*

Dylan covered her mouth with his and instantaneously began to spasm, sucking the life out of her lips and trying to remove her tongue.

"I'm sorry," he wheezed, his body bucking under her. "I tried to stop."

Hope shook her head. "But I wanted you to *go*." *But I have to get off now before I start crying.* She eased up and off, her jaw dropping to her chest. "Damn," she said.

"I have never heard you curse before," Dylan said.

Ow! "Either I have the smallest vagina on the planet," she said, hugging him, "or you are a freak of nature." She looked at the TV, where a blurry alien's legs sprouted out of a fuzzy man's head and skittered away. *That . . . that was freaky.*

He rubbed her back. "Are you okay?"

"I've been walking slowly all week," she said. "I *may* be able to walk on Monday."

"You say the nicest things," he said, "and I'm really sorry I didn't last longer than I did. I'm out of practice."

"It's actually good you didn't," Hope said. "I was in some pain."

"Oh, Hope, I'm sorry."

Hope shook her head. "It's okay. I'm out of practice, too. I hope to get lots of practice with you."

"You will," Dylan said, "but I don't want it to hurt."

You think I do? "As long as we don't run out of the help." She pointed at the bottle of K-Y Jelly. "Can you buy that stuff in bulk?" She lay on her side and bent her knees, Dylan spooning behind her. "But no more tonight. I need to recuperate."

He kissed her shoulder and put his hand on her stomach. "So do I. You took a lot out of me."

Hope felt his nose nuzzling her earlobe. "I'm glad I was finally able to . . . *jook* you."

"*Jook?*"

"You know, make love to you," Hope whispered. "It's a Jamaican word." *Taught to me by the woman who wanted to have a threesome with you and her girlfriend.*

"You *jooked* me well," Dylan said. "You're very good at *jooking.* I could *jook* with you all night long. That was the best *jooking*—"

"Dylan," Hope whispered. "Shh. I get the picture."

"Just wanted you to know," he whispered.

Hope closed her eyes. "You're pretty good at *jooking,* yourself. I may even ask you to *jook* me again . . . in a few months."

"Really?"

She pulled his hands tight around her stomach. "I'm kidding. I will be *jooking* you as often as I'm able to, and since I plan on being able to tomorrow night, you had better get your rest."

Dylan turned off the TV with the remote control. "You, too. Good night, Hope. *Rêves doux.*"

Hope smiled. "Good night, Dill Pickle." *Sweet dreams to you, too.*

I hope I'm in them.

The next morning, Dylan once again sneaked out without waking Hope, returning with breakfast from Café Shane. The two of them polished off four whole-wheat Belgian waffles topped with mango sauce, two fried eggs, a pile of home fries, and four slices of bacon.

"You were hungry," Dylan said, removing his clothes.

"Ooh, breakfast and a show," Hope said.

Dylan stood before her in only his boxers. "May I take a shower?"

"Only if I can join you," Hope said.

"I really have to hustle," he said. "I have twice the orders to process this week as I had last week, thanks to you, and if you join me, I may not get done. We at Odd Ducks pride ourselves on our ability to ship your order—"

"Okay, okay," Hope interrupted. "But I'm watching."

Dylan used extreme efficiency, lathering and rinsing furiously, giving Hope only enough time to see his sexy derriere, his hairy legs, his smooth chest, and his ripped stomach for the first two minutes. When he began washing his hair, her glasses fogged up and she tired of wiping them. In only four minutes' time, Dylan was out of the tub and the washroom, changing into a set of clean jeans, a blue-and-green tie-dyed T-shirt, socks, and brown leather hiking boots.

"I feel cheated," Hope said. "I want my money back."

He kissed her quickly. "What are you going to do while I'm gone?"

Hope pulled on his hoodie, flashing him shamelessly.

"Hope, I'll need that." Dylan stuck out his hands.

"Take it off of me then."

Dylan sighed. "It's warm enough today for a Windbreaker." He pulled a black Windbreaker from the backpack.

That didn't work. I was going to pin him to the bed for a few seconds at least.

"So what will you be doing?" he asked.

She fell back onto the bed. "I'll be fantasizing about what I *didn't* get to see because you washed yourself too fast."

He leaned down and kissed her forehead. "I'll bring back lunch. Do nothing until I get back."

"I don't want to do nothing," Hope whined. "I've been doing nothing long enough. Why can't I go with you?"

"I'll be back before you know it." He kissed her lips three times. "Bye."

After Dylan left, Hope did enough nothing surfing the TV to fall asleep, and when she did, she began to dream . . .

Where am I? A theater. The floor is sticky. That is so cliché. You'd think clichés wouldn't lurk in dreams. Hey, I'm on the big black tongue of a stage. Where's that sexy red spotlight going? It's stopping on Kiki, who sits on her stool. Let's go talk to Kiki, but she wears no clothes. She certainly looks cold. Shoot, even her toes are cute. I am wearing a tie-dyed shirt and boots. My sexy derriere is cold. "Come here," Kiki says. I go, and when I look down, I see my bare feet. Where'd my boots go? Kiki gives me a juicy kiss on the lips and turns into a djembe. That fits. She definitely has a nice, round djembe. The red spotlight travels to Angie, who lies naked on a red velvet couch. "Come here," Angie says. I go, and when I look down, I see stick figure legs holding me up. Now my drawings are invading my dreams. Angie hugs me tenderly for five minutes, smiles, and turns into a xylophone, probably because Angie has too many teeth in her head. The red spotlight leads me to a circular bed. Dylan is there! Yes! Now I'm only wearing my smock. Dylan wears a Santa Claus mask and nothing else. I know the man behind the mask is Dylan because I see his long, black hair, sexy derriere, and an elf sock puppet on his abundance. "Come here," Dylan says. I take a step toward him, but before I can get on the bed, the elf puppet says, "Answer your buzzer, Hope," and Dylan turns into a DocuTech printer spewing pictures of Justin's threesome into the air . . .

Hope woke up sweating and trying to make sense of her dream. *That was too logical to be a dream.*

She heard the buzzer.

An elf puppet warned me in a dream. It's a sign.

She pulled Dylan's hoodie down to her thighs, buzzed Dylan in, and waited by the door. *It's two-thirty. Why does it take him so long?*

She opened the door, and Dylan carried in two one-pound ginger buff wing combos from Super Wings NY.

"Are we ever going to run out of places to eat?" Hope asked, opening her box and munching on a zucchini bite.

"Not in Brooklyn," he said. "Ready for your bath?"

"At three in the afternoon?" she asked. She tore into a wing. *I am in heaven.* "And anyway, I'm eating."

"Won't you have trick-or-treaters soon?" Dylan asked. "You don't want to scare them away with your body odor, do you?"

"I smell like you."

"I have body odor, too," Dylan said. "Care to join me?"

Well, I suppose if I absolutely have *to . . .*

Within a minute of beginning their bath, they realized they would need a bigger tub. No matter how they arranged and rearranged themselves, it just wasn't going to work. Dylan went in first and rested his back away from the faucet, Hope sitting on his lap, her feet splayed out to the sides, her left foot completely out of the tub.

"This is uncomfortable," she said. "Kinky, though."

They reversed positions, and Dylan's knees banged into the faucet.

"There's a punch line here somewhere," Dylan said. "I'll think of it eventually."

They tried facing each other, but the faucet dug into Dylan's back, and Hope's feet only fit comfortably when she gouged her heels into Dylan's shoulders.

"Shower," he said.

"Yes."

Hope turned the hot knob only and adjusted the spray away from her hair. "Soap me up," she said, raising her arms to the ceiling. She expected Dylan to take his time and massage her delicate skin properly with the washcloth, but Dylan circled her several times, soaping her from neck to toes within one minute.

"I'm not a car, Dylan," she said as she rinsed.

"If your building is like mine," he said quickly, "there can't be that much hot water left after we filled this tub."

Hope nodded. "Point taken. Turn around." She soaped him from toes to ears as the water rapidly changed from lukewarm to cool. "Hair?" Hope shrieked.

"Next time!" Dylan yelled.

"Rinse!" Hope cried.

This was the first time Hope and Dylan would ever dance.

By the time Dylan rinsed off, the water had turned icy cold. Fortunately, Dylan bore the brunt of the stinging, frigid water. Dylan turned off the water and shivered, trembling even more when Hope threw him the cold, wet towel he had used in the morning.

"Sorry," Hope said. "It'll be warmer in the bed."

Hope slid under the covers first, her arms and legs quivering. Dylan left wet footprints as he went over to his backpack, took out another DVD, put it in the DVD player, and joined Hope's shuddering form.

"I'm c-cold," she said, skimming her feet up and down Dylan's shins.

He pressed several buttons on the remote control. "This will warm you up."

"Is it a steamy romance?" Hope asked.

"It's Halloween," Dylan said. "We're going to watch *Alien*, one of the scariest movies of all time."

"Is there a steamy sex scene?" Hope asked.

"Nope," Dylan said. "Just an exploding stomach, a malevolent creature, a high body count, and a hissing cat." He rubbed her back. "You're still cold."

It's cold in space.

"By the way, they had to put tape over Sigourney Weaver's nipples in one of the first scenes, and the slime on the creature is K-Y Jelly," Dylan said.

"How do you know this?" Hope asked.

"It's one of my favorite movies," Dylan said. "I know nearly everything there is to know about this movie. It's one of the first movies I ever saw as a kid."

Hope, who really didn't want to see exploding stomachs, reluctantly put on her glasses and watched Sigourney Weaver's character, Ripley, waking up on a shelf-like pod. When Weaver stood, the camera panned over her tight white top and skimpy panties.

Dangerously white women should never wear all white under-wear, Hope thought, *and the very first thing I'd do if I woke up after a month-long nap would be to brush my teeth.*

"Do you think she's pretty?" Hope asked.

"She certainly is tall," Dylan said. "Probably taller than you are."

"That's not what I asked," Hope said. "Do you think she's pretty?"

"I cannot answer this without getting in trouble," Dylan said. "All I will say is that her character has a nice body, and she will kick ass later in the film."

Hope didn't want to see Sigourney "Nice Body" Weaver kick ass. She snapped off the TV and took off her glasses, handing them to Dylan. "Oh, I was certainly scared."

"You only saw the first part," Dylan said.

"I do not want to watch a tall white woman running around barely dressed in the wrong clothes for two hours," Hope said. "If you didn't already notice, I am naked, in the buff, and wearing nothing but a frown."

He pulled her on top of him. "What would you rather do?"

She dug her elbows into his chest and propped her chin in her hands. "I'd rather talk more about your fantasies. Tell me another fantasy, the one where you're with two women." *Cold water has made me bold.*

Dylan blinked. "I don't have that fantasy."

Liar. "All men have this fantasy."

"I don't."

He's still lying, but I must move on. I have a sex life to catch up on. "Let's say you *had* to choose two women to sleep with at the same time. Who would the *other* woman be?"

"I like how you said that," Dylan said. "But I don't know who I'd choose. This isn't something I think about. I wouldn't want another woman, so I guess it would boil down to whom *you* wanted her to be."

Oh, he's good at turning things around. "That's not how it works. *You* have to choose."

Dylan sighed. "You know I'm going to ask you the same question."

Oh yeah. "And I will answer." *Somehow.*

"Okay, um . . . I would choose . . ." He shrugged. "It would have to be someone you didn't know."

"You're stalling. Who?"

"Um . . ." He shook his head several times. "Corinne Bailey Rae."

"Who?"

"Corinne Bailey Rae. She's a British soul singer and guitarist."

A singer? He wants to hook up with a singer? Hope pointed to the nightstand. "Hand me my laptop. It's on the shelf."

Dylan handed the laptop to her. He wisely didn't say anything.

She booted up her laptop and ran a search for Corinne Bailey Rae. *What kind of name is that anyway?* She clicked on "images" and saw . . .

Corinne Bailey Rae could be my twin. She's about my age, tall, thin, has thick frizzy hair, and is lighter-skinned than I am. She's not at all the kind of woman I expected Dylan to choose. I thought he'd want a more buxom woman. Wait a minute. Maybe he chose someone who looks like me because he likes the looks of me. His choice is almost a compliment to me. Let's see, she was Grammy-nominated, won a bunch of awards, married to a white musician, and she is definitely talented. I hate to say it, but Dylan made a good choice.

I'll never tell him that, however.

"We'd only need a twin bed for the three of us, Dylan," Hope said. "Why her? Besides the obvious resemblance."

"About the same time Marie left me, I read a story about Corinne's husband dying," Dylan said. "She didn't put out another album for two years, which is a lifetime in the music industry. We were both in mourning at the same time. I guess I felt a kind of kinship."

Hope shut her laptop. "Are you naturally drawn to sad people?"

"I don't think I am," Dylan said. "I saw joy in you from the first moment we talked. I didn't see sadness."

You weren't looking very hard. "Well, she seems like a very nice person," Hope said. *She actually seems like someone I'd like to meet.* She sighed. "You can ask me the same question if you want."

"First answer this question," Dylan said. "Is a threesome a fantasy of yours?"

"No," Hope said, laughing. "No way."

"Then why bring it up?" Dylan asked.

Good point. "I'm just curious. I wanted to know what you considered beautiful, I guess, and you picked someone a lot like me, which means . . . you really think I'm beautiful."

"I do," Dylan said. "Now I'm suddenly curious who *you* would pick. If you, Hope Elizabeth Warren, had to choose another person to join us, who would it be?"

"Let me think."

I should have already had an answer ready. What do the lawyers always say? Never ask a question you don't already know the answer to. I couldn't possibly choose another woman for Dylan to play with. Except for my gynecologist, every woman on earth would be a threat to my sexual self-esteem, especially free spirits like Kiki and Angie. So it would have to be a man, but it would have to be a man to compliment Dylan somehow. Who's hot and Irish? Sean Connery? No, he's Scottish. Pierce Brosnan is okay, but only when he's James Bond. Liam Neeson is a great actor, but he's huge! I know. Colin Farrell. He could almost be Dylan's twin. No, I hear he can be wild.

I got it.

"I have an answer," Hope said.

"Go ahead."

"I would choose . . . your twin."

Dylan blinked. "But I don't have a twin. It has to be a real person."

"I didn't say it had to be a real person, did I?" Hope smiled.

"But I thought . . ." He crossed his arms. "You don't play fair, *cailín*."

She pulled his arms apart and wormed her way up his chest. "You're only angry that *you* didn't think of it."

"I am," he said. "But you cheated, and because you cheated, you get no candy."

Hope grinned. "Candy? Where's the candy?"

"No candy for you," Dylan said. "You chose not to choose."

"If I give you a name, may I have some candy?" Hope asked.

"Yes."

"Colin Farrell," Hope said, rolling out of bed. "Now where's the candy?"

"In my backpack."

Hope ran to the backpack and opened the main compartment. *I have died and gone to chocolate heaven.* She dragged the backpack closer to the kitchen table, removing bags of mini candy bars: 5th Avenue, Almond Joy, Baby Ruth, Butterfinger, Milky Way, Mounds, Nestlé Crunch, Snickers, and Reese's Peanut Butter Cups.

I will eat them all and die with a cavity-filled smile on my face.

"I didn't know what you liked, so I got an assortment," Dylan said. "They don't sell any Canadian brands around here. Sorry."

Can one die of too much chocolate goodness? Has there ever been a scientific study on this? Maybe I'll start my own study.

"Can I have one now?" Hope asked, biting her lip.

Dylan swung out of bed. "I promised you that I would taste every square millimeter of your body."

I want candy. Now.

"I will let you have much more than one candy bar . . ."

This man is a god. I will listen to him. He is very wise when it comes to chocolate.

"But only if I can feed you a certain way."

Hope nodded. "Are these your props?"

Dylan nodded. "Go lie on the bed."

Hope complied with a speed that surprised her. *Candy. Now.*

Dylan carried the bag of Reese's Mini Peanut Butter Cups to the bed. He tore open the bag and began unwrapping and placing them at several strategic places on the front of Hope's body. "Stay still."

Though the candies were cold, Hope remained motionless.

After he placed the last one on her navel, he whispered, "How hungry are you?"

"I'm starving."

"Good. Close your eyes."

Hope closed her eyes. She first felt a hot kiss high on her right thigh. A moment later, she felt chocolate at her lips. She opened her mouth, felt a tongue pushing the candy in, and kissed Dylan's sweet lips. As she chewed, she felt suction first on her left nipple and then on her right. A moment later, she tasted a double helping of chocolate and peanut butter. She knew there were three on her stomach, so she chewed faster. One by one, they rose with a tender kiss to her waiting lips.

Dylan gently turned her onto her stomach and placed several more on her back and sexy derriere. He pulled her hair back. "This might be a little sticky and tricky."

He started with the ones on her back, shooting each through the side of her mouth. Two more lifted off her sexy derriere after the tiniest of bites. Then Hope felt a hot tongue moving up her right calf to her thigh to her cheek to her shoulder blade. She felt Dylan move to her other side, where he blazed another trail from her left shoulder to her left calf. She felt goose bumps over most of her body now, but they soon disappeared when strong hands massaged her neck and shoulders, the rest of him resting lightly on her sexy derriere. She felt him press, knead, rub, and dig lower and lower on her back, her hips rising involuntarily to meet his hands. When he worked and kissed her sexy derriere, she sighed.

And she felt a serious tingle.

Hope could not ignore this particular tingle.

She turned quickly and pulled him forward. "I want you," she moaned. She grabbed his hair. "Just take it slow."

She felt him enter her hesitantly, carefully, ever so gently, his finger rubbing her clitoris in a lazy circle. She dropped her hands to his sides and reached for his lower back, latching on and pressing him deeper.

Ow! Why does it hurt so freaking much! I'm feeling moister than I have been before. This isn't fair! She pushed his hips back. "I need help."

Dylan nodded, taking the K-Y bottle from the nightstand and liberally rubbing his penis.

She gripped his sexy derriere this time, and pulled him in more quickly, his finger making faster, fiercer circles, his hips backing away before plunging again. She closed her eyes and tried to imagine what he looked like, his magnificent body splitting hers in two, her heels digging into his hamstrings.

"You can start *jooking* me now," she whispered. "But please go slowly."

She brought her hands to his upper back and felt him go in and out in a slow, lazy rhythm.

"Are you okay?" he whispered.

"Yes." She raised her arms over her head and gripped the headboard. *I feel him, but I know he's holding back for my sake. I should be having my second orgasm by now.* "Give me all you've got."

At first, the pain was a dull ache, but as Dylan increased his speed and depth, Hope realized she was in agony.

"Stop, stop!" she cried, pushing down forcefully on his shoulders until he left her. She pounded the bed with her fists. "I *hate* this!"

Dylan rubbed her fists with his hands until they opened, intertwining his fingers with hers, and then he pulled her onto his chest, caressing her hair.

"I want you worse than anything I've ever wanted," Hope said, tears streaming down her face and onto his chest. "But no, I can't have you. Why does it have to hurt?"

"We could go see a doctor," Dylan said. "Just tell me when, and I'll take you."

"I don't know, I'm probably overreacting," she said. "I want it to work so badly that I'm tightening up or something. I'm probably expecting too much too soon. Sexual anorexia is a bitch." *And I created every last bit of that bitch.* "It's as if I'm losing my virginity every time we try." *I should probably go check to see if I'm bleeding.* She pushed off his chest. "Be back in a minute."

As she went toward the washroom, she felt a thin trickle of blood down her thigh. She stopped at her wardrobe, took out a pair of underwear, went into the washroom, and closed the door. When she wiped herself with some toilet paper, she saw dots of blood. *Merde! I'm spotting while I'm* not *on my period. I am so lucky.* She opened the washroom closet and stared at ancient packages of tampons and maxipads. *I might pass out from the pain of putting in a tampon.* She slid her underwear up to her thighs, unwrapped a pad, secured it, and pulled her underwear on completely.

Then she wept.

She heard a knock on the door. "Be out in a minute."

"Hope, are you okay?" Dylan asked.

No, and I don't know if I ever will be. "Yes. Just a second." She flushed the bloody toilet paper and opened the door, immediately walking into Dylan's arms.

And she wept some more.

He led her to the bed, eased her under the covers, and held her while her body shook.

"I feel so stupid," Hope sobbed. "I know it's all my fault, but I'm trying to get better, aren't I? I'm eating like a horse, I'm trying to avoid stress, and I'm sleeping more. Why am I not getting better?"

"You said you felt more tingling today, right?" Dylan asked.

"Yes."

"That's progress, isn't it?"

"I guess."

He massaged her neck. "I looked up something I have never looked up in my life the other night."

"What?"

"Vaginal dryness." He sighed. "Do you think you could have early menopause? You have almost all of the symptoms."

"God, I hope not," Hope said.

"I read about one cause that hit home with me, too," he said. "Unresolved relationship problems can dry you up, depress your libido, and keep you from being aroused."

Hope closed her eyes. "So you think I need to see my gynecologist *and* a psychiatrist?"

"It may be something simpler than doing that," Dylan said. "I will try to relax you more. A long, hot bath beforehand. A glass of wine. Music. Longer massages. Gentler foreplay, and we don't have to do the deed every time. We'll just take things slower than slow."

"Sounds like a very nice evening," Hope said, "but there are no guarantees that even that will work."

"True," Dylan said, "but I'm willing to try. I'd also like you to confront Odell in some way."

"What? I don't want to see him."

"I don't mean literally," Dylan said. "Though that might help, too."

"How am I going to do that?" Hope asked. "Find out where he and his lovely wife and perfect child live and curse him out? I would curse him out in English and in French."

"That's a little more extreme than what I had in mind," Dylan said. "I'm still getting over Marie. Every time I open my apartment door, a part of her is still there. It's as if she's haunting me." He sighed. "That's one of the reasons I've been hesitating to have you over to my place."

I know the feeling. Odell, the goblin, is still standing in my door-way. "Do you want her back?"

"No, no, nothing like that," Dylan said. "I'd just like to talk to her one more time and tell her that *she* was wrong, not me."

Hope sat up, gradually easing her back to the headboard. "I would love to scream at Odell. I have so many things to say to him."

Dylan sat up next to her. "Go ahead." He squeezed her hand. "It's Halloween, a day made for screaming."

"I mean, *really* scream, Dylan," Hope said. "I have bottled up years of aggression and frustration, and when it all comes out, it won't be pretty."

"Let it out."

"My neighbors will call the police," Hope said.

Dylan handed her a pillow. "Use a silencer. It's what I did. Since I've been with you, my pillow likes me again."

Hope twisted the pillow in her hands. "What did you say?"

"Well, after I stopped calling Marie a self-centered, narcissistic, pampered, poor-excuse-for-a-human-being, balls-slicing bitch— this usually took about ten minutes—I stuck up for myself and made a list of all the things that I did right. At first, my list was short, but over time, it became longer. If it helps you vent, I can leave for a while. Need anything from the store?"

"Ice cream," Hope said, "but I don't want you to go. I can scream at him during the week when you're not here. If I start screaming at him now, I'll scare away any trick-or-treaters I might get." *Which will mean more chocolate for me . . .* "Yeah, go get me two pints of that Karamel Sutra ice cream."

He kissed her cheek. "It *will* help, Hope."

"The screaming or the ice cream?" Hope asked.

"Both," Dylan said. "Let me borrow your keys. If I hear you screaming when I get to the door, I'll wait outside until you're done."

She watched him dress. "You really think this will work?"

"It worked for me to a point," Dylan said. "Having you in my life has cured me completely."

He's so sweet. "I just want things to work out between us down there."

He sat at the foot of the bed and squeezed her feet. "It will happen, Hope," Dylan whispered, "and when it does, I will be the one crying."

That would make me cry even more.

He glanced at the pile of candy on the kitchen table. "I want ... a Snickers bar. How about you?"

"Bring me the bag," Hope said.

He laughed. "Your hunger knows no bounds." He went to the table, took out two mini Snickers bars, and tossed the bag to Hope. "Are your keys in your coat pocket?"

Hope nodded.

Dylan found the keys. "Sweet screams, Hope."

"Boo," Hope said.

Dylan left, the door closing behind him.

Hope felt her depression return almost immediately. *You always show up at the worst times. You're the uninvited guest who never leaves.*

Hope folded the pillow and pressed it to her face, took a deep breath, and screamed.

"Odell Wilson, you fat, sloppy, stuck-up piece of *merde*!"

She jerked back from the pillow, her breath hot, her heart racing. *That felt good. Damn. I wish I could really say these things to him, but ... damn. My temperature just shot up ten degrees!*

She rose from the bed, put on Dylan's hoodie, and carried her pillow to the door. "You were a fool to walk out on me, you smelly, cold, heartless, ignorant asshole!" she screamed into the pillow.

Then she laughed. It was not a pleasant laugh. It had menace in it. It had bite. It even had a distinctive French accent.

Whack ran and hid under the quilt.

Hope held the pillow with one hand and punched it for several minutes with the other, wishing it were Odell's ever-sneering face. She stopped when she realized that no amount of punching could improve on what wasn't really a handsome face. "You weren't even that handsome, Odell," she said, "and yet you thought you were. I was so blind."

She folded the pillow, pressed it to her lips, and stalked toward her bed. "You were no good in bed, had no clue what you were doing down there, and I faked most of my orgasms!" She dropped onto the bed and buried her face in the pillow. "In fact, *vous* dick, I had all of my *orgasmes after* you left!"

Hope started to sweat. *Yes, I'm starting to sweat him out of my system. I will need another bath.*

She closed her eyes. "Oh, sure, you complimented me every now and then, but even your compliments contained criticisms. You'd say, 'You look nice, Hope, but wouldn't the black top look better?' Or 'I like the way you did your hair, but why don't you get it bleached?' Or 'Wow, those jeans really look good on you, but aren't they a little too loose?' You *never* let me be myself! You were always trying to make me into what you wanted me to be!"

She flipped over onto her back, only laying the pillow on her face now. "And you thought you were *so* smart and *so* sophisticated and knew everything about everything and I was only an Island girl refugee from Canada who knew nothing of the real world and you had to *tell* me about all the things you thought I didn't know, but I already *knew* most of them, and you know what? I didn't listen to a *freaking* thing you said because you never really said anything! I listened to you talk about nothing for two years. I could have watched TV instead. I have some news about your racist, homophobic, and prejudiced ideas, Odell, those ideas you spouted at me daily and expected me to digest and ask for seconds. They were all wrong. Wrong! Cab drivers are not out to rip you off! You just didn't know where you were going. Your boss was not an asshole because he was a Jew. You were a lazy-ass, backstabbing worker! *You* were the asshole! Asian people *can* drive. I see them every day driving just fine. Hockey is *not* a racist sport. There are black players in the NHL. Brownsville is not the hell on earth you said it was. There are people there, there's laughter there, and there's life there."

She fought back tears as she went to the window, peering out

into the twilight. "And whenever I showed the least bit of independent thought, you shot me down. I would offer an opinion, and you
would dissect it until I hated my own thoughts. It was always *your*
ideas, *your* opinions, *your* dreams! I had a working mind, and I had
dreams, too! Did you know that, you hypercritical hypocrite?
Odell, you weren't the shit—you *were* shit!"

She collapsed onto the futon. "And you know what, Oh-*Hell*, I
was pretty enough, and I *was* as pretty as the woman you married.
No, I was prettier. You need to get your muddy little eyes checked!
Maybe you married her because you could control her better, and I
wasn't just *good* at making love to you! I was *great* at it. *You* couldn't
keep up with *me*! You thought sex was only supposed to last for a
minute! I now have a man who can make sex last all day! The word
'foreplay' was not in your vocabulary! You even blamed me when
you came too soon! 'Why'd you do that, Hope?' and 'If you hadn't
done that, Hope . . .' and 'It's your fault, Hope'! *It wasn't my fault!*"

She shed a few tears. *It wasn't my fault.*

It was never my fault.

She took several deep breaths and returned to her bed. "Dylan
loves foreplay," she said. "He respects it. He worships my body
first. Dylan does some serious foreplay on me from the moment I
see him in the morning to the moment he fills me at night, and he
fills me all the way up to my spleen. Odell, you were a *rude* lover!
Yes, you were rude, inconsiderate, and ungrateful in bed! You had
no respect for me! You fed me your sixty seconds of bullshit and
expected me to like it. Dylan feeds me love twenty-four hours a
day."

Hope blinked at the ceiling.

I love Dylan.

I really love Dylan.

I hunger and I thirst for that man.

She tossed her pillow against the headboard. "I never really
loved you, Odell," she whispered, and then she laughed.

It was a soft, quiet laugh with an American accent.

"I only thought I did. I was nothing but a *kept* woman to you. I
kept my hair short for you. I *kept* my feet in flats so you didn't feel
so short. I *kept* wearing slacks and blazers instead of the jeans and
sweaters I love to look good for you—in *your* mind, anyway. You

kept control of what we watched on TV, *kept* control of where we went, what we ate, and when we ate it, and I doubt if you ever *kept* me in your thoughts for more than a few minutes at a time. I only thought I needed you. I *know* in my bones that I need Dylan." She looked at the door. "And he's bringing me ice cream." She closed her eyes. "Odell, you *never* brought me any ice cream."

She heard the key turn in the lock and ran to the door, throwing it open and launching herself into Dylan's arms, the bag he carried clunking to the floor.

"I was going to say 'trick-or-treat,' " Dylan whispered as he hugged her.

"You don't have to say either," Hope said. "Whatever you want from me is yours."

"I'd rather give you everything," he whispered.

"That sounds fair." She kissed him and felt the cool breeze wafting up the stairs and drying her sweat.

Dylan picked up the bag and closed the door behind him. "They were out of Karamel Sutra," he said.

It figures. Even the ice cream gods are against me. "What'd you get me?"

He pulled the container from the bag. "Dublin Mudslide."

"I think I like that one better anyway," Hope said.

Dylan read the label. " 'Irish cream liqueur ice cream.' That would be me. '*Chocolate* chocolate chip cookies.' That would be you. 'A coffee fudge swirl.' Hmm." He blinked. "That would be the eight or nine children we'd have keeping us up at night."

She draped her arms around his neck. *This man, this man.* "Or ten, right?"

"Right." He looked around the apartment. "I don't see anything broken. You're not a thrower?"

"No. I don't have much to throw, and if I did, I'd be afraid of hitting Whack."

"I threw a few things," Dylan said. "That's how I learned to repair drywall. I'm still fixing a few spots here and there. I threw quite a few fists."

Those scars on his knuckles might not all have been from street boxing.

Hope took off his Windbreaker, noticed it was wet, and laid it over the back of a kitchen chair. "Is it raining?"

"Bad night to be out trick-or-treating," he said. "It's supposed to rain steadily for the next three days." He glanced at his backpack. "No art in Brownsville tomorrow. It's just as well. Those kids will be so hyper from all that candy anyway." He leaned on the kitchen table. "Did you have success?"

Hope nodded. "I was successful. I don't know why I didn't do it before. I'm not the most demonstrative person in the world, you know. I'm still shy, even with myself, I guess."

"And how do you feel now?" he asked.

"I feel sweaty." She pulled rapidly on the front of *her* new hoodie to fan her chest. *Dylan will never get his hoodie back now. It's mine.* "That was work."

"It might be because of the candy," Dylan said. "Chocolate overload."

"No," Hope said. "I was *un*loading. Now I feel so alive, and lighter, so to speak. It's all because of you." She laughed. "And the screaming. Near the end, though, I stopped screaming and started talking to him. Was there a point when you stopped screaming, too?"

Dylan nodded, setting the pint of ice cream near the sink. "It took me a few hours and several pillows, but yeah, I started talking. It was the conversation Marie and I never had but should have had."

Hope rubbed her throat. "My throat is sore."

He took two spoons from a drawer. "Ice cream will cure that, you know."

Hope took a spoon. "And so will cuddling with you all night long . . ."

For the rest of Halloween and deep into Sunday morning, they cuddled, and whispered, and ate Dublin Mudslide ice cream, and even watched *Alien* all the way through, keeping each other warm as heavy rains drenched Brooklyn and an empty playground in Brownsville a few miles away.

They slept, they lingered, they snuggled, they rested.

Hope prepared Sunday dinner—pork chops and baked potatoes loaded with butter, sour cream, chives, bacon, and four different cheeses—and they ate for the first time at Hope's table.

"I'm just trying to butter you up," she said.

"You're no common tater," Dylan said.

Ouch. That pun was horrible. "I only have eyes for you."

Dylan smiled. "I wish every day was 'fry day.' "

That one was even worse.

Before he left late Sunday evening, Dylan brought Hope back to reality. "Tomorrow we're going to be very busy. In fact, starting tomorrow, we're going to be *extremely* busy for the next six weeks."

"We haven't been busy yet?" Hope asked.

"It's like a switch someone throws after Halloween," Dylan said. "Christmas is coming."

Hope smiled. "And our bank accounts are going to get fat."

NOVEMBER 2

Only 52 more shopping days
until Christmas . . .

Chapter 19

Holiday madness saluted Hope and her black, somewhat round and working umbrella on her puddle-infested, rain-swept stroll to work the Monday after Halloween. Electric snowflakes and stars, green bows, and lighted silver-and-red garlands floated over Flatbush Avenue. Even barriers for terminally unfixed sidewalks became candy canes, red and white stripes flowing from one end of the barrier to the other. Lighted artificial Christmas trees, chubby Santa Clauses, and prancing elves and reindeer stared at her through store windows plastered with "Early Xmas Sale!" and "Santa Says Save!" signs.

A rickshaw bicycle carrying a hefty human Santa driven by an overgrown human elf nearly collided with her in a crosswalk.

"Sorry," the elf said.

"Merry Christmas!" Santa yelled.

Brooklyn had become tinsel town overnight.

It's beginning to look a lot like... desperation, Hope thought. *Red, green, silver, and gold desperation. I hope these stores do well this holiday season, I really do, but it's only the beginning of November! What about Election Day? Oh. I forgot. This is America, the world's greatest democracy, where half the eligible voters don't vote. What about Veterans Day? Oh. I forgot. This is America, the world's biggest superpower, where people don't often respect the heroes who made and keep them a superpower. What about Thanksgiving? Oh. I forgot. This is America, the world's biggest consumer, where Thanks-*

giving is only a big meal overeaten during twelve hours of dreary football games.

Dylan met Hope at the Kinderstuff door wearing a fuzzy blue puppet on his hand. "Happy Cookie Monster Day," he said. After the exchange of coffee and toast, order summary, and earnings statement, Dylan kissed her—and so did the puppet.

"I didn't know the Cookie Monster had his own holiday," Hope said.

"We celebrate every holiday we can here," Dylan said. "By the way, tomorrow is Cliché Day, National Men Make Dinner Day, and Sandwich Day. I guess tomorrow will be a day to separate the men from the boys when it comes to cooking, huh?"

"How cliché of you to say so," Hope said, shaking her head. "Does that mean men will make sandwiches for dinner tomorrow? Just some food for thought."

"Only time will tell," Dylan said.

Hope sipped her coffee. "It's time to wake up and smell the coffee."

"We could make the 'Cliché Collection,' for Odd Ducks," Dylan said.

Hope bit into her toast. "It would be a piece of cake."

"You're good to the last drop," Dylan said.

"I better get to work, I'm going to be late again," Hope said.

Dylan smiled. "Better late than never." He kissed her, Cookie Monster nuzzling her cheek. "See you later, alligator."

Hope walked away before Dylan could assault her with another cliché.

While running several hundred Odd Ducks cards, Hope trained Kiki on the DocuTech *and* the Baum. Within thirty minutes, Kiki was a pro on both machines.

"A piece of cake," Kiki said.

"Not you, too!" Hope cried. "It's not until tomorrow!"

Kiki had no idea what Hope was talking about.

Justin, on the other hand, was hopeless. He found the ON button fine. After that, it was a struggle. On a machine that had only jammed a few times in three years, Justin jammed it the first time he loaded it with paper. He "forgot" to adjust contrast settings. He "didn't see" the buttons Hope pushed repeatedly because Hope was "going too fast!" He printed multipage documents out of order, commenting, "Does it really matter?" He "didn't know" he had to press the COLLATE button. He inserted the staple cartridge upside down. He even fused several different orders together, requiring Hope to waste a frustrating hour separating them.

Before she left for Kinderstuff, Hope whispered to Kiki, "Don't *ever* let that man *touch* that machine."

By the end of the week, Hope would repeat this phrase to Kiki nine more times after training Justin on the rest of Thrifty's machines.

The art class at Kinderstuff became the highlight of Hope's November days. On rain-free and windless days, they marched the children hand in hand down Flatbush to Prospect Park to paint autumn scenes on Dylan's portable easels. Hope would begin painting trees and leaves, and the kids would mimic her. *This is more like show-and-tell than teaching,* Hope thought. *I can do this!*

On cold or wet days, they stayed inside, adding to a messy, and therefore fun, charcoal, chalk, watercolor, and crayon mural depicting the first Thanksgiving. After Dylan sketched a long table and outlined the children sitting around it on a massive piece of paper ("The exact size of the right picture window out front," Dylan said), Hope gave them a choice. "Do you wish to be a Pilgrim or a Native American?" All of the children chose to be Native Americans since feathers, bows, and arrows were "easier to draw." Then they scoured hundreds of magazines for pictures of food, cutting and pasting the pictures to the table.

The resulting display in the front window of Kinderstuff stopped dozens of people in their tracks, most of them smiling, laughing, and pointing. Other than a live, bug-eyed turkey wearing a Yankees cap that Hope added at the far end of the table, the food on the table was anything but authentic Thanksgiving fare and featured spaghetti, tacos, cheeseburgers, ice cream, pudding, and breakfast cereal.

Midway through the month, they cut out and painted colossal, glittering snowflakes made out of cardboard, and Dylan hung them from the ceiling with fishing line. They made reindeer sock puppets. They even mixed, rolled out, cut, decorated, and baked Christmas tree cookies using red and green sprinkles.

Helping the children design and create oversized Christmas cards, however, gave Hope the most satisfaction because of Aniya, whose hair was just starting to return as soft black fuzz. Aniya spent two days in front of a mirror drawing a self-portrait of her smiling face and shiny head in a New York Yankees cap. Underneath the portrait, with Hope's help, Aniya wrote, "All I want for Christmas . . ." Hope copied the outside image, and Aniya traced all but the cap on the inside of the card. Then Aniya added hair, *lots* of hair, hair so thick and luxurious that it filled the inside of the card.

"I don't think we'll need a caption inside, do you?" Hope asked Dylan.

"Nope," Dylan said. "Let's do this one, Hope."

Hope smiled. "For Odd Ducks."

"And any money that comes in goes straight to her family," Dylan said. "They have a lifetime of bills to pay. Maybe this will help."

And help it did in ways Hope and Dylan never imagined it would.

Dylan featured Aniya's simple yet profound card on the main page of the Odd Ducks website. Underneath the card was a quiet plea:

All proceeds from this card will go to the Aniya Fund to help Aniya Pierre-Louis, a child in Brooklyn, New York, who has leukemia. Click here to read more about Aniya.

The link took viewers to a colorful collage of pictures of Aniya and her artwork along with Aniya's life story. Within hours of its posting, orders streamed in by the hundreds, breaking the thousand-mark barrier in only two days.

Most importantly, Dylan began receiving e-mails from people who wanted to see if their bone marrow matched Aniya's.

"This is so exciting," Dylan said, "and these people are serious, Hope. A few have already gone to Brooklyn Hospital Center to be tested."

One of the people, who chose to remain anonymous, *matched*.
Hope got a rare phone call from Dylan that evening.
"It's a match!" Dylan yelled. "Aniya's got a match!"
Yes! "That's wonderful!"
"I just got off the phone with her parents," Dylan said. "Aniya
has to go for more chemo tomorrow to prep for the transplant."
*Just as her hair was coming back. She's going to lose what little
hair she has.* "Will she have the transplant done soon?" *So she can
have her Christmas wish?*
"It all depends on how well she responds to her treatments,"
Dylan said, "but I have a good feeling she'll be home and sprouting
hair by Christmas."
Out of a somewhat guilty conscience, Hope stared at her hair in
the mirror. *If I could, I'd give my hair to that child. I wonder if I can.*
Hope surfed the Internet until she came across Wigs for Kids,
an organization in Ohio dedicated to providing wigs for children
like Aniya. She read the requirements and found that she could donate her hair—*if* she unlocked her dreads. *Each wig requires a minimum of twelve inches of hair. I know I have more than that. Dylan
has more hair than that. Maybe both of us can donate our hair.*
She had trouble imagining Dylan without hair. *He wouldn't look
like Dylan anymore, and putting a man's hair on a little girl's head is
strange.*
She pressed and fluffed her own hair, pulling several locks to
her chest. *What if Aniya didn't want a wig? She's a proud little
thing. She'd much rather wear a baseball cap. I'd be sending my hair
to Ohio anyway, so there's no guarantee she'd get my hair or that my
hair would even end up back in Brooklyn. Would Dylan like the way
I looked with short hair? For that matter, would I? I like having long
hair. I only had short hair because Odell liked short hair.*
These thoughts troubled Hope as she printed out cards nonstop, most of them Aniya's. She often had to return to Thrifty after
art at Kinderstuff and remain there after six to stay ahead of the
avalanche of orders. She and Dylan had working dinners as cards
flew off the virtual Odd Ducks shelves. They were making nearly
$4,000 a week now, an extra $8,000 for Aniya because of her sweet
card.

At this rate, Hope thought, *I'll have a total of seventy-six thousand dollars toward the beach house by Christmas. I really need to double that amount before I can even start looking. Maybe this time next year I'll be walking in sand and listening to the waves. Miracles can happen, because miracles are already happening. Aniya is going to get a transplant.*

Hope knew there was a chance that Aniya's body would reject the new bone marrow, but something about the season told her not that anything's possible but that *everything's* possible.

Aniya is going to get well.

Weekends allowed Hope and Dylan to become well, too. Every Friday night became "Reunion Night" as they reacquainted each other with the intricacies of each other's bodies, his healing hands and whispers removing the stress of the previous week.

Saturday became "Movie Day," though they rarely watched any movie all the way to the end. Hope supplied them with black-and-white classics such as *Sunset Boulevard*, Orson Welles's *Touch of Evil*, Ingmar Bergman's *The Seventh Seal*, *Top Hat* starring Fred Astaire and Ginger Rogers, Marlon Brando in *On the Waterfront*, and Humphrey Bogart in *The Big Sleep*. They ate and fed each other buttery popcorn. They finished off pints of Ben & Jerry's ice cream. They tried to make love repeatedly, each attempt ending in tears and a trip to the washroom. On Sundays, they visited the Brownsville Recreation Center's community room, re-creating the mural, the snowflakes, and the cards on successive Sundays.

Despite the stress, Hope steadily gained weight. She saw curves at her hips. A rib on either side went into hiding. She could almost pinch a centimeter near her navel.

On the third Sunday in mid-November, Hope felt confident enough to allow Dylan to watch her weekly weigh-in.

Dylan sat on the edge of the tub with a bag of popcorn. "Do I cheer or what?"

"Shh."

"Ladies and gentleman," he announced. "In this corner, weighing . . ."

Hope frowned.

"Sorry." He ate more popcorn. "This is exciting."

Hope placed one foot on the scale. "Oh, I forgot my glasses."

"I'll get them." Dylan left the washroom and came back wearing them. "I've used microscopes with less magnification." He leaned close to her arm. "You have very cute pores. Are those skin cells?"

Hope removed her glasses from Dylan's face and put them on. She stepped onto the scale. "One-fifteen!" *Yes!* "This is cause for celebration!"

Dylan lifted Hope off the scale. "At the rate I've been eating, I should have gained at least ten pounds." He stepped on the scale. "That's a long way down there. Tell me what it says."

Hope squinted. "Two twenty-five. You're almost twice my weight."

"Look again," Dylan said.

Why? Hope looked anyway. "It didn't change. Two-twenty five."

"Look closer," he said.

Hope bent down. *Oops.* "Oh, two-*oh*-five. Sorry." She straightened and gave Dylan a hug. "How are we going to celebrate all my new fat?"

"I guess we'll go out to eat," he said, leaving the washroom and sitting on the futon.

"How ironic," Hope said. "Celebrate the gaining of weight by gaining some more."

Dylan nodded.

Now he's quiet. He's only quiet when he's asleep or something's wrong. She sat next to him. "What's wrong? Did you think I'd weight more?"

"No, that's not it. I am overjoyed you've gained so much weight, and I never thought I'd ever say that to a woman." He sighed. "It's just that I'm worried. Hope, how bad is your eyesight?"

"Not bad," Hope said. "I just wasn't paying close attention."

"How bad is your eyesight, Hope?" Dylan asked.

"You want the numbers?" Hope asked.

Dylan nodded.

"At my last checkup, I was twenty-three hundred in my left eye, and twenty-two hundred in my right eye. I'm extremely nearsighted. With these glasses, though, I'm fine. If I drove—and I've never driven in the U.S., by the way—I'd probably have a restricted license of some kind."

"Are your eyes getting worse?" he asked.

"Well, I have some lattice degeneration," Hope said.

"What's that?" Dylan asked.

"It's kind of like losing your peripheral vision gradually over time," Hope said. "In other words, my field of vision is shrinking. It started about fifteen years ago, and my optometrist says I'll have to do something about it eventually."

"Could you go blind one day?" Dylan asked.

"I don't plan to."

"I don't want you to, but *could* you?" Dylan asked.

"It's always been a possibility," Hope said. She rubbed his leg. "Does my bad vision bother you?"

"Yes," Dylan said. "I mean, no. It troubles me. It worries me. I mean, whenever you take off your glasses, like in bed, what do you see?"

"Well, most of you gets all hazy and fuzzy," she said. "I'm glad you're a symmetrical man. I can always find your lips and other centered things."

"So you don't see me very well at all."

"Well, you're usually down under the covers, aren't you?" She smiled. "I like it when you're down under the covers."

"Have you ever thought of getting laser surgery done?" Dylan asked.

"No," Hope said quickly. *Lasers on soft tissue? Whose crazy idea was that? Hey, we have some delicate flesh here. Let's burn it.*

"Why not?" Dylan asked.

"Laser surgery scares me," Hope said. "It's also expensive, and my insurance won't cover any part of it."

"It's a pretty common procedure these days," Dylan said. "Millions of people have had it done, ten million at last count."

"Good for them," Hope said. "I'll be all right."

"But you're not all right, Hope," Dylan said. "You can't see me when we're intimate."

"Ah, but I can feel you," Hope said. "Trust me, I can feel you."

He turned to her. "I want you to be able to see me perfectly,

Hope, and without your glasses. That may be part of the problem of your not getting...*juteux*. What I see of you arouses me *so* much. I'm not saying that I have the greatest body, but if everything's fuzzy, you're not seeing the parts of me that *should* arouse you. At least I hope they would arouse you."

"Well, I can keep my glasses on if you want me to," Hope said. "I'll definitely have to get an eyeglass strap to hold them on while we're *jooking*."

"Your eyes are extremely important to me, Hope," Dylan said. "I love your eyes. I don't want to see you go blind. I saw a child go blind, remember? That still haunts me. Shayna would look directly into my eyes, and I knew she couldn't see me. You are not going blind on me, Hope. I want you to get laser surgery."

What?

"I am going to pay for your surgery as part of your Odd Ducks benefits package," Dylan said. "Nothing out of pocket, no deductible, no dent in your beach house fund."

"But it's not really necessary, Dylan," Hope said. "I can see fine with these glasses. You could buy me some lighter frames and the eyeglass strap. Do you think they make ones that glow in the dark?"

"Hope, please," Dylan said. "I just watched you squinting to see a scale only two feet from your nose, and you were *wearing* your glasses. I want you to see our children and grandchildren when you're one hundred, Hope, and if you really want this beach house, you need to be able to see to draw. If you can't see to draw, you can't draw and you can't make more money to go toward that beach house. I've seen you practically putting your face next to the page even with your glasses on."

"I like to get close to my work," Hope said.

"But you're straining eyes that are already in need of help," Dylan said. "Let me do this for you."

I love how he cares for me, but ... "I'll think about it."

Dylan sighed and shook his head. "What's to think about? On the one hand, you can have perfect vision. On the other hand, you can have a fuzzy boyfriend in bed and maybe blindness in later life."

"Well, let me sleep on it at least," Hope said.

"No."

Did I hear him correctly? My hearing is excellent. Let me check. "Did you say no?"

Dylan nodded. "I've already scheduled you for a consultation at the Dello Russo Laser Vision Center."

Hope jumped off the futon. "You what?"

"We're going to the eye doctor, Hope."

"No, we're not." She walked into the kitchen, rinsed her glass, and poured herself some lemonade. "Cancel the appointment."

Dylan rose, scratching his head with both hands. "Please do this for me. I held a child who couldn't see me. I won't have that happen again."

"And it probably won't, Dylan," Hope said, "and anyway, they're my eyes, not yours."

"They *are* my eyes," Dylan said softly. "Your eyes drew me to you."

Hope rolled her eyes. "No, they're not. You don't own me or my eyes. I don't want anyone cutting or burning—"

"I've already given them a down payment."

Hope blinked rapidly. "You what?"

"For the right eye, I think," Dylan said. "I'm pretty sure they do the right eye first."

"You already paid them?" *Is he crazy?*

"Yes," he said, "and it's nonrefundable."

"You're serious."

Dylan nodded.

This isn't happening. "You can't go around . . . signing people up to have their eyes ripped out without their permission!"

"That's not what they do, Hope," Dylan said. "They reshape your eyes so you can see better. Go with me to the consultation. Dr. Dello Russo will explain everything to you."

"When is the consultation?" Hope asked.

Dylan looked away. "Consultation tomorrow, surgery Tuesday."

This is really *not happening.* "You have to be joking."

"I'm not," Dylan said. He turned back to her. "It was difficult getting you in. Luckily, I taught the receptionist's kids at Kinderstuff, and she worked you in."

Hope crossed her arms. "I'm not going."

Dylan approached and rubbed her arms. "You'll be able to see clearly, Hope. You'll be able to see *me* clearly. You'll be able to roll out of bed without tripping over your cat. You'll be able to go to the bathroom at any time, day or night, without having to search for your glasses. You'll be able to see that scale correctly. You'll be able to see what I put inside you. You'll be able to see my head when I'm down there feasting on your tender flesh." He held her hands. "You'll be able to see my eyes when I kiss you. You'll be able to see us growing old together. You'll be able to see the sunrises and sunsets at your beach house when you—"

"Okay, okay, I get the point," Hope interrupted. *That convinced me. There's no reason to get a beach house if you can't see a sunrise or a sunset.* "I'll go to the consultation."

"And you'll get the surgery," Dylan said.

"I don't know, okay? Maybe."

He hugged her. "Thank you. Thank you, Hope."

I'm crying again. I thought I had cried enough in this apartment!

"Why are you crying?" Dylan asked. "Aren't we celebrating?"

"I've never had anyone care so, so fiercely for me, Dylan," Hope said. "It scares me." *Because people who supposedly care for me go away.*

"It scares me, too," he said, "but in a good way." He looked down. "I've never asked this, but what happened to your left pinkie toenail?"

Hope looked down at her foot. "I lost that nail years ago. Why?"

"You need to have a transplant," Dylan said. "I will make the appointment."

"Stop!"

"Millions have had this procedure done."

"I'll give you a procedure," she said, sliding her hands into his front pockets.

"We're going to play doctor?" Dylan said. "Does it involve suction?"

"It *may* involve some cutting," Hope said, "so take your sexy derriere to that bed and do some operating on me . . ."

* * *

Though the countless eye tests the next day taxed her, annoyed her, and scared her to no end, Hope made it through the consultation.

And she agreed to do the laser surgery.

"What was the deciding factor?" Dylan asked as they kissed in the back of another cab returning them to her place.

"You were the deciding factor," Hope said. "Everything you said made sense."

"You were so against doing it before," Dylan said. "What's the real reason?"

Hope looked out the window. "Something the doctor said."

"And that was ..."

"Dr. Dello Russo said you have to take total care of me for twenty-four hours after the surgery," Hope said.

"Haven't I been doing that?" Dylan asked.

"Not on a Tuesday night," Hope said. "You have not been out of my sight, pun intended, since three o'clock Friday. I will have this surgery done tomorrow. That means I will be with you through Wednesday evening, a total of over one hundred and twenty consecutive hours with you."

"It has seemed like *such* a long time," Dylan said. "One hundred and twenty hours!"

"I can still do surgery on you with my eyes closed," Hope said. "Be careful how you talk to a woman about to have her eyes cut open."

Early Tuesday morning, after a nervous cab ride with no kissing, Hope gripped the skin off Dylan's hand as she sat in a reclining chair, Dr. Dello Russo and a nurse prepping instruments and machines around her.

"Is it okay if he stays?" Hope asked the doctor.

"Sure," Dr. Dello Russo said, "but he will have to sit over there." He pointed to a chair a few feet away.

Hope reluctantly released Dylan's hand, and he sat in the chair.

"Are you excited?" Dylan asked.

That's not the word I'm feeling. Mortified. Terrified. Petrified.

"I am," Dylan said. "I wouldn't miss seeing this for all the world."

"Ha," Hope said. "Dr. Dello Russo, get this man out of my sight."

Dr. Dello Russo chuckled. "I have heard that one before." He removed Hope's glasses. "Say good-bye to your glasses."

"Bye," Hope whispered.

"Are you ready?" Dr. Dello Russo asked.

No. "Yes."

Dr. Dello Russo first numbed Hope's eyes with several drops of solution. Once Hope had no feeling in her eyes, the nurse cleaned Hope's eyes thoroughly before using lid speculums to keep her eyelids open.

"Are you okay?" the nurse asked.

No. "I'm fine."

Then came the suction.

What was blurry before became blurrier. *Hello, fuzzy world. Miss me?*

"What do you see, Dylan?" Hope asked.

"I'm watching your eye on the monitor," Dylan said, "and it is the biggest brown eye on earth. It looks like a planet. Planet Hope. No, it looks more like the rings of a tree."

Planet Hope. The Hope's Eye Tree.

"Let us begin," Dr. Dello Russo said.

It was good that Hope couldn't see or feel the doctor's scalpel.

Dr. Dello Russo cut a round flap in Hope's right cornea, then told her to stare at a light. A moment later he said, "We're reshaping your right cornea now."

Hope didn't feel a thing. *Is the laser on? Is this the surgery? Shouldn't there be smoke?*

A minute later, Dr. Dello Russo replaced the flap he cut and secured a shield over her right eye.

After he repeated the entire procedure with her left eye, Hope felt the reclining chair raising her slightly.

"I'm done?" Hope asked.

"Yes," Dr. Dello Russo said. "I will see you in twenty-four hours."

Now he's *making jokes.*

"What about the other thing," Dylan said. "What about the lattice degeneration?"

Dylan, let's just go. I don't like this darkness.

"We will worry about that later," Dr. Dello Russo said. "Now see this woman home."

He's still making jokes!

Dylan helped Hope from the chair and placed her hand on his elbow.

"Blind woman walking," she whispered, her heart racing.

"We'll take it slow," Dylan said.

Hope grasped his elbow with her other hand as well. "I'm scared," she whispered.

"I won't let you out of my sight," Dylan said.

Hope wished she could see so she could hit him somewhere soft.

After a relatively curse-free, horn-free cab ride to her apartment, and after a dizzying walk up the stairs to the second floor, Dylan led Hope to the kitchen table and seated her in a chair.

"I'd rather lie down," Hope said.

"You haven't eaten yet today," he said, somewhere to her right.

"I am kind of hungry." She felt the coolness of the table in front of her. "Where's the food?"

"I'm feeding you," Dylan said. "Open wide."

This could get very sticky.

For the next half hour, Hope's sense of taste went into overdrive. Dylan fed her grapes and apple slices, pieces of a cheese omelet, and a piece of toast soaked in butter. For "dessert," he fed her a mini Milky Way bar with his lips.

It was the best breakfast Hope had ever eaten.

Dylan led her to the washroom, where he reluctantly allowed her to brush her own teeth and take care of her own business, and then he carried her to the bed, where she allowed him to remove all of her clothes.

"We're going to play a game," Dylan said. "It's called 'Body Part Identification,' and you are the star."

"I am going to like this game," Hope whispered. *Very much.*

"First, I will touch you in certain places," Dylan said. "You must correctly identify these places or you will lose points, and if you earn enough points to go to the bonus round, I will have you touching some of my places. Do you *feel* up to it?"

"Just feel me up, Mr. Healy," Hope said.

Hope immediately felt his finger circling her navel.

"What's this?" he asked.

"My *ombilic*," Hope whispered.

"Correct," Dylan said. "I think."

Hope felt two fingers tracing a path from her knee to her sexy derriere.

"Please identify."

"*Mes cuisses,*" Hope whispered.

"Wrong answer," Dylan said. "The correct answer is your silky, sexy thighs."

"Oh, I knew that one," Hope said, snapping a finger. A moment later, she felt two hot hands caressing her breasts gently and teasing her nipples to hardness.

"And these?"

Oh, that feels so nice. "*Mes seins et mamelons,*" Hope whispered.

"You're only half right," Dylan said. "They are melons."

They're getting there. My bras have been noticeably tighter. She soon felt his unmistakable lips on hers. "*Mes lèvres,*" she whispered before he could ask. She felt his tongue moving down between her breasts, his hair tickling her nipples, his tongue stopping briefly at her navel before lingering much lower.

"*Mon clitoris,*" she whispered.

She whispered this for the next fifteen minutes, and at times, she felt a stirring, a tingle, an echo of a feeling she once used to have. *I know I am close to a breakthrough. It won't be long now. I'm not going to cry.*

"Let me feel you now," she whispered.

"You've earned your way to the bonus round," Dylan said.

Yay! She heard a zipper. She heard a sigh. She felt something large, full, and hot in her hand. "Is that your forearm?"

"No."

She squeezed gently. "Your leg?"

"No."

She squeezed it harder. "Your foot?"

"No."

"Ah," Hope said. "Then it must be *mon pénis*."

"Yes."

"*Je veux que vous couvriez votre pénis avec la gelée K-Y et me fassiez l'amour maintenant,*" she said, widening her legs to welcome him.

Dylan didn't have to be told—in any language—twice.

Hope sat again in the reclining chair.

Hope again gripped the skin off Dylan's hand.

"Keep your eyes closed until I tell you to open them," Dr. Dello Russo said.

She felt the shields leaving her eyelids and something like a wet wipe removing the crust around her eyes.

"Okay," Dr. Dello Russo said. "You may feel sand or grit, and the lights may appear as crosses to you, especially when it is dark. You may open your eyes now."

Hope opened her eyes. After an initial panic because of the darkness in the room, Hope turned her head from side to side. *I can see! Wow. I have high-definition vision! Oh my God, I can see!*

"What time is it?" Dr. Dello Russo asked.

Hope focused on a round clock at least ten feet away. "Nine-twelve and twenty-six seconds." *Yes!*

"Please read the letters on the ninth line of the chart directly in front of you," Dr. Dello Russo said.

Hope focused and read line *ten* instead, and she read the letters flawlessly. "I don't take directions very well," Hope said.

"Look to your left," Dr. Dello Russo said. "Do you recognize this man?"

Hope turned her head to look at Dylan. *Time to play a little trick.* "No. Who's he?"

Dylan's eyes widened as he stood. "Come on, Hope, stop playing."

"Who are you?" Hope asked, shrinking away from him.

Dylan reached for her hand, but Hope pulled it out of his reach.

"Hope, it's me, Dylan. Don't you recognize me?"

Hope widened her eyes. "Dylan?" She looked at Dr. Dello Russo and the nurse. "*He's* Dylan?"

They nodded.

Hope turned slowly back to Dylan. "Dylan, is it really you?"

"Yes," Dylan whispered.

"Oh my God, Dylan!" Hope yelled.

"What?" Dylan said, his eyes as big as planets.

"You're white!" Hope shouted.

Dr. Dello Russo and the nurse laughed loudly.

Dylan did not.

NOVEMBER 19

*Only 35 more shopping days
until Christmas . . .*

Chapter 20

As soon as Hope walked into Thrifty the next day after five days' absence, she realized that she didn't need to come. Kiki, wearing a rainbow-colored smock, was already cranking out copies in the back.

"You should be home resting from your surgery," Kiki said, rushing to the counter. "You did not need to come in."

"Habit," Hope said.

"We must break you of this bad habit," Kiki said. "How did it go?"

"I can see," Hope said. "Perfectly."

Kiki posed. "Do I look even more beautiful?"

Hope laughed. "I can certainly see more of you."

"And this is a good thing." Kiki tightened the smock around her. "You like?"

"Sure beats mine," Hope said.

"Really," Kiki said, "you do not need to be here. You should be in your bed."

"It's okay," Hope said. "I will take off tomorrow."

"You rest and work the register today," Kiki said. "I have got the hang of these machines."

Hope cut her eyes to the office door. "What about . . ."

Kiki shook her head. "I have banished him to the self-serve machine." She smiled. "I do not wish to be mean, but you look so much sexier without your glasses."

"Thank you," Hope said. "I feel sexier."

"And you look . . . fuller," Kiki said. "Your face. It is not as severe."

"I have been eating very well," Hope said.

Hope walked around the counter and saw more than two dozen bags with "Odd Ducks" written on the work orders. *Dylan must have been sending these to the mainframe all week.* "Kiki, did you do all these?"

"Of course I did," Kiki said. "You taught me well. Miss Aniya's cards are still doing well, and those sexy cards are so daring, and yet they are selling very well. I have a suggestion. You must come up with something for two women, yes? Do not leave us out at Valentine's Day."

Hope blinked, still feeling some grit in her left eye. She put some lubricating drops into her eyes. "It's sort of out of my experience, Kiki."

"No, it is not," Kiki said. "Do you and Dylan kiss?"

"Yes."

"Do you and Dylan taste each other?"

A lot. "Yes."

"Do you and Dylan cuddle, spoon, and massage?"

"Of course."

Kiki shrugged. "I have just described being with a woman." She took a card from a bag. "This one says, 'I will stick with you through thick and thin.' Simply draw two women on your cover and that will work. Even 'Get on the stick' can work, yes? We do occasionally stick it to each other. If you do this, you will open up a whole new market."

It wouldn't be too hard to do. "Noelle" is going to be on all teams, now. "I will. That's a great idea."

"What can I say?" Kiki said. "I still know best. It is good to have you back." Kiki started another order. "Justin has not been out of the office for more than a few minutes since you've been gone." She stepped back and winked. "If you were to disappear, he would never know. Go down early to Dylan. Take him lunch for a change."

"I would," Hope said, "but they're on a field trip to the Prospect Park Zoo today. We are going out to celebrate my new eyes this evening. I'd love to leave early so I can go prepare."

"You go," Kiki said.

Hope nodded. "You seem to have everything under control. How many of Aniya's cards have you done?"

"Over four *thousand*," Kiki said. "There was not enough room out here so I had to put them in the storeroom. When will Dylan be by to pay for them and get them out of here?"

Hope smiled. *He won't. I will.* Hope pulled the Odd Duck credit card from her purse, and then she hesitated. *Twelve orders out here, over three thousand dollars' worth in the storeroom. Does this little card have enough on it to pay for it all? It should. Let's find out.* She handed the card to Kiki. "You ring it up. I can't watch." *Be good to us, PayPal. Please.*

Kiki totaled the damage, her eyes popping. "A little over four thousand dollars."

Hope nodded. "Swipe it."

The charge went through without a hitch.

"How much are you two making?" Kiki asked.

We're up to at least fifteen thousand dollars each, but I can't share that with Kiki. "A lot." *I need to get these cards home to my place.* "Kiki, I'm getting a cab now and taking all these orders off your hands."

"A good idea," Kiki said. "I will help you."

A cab ride and three trips up her steps later, Hope was in her kitchen, surrounded by bags of cards. *Maybe Dylan will want to package and stuff them here since they're already here and there are too many of them for him to carry home.* She sighed. *He'll just get another cab. I don't have the addresses, I don't have the labels, I don't have the envelopes, I don't have a printer . . . Still, he'll have to come up to my apartment on a Thursday night, and I will do everything in my power to keep him here all night.*

So I will have to dress sexy for this celebration dinner.

She opened her wardrobe and frowned.

I only have one somewhat sexy dress, what my mother would call "dan dan." This is what I must wear.

She held up a Marc Jacobs silk navy-striped lamé dress with a ballerina neckline and self-tie belt. *I think I wore it once to some forgettable business banquet or other with Odell. I spent far too much for it, but I was stupid then.* She modeled in front of the skinny mirror on the washroom door. *I might fill it.* She put it on.

Okay. Nothing spectacular. It makes my arms and legs look so much longer than they are.

She slipped on her only pair of black flats. *Odell was so upset my flats didn't match my dress. The horror! Damn, Odell, you spend a thousand dollars on a single piece of clothing. There isn't much money left for matching shoes, you know?* Hope frowned. *I don't want to wear this dress. It reminds me too much of Oh-Hell, and it probably even smells like him. Dylan might appreciate it, but . . .*

She stood sideways in front of the mirror and stuck out a hip, pursing her lips. *I could be a model. I'm bony enough, and I certainly have the legs. Not having a pinkie toenail might be a problem—*

Her phone rang.

Whack purred.

Hope stepped into the kitchen. "So now the phone makes you purr." She picked up the receiver. "Hello?"

"*There* you are," Dylan said. "I called Thrifty, and Kiki said you had left, but she wouldn't tell me why. Are you all right?"

"I'm fine," Hope said. *I love that he is concerned for me.* "I decided to come home early." *With over five thousand greeting cards to lure you into spending a Thursday night with me.* "How's the zoo?"

"Fun but cold," Dylan said. "Wish you could be here."

"So do I," Hope said. "Have you heard anything about Aniya?"

"I called and talked to her mother this morning," Dylan said. "She's doing great. She's happy you can see now."

"What did you tell her?" Hope asked.

"Just that you had to be blind to go out with a man like me," Dylan said.

"You're funny," Hope said. "How is tonight going to work? I'm obviously not at work. Where are we eating? And what should I wear?"

"I will be by your apartment at six-thirty sharp," Dylan said. "We're eating Italian, and that's all I'm going to say. Dress any way you like."

"What are you wearing?" Hope asked.

"Tan chinos and a blue oxford," Dylan said. "I have to dress up for outings like this."

I can't possibly wear this dress now.

"Gotta go," he said. "Ramón needs to use the little boy's room. See you soon."

"Bye."

Hope hung up.

Whack purred.

"You knew it was Dylan, didn't you?" Hope said to Whack.

Whack rubbed against her legs, and then Whack stood on her back legs, claws extended, and latched onto the hem of the dress.

"What are you doing?" Hope asked. She scooped Whack from the floor. "You want this dress?"

Whack purred.

Hope blinked. "You purred for me."

Whack batted a paw at the ballerina neckline.

"You obviously don't like this dress, do you?" Hope asked.

Whack purred.

"Maybe you even *hate* this dress," Hope said. She laughed. "It's yours." She set Whack on the floor and slipped out of the dress, tossing it onto the bed.

Whack circled Hope once more, then bounded across the floor to the bed, leaping onto the dress—and shredding the living lamé out of it.

I wish I had a camera! This is too much! She sat next to Whack on the bed, petting her from head to tail, as Whack reduced a thousand wasted dollars of a party dress to shreds.

"Good girl," she whispered.

Whack purred . . . and continued to shred.

Hope waited outside her apartment building wearing her brown coat over her tightest jeans, a white wool sweater, and her flats. After a cab dropped Dylan off, they walked by red, green, gold, and silver Christmas lights shining like crosses to Hope's eyes to Cambridge Place and Locanda Vini & Olii, an old pharmacy converted to an intimate, quiet Italian restaurant.

"Why'd you meet me outside?" Dylan asked as they sat.

Well, there's this shredded dress all over the apartment, and, oh, there are over five thousand greeting cards hiding up there, too. "I was hungry."

"I hear this is a good place to satisfy all your hungers," Dylan said.

Not all of them.

Dylan bought a bottle of Barolo "Case Nere," rated *due bicchieri* by *Gambero Rosso.*

Their waiter told them that *"due bicchieri"* meant "two glasses."

Hope had two glasses of wine by the time they finished their antipasti of marinated mixed olives, cured fish, shrimp, and sardines.

I am already buzzing, Hope thought. *That was only the first course. I should slow down, but this wine is warming every square centimeter of me.*

Lamb prosciutto with pear rosemary marmalade preceded ricotta and thyme ravioli. Cheeses and caramelized onion marmalade followed grilled Piedmontese beef and roasted potatoes.

Hope held out her glass at the end of the meal, and only a trickle splashed into the bottom of her glass.

"We killed it," Dylan whispered.

I killed it. Dylan only had two glasses.

"Are you all right to walk?" he whispered.

Hope looked at her legs. *I see them just fine. I only sort of feel them.* "It's only a short walk to my apartment."

"But the night is young," Dylan said. He smiled and held her hand. "I'm not working tomorrow, are you?"

I like this man. He falls into my evil clutches so easily. "I hadn't intended to."

"We could get a cab and go somewhere," he said.

Anywhere with you, as long as we end up in my bed. She sipped the last drops of her wine. "Let's go."

They only held hands after getting in the cab, but Hope didn't mind. *My breath is a mixture of fish, garlic, and wine. I wouldn't kiss me either.* She was overjoyed to be out at night in Brooklyn on a Thursday night with nothing but time and a good man on her hands.

"Where to?" the driver asked.

"The two thousand block of Pacific Street, Crown Heights," Dylan said.

Hope exhaled. "We're going to your place?"

Dylan nodded. "I have finally repaired all the holes in my walls. I know I should have had you over before, but remodeling takes time."

Hope's flats danced. "It's about time." She remembered the cards. "Oh, but I already took the cards Kiki ran to my place. Over five thousand of them."

Dylan tapped the driver's shoulder. "Change of plan. Corner of Washington and Eastern Parkway, then Pacific Street."

The driver nodded.

"Five thousand?" Dylan asked as they started moving.

"Four thousand of them were Aniya's," Hope said.

"We need to hire her as another Odd Duck," Dylan said. "That child has made over twelve grand already."

While Hope buzzed dreamily in the cab, Dylan retrieved the cards from her apartment in one trip, piling them into the cab's trunk.

Ten minutes later, they walked up four flights of stairs to Dylan's floor, Dylan again carrying all the bags of cards.

"It looks as if we've been shopping," Hope said, leaning on Dylan's shoulder.

Dylan stopped Hope at the top of the stairs. "Which apartment is mine?"

Hope saw four doors, but only one had a wreath, a large round wreath with a velvety red bow. She pointed. "That has to be your apartment. Is that a real wreath?"

Dylan nodded. "Nothing but the real thing for me."

"I can smell it from here," Hope said, pulling him toward the door.

Dylan set down the bags and took out his keys. "I have to warn you before you go in. What you are about to see might blind you."

"Never again," Hope said. "Open the door, Mr. Healy."

When Dylan opened the door, a winter wonderland lit up in front of Hope's eyes.

I have died and gone to Christmas land, Hope thought, stepping inside. *Santa himself might live here!*

Tiny white Christmas lights blinked and raced across walls and the ceiling and wrapped around pillars illuminating rooms on either side of her, each room overflowing with Christmas. Santa, Frosty the Snowman, and Rudolph perched on a fireplace mantel to her left, three huge red stockings dangling below and topped with glittering names: "Dylan," "Hope," and "Whack."

"My cat gets a stocking?" Hope asked.

"Why not?" Dylan said. "Cats need toys, too." He brought in all the bags and shut the door.

Unlit candles and snow globes filled shelves and window ledges, a nativity scene sat on a coffee table in front of a long white couch brimming with red-and-green-striped pillows, and sleighs and holiday tins filled with candy called out to Hope from the top of a bookcase filled with angel and shepherd figurines.

Her eyes focused on an eight-foot-tall Christmas tree blazing bright red and green lights next to the fireplace. Ornaments of every shape and size, most obviously handmade by children, covered the tree. "Is that real?"

"Can't you smell it?" Dylan asked.

Hope sniffed the air. *Oh, that is pine, and I am feeling fine.*

"Look behind you," Dylan said.

Hope turned and saw all of their greeting cards taped to the back of the door in the shape of a Christmas tree, "Siamese Snow Angels" at the top. "So *that's* what you do with greeting cards."

Dylan ushered Hope to the couch, seating her at one end. "May I get you something to drink? I have some more of that fine Brooklyn tap water."

"Wine, if you have any," Hope said. *This is amazing. He even has all his windows decorated with lights and that spray snow stuff.*

Dylan left and returned with a single glass of red wine. "It won't be as nice as the Barolo." He handed her the glass.

Hope took a sip. *I can barely taste it.* "You aren't having any?"

"That's all I have," Dylan said.

She leaned back into the couch, kicking off her flats. "Are you trying to get me drunk?"

"Maybe." Dylan winked. "So, what do you think?"

Hope smiled. "Unexpected, but then not really." She motioned to the tree with her glass. "Where'd you get your tree?"

"At the Christmas tree stand on Flatbush and Seventh last week," Dylan said. "You've probably walked right by it and didn't see it."

Because I don't go looking for Christmas.

Hope let her eyes continue to roam, drifting over the skinny kitchen with breakfast bar and two stools to the right, the shiny dark hardwood floors everywhere she looked, and the lights blinking in the windows.

She pointed to the short hallway. "What's down there?"

"Take a look," Dylan said. He held out his hand.

Hope finished her wine, set her glass near the manger of the nativity scene, and took his hand, and they walked the hallway to a door on the right. She opened it and saw an office, with computers, scanners, and printers in abundance, a rolling chair in front of a drafting table looking out at a literal wall of ceiling-high windows, and boxes of envelopes in all sizes sitting neatly stacked in the corners.

She closed the door. "No work tonight," she whispered. "Nice and neat, though."

"It isn't always that neat," Dylan said.

She turned her attention to the room across the hall. "Your bedroom?"

Dylan nodded.

Let's see where we will be jooking later. She stood in the doorway. *Neat, tidy, TV on a dresser, large mirror facing a queen-size bed.* Hope blushed. *He has a mirror facing his bed. I will be seeing us in action later. Two more doors. The one on the left has to be the washroom. What's behind the other door? Let us go see.*

She drifted to the door on the right, opening it. *Ah. Clothes. Flannel. More hoodies to steal. A collection of paint-spattered pants. Sweaters. Sweatshirts. A dozen pairs of shoes and boots. These clothes will look so nice on me.*

Hope walked past Dylan and back to the couch, falling into a pile of pillows. "But Dylan, you have no presents under your tree."

I mean, really, it's not even Thanksgiving. Who even has a tree up by now?

Dylan stood next to the fireplace. "I haven't wrapped any yet."

Wrapped any? What? "Why are you way over there?"

"We have some business to attend to, Miss Hope," he said. He took out a memo pad and readied a pen. "What do you want for Christmas?"

"A beach house," she said.

"Allow me to rephrase my question," Dylan said. "What do you want for Christmas that I can afford?"

Hope sighed. "Sit with me." *While my buzz is still buzzing.*

"I'm trying to make a list here, Hope," Dylan said. "You'll only distract me."

"Isn't that the point?" Hope asked.

"Humor me," Dylan said. "What do you want for Christmas?"

"Well," she said, "you've already given me my sight."

"Dr. Dello Russo did that," Dylan said.

Hope lay back, the pillows so soft on her back. "You paid for it. You convinced me to do it. Sorry I gave you such a hard time."

"It's good that you've finally seen the light," he said.

"Ha." *He's so cute, but he's so far away.* "I see lots of lights. How can you sleep?"

"I turn them off at night, Hope." He tapped the pen on the pad. "So, what can I get you to wrap up and put under that tree?"

"A new toque."

"All right." Dylan wrote it down. "Color?"

"Colorful," Hope said.

Dylan nodded. "Colorful. What else?"

I am lying on his comfortable couch in a very fetching pose, and we're talking about toques. "What else? I don't know, a new . . . pair of . . . socks."

Dylan wrote it down. "What kind?"

Hope sat up slowly. "I'm joking with you, Dylan. I don't need socks, and if I did, I'd go out and get them like most normal people. I won't wait for someone to give them to me at Christmas. I can't let my feet freeze off, can I?"

"No." He made a mark on his pad. "What else can I get you?"

You can get your sexy derriere over here. "I don't want anything. Really. I have everything I need right here in Christmas land with you. We are definitely celebrating Christmas here. Does your fireplace work?"

Dylan tapped his pen on the memo pad. "No. It's just for show. Okay, the space under the tree will contain one toque on Christmas morning. I have to put more than just one toque there, Hope. How about an entire new wardrobe for your new body? I could get you clothes from head to toe."

"Not necessary," Hope said. "Don't I look good in whatever I wear?"

"Yes, of course."

Hope rested her head on a pillow. "And I will be stealing your clothes. I love flannel, by the way. I will be borrowing a shirt later."

"Could I maybe get you a sweater at least?" Dylan asked.

Hope rubbed at her face. *My face is so hot. That wine was nice.* "I don't need a sweater, Dylan. If I need a sweater, I'll go out and buy one."

Dylan closed his memo pad. "Don't you want me to get you anything for Christmas?"

Hope shrugged. "Not really. I just want you." *Now, as a matter of fact. Right here on this Christmas couch. I'll prop up some of these cushions under my hips . . .*

Dylan wiped at his lips. "Are you serious about that?"

Hope nodded. "Yep."

He shook his head. "But it's Christmas, Hope."

"It's not even Thanksgiving, Dylan," Hope said.

"I like to get started early," Dylan said. "I don't want to rush in December."

"I've never met anyone who had *this*," Hope said, throwing out her hands and looking around, "much less all *this* before Thanksgiving." *Am I making sense? Why are my hands flopping around so much? Maybe it's because I had an Italian dinner.*

Dylan sighed. "I wanted to impress you."

Hope shrugged. "You did."

"I was hoping to get a better idea of what you wanted tonight, Hope," Dylan said. "I know it's not so much the presents themselves that make Christmas. It's the act of giving. I am the giver, and you are the give-ee."

"You give me your love every day," Hope said. *I said the L-word. The wine has loosened my tongue. Now if I could only feel my tongue.* "I don't need anything more."

"You don't?"

Hope shook her head.

"Even if any present I give you would be the manifestation of my love?"

Ooh, that was a big word. "Manifestation." He should not be using five-syllable words when I'm buzzing.

"I want you to unwrap my love on Christmas morning, Hope," Dylan said. "Tell me what I can wrap up for you."

That was an easy question. Hope smiled. "Yourself."

Dylan sighed. "Why do you have to be so difficult?"

Hope squinted. *Is he getting angry? I've never seen him get angry. It's just amazing what you can see in this apartment.* "Dylan, I just want to snuggle."

"I want to snuggle, too, Hope," Dylan said, "but I need to do this first. I love giving gifts. I haven't had anyone to give Christmas gifts to in years, and now that I do, the receiver of my gifts doesn't want to get any."

I do think he's pissed. Red face. Vein in forehead. Restless hands. Darting eyes. I'll just let him talk it out of his system.

"I want to give you whatever you want. I want to give you gifts that *I* think you want, you know, surprises, unexpected gifts you open Christmas morning and say 'Dylan, you shouldn't have!' and 'Dylan, how did you know I needed that?' and 'Dylan, I've been wanting this!' "

Now he's getting louder. "But it's not necessary."

Dylan moved in front of the tree. "It is to me. I want to buy you a whole bunch of little stocking stuffers, wrap every one of them, and fill your stocking to the very top."

Hope chuckled. "You wrap the stocking stuffers? Why?"

"I know it's a shameless waste of wrapping paper, but I do it because I like to," Dylan said. "I want to shower you with gifts. Please let me."

"But I have everything that I need," Hope said.

"Look, Hope," Dylan said, "Christmas isn't strictly about need. It's more about wants, wishes, and desires. I want to help you fulfill your wants, wishes, and desires."

Hope shrugged. "You do that every day. Let's just keep Christmas small, okay? It's only the two of us, right?" *Now he's staring at me with those brown brown eyes of his. What did I say?*

"You want to keep Christmas . . . small?"

Oh, that's what I said. "Yes. I want to keep Christmas small. Aren't we both saving for bigger dreams? What about Art for Kids' Sake? If we start wasting our money now—"

"Wasting?" Dylan interrupted.

Oops. I should have said "spending" or "using."

"Are you saying that giving gifts on Christmas Day is a waste?" Dylan asked.

Hope wiggled her hands in front of her. "I meant spending, not wasting."

He scratched his head. "You made yourself perfectly clear."

Now he's looking away from me. Hey, Dylan, I'm over here. "I just think we shouldn't spend a lot at Christmas so we can reach our ultimate goals."

Dylan slumped into the other end of the couch, rubbing his hands together. "Okay, I understand about saving money for a dream, I really do. I've been putting away money for five years. You've been saving longer for your beach house. I get it. Money is obviously more important to you than properly celebrating Christmas."

Now I'm *getting a little angry.* "It's not about the money, Dylan."

"So what's it about, Hope?" Dylan asked.

"I'm saying that we should *save* our Christmas money so that our *ultimate* dreams and goals will occur *sooner.* If we spend *less* today, we'll have *more* for tomorrow." *I am making so much sense tonight.* "I *refuse* to go overboard." *Here's another great idea.* "I know what we can do. We'll have a budget."

"What?" Dylan jumped off the couch. "A budget?"

Hope blinked. *I am definitely getting his Irish up. It's actually kind of sexy. He's making me hot.* "Yes, a budget. We'll both agree to spend no more than a certain amount on each other, say, five hundred dollars."

"You want to put a *budget* on Christmas."

Hope wrinkled up her lips. *The word "budget" is not an evil word.* "Yes. If more people did it, there would be fewer broke people at the end of January." *Oh, now his face is another shade of red. It almost matches the lights on the tree.*

"But that's like putting a budget on my heart, Hope!" Dylan shouted.

Oh, that was deep. Loud but deep. It sounds like a future greeting card.

"What if what I want to give you adds up to *more* than five hundred dollars?" Dylan asked.

Hope sighed. *I have to explain everything.* "Then *you'd* be over budget, and then *I'd* feel obligated to go over budget, and then we'd go back and forth like that until we spent too much money on each other."

Dylan sat next to her, taking her hands.

Now we're talking. Rub on my legs, too, Mr. Healy.

"I wouldn't care, Hope," Dylan said. "It's the giving that matters to me, not the monetary amount. I can't believe you want to put limits on what I want to give you. That defeats the purpose of giving. I give because I can. I give because I want to. I give because you mean so much to me, and now you say I can only spend five hundred bucks on you. I will not budget *anything* where you are concerned. I probably won't even add up the receipts until after Christmas."

That's not a good idea. That's a good way to overdraw your bank account. Oh, his hands are so hot! "You actually *like* to go Christmas shopping?"

"I *love* to go Christmas shopping," Dylan said.

There's that word again. Ooh, he is so passionate! Put your hot hand on my heart!

"I *love* finding that perfect gift," Dylan said, squeezing her hands harder. "I *love* the hunt, the hassle, and even the crowds, because it tells me that here are bunches of giving people around me all trying to be giving at the same time."

"That's not what *I* see," Hope said, shifting in the pillows. "I see an unruly *mob* buying things they *don't* need with money they *don't* have."

"Wow." Dylan's chin dropped to his chest. "I don't know what to say." He looked up. "Christmas is simple to me, Hope. You find out *what* someone desires, you *find* those desires, and you *give* those desires, and you never count the cost." He released her hands and slid off the couch, walking to the mantel. "You never count the cost," he seemed to say to a snow globe. He turned. "Are you going to give me a wish list?"

I don't know if I like his attitude. He sets my hands on fire and then he leaves. "Do *you* have a list?"

Dylan dug into his pocket and took out a folded piece of paper. "Here." He handed it to her.

Hope unfolded the paper and read the list:

- 2 small portable easels, tempera paint (all colors), and paintbrushes (assorted) for Brownsville Rec
- sketch pads and good mechanical pencils for Odd Ducks
- ergonomically correct desk chair (for my aching back!)
- new hoodie to replace the one Hope stole and won't give back!
- assorted restaurant menus from Manhattan, the Bronx, Staten Island, Queens
- a new hairbrush that's kinder to my scalp
- another dinner at The Islands
- painter's pants for art at Kinderstuff
- waterproof winter gloves
- a used car with character
- peace on earth!

I should have expected him to have a list already. I shouldn't have called his bluff. Dylan lives for Christmas. It's a simple list, but most of what he wants involves other people—including me.

Hope shook the paper in her hands. "But I could get you all this tomorrow or sometime this week. Well, maybe not the car. *You* could buy yourself all of these things well before Christmas if you wanted to."

"That's not the point, Hope." He reopened the memo pad. "I've been making a list of what I think you might want since my first visit to your apartment."

That was a month ago! We weren't even boyfriend and girlfriend then!

"I was hoping you'd give me some ideas tonight that might match my list—you know, *confirm* what I would get you. You've already helped me out." He ran the pen through a few items brusquely. "You've simplified things. Thanks."

Now he uses sarcasm? "Dylan, I do not *need* anything. How many times do I have to tell you that?"

"I said *want*, not need," he said. "Look at my list. I can get by without all those things, but I'd be overjoyed to have them as gifts." He took a deep breath. "We'll try again." He looked at his memo pad. "How about a new kitchen set? I saw one the other day that I could refinish. Nice walnut. Four sturdy chairs that won't wobble."

Hope folded up his wish list and set it next to the nativity scene. "Why? We eat mostly in the bed."

Dylan made another line in his memo pad. "How about a new TV, something bigger, a widescreen. So we can enjoy our movies more."

"We hardly ever finish a movie," Hope said, "and I hardly watch TV when you're not there."

Dylan scratched it out. "A car."

He thought I'd want a car? "I don't want to drive around Brooklyn," Hope said. "I'm safer on my feet." *As long as elves driving Santa Clauses in bicycle rickshaws watch where they're going.*

Dylan drew a large X this time. "New boots."

Now he makes big *marks on his little paper.* "My boots are just fine," Hope said louder. "They're still waterproof."

Dylan sighed and didn't move his pen. "An umbrella."

"Mine still works," Hope said even louder. *If I tilt it and lean to the right.*

Dylan flipped a page and smiled. "Food! I can buy you food! Canadian food. BeeMaid Honey and Caramilk bars. Mackintosh's Toffee. I can order it online and have it shipped directly to your door."

Hope blinked. *That wouldn't be too bad.*

"Or one of those massager shower heads."

That might be nice, but ...

"A Kindle gift certificate," Dylan continued. "Gift certificates to Tim Hortons. A trip to Edmonton to visit your family. A trip to the Bahamas or to Trinidad."

He would give me all that? None of those are practical gifts, but I cannot tell him that. "Dylan, they're all wonderful gifts, really. But isn't it enough that we have each other?"

Dylan tore out several pages, balled them up, and rolled them under the tree.

Now he crumples my gift list in front of me? This is not acceptable!

"Hope, all I wanted was to put something under the tree that says 'From Dylan to Hope.' That's all. Instead, there's only some crumpled paper." He flipped a page. "I want you to tell me, *now*, what you would like me to put under that tree. I will purchase whatever it is. I will wrap the *hell* out of it. I will *not* tell you what it is. You will open it Christmas morning, and maybe it will make you happy. Tell me what you want."

He is too serious about all this! "I told you what I wanted. I want a beach house."

Dylan closed the memo pad and shoved it into his back pocket. "On a night when we should be celebrating, *you* decide to be difficult."

I will not sit for this any longer. Hope stood. *I almost stood too fast. Whoo. It must be the altitude.* "I am being difficult? *You* are being difficult. You want Christmas to be your way or *no* way! Did it occur to you that maybe I *don't* want to celebrate Christmas the way you do?"

"Why do you hate Christmas so much?" Dylan asked.

Now he is being crazy. "Hate" is such a strong word. "I don't ... hate Christmas."

"You do, Hope," Dylan said. "You make fun of Christmas traditions."

"What traditions?"

He pulled out his memo pad, slapping it into his palm. "This.

This is a tradition. Making wish lists." He waved his arms. "This. Everything you see around you. This is a tradition. Shopping is a tradition. Giving without counting the cost is a tradition. Searching for the perfect gift is a tradition." He turned away. "And you hate all of it."

"I don't . . . I don't hate it all," Hope said, sinking back into the couch. *Do I?* "Maybe I don't see the point of these traditions. I didn't have many of these traditions growing up, okay?"

"I'm . . ." He sighed. "You won't let me be the giving man that I am. That's the bottom line. I want to say, 'Bah humbug to you.' I want to say, 'I'm getting you gifts whether you like it or not,' but if I did, I would be ruining the *spirit* of Christmas. Hope Warren, if you ask for it and I can afford it, I will get it for you because I love you."

The apartment was silent.

Hope held her breath.

"I love you, Hope," Dylan said, his eyes shining. "I have loved you and wanted to tell you. It's why I started your list. Let me *prove* my love to you, even if it's in a bunch of small little packages under the tree."

He loves me. He made a list of his love, but now it is balled up under the tree. How important was that list then? "You've already proven your love to me in every way. You are the most loving man I've ever known." She rose from the couch and took a step toward him. "You don't need to show off one day of the year to prove anything to me."

Dylan backed away. "Show off? You think giving is showing off? Okay, I'll agree with you. I do. I *need* to show off. I didn't always have the opportunity to give anyone anything when I was a kid. I do now. I had some *rotten* Christmases, nine of them in detention with no family around me at all."

"And I had eight in a row completely alone," Hope said. *I am sobering up. Some celebration this has been.* "I was *completely* alone for the last *eight* Christmases."

"*That* was your *choice.*" Dylan nodded his head rapidly. "You *chose* to be alone. I spent the last five Christmas mornings at the Salvation Army Man Shelter."

Hope shook her head. "Oh, you are such a saint. Saint Dylan, the faithful and loyal."

Dylan took a step toward her. "I went to that shelter because I didn't want to be alone on Christmas morning! You obviously *like* to be alone!"

Hope stepped back, leaning against the couch. *No, I don't. I hate being alone.*

"It doesn't take a saint to serve breakfast and hand out blankets and hot chocolate," Dylan said. "Anyone can do it, and it's the *right* thing to do on Christmas Day. It is *right* for me to give you gifts, and no matter how much you hate Christmas, I will *give* you those gifts whether you want me to or not!" He shoved his hands into his pockets and stared at the floor. "I'm . . . I'm going into the office to sort out the cards and start packaging them. I'm sure we've had some more orders to print out, too. If you want me to, I'll . . . I'll call you a cab. I'm sure I've ruined the evening." Dylan collected the bags at the door and disappeared down the dark hall.

In a moment Hope heard "Joy to the World" echoing loudly down the hallway, and then the song faded to a whisper when a door closed.

He turned on the music, and then he shut the door to keep me from hearing it. I kind of like that song, yet here I sit in silence, smelling pine and looking at the lights on the ceiling with tears in my eyes.

She looked across the room at the Christmas tree. *He cut the branches off the bottom of his tree almost two feet high. Deddy used to say, "De more branches at de bottom yuh don' see, de more presents yuh will see." Deddy always left lots of space under our tree.*

She wandered over to the tree and smiled at the decorations. *Look at all those ornaments made by Dylan's little artists. Pictures. Faces. So cute. They're Dylan's adopted family, and they share Christmas with him right here in this room. No wonder he puts his tree up so early. He wants to be less alone. There's so much love here.*

She stooped and gathered the balled-up paper, smoothing out each page. *He kept a list all this time, adding to it, thinking of me. I don't really need any of these things, but he thought of me when he made this list.*

I have ruined this evening.
Maybe I should go.
She heard a door open and then footsteps.
Dylan returned to the room with a piece of paper and handed it to Hope. "These are the orders for tomorrow. I'll e-mail any more that come in. I'm taking tomorrow off."
No toast, no jam, no kiss?
"I want to do some shopping," he said. "Are those my lists?"
Hope nodded.
He put out his hand.
Hope handed them to him.
"I'll stop by Thrifty by six to pick up the orders," Dylan said. "And if you're working, I could walk you home if you still want me to."
Yet he still wants to walk me home. Hope's eyes filled with tears. "There is something I really want for Christmas."
"What?" Dylan whispered.
"And it's not a beach house, I promise you." She watched a tear fall to the floor. "I want you." She saw Dylan's hand reach out to her, and she took it.
"You already have me, Hope," he said. "You don't have to ask for what you already have."
She rubbed her thumb on his palm. "But I get the feeling I am losing you. Right now."
"You haven't lost me, Hope," Dylan said softly. "I'm sorry if I said anything to make you think that. I've been only thinking of what *I* wanted to do this Christmas. I didn't consider your feelings. I'm sorry. I understand everything you said, and you made a lot of sense. When I've been able to, I've always overdone it at Christmas, and I'm sure that's why Art for Kids' Sake doesn't exist yet. You were blind for a day so you could see. In order to give Brooklyn a day care for the arts, I have to be *less* giving. You're right, and when I'm shopping tomorrow, I'll . . . I'll count the receipts as I go. Five hundred, right?"
Oh, my heart is breaking. I've changed him into me! "No."
"Higher? Lower?"
"No!" Hope shouted, staring into his eyes. "Whatever you want to spend, Dylan Healy, you *spend*. I just don't know why you want

to spend so much . . . on me." She stumbled into his arms. "I don't deserve you, Dylan. I *don't* deserve you."

Dylan held her while she sobbed. "You don't really think that."

She wiped her eyes, then clung to his shoulders. "I do. I didn't think I deserved *anybody*, and then you came along. *You* are my dream. *You* are my wish for Christmas. You are the *only* item on my wish list. I want *you* for Christmas. I want you wrapped up under my tree. I want to open you up on Christmas morning, and I want to hold you for the rest of my life." She looked down.

"And I'll never need batteries," Dylan said.

Hope's eyes darted up to his. She saw his smile, and then she laughed. "How do you *do* that?"

"Do what?"

"You say the most *random* things at the right moment to make me smile and forget to be sad."

He kissed a tear on her cheek. "I like to make you smile. You know we have to make that card. 'True love never needs batteries.'" He rested his forehead on hers. "And that's what we have here, Hope. True love. I love you."

Yes, this is right, this is so right. "I love you, too. I love you so much."

They held each other, dancing together for the second time in their lives, as the faint whisper of "Hark, the Herald Angels Sing" glided down the hallway while lights raced all around them.

Hope felt heat rising from her toes to her nose. "Dylan?"

"Yes?"

"I want you so badly. Right now. Do you want me?"

Dylan swept Hope off her feet and carried her to his bed, falling with her onto the bedspread. Hope felt his heat, felt his hair, felt his hands, felt her clothes vanishing, felt his tongue moving lower and lower, and for a moment, she felt something tingle.

The tingle turned into a spark.

She began to pant softly while his hands caressed her breasts and his tongue circled her navel before disappearing and landing on her thighs, his fingers probing, touching, entering.

There it is . . . there it is . . .

As his tongue began tasting her, the spark intensified and threatened to ignite.

Oh God, please, oh God, please . . .

She closed her eyes as fire spread from Dylan's lips to her stomach and raged out of control, her hips quivering uncontrollably, her lips buzzing.

Oh, yes, I'm baaaaaaack! I have missed this, oh yes!

"Dylan, come back up here!" she cried.

He scrambled to cradle her face. "Are you okay?"

"Oh yes." She laughed. "*Orgasme.*"

"*Orgasme?*"

"Huge, hot, I'm still on fire, and I'm so *juteux* I'm a freaking waterfall." She pushed him onto his back. "I want to go for a ride." She guided him into her and eased down. *We're doing it, yes, we're sliding and gliding and riding and I am gloriously slick and sweaty and I'm in ah-go-nee without being in agony!* "Dylan, we're *jooking!*"

Dylan nodded.

Hope froze. She distinctly heard "Silent Night."

"Can you change the song?" Hope asked. "I don't think tonight is going to be very silent."

"No," Dylan said. He dipped out from under her.

"Hurry!" she cried. A moment later, she heard "This Christmas" blasting from the office. *At least it has a little bass to it.*

Dylan slid under her. "Sorry. It's all I've got."

"No, it isn't," she said, resuming her ride. *Yes! He still fits!* "You like my sexy derriere, don't you?"

Dylan nodded.

"Do a little grinding," Hope whispered.

Dylan sat up and grabbed Hope's sexy derriere, forcefully moving her entire body forward and backward.

My grindsman! My champion!

"Quick," Hope said. "Get behind me and play my *djembe.*"

Dylan pulled her off the bed and moved her to the mirror. "I want to see your face," he whispered, "and I want you to see mine."

As Dylan gave her sexy derriere the pumping it had been missing, Hope watched her man move, watched him tap-tap her *djembe*, watched him pull her hair, watched him thrust until the entire dresser shook.

Hope Warren was in intense ah-go-nee as Dylan Healy jingled all of her bells.

During one furious moment, their eyes locked.

Dylan smiled.

Hope laughed.

With one final thrust, they closed their eyes . . . and they sang.

In the afterglow hours later, after they had christened every room and even the closet, after they had labeled, stuffed, and packed hundreds of envelopes and boxes, they lay facing each other under the covers with only their fingers touching as a single candle flickered on the dresser.

"I wish I could fit your beach house under the tree," Dylan said.

"I wish I could fit Art for Kids' Sake under there, too," Hope said. "Maybe this time next year."

Dylan nodded. "So what have we decided to do this year? I think we should stay small."

"You sure?" Hope asked.

"Yeah," Dylan said. "Little things can still mean a lot. They're easier to wrap, and we'll need less wrapping paper. They're also easier to fit under the tree, and I'd like to give you a bunch of small presents. The more presents you have under the tree, the longer Christmas lasts."

"I like that idea," Hope said. "Are you still taking tomorrow off to go shopping?"

"Yes," Dylan said, "and I want you to come with me."

"Thank you."

"We'll make a day of it."

Hope sighed and looked at Dylan's Mickey Mouse watch, which somehow had stayed on his wrist despite their manic lovemaking. "This is just a minor critique, Dylan, but it's really strange to see Mickey Mouse smiling and waving at me while I'm having *orgasmes*. I've never asked, but why do you wear a Mickey Mouse watch? Is it for the children?"

He wiggled his wrist until he could see the watch face. "Despite its humble appearance, this watch is important to me. It's the only present my mother ever gave me for Christmas that wasn't socks,

T-shirts, underwear, or a toy I'd break in a day. To tell the truth, I don't know if she bought it or stole it, but she gave it to me, and it let me know she really cared about me for at least the time it took her to get it. She was thinking only about me. This watch is Dylan's and no one else's. Only Dylan will wear this watch. So it's more than a watch. It's a memory of the best Christmas I had as a kid. I may even wear it if it stops working."

I can't get him a new watch now. I can get him a watchband that will keep that watch from ever falling off, a watchband that will protect his memories. "Won't it be strange to be shopping for each other when we're *with* each other?"

"So we'll just go window-shopping."

That's so romantic. Window-shopping is romance while you walk.

"And we'll get out of the city, too," Dylan said.

Get out of Brooklyn? When's the last time I was out of Brooklyn? "How?"

"I've already rented a car from an auto repair shop a few blocks down from here," Dylan said. "The car won't be pretty, but it will get us there."

"You already rented it. When?"

"When I left you alone a few hours ago, I made the call." He pulled her to him. "I promise not to leave you alone again. I was so lonely."

"Me, too." She kissed his chin. "Where will we go?"

"Wherever we end up."

"*Nous irons où que la route nous prenne,*" Hope said. "We will go wherever the road takes us. Normally I'd say that's too random, but I'm beginning to like random." She grazed his chest with her nails, sliding them lower and lower. "Let's go for another ride. I like you in my back seat. I like watching you in that big rearview mirror."

Dylan smiled. "I like that, too."

"And the only directions you can give me are 'Go' and 'Faster.' " She crawled out of the bed and rested her elbows on the dresser. "Ready to start my engine?"

He joined her.

Hope felt his readiness immediately. "Damn, Mr. Healy," Hope whispered. "I really like your stick shift. Feel free to use overdrive. Full . . . speed . . . ahead . . ."

I hope we don't break this nice dresser!

Oh, yes! I am all better now!

Love has found me, and I intend to ride this ecstasy long into the night.

NOVEMBER 20

Only 34 more shopping days
until Christmas . . .

Chapter 21

Hope and Dylan enjoyed precisely two hours and four minutes of sleep before Dylan's red, white, and green Christmas alarm clock, its hands moving around Santa's face, played "Here Comes Santa Claus" at six AM.

Hope was not amused.

"Why so *air*-lee?" Hope whined from the bed as she looked into the big mirror over the dresser to watch Dylan shave in the washroom.

"It's not early," Dylan said, "and I don't always say '*air*-lee,' *cailín*. I only say '*air*-lee' when I'm flirting." He ran water over his razor, tapping it against the sink. "I actually got to sleep in an hour later than usual. Come get in the shower. I'll join you in a minute."

"I need to brush my teeth first," Hope said, "and what am I going to wear?"

"There's a new toothbrush in your stocking already," he said, "and I thought you were going to steal my clothes."

Hope laughed. "You already got me a toothbrush."

He nodded, checking his chin in the washroom mirror. "I even wrapped it."

Hope grabbed the first hoodie hanging in Dylan's closet, wiggled into it, and wandered to the fireplace. She peeked into Dylan's stocking. *Empty. I am supposed to fill this. Why'd he buy such big stockings? I have lots of shopping to do.* She peeked into Whack's stocking and saw an unwrapped stuffed mouse, a ball, and some cat treats. *Funny. He buys presents for a cat that isn't his.* She opened her stocking and found the wrapped toothbrush and the unmistakable shape of DreadHead Dread Butta among an assortment of small packages. *That has to be gum, and that's a candy bar of some kind, and that looks like lip balm, and that looks . . . I have no idea what that is. Nail clippers?* She unwrapped her toothbrush and went into the washroom to find Dylan already in the shower.

"I was hoping you would wash me," she said, furiously brushing her teeth. *I still taste the garlic and the wine from last night.*

Dylan stepped out, the shower still running, a towel already wrapped around his waist. "I sometimes run out of hot water here, so hurry it up." He kissed her cheek. "Good morning. I'm going to get breakfast started."

Hope pouted. "What are we having?"

"A surprise," Dylan said, and he left the washroom.

Hope stood in the shower and let the water roll off her body. She had no strength to do anything more than hold the bar of soap in the stream and hope it did the trick. She eventually used a washcloth to soap herself, borrowing Dylan's razor to shave her legs, sneaking it back into his medicine cabinet when she was through.

After wrapping herself in several towels, she went to Dylan's closet, put on a blue-and-black flannel shirt over some seriously overwashed light-blue jeans that nearly fit her hips, and then the hoodie she had borrowed before. She raided his top drawer for a pair of long tube socks before realizing she had no boots, only flats.

I will just have to be a fashion misfit today. What is that heavenly smell?

She followed the aroma to the kitchen, where Dylan stood over his skinny stove fixing pancakes.

"A pair of your pants almost fits me," Hope said, turning side to side. "Isn't that amazing?"

"Turn around," he said.

Hope turned.

"I still have those?" he said. "I haven't worn them in fifteen years."

She sat on a stool in front of a raised counter. "This counter reminds me of work. You don't have much of a kitchen."

"I don't need much," he said, turning and setting a plate before her.

Hope looked down at a three-pancake "snowman" complete with chocolate chip eyes and mouth. "Where's his hat?"

He slid a bottle of maple syrup to her. "The wind took it. Eat up. It's going to be a long day."

Hope doused her pancakes in syrup and started eating. "Where are we really going?"

Dylan shrugged and brought over his plate, circling his pancakes with syrup. "Away," he said, and he wolfed down the snowman's head whole.

"You just ate Frosty's head in one bite," Hope said.

"Well, you're nibbling on his derriere," Dylan said.

Such a pleasant thought. "Are we in a hurry or something? This is a day off for me. I want to enjoy it."

"I want to get out of Brooklyn as soon as possible," he said. "I really don't want to get caught up in any traffic."

"Do you think we'll be doing a lot of walking?" Hope asked. "I only have my flats."

Dylan stuck the last hunk of pancake into his mouth. "Just a sec." He left the kitchen, returning a minute later with a present. "I hope you like them."

Hope stared at the box. "You already bought me boots?"

Dylan frowned. "How did you know?"

Hope bit her lip. "It was on the list you made."

Dylan nodded. "Open them, put them on, and let's go."

She tore through the penguins on the wrapping paper and read the end of the box. *"Kenetrek Women's Hiker, size 7.0."* "These are my boots—I mean, *these* are the boots I wear. How did you know?"

"I snoop," Dylan said. "Whenever you were sleeping at your apartment and I couldn't, I wrote down sizes and brands. Try them on."

She opened the shoebox and tried on the right boot. "Perfect." As she put on the left, she said, "Does this mean that you're giving me *everything* on the list you made?"

"No," Dylan said. He smiled. "Not all of it."

"You've already been shopping for me," she said.

"Right."

Hope stood. "When did you buy these?"

314 • *J. J. Murray*

"About a month ago," he said. "The Internet has been kind. Are we ready?"

What else is already here? "So if I wanted to wear a sweater today . . ."

Dylan looked away. "We need to be leaving."

He already got it for me, and it's somewhere in this apartment, and if he snooped around my wardrobe, he bought me . . . "It's a Pollen Sweater, isn't it?"

Dylan shook his head. "I shouldn't have read you that list. Would you like to wear it today, Hope? Or can you wait until Christmas morning?"

Is he kidding? "What color did you get me?"

"Merlot," he said.

Ooh. Sexy. I love that shade of red. "What size? My other Pollen Sweater hung on me."

Dylan sighed and looked at the ceiling. "I'll get it for you. Wait here. I don't want you to see what else I got you."

I'm getting another Pollen Sweater! They are so nice. They're all wool, but it's itch-less wool you can actually wash in a washing machine.

Dylan returned with a plastic bag. "I hadn't wrapped it yet." He tossed it to her. "Merry November Christmas, Hope."

Hope checked the label. *He got me a small! Oh, this is going to hug my body so tightly!* "Excuse me while I change."

She ran to Dylan's bedroom, threw off his hoodie, ripped open the plastic, and put on the sweater. *All right. Look at that curvy thing. She looks* good *in merlot. I almost don't want to cover this* femme sexy *with a hoodie. Maybe he got me a new coat. Was a coat on his list? I know he has seen my brown coat countless times. Oh my goodness! He may have gotten me another alpaca coat!* "Oh, Dylan . . ."

Twenty minutes later, Hope left Dylan's apartment grinning and wearing her new Hilary Radley alpaca coat, the putty color providing a nice contrast to her merlot sweater, dark-blue Hudson Beth Baby jeans, and dark-brown Kenetrek hiking boots. It might only have taken five minutes for her to change, but Hope had to thank the man responsible for her new outfit by kissing him repeatedly on his face, neck, and lips for the next fifteen minutes.

She fiercely held Dylan's hand as they walked toward a tan 1987 Cadillac Deville parked at Saratoga Auto Repair.

"That is a beautiful car," Dylan said. "Isn't it?"

Okay, it's a Cadillac, and it's huge. It has wire wheels and mostly leather seats. The antenna is a pretzel, and most of the chrome is gone from the bumpers. The headliner is sagging a bit in the back seat, and bird droppings cover the roof like a Jackson Pollock painting.

It's there.

It's in front of me.

It is car-like.

It scares me.

"It's nice," Hope said. "Sure looks roomy."

Dylan started it up, a bilious blue cloud filling the air. "Look," he said. "The speedometer only goes up to eighty-five."

They soon found out why.

The Cadillac stuttered east on Atlantic Avenue and south on Pennsylvania Avenue. It lurched through light traffic east on the Belt Parkway. By the time the car warmed up on the Southern State Parkway east of North Merrick, it shook at any speed over forty, and it finally hit on seven of eight cylinders just past Belmont Lake.

"At least it has good brakes," Dylan said.

Please stop hitting them! You're slowing its momentum! Hope cracked her window several inches. *I hope we get there soon so I can stop breathing fumes.* "Are we almost there?"

"Almost," Dylan said. "Another half hour or so." He winked.

"You know where we're going, don't you?' Hope asked.

Dylan nodded. "I'm not as random as I appear to be." He rubbed her shoulder. "I've never asked this, but how's your family?"

"I've known you all this time, and this is the first time you've asked about them," Hope said. "Why do you want to know about my family now?"

"Truthfully, I was afraid," he said, staring straight ahead. "The last *Island* family I dealt with was a mess."

"Not all *Island* families are the same, Dylan," Hope said.

"Let's just say that Bermuda will not be on any vacation itinerary in my future," Dylan said. "Marie's mother was meddling, obstinate, headstrong, and always had to be right—and that was the *first* time I ever spoke to her. She only got worse. Marie's deddy wasn't her real deddy, so he rarely said a word to me. He made lots of faces, though."

"How meddling was her mother?" Hope asked.

Dylan sighed. "That *vooman* made arguments out of nothing, out of t'in air, and she tried to win every one of them no matter how petty. 'Nice day,' I'd say, and she'd say, 'What be nice 'bout it wit' all de pain in de *varld*?' She was so coldhearted she could hold a grudge against herself. That *vooman* was so evil she could have an argument with herself and then not speak to *herself* for days."

Hope laughed. "She sounds . . . colorful."

He shook his head rapidly. "When you told me you had Island roots, Hope, I decided to not ask about your family."

"Don't worry about my family," Hope said. "We're not close, and I doubt my mudda would ever argue with you. My mudda was the quiet one. My fadda, not so quiet. He would argue with and fatigue, or ridicule, you. They left me to myself as a child, but only if I continued to worship them. When I stopped bowing down to them, *that's* when they tried to control me, but by that time I was already in the States."

"When's the last time you spoke to them?" Dylan asked.

Hope turned up the heater, and she felt no difference in the temperature. "Just before I became a citizen, so about five years ago. My fadda tried to talk me out of it. 'Doh ge' meh vex, nuh,' he said. 'You walkin' with yuh two han' swingin'.' He didn't think I was making any money, which was true. He called me *bubu*, *dotish*, *bazodee*, and *vi-ki-vie*. He basically called me stupid and confused, and he said I was a freshwater Yankee full of backchat."

Dylan seemed to shudder. "You were sounding like Marie's mother just then."

"I can still turn on that Island accent," Hope said. "Obviously, I didn't listen to him." She sighed. "All that happened right around Christmas, too. Lots of things end during the holidays, don't they?"

"They can also begin," Dylan said.

"True," Hope said.

"Have you tried contacting them recently?" Dylan asked.

"No, and I really haven't missed them," Hope said. "I was never really a part of my family because I was born so long after my sister. I get a Christmas card occasionally from her. It's usually a picture of her and her husband posing in front of some new painting in their condo. Very depressing. What about your family?"

Dylan turned onto the Robert Moses Causeway. "My remaining family is a brother named Conor doing life at Sing Sing. He went into prison on a theft charge, and he killed a man inside within a month over a cigarette." He sighed. "A single cigarette."

"Do you ever visit him?" Hope asked.

"Once, but that was a horror show," Dylan said. "I'll never go back. Conor and I have nothing in common. He's about fifteen years older than I am. I do send him Christmas cards every year— and two cartons of cigarettes, just in case he's feeling murderous."

Dylan exited and got onto Montauk Highway. "Look out your window. Can you see the water?"

Hope saw snatches of green and blue. "Is that the ocean?"

"That's the Great South Bay," Dylan said, "and we are going to take a water taxi from Bay Shore to a little town called Kismet on Fire Island." He checked his watch. "And if this beast can go a little faster, we'll catch the next water taxi over."

"We're going to the beach?" Hope asked. "In November?" *That's random.*

"I want to see the ocean," Dylan said, smiling. "Don't you? No crowds. We may be the only visitors. We can explore the scenic town of Kismet in a couple hours." He winked. "It is our fate to go to Kismet."

They barely caught a ride on the *Fire Island Flyer* from the terminal off Maple Avenue in Bay Shore, and despite the chill and Dylan snapping pictures of her hair dancing in the breeze, the ten-minute, occasionally choppy boat ride exhilarated Hope as they sped over shallow green and gray water toward the black-and-white Fire Island Lighthouse. The boat deposited them onto the pier in Kismet, and they walked down Pine Street and took Bay Walk to the Kismet Market.

It's so quiet, Hope thought. *Where are the people? One grocery store, one pizzeria. We're not in Brooklyn anymore.*

"Quiet town," Dylan whispered.

"I'll say," Hope whispered. "Why are we whispering?"

"We don't want to wake anyone," Dylan whispered.

"Why are most of the buildings light blue?" Hope asked.

"Must be a Kismet thing," Dylan said.

They checked out the menu posted on the wall outside the Kismet Inn in front of the marina, where a dozen or so boats were tied up and rocking in front of a small beach.

"Can we eat here for lunch?" Hope asked. "I want to try this seafood salad."

"Sure," Dylan said. "It's either here, the pizza place, or Surf's Out." He pointed to a nearby restaurant. "Those are our choices."

Hope sniffed the air. "I love the smell of the ocean."

"Let's go see it," Dylan said.

They walked down Oak Street past the Kismet Fire Department.

"Not many windows to shop here, Mr. Healy," Hope said.

"Maybe we'll just look in some windows," Dylan said. "Beach houses have lots of windows. We could do some beach house walk-bys, and if nothing else, we can kick up some sand."

Hope took his arm. "I don't care what we do." *As long as I'm with you.*

"They say this town is more laid back than Ocean Beach," Dylan said. "Ocean Beach requires you to get a permit and a license just to ride a bicycle, and you have to keep your yard perfect or face fines. All cats in Ocean Beach have to wear bells. You can get a fine or even jail time for being too loud or cursing in Ocean Beach. Not here."

"Damn," Hope said. She looked around. "And I wasn't arrested. I like this place."

No one in my apartment building, however, can ever visit Ocean Beach. They'd be locked up getting off the boat.

"I don't see anyone," Hope said, looking at small but well-tended houses with picture-postcard yards.

"I guess this is what you get in the off-season," Dylan said. "We have the whole town to ourselves."

"I like it this way," Hope said. "It's peaceful, and you don't have to look six ways before crossing the street."

The beach appeared at the end of Oak Street with fences holding back the dunes.

Hope smiled and took a deep breath. "Just look at that view. Nothing but ocean, waves, and sand."

"I hear there's a nude beach somewhere around here," Dylan said.

"Really."

"I'm sure they won't be active today," Dylan said. "A tad bit chilly. Come on."

They walked the beach as far as the Fire Island Lighthouse, and on the way back, they looked at houses.

Hope was disappointed. "Most of these houses are too far from the beach," she said. "You might be able to see the ocean from your roof. The closest ones to the water, though, have to cost millions, and they're no bigger than your apartment."

They passed what looked like a shack high up on a dune.

"And that one has to have a nice view of the ocean," Hope said, "but look how tiny it is. It could be a storage building with windows. So lonely. It probably doesn't even have plumbing. It's no more than a cottage, and it has to be smaller than my apartment."

"It's for sale," Dylan said.

"That sign is ancient," Hope said. "I'm sure there's a reason no one has bought it."

"Maybe Hurricane Irene swamped it," Dylan said.

"Probably," Hope said. "I'll bet the land is worth a hundred times the value of the house."

They turned up Bay Walk and saw a monster of a beach house.

Wow, Hope thought. *Now* that's *what I'm talking about!* "I want it."

"That's awesome," Dylan said. He took out his camera. "Go to the mailbox and act like you're getting your mail."

Hope flipped open the mailbox, posing and pointing at the house.

Dylan took the picture. "What do you think? Four, five bedrooms?"

"At least." She smiled. *That's more of a mansion than a beach house. Easily three or more million dollars.* "And that's a chimney. It has a fireplace. And look at that deck. It goes all the way around."

"I'm guessing you like that one the best so far," Dylan said.

Hope nodded. "Buy it for me."

"How much do you think it would be?" Dylan asked.

"Let's say it's three million, give or take," Hope said. "A twenty percent down payment would be about six hundred thousand dollars. Your mortgage payment would run at least fourteen thousand a month." *Who on earth has that kind of money? If Dylan and I pooled our Odd Ducks money, we could only afford to live there for sixty days.*

"I wonder if they rent it out in the off-season," Dylan said. "That might be fun."

"But I want it all the time," Hope said, pouting. "Win the lottery for me."

Dylan pulled her up Bay Walk. "I'd rather win your heart than the lottery."

"You already have," Hope said. "But could you at least try?"

Dylan laughed. "Let's go eat."

Hope and Dylan were the only couple eating at the Kismet Inn, and in less than half an hour, they had eaten baked clams, seafood salads, and bowls of Manhattan clam chowder.

"You ever have the feeling you're being watched?" Dylan whispered.

Hope nodded. "Must be your long hair. They think you're someone famous."

"Ha," Dylan said. "It's you they think is famous, not me. That outfit really looks great on you."

"So glad I opened it early."

Dylan sat back and sipped some lemonade. "What do you require in your beach house?"

"What I just saw," Hope said.

"The last one?"

Hope nodded.

"It was nice, but that wasn't my question," Dylan said. "What would be the bare minimum you'd need for your beach house?"

"Well, I have to be able to see the ocean from any room in the house," Hope said. "That's a given."

"Bedrooms?"

"At least one, two would be better," Hope said. "It would have to have at least one washroom with a tub big enough for the two of us, a nice big kitchen, a great room with a fireplace, oh, and a deck to eat out on." She pushed back from the table. "That's all."

"And how much would you expect to pay for such a house?" Dylan asked.

"More than I will ever make in my lifetime," Hope said. "It's just a dream, Dylan. Really."

"It's fun to dream," Dylan said.

"Yes." She smiled. "Every day is a dream with you."

After a return trip to Bay Shore in the water taxi, and after a few tense minutes waiting for the Cadillac to start, Hope pushed up the center armrest and fell asleep while leaning on Dylan's arm, and she had another dream . . .

Hey, this is a nice house. I wonder whose it is. Oh yeah. It's mine. This is a dream house. I own every house in my dreams. Nice view. That water is so blue, and it's warm. Let's walk outside on that deck. Is that a tropical island offshore? Palm trees everywhere. I must be thinking of the Caribbean. I shouldn't have eaten the clam chowder. People on the beach are waving to me. Who are they? "Come on down," they say. I leave the deck and notice I'm naked. Well, so are they. A nude beach is in my front yard. As soon as my foot hits the hot sand, a cat looking very much like Whack crosses my path. "Hey, Whack!" A moment later, a policeman runs up to me and arrests me for indecent exposure and for not belling my cat, and then he adds an assault charge when I curse him out in French . . .

She awoke with a start. "We there yet?" she asked lazily.

"Almost," Dylan said. "You were dreaming. Was it a good dream?"

The house was nice. "I was arrested for indecent exposure at a nude beach."

Dylan laughed. "Are all your dreams so ironic?"

"Sometimes," Hope said. "It was Whack's fault. She wasn't wearing a bell." She looked out the window and sat up straighter. "Isn't this Washington Avenue?"

Dylan nodded. "Almost there."

"We're not going back to Christmas land?"

"Nope," Dylan said. "We have to christen your apartment."

Hope stretched. "Yes, we do."

Once inside her apartment, Dylan handed Hope a sprig of mistletoe.

Another prop!

"Wherever you put it," he said, "I have to kiss it."

I like this holiday game very much. "You've been carrying a piece of mistletoe with you all day," Hope said, backing away toward the bed, unzipping her jeans.

"Two, actually." He withdrew another sprig from his pocket, his pants dropping to the floor a second later. "I have one, too." He pulled her new sweater over her head.

"Ah. So all I do is ..." She touched her mistletoe to her stomach.

Dylan kissed her stomach while Hope removed his shirt.

Dylan stood and touched his ear with his sprig.

Hope kissed his ear while removing his underwear.

"What if I touch something you *could* kiss, but it would be better that you did ... more?" She waved the mistletoe in the air as Dylan unsnapped her bra and tore off her panties. "I mean, what if I wanted you to do more than kiss it?"

"Tap it twice," Dylan said, removing his underwear. "Tap it twice, and I'll do something nice."

She knelt on the bed. "I intend to tap things twice all weekend."

Dylan nodded. "Tap-tap," he whispered. "Tap-tap."

My djembe *rejoices!*

"Let's play some music ..."

NOVEMBER 25

*Only 29 more shopping days
until Christmas . . .*

Chapter 22

With Kiki's help at the DocuTech and the Baum, Hope had spent the three days before Thanksgiving in relative peace. Though Aniya's card was still breaking all Odd Ducks records, orders for their other Odd Ducks Christmas cards had dwindled to only ten or fewer a day. Hope felt some sadness but not much.

Sales of her new "Sister Love" cards were increasing daily.

When Kiki had seen the cover of the first "Sister Love" card, she had cried and given Hope a long hug. "Why, that is me and Angie on this card! Oh, and it says, 'I will stick with you forever' inside."

Aside from the stick figure bodies, the resemblance was obvious. "Kiki" was short with curly hair and a *banduu*, and "Angie" was tall with straight hair and too many teeth.

"You should do these in color, you know," Kiki said on Wednesday. "You must put a rainbow *banduu* on my character."

"That will increase our costs, Kiki," Hope said, watching the clock. *Ten more minutes, and I am off for four consecutive days of bliss. I hope Dylan has plenty of groceries because I intend to blockade his door with the Christmas tree. Oh, and unplug his TV. No football games for us. Just . . . games. I hope Dylan brings what's left of the mistletoe. What could tapping three times signify?*

Justin burst from his office looking more composed than usual, his purple shirt tucked in, and his tan khakis less wrinkled. "Mr. Yarmouth is making a surprise visit at six." He stood smiling, his arms behind his back. "That's in ten minutes."

"I don't mean to be picky," Hope said, "but if it's a surprise visit, how do you know when he's coming?"

Justin began to speak and stopped. "Um, I knew he was coming today, I got an e-mail memo, and since the workday is almost over, I'm, um, expecting him to surprise us any minute now."

"So it was not a surprise to you that he was coming," Kiki said.

"Um, right," Justin said.

"So where is this surprise?" Kiki looked at Hope.

Hope shrugged. "I guess the surprise is on us." She turned to Justin. "What is this surprise meeting that really isn't a surprise meeting going to be about?"

"All I know is that it concerns the future of the store," Justin said, "and it is mandatory that we all be here." Justin cut his eyes to Hope. "It may involve bonuses."

Is he kidding? Doh make joke, Justin, yuh makin' joke!

Since it was, however, the first mandatory meeting of any kind in Hope's ten years at Thrifty, she began to worry. *This meeting sounds ominous. Is Thrifty closing? We're doing all right. Maybe Mr. Yarmouth is retiring and has sold out or is selling part of his interest in the store. Or maybe, someone is getting fired.*

Someone wearing purple.

Someone tall, regal, and white-haired entered the store wearing a gray, worsted three-piece suit and black tie, his long black umbrella tapping the floor, dark eyes under bushy silver eyebrows scanning the store.

This someone was Mr. Cyril M. Yarmouth.

He is getting so old, Hope thought, *but he's definitely still spry.* "Good evening, Mr. Yarmouth."

Mr. Yarmouth nodded to Hope. "Miss Warren, so good to see you." He nodded at Kiki. "And you, Miss Clarke."

Mr. Yarmouth still has his English accent. I suppose it's charming. Okay, it is.

At six, Justin locked the front door and turned the sign the moment Dylan appeared at the door.

Hope held up one finger, and Dylan nodded, leaning against the parking meter on the sidewalk.

"Have we been busy today, Mr. Tuggle?" Mr. Yarmouth asked.

"Um, yes, sir," Justin said. "We've been, um, cranking 'em out all day."

"Good, good," Mr. Yarmouth said. He moved toward the counter, stared a moment at the ficus plant, and laid his umbrella on the counter.

"Would you like a chair, Mr. Yarmouth?" Kiki asked.

"Certainly," Mr. Yarmouth said.

Kiki rolled out Hope's swivel chair, and Mr. Yarmouth sat.

"Have you told Miss Warren of the changes, Mr. Tuggle?" Mr. Yarmouth asked.

Changes? What changes?

"Um, no," Justin said. "I was waiting for you to arrive." Justin turned to Hope. "Um, Miss Warren, you have to stay until closing from now on, or, um, you're fired."

"This is ridiculous!" Kiki shouted. "Hope practically runs this store!"

Wow. Yet for some reason, getting fired doesn't bother me a bit.

"Yes, Miss Clarke," Mr. Yarmouth said, "for the last ten years, Miss Warren has done a superlative job of keeping this store going. I know this well. And at no time, Miss Warren, have you asked for a raise or a promotion. You are a good, steady worker. And until this fall, you hadn't asked for any time off for a sick day or a holiday. When Hurricane Irene hit on Sunday, you were at work on Monday. I could always count on you."

"But not anymore," Justin said.

Why am I being so silent? I should be airing out all of Justin's foolishness.

Mr. Yarmouth poked out his chin. "I understand you are now working down the street from three to five o'clock every day teaching art to children and using some of your accumulated sick and vacation days." He folded his hands, his fingers long and manicured. "Is this correct?"

Hope nodded.

"Are you planning, Miss Warren, to make your teaching job there permanent?" Mr. Yarmouth asked. "Because if you are, I urge you to make a career change and work there all day. This way I can hire another worker who will be *here* all day. I cannot afford to have problems because you are not here through the end of the business day."

"What problems?" Hope asked.

"We are in danger of losing HSBC Bank because of your absences," Mr. Yarmouth said. "They were highly displeased with their annual Christmas cards this year."

What? "I didn't run any Christmas cards for HSBC."

"Um, yeah, Hope," Justin said. "They came in last week. You weren't here all day, and Kiki left early for some reason. The HSBC man brought them in and said he needed them immediately, so I ran them. I thought they looked fine, but they weren't."

"What was wrong with them?" Hope asked.

"The Christmas tree was blue, not green," Mr. Yarmouth said, "and the word 'Merry' was spelled M-R-E-R-Y. HSBC has already sent them out. Their employees now have them."

Hope stared at Justin. "Are you dyslexic *and* colorblind?"

"Um, yes," Justin said. "I mean, I'm colorblind, but I'm not dyslexic. I didn't, um, proofread anything."

"I still don't see how this is my fault," Hope said. "Mr. Yarmouth, you hired a colorblind person to work in a copy shop?"

"Traditionally, this shop has been a black-and-white operation," Mr. Yarmouth said. "I did not see any harm."

Hope went to the mainframe and tried to pull up the HSBC card. "It isn't here."

"Right," Justin said. "They gave me the original."

"Do you still have it?" Hope asked. "If you do, I can fix it."

"Um, I gave back the original," Justin said. "I know, I know, I was supposed to file it in case they needed more."

"So their copy *came* to you with a blue Christmas tree," Hope said.

"Um, no, that's just the thing," Justin said. "I'm sure it was green, but I must have hit the wrong buttons back there."

Hope shook her head as she moved back to the counter. "How is *any* of this my fault, Mr. Yarmouth?"

Mr. Yarmouth sighed. "If you had been here, Miss Warren, you would have caught HSBC's spelling error and not pressed the wrong button Justin must have pressed. Justin tells me you trained him on the machine, so it is ultimately your fault, not only for not being here but for not training Justin properly on the machine."

Doh ge' meh vex, nuh! "I'm *not* Justin's boss! It was *never* my job to train him at all. He should have come to this job knowing how to run *every* machine, and I told him if he *ever* had a problem to give me a call and I would have come here to solve it or at least talked him through it over the phone."

Mr. Yarmouth shook his head. "Justin is management. It is not his job to make copies. It is your job. In an attempt to keep HSBC's business, I did not charge them for the mistake, but I get the distinct impression that they will not be a client much longer. That will leave us with Brooklyn Borough and this Odd Ducks greeting card company as our only major clients." He adjusted his tie. "Do you have anything to say, Miss Warren?"

Hope looked at Dylan, who was smiling at everyone walking by the store. *I'm in a pickle, Dill Pickle. I may need your help soon.* "According to the employee handbook, Mr. Yarmouth, I am entitled to use my sick and vacation days at *any* time. The handbook is *very* clear on that. I was entitled to hours and days off, and I took them. It is not my fault that you have hired an incompetent for a manager."

"It is true you are entitled to these days," Mr. Yarmouth said. "But you will have no days to use if you are no longer employed here. If you wish to remain employed here, Miss Warren, you will cease and desist your artistic afternoons and, I'm told, your Saturdays off, too. Am I making myself clear?"

Justin's mistake could cost me my *job? Oh, I am sorely vexed now.* She walked around the counter, nodded at Mr. Yarmouth, and went to the door. She opened it and said, "Dylan, could you come in here a minute?"

Dylan walked in. "What's going on?" he whispered.

"I need you to hear this," Hope said. She shut and locked the door.

"He's not an employee here," Justin said. "He can't be at this meeting."

Hope went to the counter and hopped up on it. "I will make that clear in a moment." She looked at Mr. Yarmouth. "I am co-owner of Odd Ducks Greeting Cards." She nodded at Dylan. "My boyfriend, Dylan Healy, is my partner. We are your third biggest clients, and we are going to have explosive growth in the future. We have sold nearly fifty thousand greeting cards so far this year, every one of them printed here." *This is the scary part.* "I used my employee discount, which the employee manual says I can use at any and all times."

Mr. Yarmouth actually smiled. "And how much has your discount cost me, Miss Warren?"

"Roughly ten thousand dollars," Hope said, "but we've also paid you forty thousand dollars, money that could have been spent elsewhere."

Mr. Yarmouth nodded. "Please continue."

"She cost us ten grand!" Justin yelled. "You are so fired."

"Shush, Justin," Mr. Yarmouth said. "Continue, please, Miss Warren."

"You cannot legally dictate what I can and cannot do with my sick and vacation days, Mr. Yarmouth," Hope said, "since the procedures for using them are clearly stated in the employee handbook you wrote. I will be going to Kinderstuff daily to work with those children. I will also be taking every Saturday off that I can. If you still choose to fire me, go ahead, and in one night, you may have lost two of your three biggest clients."

"Remarkable," Mr. Yarmouth said. "You have created a business within a business." He smiled at Dylan. "And is it profitable, Mr. Healy?"

"Yes, sir," Dylan said. "We have a sixty percent profit margin on each card."

Mr. Yarmouth smiled at Hope. "*Very* impressive. Very impressive, indeed. How do you make your sales?"

"Through the Internet," Hope said. "People visit our site, choose and pay for their cards, and we print and mail them." She pointed behind her. "Every one of our cards is in the mainframe for instant printing."

Mr. Yarmouth leaned forward in the chair. "This means your cards are always here in electronic form. There would be nothing physical to store, and if you ever ran out ... Forgive me. Old habit." He smiled. "Would you consider selling your cards here? What if we provided you with a rack or a wall to display them?"

Hope looked at Dylan.

Dylan shrugged.

What's the catch? "You're talking about turning part of this store into a card shop," Hope said.

"Yes," Mr. Yarmouth said. "Those racks of dusty stationery have been here for years. They are from another time, another age. Your cards, however, would move off those racks if people could see them." He sat up straighter. "I would like to display your cards at this store, and all I ask in return is fifty cents per card sold here." He smiled. "I think that is a reasonable amount."

Hope shrugged at Dylan. "What do you think?"

"Well," Dylan said, "it will save us some trips to the post office." He squinted. "Not nearly as high volume, but word of mouth always works, and you can't beat free advertising. We could *add* fifty cents to the price of the card here to keep our margin."

I asked him what he thought, and he thinks out loud. That's my Dylan.

Dylan joined Hope at the counter. "What if we advertise 'Printed at Thrifty Digital Printing, Brooklyn, New York' on the back of every card and even added your website address. Would you accept thirty-five cents per card if we did that, Mr. Yarmouth?"

Mr. Yarmouth's eyebrows moved up and down. "Free advertising is always good, but I would also expect you to link your website to mine, Mr. Healy. For larger orders or for easy pickup in downtown Brooklyn, that sort of thing. And somewhere on your website it should say, 'Thrifty Digital Printing: Exclusive printer of Odd Ducks Greeting Cards.' "

I can't believe this is happening! I was about to be fired, and now I'm about to open a card shop inside *a copy shop.*

"That sounds fine, Mr. Yarmouth," Dylan said, "but I'd like to add another wrinkle."

What is this wrinkle? Let's get this in writing and go celebrate!

"Hope," Dylan said, "since all our cards are already here, couldn't we personalize any card for anyone who comes into the store? You know, the recipient's name on the cover, the sender's name inside, perhaps even an extra typed greeting. We could even scan in a family picture, say, one of a couple sitting in front of a painting."

I'm sure that sounded random to Mr. Yarmouth, but I understand. "Anything like that is possible, Mr. Yarmouth," Hope said. "We could even take the picture of the buyer right here at the store and scan it into the card immediately."

Mr. Yarmouth nodded vigorously. "Personalized greeting cards, made-to-order while you wait. We will put that sign in the window." He turned to Dylan. "I was just about to fire your girlfriend, Mr. Healy."

Dylan blinked.

"Since she may be the future of this store, I cannot do that, but . . ." He stood and collected his umbrella. "Miss Warren, you may have your Saturdays, but I *will* need you during the week at least until you are satisfied that Justin here is proficient on *every* machine."

I am going to miss those children so much! Justin is bubu, *dotish,* bay-it. "That may take a long time, Mr. Yarmouth. It would be simpler if . . ." Hope shot a glance at Kiki. "It would be simpler if you fired Justin and hired Kiki as manager. The two of us can run this store without him, and that will save you his salary and benefits and increase your profit margin considerably."

Mr. Yarmouth blinked. "That would not be a good thing."

True. It would be a great *thing.* "Why? He's costing you money! He's a waste of space. He hides in his office. On a day we were both sick, he closed the store for the day. He contributes nothing to the running of this store and *his* mistake, *not* mine, may have cost us the HSBC account."

Mr. Yarmouth sighed and shook his head at Justin. "I know all this, Miss Warren, but he is my sister's child. I would not be welcome at her house for the holidays if I fired him."

Hope looked from tall, regal Mr. Yarmouth to short, sloppy Justin. *There is absolutely no resemblance. At least I know now why Justin was hired.* "At least give Kiki a raise. She's been here six months and can run every machine in here as well as I can."

"Done," Mr. Yarmouth said. "How does a dollar an hour raise sound, Miss Clarke?"

Kiki nodded and smiled. "A dollar is fine. Thank you, Mr. Yarmouth."

Mr. Yarmouth leaned on his umbrella. "You will have your cards displayed soon?"

I am off until Monday. "I can have them up by noon on Monday," Hope said. "All kinds. Christmas, New Year's, Hanukkah, general, love, even Valentine's Day cards."

"I will have them displayed on Friday," Kiki said. "I will make, say, five of each."

"You don't mind, Kiki?" Hope asked.

"It will be fun," Kiki said. "We must have them up in time for the Black Friday sales."

"Splendid," Mr. Yarmouth said, beaming. "And make a special sign for the window. 'Odd Ducks: Personalized greeting cards made-to-order while you wait. A Thrifty Digital exclusive.' "

"Good idea, Uncle Cyril," Justin said.

"I know it is a good idea because it is *my* idea, Justin," Mr. Yarmouth growled. "If you were not my sister's son . . ." He smiled at Dylan. "I trust you will be able to write up our contract, Mr. Healy."

"I will," Dylan said.

Mr. Yarmouth nodded at Hope. "I look forward to a prosperous year, Miss Warren."

Mr. Yarmouth pivoted, strode to the door, unlocked it, and walked across Flatbush to the subway entrance.

Hope shook her head at Justin, put on her coat, gave Kiki a hug, and left the store.

"This is great!" Dylan said, pulling her close as they walked. "Our own front-right corner of a store."

"Yes," Hope said, "but I am going to miss those children so much, Dylan. You know I won't be able to get away even if Justin learns all the machines. He is an ee-dee-ot."

Dylan put his arm around her. "You can teach him."

"I don't want to teach him," Hope said. "I want to teach art."

"And it's about time I heard you say that," Dylan said.

Hope pouted. "I was just starting to feel the Christmas spirit, too."

"You?" Dylan said. "Hope Warren, the hater of all things Christmas?"

"Doh ge' meh vex, nuh," Hope said.

Dylan shuddered. "We will do everything we can to have you excited about Christmas from now on."

"It's a hopeless cause, Dylan," Hope said.

"It can't be hopeless," Dylan said. "We're about to enter the season of hope."

She grabbed his sexy derriere. "As long as you enter me often, Mr. Healy."

NOVEMBER 26
THANKSGIVING DAY

*Only 28 more shopping days
until Christmas . . .*

Chapter 23

Dylan instituted "Operation Advance Hope's Holiday Happiness," or "Operation AHHH," on Thanksgiving Day with a vintage Christmas movie festival at Hope's apartment.

At first, Hope didn't say "ahhh."

She said, "Eh?"

Hope "fatigued" *Santa Claus Conquers the Martians*, arguably the worst movie ever made. "The Martians watch TV! That makes them as *stupide* as us, and those ray guns are obviously children's toys, and why would anyone kidnap Santa? Who would pay the ransom? The elves? They don't get paid, do they? Dat movie be *lime*."

Hope didn't think, however, that *Babes in Toyland* starring Laurel and Hardy was "lime" or a waste of time. She loved Ollie Dee and Stannie Dum, the creepy cat playing a fiddle, the monkey dressed as a giant mouse, and the old-fashioned nightgowns the three little pigs wore. She even played a scene several times where a life-size toy soldier blinked. "See! He blinked! I *knew* he was alive."

Hope became a weepy *gyurl*, however, while watching *Miracle on 34th Street*, a Christmas classic that "proved" the existence of Santa Claus because of all the letters Santa received every year.

"I believe, I believe, it's silly, but I believe," Dylan said, echoing the little girl in the movie. "Did you ever send a letter to Santa?"

"No," Hope said. "I never believed that some fat white man in a red coat at the North Pole was ever going to visit me. Did you ever write to him?"

"Every year from when I was five until I was eleven," Dylan said.

"Did you ever get anything you asked for?" Hope asked.

"Nope, but I think it had something to do with our apartment," Dylan said. "It didn't have a chimney."

On Thanksgiving, Hope proved she could cook and turned her kitchen into a Bahamian restaurant. Because she could find no fresh conch at any of the fish markets within walking distance of her apartment, she prepared ham loaf topped with brown sugar, dried mustard, and crushed pineapples. They feasted on the loaf with pigeon peas and rice with bacon, black pepper, thyme, tomatoes, and onions. Dessert was almost a disaster. She had none of the ingredients for black cake like lime rind, prunes, currants, cherry brandy, Angostura bitters, or the most important ingredient, *rum*, and she didn't have the three to five days' soaking time to prepare it. Instead, she threw together a baked banana custard.

Dylan declared it "*délicieux.*"

Dylan, his taste buds sated, his belly full, soon became Hope's stuffing quite often throughout the rest of Thanksgiving Day.

Hope liked her stuffing. She even asked for seconds and thirds.

"We're going shopping tomorrow," Dylan said as they watched a rerun of Santa's arrival at the end of the Macy's Thanksgiving Day Parade.

"I don't want to," Hope said. "Not on Black Friday."

"Why?" Dylan asked. "It's the traditional start to the holiday shopping season."

"It's dangerous," Hope said. "It's like Boxing Day in Canada only sometimes with real boxing in line. I'm staying put."

"I've been out on Black Friday on many occasions, and I've never been punched," Dylan said. "Pushed and shoved out of the way a few times but never assaulted. It won't be that dangerous. Crowded, yes. Dangerous, no."

Hope jabbed Dylan's nose lightly with her fist. "I've seen all the videos online, Dylan. I watched a man punch out another shopper in a Best Buy, and that was down in Virginia, where people supposedly have manners. I've seen unruly mobs trampling people and breaking doors at Walmart. I saw a group of shoppers trying to kill each other over some gift certificates released from the ceiling of a mall in California. A crowd not far from here in Valley Stream once crushed a Walmart worker to *death*. A Toys for Tots volunteer—a volunteer!—was stabbed by a shoplifter in Georgia. And you say shopping on Black Friday is not dangerous?"

Dylan blocked Hope's next jab. "We will not be going to any of those stores, Hope. In fact, I think we'll only go to one. It's a small place, but it's big on gift ideas."

"Where is it?" Hope asked.

"On Atlantic Avenue in Boerum Hill," Dylan said. "It is a very cool store that features Brooklyn artists and artisans."

Hope rolled away from Dylan and snapped off the TV with the remote control. "I am not setting the alarm clock. I refuse to do any shopping before the sun rises."

Dylan moved in behind her. "We'll sleep in then," he whispered. "We'll have to, actually. I haven't sampled enough of your pumpkin pie."

"But I didn't make you any pumpkin pie."

Hope felt something abundant prodding her sexy derriere.

Oh, I guess I did.

It is kind of round and brown.

I am so very thankful this year . . .

The next morning at the reasonable hour of ten AM, Hope and Dylan, fortified by leftover baked banana custard and Prospect Perk Café triple-triples, strolled up Flatbush to Atlantic Avenue.

This was Hope's kind of store.

She saw art, photography, imaginative bags, handmade jewelry, avant-garde clothing, delicate paper products—and a rotating display of Odd Ducks cards.

"Look at this!" Hope cried, turning the display. "What are they doing here?"

"We're Brooklyn artists, too," Dylan said. "They order from us all the time."

Hope spun the display. "It seems more real to see them like this." She pointed to the price at the top of the display. "Four dollars?" she whispered.

"They have to make a profit somehow, don't they?" Dylan whispered.

Dylan showed Hope an assortment of delicate Katrina Lapenne braid rings, the metal woven together like thick thread.

Hope picked up a small 14K gold ring. *So light. So delicate.*

"Try it on," he said.

You don't have to ask me twice. She slipped the ring onto her left ring finger. "It's beautiful and so light I can barely feel it on my finger."

"Don't take it off," Dylan said. He took her hand and led her to the cashier.

"You're buying this for me?" Hope whispered.

"Another early Christmas gift," Dylan said. "I hope you don't mind."

Hope shook her head. "I don't."

Dylan paid for the ring and led her outside, turning and facing her. "Hope, it's not only an early Christmas gift. It's a promise ring. I promise to love you. *Mon coeur entier pour ma vie entière.* My whole heart for my whole life." He kissed her gently. "Did I say it right?"

Hope nodded. *"Je promets d'aimer vous et aucuns.* I promise to love you and no others," Hope said, embracing him. "This is so sweet." *It fits me perfectly now, and when I gain even more weight and my fingers start to swell, it will never come off.*

"In ancient times a promise ring was considered a placeholder," Dylan said.

"It was?" Hope smiled. "A placeholder for what?"

Instead of answering, Dylan whistled "It's Beginning to Look a lot Like Christmas."

He's beginning to look a lot like my future husband!

Hope's tiny gold ring sparkled in the sunlight as they returned to Flatbush, Dylan stopping them in front of the still empty building across from Thrifty.

"I'm feeling lucky," he said. He took out his cell phone and called the number on the "For Lease" sign.

He also squeezed Hope's hand tightly.

"Hello, yes, I'm calling about the property you have for lease on the corner of Flatbush and Nevins Street," Dylan said. "Yes, sir, I was hoping to get into that space by the end of January. What are you asking per month?"

Hope felt Dylan's hand loosen.

"I'll have to get back to you on that," Dylan said. "Thank you for your time." He closed and pocketed his phone. "The monthly lease just went *up*, not down. They now want twenty-*five* grand a month instead of twenty. It's madness." He sighed and looked once more through the bottom-floor window. "All that glorious space going to waste."

"Maybe this is a sign that Art for Kids' Sake doesn't belong here," Hope said.

"I was so sure," Dylan said. "You would have been just across the street, the bank is a few doors down, the subway is right here in front of us, Fulton Street is right there . . ." He shook his head and sighed. "This is the *perfect* location, and yet it's out of my reach." He smiled. "I dream too big sometimes, don't I?"

Hope kissed his cheek. "I like your dream. You just need to look at it more realistically." She stepped back, shielding her eyes and looking up. "That is a huge building, Dylan. Fifty students wouldn't be enough to fill it."

"I know," he said. "I have to start small somewhere first. That seems to be the theme this Christmas. Small presents."

"And big dreams," Hope added. "Start small and build up to your dreams." She looked again at her ring. *This tiny, beautiful ring is just the beginning of a lifelong dream.*

I hope.

"Let's go see what Kiki has done with our cards," Hope said.

"You want to go to work on a day off?" Dylan asked.

"It will be a first."

They crossed Flatbush and tried to enter Thrifty, but a crowd of women prevented them from getting farther than two steps into the store. Hope saw Kiki running back and forth from the DocuTech to the counter and Justin taking pictures with a digital camera in the back.

What's going on?

"Excuse me," Hope said to the woman in front of her.

"Wait your turn," the woman said, clutching several "Sister Love" cards.

"I work here," Hope said, shedding her coat and handing it to Dylan.

"It's about time *someone* did," the woman said. "I've been waiting in line for thirty minutes."

"Go to work," Dylan said. "I'll just . . . do a little selling."

After the woman and several others stepped aside, Hope made it to the counter.

"Put on your smock, Miss Hope," Kiki said, ringing up a huge stack of Odd Ducks Christmas cards. She pointed behind her. "You run that machine!"

"Say cheese!" Justin said, the flash blinding two women holding each other next to a wide sheet of green paper. "Hi, Hope. I hope you can keep up with me." He smiled at the couple. "It won't be but a few minutes, ladies. Kiki will call your names when your cards are ready."

"What exactly do you need me to do?" Hope asked Kiki.

"Keep running five of every one of your Christmas cards in that computer, and *twenty* of every 'Sister Love' card," Kiki said. "We keep running out of them. Look at all the sisters in love in here! They all want to make personalized picture cards for Christmas!"

Hope looked around. Except for Dylan and Justin, only women stared back at her, many of them holding hands.

Kiki is always right.

"Hope, pay attention!" Kiki said.

"Sorry," Hope said.

"Get Dylan to help you restock them." She waved at Dylan. "Priority one is doing the orders Justin is taking. We are falling behind." She lowered her voice. "Justin is actually a decent photographer. Who knew? He will give you a flash disk, and you will insert the picture on the inside of the cards before printing."

"But isn't it in black and white?" Hope whispered.

"They look *very* good in black and white," Kiki said. "We will have to see about color in the future, but not today. Now go! Go!"

Thrifty Digital Printing became the Odd Ducks Greeting Cards capital of the world for the next *six* hours, and the entire staff stayed well past six to accommodate the last groups of women wanting personalized photographic Christmas cards. While Dylan flirted, stocked displays, played the salesman, and brought in five dozen wings and sodas from Buffalo Boss, Kiki kept the register humming, Justin filled the store with flashes, and Hope worked the DocuTech and Baum relentlessly.

At 7:07 PM, Justin locked the store while Kiki totaled the day's receipts.

"This cannot be right," Kiki said.

Hope rested in her chair, Dylan sitting on the counter and munching on a hot wing. "If it's a big number you've never seen before," Hope said, "it's the right number."

"We sold over forty-three *hundred* cards today," Kiki said breathlessly. "This store made over sixteen *thousand* dollars in *one* day."

Which means Dylan and I made over eight thousand dollars in one day!

Kiki shook a finger at Hope. "You are coming in tomorrow, and I do not care if you and Dylan have plans to make triplets. Word is going out tonight all over Brooklyn, and sisters in love will be coming in to get personalized 'Sister Love' cards all day tomorrow, and if you are not here, I will track you down and drag you here whether you are wearing clothing or not."

"I don't know, Kiki," Hope said. "I was so looking forward to a quiet day of making triplets."

Dylan slid off the counter shaking his head. "We will be here, Kiki. I'm thinking . . . curry goat and jerk chicken from The Islands for lunch and Basil Pizza for dinner." He massaged Hope's shoulders, whispering, "We can't afford *not* to be here, can we?"

That feels so good. "Add oxtail soup and some of those basil fries, and I'm in." She smiled at Justin. *Another first.* "You missed your calling, Mr. Tuggle. You take a mean picture."

"Oh, I do some photography on the side," Justin said. "I'll bring my Nikon tomorrow."

Hope nodded. *So maybe Justin was in his office looking at pictures that he had taken.* "What kind of photography do you do?"

Justin blushed. "Um, portraits, um, couples, group shots, that sort of thing."

Um, porn.

"Is business good?" Dylan asked.

"It's steady," Justin said.

Porn is like that.

"Well," Dylan said, "perhaps you can do our portrait one day."

Okay, no. Oh, Kiki, please don't—

Kiki laughed. "I would *love* to see the picture Justin takes of you two. Do you also do two women, Justin?"

"Sure," Justin said, "and my rates are very reasonable."

"Am I missing something?" Dylan asked.

Hope sighed. "You want to tell him, Justin, or should I wait and tell him when I get home?"

"I don't mind telling him," Justin said. "I specialize in artistic nudes. If you would like to see some of my work, we could step into my office."

Hope snatched Dylan's hand. "That won't be necessary, Justin." *Dylan has already seen some of your work.* She grabbed her coat and pulled Dylan out of the store.

"What's all this about?" Dylan asked.

"Justin does artistic nudes bordering on porn," Hope said. "Remember that day in his office?"

"Oh. *Oh!*" He was quiet for a moment. "So does that mean those three were only *posing* for that picture?"

"I don't think so, Dylan," Hope said. "That looked like an action shot to me."

Dylan was silent for a few moments. "Want to do a few action shots with me? I have a camera. It's not a Nikon, but I know we would look smashing in front of the Christmas tree."

Hope smiled. "Do you want to trim my tree? I want to deck your halls, Mr. Healy."

"With boughs of holly."

Oh . . . yes.

After a night in front of and twice slightly *under* the tree at Dylan's apartment, and after reviewing the pictures they took in the mirror in Dylan's room, they returned to Thrifty early Saturday morning. A line of women had already formed all the way up Flatbush to Fulton Street, still others trickling across the street from the subway entrance.

"Are you ready?" Dylan asked.

"Maybe they're in line for breakfast at Golden Krust," Hope said.

"They're facing *this* way," Dylan said.

"I know," Hope said. *We may run out of paper!*

"You might want to open earlier than ten," Dylan said.

Hope nodded. "We need to open *now*." *Impatient women plus long line equals trouble.*

She approached the door and smiled at the first couple in line. "I work here."

"You the manager?" the shorter of the two asked. "There are two people already inside, and they refuse to open the door."

"We usually open at ten," Hope said, "but we'll try to open earlier today."

"So when are you opening?" the other woman asked. "We got places to go."

"Soon," Hope said. She peered inside and saw Kiki already at the DocuTech and Justin readying a fancy camera on a tripod to her right in front of a tall gray screen. She knocked on the door.

Justin came smiling to the door, and Hope noticed he was wearing nice jeans and a NYU sweatshirt. "Hi, Hope."

He remembered my name. "We need to open soon."

Justin stuck his head out the door. "Wow!" He nodded at the first women in line. "We will be opening in five minutes. Are you here for personalized picture cards?"

The women nodded.

"Pictures to the right, regular card orders to the left," Kiki said.

Justin opened the door, and Hope and Dylan stepped inside as a murmur swept through the crowd. "Dylan, good to see you."

Dylan pulled out one of his trusty memo pads. "I might be able to speed this up if I walked the line and took down some information. Then all they have to do is give you the page and sit for the picture."

"Great idea," Justin said.

Dylan kissed Hope on the cheek. "Ready to rock and roll?"

This is amazing! "Let's rock."

Ten hours later, they broke Friday's record by $6,000.

They almost ran out of thirty-two-pound paper.

To celebrate, Hope and Dylan took Justin and Kiki out for stuffed meat pizzas and dozens of garlic knots at Not Ray's Pizza on Fulton, and after Angie showed up, it turned out that Justin, of all people, was the life of the party.

"I graduated at the very *bottom* of my class at NYU," Justin said cheerily. "Not many people can say that. I was the *worst* in my class, and I didn't even get to walk with my class. I was on the six-year plan. The Yarmouth and Tuggle families then tried to make me employable for the next ten years in meaningless jobs within the Yarmouth conglomerate." He smiled. "It's not much of a conglomerate. My uncle owns a copy shop in Brooklyn, a trucking company out in Ronkonkoma, two pubs near Times Square, and a pub in Queens. I spent most of my time *not* working at the pubs." He patted his stomach. "I drank up a lot of the profits."

"How'd you get so good at photography?" Hope asked.

"I have no idea," Justin said. "Actually, I do. I was the one who took all the family portraits and pictures, mainly because they didn't want me in the picture. They didn't want any proof of a Tuggle who didn't become a success in America."

Hope watched Dylan interacting with the others, and she felt so proud. *Dylan is so giving, loving, and caring, and it doesn't matter who he's with, whether it's a child, a perverted photographer, a bisexual Jamaican in love with a Hungarian lesbian, or me. He gives everyone time, and it's not an act. Some people act as if they're listening. Dylan listens. He treats everyone he meets with respect, honesty, and humor when he could have easily ended up like his brother—or worse.*

The man I love is an American success story, one of those stories you never read about.

Once Dylan left after a long day of Sunday snuggling and two pints of Ben & Jerry's ice cream, Hope had a heart-to-heart with herself.

I have been so selfish. Dylan sacrificed his money for my eyes and he has spent so much on food and my gifts! He has always put my life and health in front of his. My beach house is not nearly as important to me anymore. One day, I'll get one, even if I can only rent it for a week. That's why they call them "dream vacations," right?

Everyone's dreams shouldn't stay out of reach forever.

I can put Dylan's dream in his grasp.

With the money we made this weekend, I will have close to eighty thousand dollars in my beach house fund.

Which is now officially Dylan's dream fund.

I don't deserve a dream house.

Dylan deserves his dream.

I'm going to make Dylan's dream come true.

Hope searched the Internet, Craigslist, and real estate websites for the rest of the night and vowed to inquire about the vacant office building across from Thrifty first thing in the morning.

Maybe I can talk those fools down, but even if I can't, I'll give them a piece of my mind.

The next morning, with Kiki running late, Hope called the number on the "For Lease" sign across from Thrifty.

"Hello, I am inquiring about leasing a vacant property fronting Flatbush at Nevins Street."

"That property is a hot one right now," an annoying man said.

He sounds like Mickey Mouse.

"I'm fielding *dozens* of calls *every* day for that space," he squeaked. "For twenty-seven five, you can move right in today."

What? "It was twenty-five thousand on Friday!" *This is absurd!* "Why have you upped the price?"

"The property is hot hot hot!"

You're not not not! Because you received some random phone calls, you upped the price. Did any of those people call you back? I doubt it!

"That building has been cold and vacant for two years," Hope said. "How is *raising* the lease price going to get it filled?"

"The economy is coming back," the man said. "All the signs point to it."

"Which ones?" Hope asked.

"Unemployment is dropping," the man said. "Didn't you see today's *Times*?"

"That employment data is a joke," Hope said. "There are thousands of seasonal workers out there who will be out of jobs as soon as stores do inventory in January. Employment always goes up during the holidays."

"Well, Black Friday was a godsend for Brooklyn businesses this year," the man said. "And the *Times* says so. The numbers this year are *off* the charts."

And you are out *of your mind.* "What are they basing those numbers on?"

"The *Times* said stores were especially crowded Friday."

That doesn't mean those crowds of shoppers bought a lot of stuff! "I've lived in Brooklyn for ten years. A vast majority of the businesses in Brooklyn are small, family operations. You think any of these families can afford that building for what you're asking?"

"They'll have to, won't they?" the man said. "What is your name? I'd like to send you some more information."

My name is Angry, and your name is Stupide. "What if Chase Manhattan Bank vacates the other half of that building? I've seen fewer and fewer employees going into and coming out of there these last few months. What is going to anchor that property if Chase leaves?"

"That building is *prime*, Miss . . . I didn't catch your name."

Because I didn't throw it. "Just two months ago it was at twenty thousand a month. Friday, it was at twenty-five. Today, it's at twenty-seven-five. Will it be at thirty thousand tomorrow?"

"It *might* be. The phone has been ringing off the hook."

Hope sighed. "Did it ever occur to you that people like me are calling to find out what you're asking, and that once we hear your ridiculous, inflated lease price, we *won't* call you back? You're pricing that building into *permanent* vacancy."

"Well, Miss . . . um, I still didn't get your name."

You're still not getting it.

"What might you be able to afford?" he asked.

"I might be able to afford twenty, but even that's a stretch."

"What did you have in mind for putting in that space?" he asked.

"Art for Kids' Sake," Hope said, "a day care center for the arts for preschool children."

"A day care center?" he said with a laugh. "In that *pristine* space? You're joking! That's seven thousand modern square feet of prime *office* building, and you want to waste it on some kids."

"If I offer you nineteen—"

Click.

Bay-it. Hope hung up the phone. *I wouldn't want Dylan's dream to be there anyway if we have to deal with that fool!*

Kiki arrived a few minutes later. "Are you okay?"

Hope nodded.

"You looked vexed."

Just angry with "Mickey Mouse" and his foolishness. Hope turned to the mainframe. "I'm fine."

After sending the overnight Internet orders to the DocuTech, Hope surfed the Internet looking for properties for several hours before finding a new Craigslist listing at 1001 Flatbush Avenue that came loaded with pictures and information.

It's definitely an older building with lots of brick. Three floors with full basement apartment. He could live there. We could live there and save ourselves rent payments. I wonder when his lease is up. Mine is up at the end of December. Nine tall windows face Flatbush to the west, but they're all bricked in. If we knocked out the bricks, there would be plenty of light from about one o'clock to sundown. Fifty-six hundred square feet, or fourteen hundred square feet per level. Adequate parking around back, and it's just around the corner from the Loew's Kings Theatre restoration.

Art for Kids' Sake can be part of a cultural revival on Flatbush Avenue.

Hope used Google to map it. *There's a jeans and sneakers store on one side, a beauty supply store on the other, and a Golden Krust right across the street.* She also found a Staples half a block away.

This is a great *location. "Contact Mr. Vacca." What kind of name is that? I wonder why a lease price isn't listed.* She sighed. *Because it's probably too much.*

But if I don't call and I can afford it, I will hate myself. She smiled at Kiki. *I need some privacy. I can't have gossipy Kiki knowing anything about this.* "Kiki, are you hungry?"

"I could be," Kiki said.

"Your choice this time," Hope said.

"No Chinese burritos?"

"No."

Kiki smiled. "Jerk chicken combos from Golden Krust, okay?"

Hope nodded and gave her a twenty. "My treat."

Kiki snatched the money. "Thank you."

"Take your time." *Please.*

The second Kiki left, Hope dialed the number in the ad.

"Ideal Properties Group, this is Johnny Vacca."

Definitely an older Italian man. "Hello, I'm Hope Warren, and I'm calling about a property you have listed on Craigslist at one thousand one Flatbush Avenue."

"Ten thousand a month, you pay all utilities, two-year lease minimum. Are you interested?"

The money's okay, but that's a long lease. What if Dylan needs to expand or move to another space? "Yes, I'm interested. How old is the building, Mr. Vacca?"

"Built in the thirties and built to last."

"How long have the businesses on either side of the property been there?" Hope asked.

"I'm not exactly sure, but there's always been something in those buildings since I was a kid. What will you use the building for?"

Hope crossed her fingers. "A day care center for preschool children that emphasizes the arts."

"Interesting."

At least he's not laughing at me. "How long has the building been vacant?"

"Close to nine months. A wireless company found a smaller space up the street when the lease ran out. They were foolish, if you ask me. There are now four wireless companies in the same block."

At least they didn't go out of business. "So ten thousand a month ..."

"Two-year lease."

That's nearly a quarter of a million *dollars over two years! This has to be where I act hesitant.* "I'm not sure ..."

"Do you have a counter offer?" Mr. Vacca asked.

Yes, give it to us rent-free for a year, and we'll pay you ten percent of what we make. Right. Here goes ... "Nine thousand a month and throw in all utilities on a one-year lease."

"That's ... Miss Warren, you sound like an educated lady, but I have to say this. Are you crazy?"

I used to be. I think I'm sane now. "If you agree to my terms, Mr. Vacca, I'll pay you ..." She nodded. *Here's where a sacrifice feels right. It feels good.* "I'll pay you five months plus the security deposit up front at nine thousand a month."

Maybe I am *crazy! That's fifty-four thousand dollars! I'll only have twenty-six thousand left, but if we lived— I mean, if Dylan lived... No. If* we *lived in the basement, we wouldn't have rent or utilities payments.* "But only if you give us a one-year lease and pay all utilities."

"You have fifty-four K lying around?" Mr. Vacca asked.

"Yes." *It's been lying around waiting especially for this moment. All this time I thought I was saving that money for my dream, only it wasn't my dream. It was* Dylan's *dream all along.*

"And you can pay me this money when?"

He sounds very interested. Money does talk in America. "I can hand you a cashier's check for that amount tomorrow."

"Tomorrow?"

"Tomorrow." *That wonderful word!* "Mr. Vacca?"

"You have my attention, Miss Warren," he said. "How can I contact you?"

Hope gave him her home and work numbers.

"You're low-balling me, Miss Warren, but I like how you negotiate, and I like your idea. You know, once the Kings Theatre is back to its original splendor, that block will be jumping again."

"That's what we're counting on, and that's what we want to be a part of." *I keep saying "we." I'm seeing Dylan and me as a team, a couple, as lifelong partners. I can't keep my feet still.*

"How's this: ninety-five and water only, two-year lease."

He caved in that quickly! I'm winning. I think. Should I accept this compromise? My parents didn't raise me to compromise on anything. Okay, I compromised on Odell, and look where that got me. "I have to stick to my offer, Mr. Vacca. You could have fifty-four thousand dollars in your hands tomorrow. Give me a call if you'd like to reconsider."

"Don't go looking anywhere else, Miss Warren," Mr. Vacca said. "I have to run this by some of my people. Thank you for calling. I *will* be in touch."

Hope hung up the phone, and her hands began to shake. *I don't know what I'm doing, but it feels right. Please call back! Please call—*

Oh merde!
My period? Not now!
Wait.
My period!
Yes!
I'm all the way back now.
This is so wonderful!
But it has to come now? At this freaking *moment when I'm on the brink of Dylan's dream?*

Hope rushed to the washroom, where she still had a stash of tampons and panty liners in a cabinet. *Do I call Dylan with the good news? Hmm. Does a woman call her boyfriend to tell him her long-lost "friend" has returned? And with a vengeance. Wow. And ow. I have not missed this. I mean, I have, but . . . ow.*

Food always helped me. I need food. Where is Kiki with our lunch?

Kiki banged in the door with their food minutes later, and as she arranged it on the counter, she stared at Hope. "Are you all right? You look sick."

"I just started my period." She opened the Golden Krust container and dug into her jerk chicken.

Kiki spooned some red beans and rice into her mouth. "You were worried your period would not come? Or are you sad your period came?"

Oh, she is so nosy! "I don't know if you noticed, but I used to be really thin."

"You are not skinny now," Kiki said. "You are the picture of health. Love has made you strong."

Love has made me well. Love has made me sane. "I had anorexia, Kiki."

Kiki blinked. "Black women do not get this disease."

"This one did," Hope said. "This is my first period in about fifteen months."

"I did not know such a thing was possible," Kiki said. "You look so fit now."

Because I've been eating over twenty thousand calories a week. "I feel fit, and it's because I've gained weight and gotten healthy that

I'm working down there again." *And working well. I have not missed this freaking pain.*

"I never thought I would ever say this to another woman," Kiki said. "I am overjoyed you had your period today." She laughed. "And I hope you get many more."

"Thank you." *Although one day, and maybe soon, I hope to be late for at least nine months.*

The afternoon training session with Justin went well. Hope watched as he took apart and cleaned the self-serve copier.

"I've been reading the manuals," Justin said. "I can actually run them all, you know."

"You've been dogging it," Hope said. *That's one American phrase I'll never understand. Dogs are more active than cats. They should say, "You've been catting it."*

"Yeah," Justin said. "I get sidetracked by my other job too easily. If you and Dylan are ever interested in my services, let me know."

"You take normal pictures, too, right?" Hope asked. *Like engagement pictures or wedding pictures or baby pictures . . .*

"I could," he said, "but I get more money doing the other kind."

What are they called? Oh. The "money shots."

"Kiki and Angie are getting theirs done," Justin said.

"With their clothes on, right?" Hope whispered.

Justin squinted. "Not sure. I think Kiki is more interested than Angie is. We'll see." He shut the machine and turned it on. "All cleaned and fixed."

"Justin, could I *please* go to Kinderstuff at three today? I haven't seen those children in a long time."

"Sure," Justin said. "But only . . ."

I knew there'd be a catch. "But only if I . . ."

Justin looked out the front window. "Could you maybe write a letter or call my uncle? You know, to let him know that I'm not useless."

"I'm sure he's seen the sales figures from the weekend," Hope said.

"Yeah, but he thinks that you run the place," Justin said. "If he heard what *I* did over the weekend, he might, you know, think better of me."

"I'd be happy to make that call," Hope said. *Just not today.*

Justin nodded. "I'm, um, I'm really sorry I've been such a bad boss. I looked at this copy shop as the end of the line, you know? I kept expecting to screw up worse than I already have and go back to some loading dock in Ronkonkoma, but you kept everything going and made me look good. I'll try to be more, um, managerial from now on. Oh." He pulled a business card from his shirt pocket. He handed it to Hope.

"Tuggle Photography. For the best in discreet, intimate photography."

"In case you know anyone who might be interested in my services."

I know no one.

"I handed out a few of these this past weekend," Justin said, smiling, "and some of them called back. So if I disappear . . ."

Hope nodded. *I will try not to think about it.* "I will know where you *aren't*."

The phone rang four times between one and two, none of them Mr. Vacca. Hope began to worry. *Maybe he's still at lunch.*

At 2:17 PM, Kiki picked up the ringing phone. "Phone for you," Kiki said. "A Mr. Vacca. He sounds Italian."

Hope took and covered the receiver. "Please don't eavesdrop."

"It is not in my nature *not* to listen," Kiki said from her stool.

"Please," Hope said. "Could you take a walk?"

"You do not trust me with this secret?" Kiki asked.

"No."

Kiki laughed and hopped off the stool. "I would not trust me either. It must be a big secret. I will leave you two alone."

Once Kiki left, Hope sat on the stool. "Sorry to keep you waiting, Mr. Vacca."

"I have a new offer for you, Miss Warren," Mr. Vacca said, "and I want you to know that I am cutting my own throat. Ninety-five and all utilities, two-year lease."

All utilities? Is he crazy? I'm thankful he's crazy, yes, but he has to do something about the other two items. "I'm still not sure. We're just beginning this thing, Mr. Vacca."

"Is it the lease amount that's holding you back?" he asked.

"That and the length of the lease," Hope said. "If we are successful, and we will be, we may have to expand or move to a larger space. We don't want a lease to tie us down. Don't tie us down, Mr. Vacca, and we'll be the best tenants you've ever had. I'll restate my offer. Five months plus security deposit at signing, one-year lease, all utilities."

"As is."

That sounded gloomy. "Of course. And we reserve the right to fix it up any way we see fit. If we see a wall we don't like, we knock it down. If we see a window that needs opening, we open it."

"You will need new carpet," Mr. Vacca said. "The first-floor carpet is stained."

"There are hardwood floors under the carpet, right?" Hope asked.

"Right."

"We actually prefer hardwood floors," Hope said. "They're easier to clean up."

"And the furnace is forty years old."

Brr. "If we replace it, would you take it off the lease payment for that month for the inconvenience? It will only add value to the property."

"I might," Mr. Vacca said. "I should. That's a drafty building for children. It mostly needs paint."

"And we'll have children who will help us do it," Hope said.

"You really are putting a children's art center and day care there," Mr. Vacca said.

"Yes."

"Until you told me, I had never heard of such a thing," Mr. Vacca said. "Not so much with the books, huh?"

"No, sir," Hope said. "We want creative, active learning all the time."

"I learned most of what I know by doing it," Mr. Vacca said. "How much will you charge?"

I have to be careful here. Dylan wants no more than one-fifty a week, but that's just not realistic. "No more than two hundred a week."

"And reasonable, too," Mr. Vacca said. "I have grandchildren who would like such a place. Maybe I could pay you in advance, say, for the first month?"

A client already? Will we be ready? "Mr. Vacca, we're not ready to begin immediately. We couldn't possibly open our doors before the new year."

"Oh, I figured you wouldn't be, but you sound determined, and if you make it work, you're going to have plenty of applicants at two hundred a week."

Plenty of applicants. Wow. We have so much to do! We have to make and print applications, contracts, emergency forms . . . but here I am at the place to do them all at a fifteen percent discount. I am obviously in the right place for the first time in my life.

Maybe I've been in the right place all this time.

"Here is my final offer, Miss Warren," Mr. Vacca said. "Fifty thousand at lease signing for one year, nine thousand a month, all utilities paid, and I will strip out all the carpet for you. This amount includes one free month for my grandson Joey, who is very good at drawing."

What did he say? Fifty? What? "You said you had grandchildren."

"A set of twins, twenty-two months old," Mr. Vacca said. "So beautiful you would cry to see them."

They're part of our future! Wait. His math is wrong. "I'm not following your math, Mr. Vacca. I'm missing thirty-two hundred somewhere."

"Consider it a discount for a great idea," Mr. Vacca said. "There are nine windows that have been bricked in. There are no windows behind that brick. I will remove the brick and put in the windows at my cost."

"You will?" *Why would he do that?* "Mr. Vacca, you sound like a very intelligent man. Why would you do that?"

"It's Christmas, Miss Warren. Besides, I don't see how my grandson can make masterpieces without light, and I also want to keep the electric bill down since I'm paying it. Come to my office on Third Avenue in Gowanus and sign the papers as soon as you can, and bring that cashier's check."

Hope wrote furiously on some scratch paper. "Should I make the check out to Ideal Properties Group?"

"No, make it out to me. Johnny Vacca."

What? "You own the building?"

"Yeah. My *nonno* used to have a shoe shop there. He made his shoes and boots from scratch. The finest leathers from around the world. Everything made by hand. He could repair any shoe good as new, and the shoes he made are still walking the streets of Brooklyn. He'd be proud to have your business there, and so will I. What will it be called?"

"Art for Kids' Sake," Hope said.

"Great name. You mind if I talk it up around here? There are plenty of agents here with kids, and they're always complaining about day care costs."

"Sure, just . . . tell them it will be affordable," Hope said. "We haven't set the weekly costs yet."

"I understand, Miss Warren," Mr. Vacca said. "I look forward to meeting you tomorrow."

This is all so overwhelming! "I don't know what to say, Mr. Vacca."

"Say Merry Christmas."

Hope smiled. "Merry Christmas, Mr. Vacca." *No "Merry Freaking Christmas" from now on for me.* "And thank you so much. See you tomorrow."

She returned the receiver to the phone.

She looked at her hands.

They weren't shaking.

Why aren't my hands shaking? They should be! I am about to be on a nine-thousand-dollar-a-month lease!

No. I am about to give the man I love a dream.

Kiki returned to the store munching on a sugar bun and carrying a Golden Krust bag. She handed Hope a sugar bun and a container of fried plantains. "You need your sugar."

Hope bit into the sugar bun. *It's still warm! Sugar! Cinnamon!* "Thank you."

Kiki raised an eyebrow as she chewed a plantain. "So this secret of yours. What can you tell me?"

"Nothing," Hope said. "It's a secret."

"I brought you sugar buns and plantains," Kiki said. "You must tell me something."

Miss Nosy Sugar Buns is trying to bribe me with plantains and sugar buns she bought with my *money.* "I can't tell you anything concrete yet," Hope said. "There's still more I have to do." *Tomorrow is going to be a* huge *day.*

"You will tell me this secret eventually, yes?" Kiki asked.

"Yes." *After it has already happened.* "Tomorrow I will be coming in late. Is that okay?"

"Do not sweat it," Kiki said. "I got your back."

Hope felt a twinge in her back. *Dylan will be massaging my lower back tonight. My friend demands it.*

Hope arrived after three at Kinderstuff, and the children were hard at work decorating stockings with glitter. Ramón gave her a hug, but the rest of the children ignored her because they were so intent on telling Dylan what they wanted for Christmas.

"I want a Harry Potter Lego board game ... I want another Xbox Kinect cuz mine broke ... I just *have* to have a Sing-a-ma-jig ... a dancing Mickey Mouse ... a unicorn pillow pet ... I'm getting Stinky the Garbage Truck ... My mama won't let me have another Nerf gun cuz the cat's scared of it ..."

After they left, Hope leaned against a wall, pressing her hands into her back.

"You okay?" Dylan asked. "You look kind of ... pale."

"I had my period today," Hope said.

"That's ... that's ..." Dylan sighed. "I don't know if I'm supposed to say it's great or that's too bad."

"It's great, but I'm in some pain," Hope said. "It does mean that I'm a whole woman now." *Which brings up an interesting point.* "And that means," Hope whispered, "one of us will have to provide some birth control."

"Or not," Dylan whispered.

Hope blinked. "Or not. Sure."

Wow. This man has just said "or not" to me. Okay. All right. That means we're going to make us a baby and soon. This calls for a celebration!

"Can we go somewhere to sit and eat tonight?" Hope asked. "I am starving."

"I know just the place," Dylan said.

They ate at Bacchus, an affordable French restaurant on Atlantic Avenue, and it was exactly what Hope needed. She slurped onion soup topped with shredded Swiss cheese. She enjoyed her escargot in garlic and star anise butter, crispy goat cheese and pear beggar's purse with fig relish, and duck *rillettes* with apple and onion chutney with toasted country bread. She had a little difficulty with the mussels in tomato and herb sauce, but she muscled them down along with an order of French fries and two glasses of Muscadet.

As soon as she finished off her crème brûlée, she came up for air long enough to ask, "Can we get some chocolate mousse to go? I'm still hungry."

Dylan bought her an entire chocolate mousse. "You know, in case you need a midnight snack."

After Dylan walked her home, his hand rubbing her lower back the entire two-mile trip, Hope went immediately to the Internet to check out Johnny Vacca. *Just in case.* Searches at LinkedIn.com, Facebook, and the Ideal Properties website painted a rosy picture of Mr. Vacca. Testimonials touted him left and right: "I am impressed with his integrity, professionalism, intelligence, efficiency, and good humor . . . He was attentive and patient, the kind of real estate agent that seems rare this day and age . . . Mr. V only showed me what I wanted within my price range and nothing else."

Mr. Vacca, you're about to make me and Dylan—and all the children he will inspire—very happy.

The next morning, the first day of December, Hope woke early so she could walk to 1001 Flatbush Avenue before work.

She was, in a word, "underwhelmed."

The windows were dirty, the sidewalk cracked and strewn with trash. She rubbed a small circle in the dirt-encrusted window. Through the gap, she saw ratty green indoor/outdoor carpeting, a reception area to the left, a hallway with several doors, a decent open space on the right, and a stairway going up along the right wall.

Not great, but not horrible. The carpet will go. I have to go on faith about the upper two floors and the basement. She turned and looked at a tall oak tree climbing out of the sidewalk. *At least we'll get to see this tree changing throughout the year.* She looked up and down the street. *We have the tallest tree on the block.* She patted the tree. *And if a hurricane named Irene couldn't knock you down, our little artists won't bother you a bit.*

She rushed back up Flatbush to Kinderstuff for her morning toast and kiss.

Shoot. I forgot Dylan's coffee.

"I don't like drinking caffeine when I'm on my period," she whispered. "I should have gotten you some, though."

"No, it's okay," Dylan said. "I haven't been sleeping very well lately. You seem out of breath. Are you okay?"

"It's colder today," Hope said. "My lungs aren't used to it, I guess."

"Is there any mousse left?" Dylan asked.

"Yes," Hope said. "I wasn't that hungry. You better come over tonight if you want to get some, though."

"I will." He kissed her. "Something light tonight?"

"Soup and sandwiches," Hope said. *We're so domestic.*

"Sounds good."

Hope left slowly, looking back often, until Dylan closed the door. As soon as she was sure he wasn't watching, she left Flatbush and trotted down Bergen, past Bark Hot Dogs, to Fifth Avenue. Four blocks later, she was inside a Chase Manhattan Bank about to change her life forever.

She wrote out the withdrawal slip, counted the zeroes, and handed it to the teller. "I'd like a cashier's check in this amount"—she pointed and did not say the number—"made out to Johnny Vacca—that's Johnny V-A-C-C-A."

The teller nodded. "One moment, Miss Warren."

Holy cow! Hope thought, wondering about this particular American phrase. *What's holy about a cow? Oh, I know Hindu culture venerates cattle, but holy cow! But why am I thinking about cows when I'm about to walk over a mile across Brooklyn carrying a piece of paper worth fifty thousand dollars!*

The teller handed her the cashier's check. "Are you getting a house?"

"No," Hope said. "A dream."

She folded the check once, put it in her front jeans pocket, and then checked its location about fifty times as she took Degraw Street to Third Avenue. She didn't run exactly. It was more of a paranoid race-walk highlighted by long strides and hair whipping back and forth as she surveyed the scene ahead of her.

Once inside the gray Ideal Properties office, she relaxed somewhat and asked the receptionist to see Johnny Vacca.

"I'll see if he's here," she said.

I didn't think to call ahead! What if he's not here? What if he won't be in until this afternoon? If I'm not at Kinderstuff later, how will I be able to explain that to Dylan?

"Mr. Vacca will see you now," the receptionist said. "Second door on the left."

I worry entirely too much. I have to stop doing that. Things are working out.

Hope rose, took two long strides, knocked, and entered Mr. Vacca's office. A pair of white plastic chairs sat in front of an industrial gray desk, Mr. Vacca turning to Hope in a rolling chair in worse shape than Hope's chair. *Gray hair, black mustache, black polo, gray slacks, black walking shoes, wrinkled brow.*

"Miss Warren, thank you for coming," he said.

Hope sat. *Mr. Vacca's gray hair matches his pants, and his black polo and shoes match his mustache and eyebrows. I wonder if he does that on purpose. He has clear blue eyes. Piercing. This is a handsome older man.*

"Like the office?" he asked.

Not really.

"You can be blunt, Miss Warren."

"It's . . . spare," Hope said, trying to be nice. "And please call me Hope."

"You're too kind, Hope," he said. "There are a dozen of us that share these offices, and no one could agree on how to decorate them, so we went with industrial dull and depressing. None of us are ever in the building for very long, though."

"I hope you haven't been waiting too long," Hope said.

"Just got here."

"Oh." Hope took out the check and handed it to Mr. Vacca. "I have never walked so far with so much money before."

He opened his briefcase and took out a file folder. "When we spoke, you kept saying 'we.' Do you have a partner?"

In many wonderful ways. "Yes. I'm trying to keep this a secret from him, but I should have mentioned his name to you. Your building is a Christmas gift for my boyfriend Dylan Healy, the founder of Art for Kids' Sake."

"Most guys ask for a Ferrari or golf clubs," Mr. Vacca said. "He asked for a building?"

"Kind of," Hope said. "I'm trying to get him his lifelong dream. May I add him to the lease after I show him his new arts center?"

"Of course," he said. "I have to ask a few standard questions. Are you both employed?"

"I've worked for Thrifty Digital Printing for ten years, and Dylan has worked at Kinderstuff for fifteen years. He'll leave Kinderstuff, of course, once Art for Kids' Sake opens. I will still be working at Thrifty, for the time being, but I plan to teach at Art for Kids' Sake full time one day." *Now I'm thinking out loud.*

He nodded. "Will you two be occupying the building?"

"Occupying," Hope whispered. "Oh, are we going to live there?"

"Yes."

"I hope so." *I can't believe I said that out loud!* "I know it would be most cost-effective for us to do so." *Wow. I am almost forcing Dylan to leave Christmas land. What if he doesn't want to go? I am assuming so much. We seem to be moving toward moving in together. Maybe this will simplify the struggle.*

"When are you showing him his dream?" Mr. Vacca asked.

"I'd like to give him this present on Christmas Eve, if it's possible," Hope said.

"It's more than possible," he said. "The people I had to consult before okaying this deal are my family. They recommended that I start the lease once you opened for business, no matter how long it takes, and don't be surprised if you have a bunch of my relatives applying first."

"I hope you have lots of relatives, Mr. Vacca," Hope said.

"We do," he said. "Christmas takes forever."

I would love for Christmas to last that long!

"So, if you initial here"—he turned a sheaf of papers toward her—"we agree to leave the lease starting date blank until the business officially opens."

Hope initialed the space. "I hope no later than the end of January."

He pointed to X's on several sheets, and Hope signed her name.

"You seem motivated, Miss Warren," Mr. Vacca said. "I wouldn't be surprised if you were up and running the day after New Year's."

Hope began filling out an information form. "Mr. Vacca, my apartment lease is up at the end of this month, so I won't have a permanent address to put down here. May I..."

"Certainly," Mr. Vacca said. "That apartment in the basement is very nice. Quiet, insulated and paneled, thick carpet, spacious, built-in bookshelves, warm, two bedrooms, big kitchen. My *nonno* loved to cook."

I will be living at 1001 Flatbush Avenue, Hope thought. *I'll have to give notice to my current landlord, fill out change-of-address forms, start boxing up stuff—*

I don't want to think about all that now. One small step at a time.

"Twenty-two days," Mr. Vacca said. "I don't think I could keep a secret that long."

Hope finished the form and handed it to Mr. Vacca. "This is the season for secrets."

Mr. Vacca handed her a set of keys, each labeled with two numbers. "First number is the floor, second is the door. B for basement. All the locks should work fine, but if they don't, give me a call."

Hope clutched the keys and started to tear up. "Sorry. These"— she shook the keys—"make everything real." She exhaled and wiped at her eyes. "This is one of the biggest moments in my life."

"I imagine there will be bigger ones," he said. "I rode by there last night. I'm going to do something about the sidewalk. You see that tree?"

"Yes."

"The roots are buckling the concrete," he said.

"I love that tree," Hope said.

"Oh, I'm not cutting it down," Mr. Vacca said. "The city planted that one over a hundred years ago, and they fine you if you harm them in any way. I'll get a crew to break up the concrete and pour some more, if the weather cooperates. We might have to wait until spring."

"That's okay." Hope examined the keys. "Which one opens the entrance door?"

Mr. Vacca squinted. "Should be the newest one, the only one without a sticker on it."

Hope found it. "Thank you so much for doing all these things for us." She stood and offered her hand.

Mr. Vacca shook it firmly. "You are giving the man you love his dream. My *nonno*'s dream of owning his very own store sixty years ago is the reason I'm here today. *And* you just brought me fifty K. It's the least I can do."

Hope checked her watch. *It's eleven already?* "I have to be going."

"Merry Christmas, Miss Warren," Mr. Vacca said.

"Merry Christmas, Mr. Vacca."

Hope raced as fast as her weary legs could carry her back to Thrifty. *By the time I get there, I will have walked at least seven miles since eight o'clock this morning. I have burned off over four hundred calories. I should be huffing and puffing, but I'm not. Why is that? What did Kiki say? Love has made me fit. That must be it.*

Hope entered the store, and all was quiet.

Kiki sat reading the *Times*. She looked up. "You are very late," she said, folding the paper and setting it under the counter. "Justin is very mad."

"No, he isn't," Hope said. "Is he even here?"

Kiki rolled her eyes. "He is on another assignment."

"At eleven-fifteen in the morning?" Hope grimaced.

"Maybe someone is trying to surprise her lover," Kiki said, blinking. "Did everything go okay?"

Better than okay. "Yes." She took off her coat. "Everything went okay." She smiled. "Are all the orders caught up?"

"Yes." Kiki picked up the paper. "Someone does work here, you know."

Hope turned her attention to the mainframe, where she created a simple sign:

ART FOR KIDS' SAKE
Dylan Healy, founder

She printed it out, folded it once, and stuck into her coat pocket. *On Christmas Eve, I'll tape it up to the front window, and then he'll see it, lift me high into the air—*

Hope felt someone Jamaican staring at her back.

"What, Kiki?" Hope said, spinning around.

Kiki squinted. "You are far too happy for someone on her period. Why are you so happy, Hope?"

Hope spun away from Kiki. "It's a secret."

"Are you engaged?" Kiki asked.

Hope spun back. "No. What makes you think that?"

"You have been wearing that ring," Kiki said, "and I have been too busy to ask."

"And it's so unlike you," Hope said. "It's a promise ring. Dylan has promised to love me and only me."

Kiki sighed. "I knew it was not an engagement ring. I thought Dylan would get you a much finer ring."

"It *is* a fine ring, Kiki."

"Too small, no diamond," Kiki said. "What could it be then? You were gone all morning, and you were rushing around." She snapped her fingers. "You are getting a house!"

Close. It's a dream with a basement apartment. "No."

Kiki frowned. "You are moving in with him?"

I hope so. "No." Hope turned away. "It's a secret, Kiki. Leave it alone."

"You have won the lottery!" Kiki cried.

Hope shook her head, scrolling down the list of finished orders on the screen. "Would I be here if I had won the lottery?"

"Well, we know you are not pregnant," Kiki said. "What else is there to be happy about?"

Hope laughed. "Everything, Kiki. It's Christmas, and I'm happy."

"Can I assume it involves Dylan?" Kiki asked.

That woman is not going to leave me alone! Hope spun slowly to face Kiki. "Yes, it involves Dylan, and that is all I'm going to tell you."

Kiki stared at Hope. "And what of this strange Italian man calling? Does Dylan know of this man? How would Dylan react if he knew a strange Italian man was calling you? Oh, and what would Dylan think if he knew that you ran out and *met* with this strange Italian man this morning when you should have been at work? I think I may bring these things up when Dylan arrives. Dylan is my friend. I will hold no secrets from him."

I have had enough of this! Hope stood. "Me nuh put up with yuh farseness, Kiki Clarke!"

Kiki dropped the newspaper.

Where is this coming from? I sound like my mother and grand-mother. Did they feel this powerful, too? "Nuh more wit' yuh farse-ness, Kiki!"

Kiki slid slowly off the stool. "Me farseness?"

Hope put her hands on her hips. "Yuh meddlin', dotish *vooman.*"

As Kiki's mouth dropped open, she began wagging a finger in the air. "But a wha di rass fi tak 'bout? Listen to yuh with yuh facety talk! Nex' t'ing yuh know, me be vexed!"

What the freak am I talking about? Oh, she's not saying that to me! "Facety talk! Yuh nuh go be vex! Yuh nuh gon' frig up me sur-prise!"

"Frig up?" Kiki threw out her chin. "Yuh nuh 'ave brough-tupsy! Yuh buttu!"

What? I have no home training? "Yuh nuh got broughtupsy, Kiki! Yuh a *maco* and a sip sip!"

Kiki shook her head rapidly. "What be dis sheggery? Yuh bol' face beti, now she boof me, why she cos jhanjat so? Go dey, gyurl!"

Now she is saying that I'm rude? That I'm causing trouble? "Go dey, gyurl!" Hope growled, stepping inches from Kiki's cute little sneakers. *I could crush both her feet with just one of my boots!* "Yuh be *bazodee!* Eh! Eh! Yuh stickin'! Eh! Eh! Yuh *rude*, gyurl!"

"Yuh got hard ears, always give me da cut eye, Miss Natty Dread," Kiki scowled.

"Miss Natty Dread!" Hope shouted. "Jeez-an-ages! Yuh biggety, wining an' makin' style and shakin' yuh front like a *femme desserrée* for the customers whole day!"

Kiki squinted. "Like a what?"

"Like a loose *vooman*, yuh *jagabat*," Hope said, her growl becoming a snarl. "*Vous tremblez vos seins et votre derrière à n'importe quoi ce qui entre de ce magasin, en incluant Dylan!*"

"No fair!" Kiki shouted. "English or Island! No French!"

Hope put her face in Kiki's face. "I'll speak *American* then. What?"

Kiki stepped back. "Every hoe a dem stick a bush."

Hope leaped forward. "Yuh call me a ho, yuh freshwater Yangkey?"

"Damn, Hope," Kiki said, stepping behind the stool. "What I said means whatever floats your boat."

"What? 'Every hoe a dem stick a bush'? Dey nuh 'boat' in dat phrase! Dat bubu!" Hope slapped the top of the stool. "Do so eh like so! Hog know where ta rub he skin. Yuh nuh bully *me*, Kiki Clarke!"

Kiki closed her eyes. "Oh, Lawd, gyaal bright! Why fi galang so? Tek set pon you, lef mi nuh. Gyaal, gwaan!"

Hope moved the stool out of the way, pinning Kiki to the counter. "Me *not* annoying. Yuh be *queen* of annoying around here. Yuh shake yuh tot tots and *boomsie* at anyt'ing dat come in here, including Dylan!"

"I do *not*!" Kiki cried. "That is the way I am to everyone!"

"Then you are annoying to *everyone*!" Hope sneered.

Kiki looked up at Hope. "Let me by."

"No." Hope balled up her fists. "Yuh goin' to tell me yuh weren't considering a *ménage à trois* with *my* man? Yuh were, Kiki Rafiki. Yuh go be vex, nuh. Don't *piss* me off today, Kiki! I'm *happy*!"

Kiki closed her mouth.

"This is the *happiest* I have *ever* been in my entire *life*!" Hope shouted.

Kiki smiled.

Hope frowned. "Check yu'self befo' yuh skin yuh teet, Kiki Clarke! All skin teet eh laugh!"

Kiki bit her lip.

Hope stared. *She is* not *about to laugh at me!*

Kiki cackled. "And you *sound* so happy, too!"

Hope took a breath and stepped back. "I *am* happy."

368 • *J. J. Murray*

Kiki continued to laugh, slapping her hands on the counter, tears coming out of her eyes. "Me mek eyewata!" she cackled.

Hope smiled, bit her lip, and howled with laughter, falling back into her chair and shaking.

Kiki wiped her eyes. "I did not know you had that *in* you, Hope. I thought you were going to *vank* me."

"So did I," Hope said, breathing heavily. "I was about to give you some licks. I'm so sorry, Kiki."

Kiki shook her head. "Do not be sorry. I deserved it for prying."

"I don't understand why I said all those things," Hope said. "I've been holding it back for so long. I can't believe it spilled out like that."

"Why have you kept that *ooman* quiet?" Kiki asked. "She be a trip all de way fi de islands, mon. I am not sure which island. You were Bahamas, you were Trini. Maybe you are from them all."

"I don't honestly know why I went off like that," Hope said. "It's as if something flipped a switch inside of me."

Kiki shook her head. "Oh, Hope. You know why. You have always known why."

Hope nodded. "I have. I don't know why I haven't admitted this before. Kiki, I was ashamed. I was genuinely ashamed. I've been trying so hard to fit in here. I guess I wanted to sound American."

Kiki laughed. "Even Americans do not sound American! Find me one person in Brooklyn who speaks American. Find me one person in America who speaks American. There is no such thing as speaking American. All of us, all of them, everybody—*all* of it is American. That is what America is for. America is for being who you really are and damn them all if they do not understand what you say." She nodded. "You are a powerful *ooman*, Hope Warren. I would never want to be your enemy. It felt good, yes?"

It felt great! "It felt good to let go. It felt good to be . . . myself."

Kiki stepped over to Hope. "Stand up, *ooman*."

Hope stood.

Kiki hugged her tightly. "I am *really* beginning to like you, Hope."

Hope held Kiki close. "I'm beginning to like me, too."

Kiki stepped back. "Would Dylan approve of such talk?"

"I doubt it," Hope said. "It might remind him of an old Bermudan girlfriend's mother."

Kiki's eyes popped. "Dem da *vurst!*" She laughed. "He might like to hear your patois, but do not overdo it. You will scare him as you scared me."

"You weren't really scared, were you?" Hope asked.

"You are tall with longer arms," Kiki said. "I would have been no match."

"I wouldn't have hit you," Hope said. "Very hard." She laughed. *I'm laughing! Wow! I'm laughing at work!* "I'll stick to French with Dylan. He loves to hear me speak French. He's even speaking Irish to me."

"Because he is an Island man, too," Kiki said.

Hope blinked. "You're right." *I have never thought of him that way. Dylan is from de Islands, too, mon.*

Kiki returned the stool to its rightful place. "You are really not going to tell me your secret, are you?"

"Me mus' have bad ways 'bout dis, Kiki," Hope said. "Just know that it's *really* important, okay?"

"Too important to tell me?" Kiki poked out her lower lip.

"Yes," Hope said.

Kiki laughed. "You really think I'm a sip sip?"

Hope nodded.

"I would only tell On-Gee and a few . . . *hundred* other people. You must call me Christmas Day with this news. I will not be the last to know."

If I don't show up for work for, say, the rest of my life, you'll know, Kiki. "You won't be the last to know."

"Good," Kiki said.

Now all I have to do is keep from slipping and telling Dylan for the next twenty-two days.

I can't frig up the best present I may ever give!

DECEMBER 2

Only 22 more shopping days
until Christmas . . .

Chapter 24

After feeding Dylan grilled cheese sandwiches and home fries and falling asleep to his massage by eight the night before, Hope was bright-eyed the next morning as she went through her routine.

She also remembered to bring Dylan his coffee.

Dylan met her with a bear hug inside the door of Kinderstuff. "Good morning."

"Good morning," Hope said, releasing her grip and handing him the coffee.

Dylan pointed at a plate containing two slightly burned pieces of toast. "Sorry, but they're a little burned."

They're not burned. They're charred. "What happened to my breakfast?"

"I can explain," Dylan said. "I put Ramón in charge of your toast this morning. He has a crush on you, by the way. Anyway, the phone rang, and they must have popped up, and I think Ramón cooked them again."

I'm still hungry, though. Cook me more. "Okay . . ."

"Aniya's mama is the one who called," Dylan said. "Hope, Aniya is going to have her transplant tomorrow."

"That's fantastic!" *I hope Aniya returns quickly. She always cooked my toast just right.*

"Her parents believe Aniya can be out of the hospital by Christmas," Dylan said, sighing, "but that might be overly optimistic."

"What do you think her chances are?" Hope asked.

"I wish I knew," Dylan said. "I hope she's home by then."

"She will be." *This is the season for miracles.* Hope kissed his cheek. "We'll have to go visit her."

Dylan nodded. "And we won't go empty-handed. We'll have to get her some gifts in case she has to spend Christmas in the hospital."

"Just tell me when," Hope said.

Dylan blinked. "You *want* to go shopping now?"

"Yes." *After you've made the biggest purchase in your life, the rest is* un morceau de gateau, *a piece of cake.* "Could I have some toast that doesn't look like a hockey puck now, please?"

Dylan and Ramón remade the toast, and it was as brown as Dylan's brown brown eyes. Hope hugged Ramón.

Ramón giggled. "*Hasta luego, Hope.*"

"In English, Ramón," Dylan said.

"No," Hope said. "I understood you perfectly, Ramón. You keep singing that American."

Ramón looked away. "Is not American."

Hope knelt before him. "Anything you speak in America is American, and don't ever let anyone tell you anything different."

"Okay," Ramón said. "Like your toast."

"I will *like* my toast," Hope said. "How do you say 'Have a great day'?"

"*Tienen un gran día!*" Ramon shouted.

"*Tienen un gran día!*" Hope shouted back. *I think I made him blush.* She stood and kissed Dylan. "I'll explain later. *Ayez un jour grand.*"

"*Mol an oige agus tiocfaidh said,*" Dylan whispered. "Praise the young and they will flourish."

"You have beautiful thoughts," Hope said. "*Ciào!*"

"And now you're speaking Italian," Dylan said.

"Nope," Hope said, "I'm speaking American."

As she walked to Thrifty, a poster took shape in her mind. She'd make a map of Brooklyn showing stick people saying hello in all the languages spoken in Brooklyn.

It's going to be a huge poster! Since Hope had lived in Brooklyn, she had heard "*heyello,*" "*oi,*" "*ni hao,*" "hi," "hey," "yo," "*salem,*" *"allo," "hallo," "shalom," "ciào," "yow wah gwaan," "salaam," "hola," "pryvit," "qué pasa," "jambo,"* and "greetings."

I know there are dozens of others, and at the top of the poster it will say "Brooklyn: American Spoken Here."

She walked by people from all over the world every day, and they were all Americans. *America is not a melting pot,* Hope thought. *It's a stew, and we all add the spices. English may be the base of this stew, but the rest of us make it taste good.*

After cutting hundreds of tiny snowflakes, drowning them in glitter, and pasting them to the front window at Kinderstuff, Hope found a way to walk Dylan past 1001 Flatbush Avenue.

"Exercise is good for my period," she said. "I want to go for a long walk."

"Okay," Dylan said. "Where to?"

He's so agreeable. Now what did I pass down there? A Burger King and a McDonald's. "How about . . . McDonald's?"

"Really?"

"I love their fries," Hope said, "and we can walk through the park."

Dylan pointed up Flatbush. "There's a McDonald's up the street from here."

The Golden Arches are inconveniently everywhere! "I need to work up an appetite first. Let's go."

They walked down Flatbush and through the Grand Army Plaza and through Prospect Park, pausing to look through black iron fencing at the Prospect Park Zoo.

"Did you have a good day?" Dylan asked.

"Yes," Hope said. "You?"

"I had trouble concentrating," Dylan said.

"Why?" Hope asked.

"I was thinking about Aniya," Dylan said.

"Let's visit her this weekend," Hope said.

Dylan kissed her cheek. "That's one of the reasons I love you." He looked up Empire Boulevard as they crossed. "There's a McDonald's up there."

Wrong one. "I'm still not hungry. You?"

He shook his head. "I can wait."

When they found the "correct" McDonald's near Snyder Avenue, it was sandwiched between a Sprint store and Sleepy's mattresses. *Now I am hungry. I hope the service is more sprint than sleepy.*

Hope was wrong.

It took fifteen minutes for their Big Mac meals to appear ("miraculously," Dylan said) at the dirty counter, there were no condiments, and there were no clean tables.

The fries, though, were deliciously greasy and salty.

"Let's go see how the Kings Theatre is looking," Hope said.

They carried their bags and sodas a block south, and as they approached *their* oak tree, Hope noticed clean windows at 1001 Flatbush. She slowed and saw hardwood floors instead of carpet. *Mr. Vacca has been busy! The floors need some polish, but otherwise—*

Dylan was several steps ahead. "The theater's up a bit farther."

Hope nodded. *And you've just walked past your future dream, Dylan Healy. We'll catch it on the way back. That's what happens with future dreams sometimes. You walk right past them without knowing it, and those dreams are often in the last place you look.*

There wasn't much to see of the Kings Theatre, four stories of scaffolding and tarps hiding the facade, the marquee only a metal shell of tubes and wires hanging above the sidewalk, the front windows heavily taped and soaped.

Dylan finished his Big Mac. "It looks tarpy, wiry, and soapy."

"When's it supposed to open?" Hope asked, stealing several of his fries.

"Soon," Dylan said. "Maybe this spring. They think they can do two hundred live performances in there annually. Four thousand seats."

"I want to be at the opening," Hope said.

Dylan smiled. "So do I. It's a date."

She took his hand. "Let's go back now."

This time, Hope stopped and looked in the window at 1001 Flatbush. "I hear this one's been leased."

Dylan put his hands around his face and peered through the window. "How'd you hear that?"

"I've been looking online for you, Mr. Healy," Hope said. "I saw this property on Craigslist. It was there one day, and it wasn't there the next. I assume that means it has been leased. You ever look at this space?"

Dylan nodded. "Once. The guy wanted too much, something like twelve grand a month."

Twelve thousand? I stole this building!

"Too much sentimental value, he said," Dylan said. "Been in his family for three generations. Right."

It's about to be in our family, too. Sort of. "It has character, doesn't it?"

Dylan shrugged. "Could be nicer inside for twelve grand. At least he got rid of the puke-green carpet."

Dylan actually visited this space? "I wonder what's upstairs," Hope said.

"Two open floors, decent space," Dylan said. "No light, though."

"That isn't good," Hope said, her eyes wandering up to the bricked-in windows. "I wonder where people would park."

"Parking lot's on the other side," Dylan said. "Not much of one. A few spaces. Ready to go?"

"Sure," Hope said, taking his hand. "Twelve thousand, but right on Flatbush, though."

"I'll keep looking," Dylan said.

It is so hard not to say anything! "Oh, you'll find it, Dylan." *I'll even hand you the key to it.* "Besides visiting Aniya, what are we doing this weekend?"

"For Operation AHHH?" Dylan asked.

"Ah, yes," Hope said. "You seem to need a little cheering up, too."

"I'm fine," Dylan said. "Really."

She rubbed his back. "I know you are. So, what's the plan, man?"

He pulled out his memo pad.

Hope laughed. "You're kidding. You wrote it down?"

"I write everything down," Dylan said. "I have hundreds of these memo pads in my apartment. In a few centuries, an archaeologist will excavate wherever these end up and piece together my life. I'm sure it will make the *National Geographic*."

"Right." She leaned closer to look at the page. "So what's it say we're doing?"

"Everything we can do in Brooklyn before Christmas given our work schedules," Dylan said. "Your weekends are about to get very busy."

On the first weekend in December, they took the B65 bus from Bergen and Washington to Smith Street in "BoCoCa" (Boerum Hill, Cobble Hill, and Carroll Gardens) to shop.

At Brooklyn Bead Box, Hope bought pounds of beads and stones and meters of string and wire for Kiki. "For when we're not busy so I can keep her from getting into my business," Hope said. "I mean, she's already loud. Why not make her louder?"

Dylan bought Whack some cat toys at Beastly Bites.

"She won't play with them," Hope said.

Dylan didn't think it would hurt.

At American Apparel, Hope picked out several Brooklyn hoodies in green and blue for Justin. "I have to do something to retire Justin's purple belly shirt."

Dylan pouted.

Hope bought him another hoodie.

In *her* size.

After eating shish kabob at Zaytoons, they went to Modell's, where Dylan ordered a personalized Yankees jersey with "Pierre-Louis" and the number one on the back. "Aniya's been asking for one for the last two Christmases," Dylan said. "I already got her Yankees–Red Sox tickets, home side, first series in the spring."

"What did that cost?" Hope asked.

"Why not get her some of these?" Dylan asked, pointing to a display of Yankees leather and platinum bracelets.

"That much?" Hope asked.

Dylan nodded. "I'm kind of hoping she takes us along, but she has a baseball-crazy family."

Hope chose two different leather bracelets.

"Where to?" Dylan asked.

"Jay Street," Hope said.

At W. C. Art & Drafting Supply, Hope priced drafting tables and found a nice set of charcoal pencils and several sketchbooks.

"Who are they for?" Dylan asked.

The drafting table is for me eventually. That kitchen table kills my back. "For Aniya the artist," Hope said.

They wrapped Aniya's gifts at Dylan's apartment and took them in a cab to the Brooklyn Hospital Center, which was only a few minutes' walk from Thrifty. *I know where I'll be on my lunch breaks until Aniya gets out.*

Dr. Mishra, Aniya's doctor, met with them and Aniya's parents, Violine and Georges Pierre-Louis, in the pediatric ICU waiting room.

Hope hugged Violine. *It's like looking at an older Aniya. Violine has those big eyes, too. So pretty.*

Georges shook hands with Dylan. "It is good to see you again."

"How is she?" Dylan asked.

"She is very sleepy," Violine said, "but she is doing well."

Dr. Mishra, who was lithe and dark with a thin nose and long black hair, nodded. "She is still very weak," she said with a slight English accent. "Try not to excite her too much." She smiled. "Though I am sure you will. Presents! She will be so happy."

"She has been asking about both of you," Georges said. "She talks of no one else. Oh, she still talks about baseball."

Dylan held up the bags of presents. "Is it okay to take these in?"

"After you show them to her," Violine said, "we will take them home."

"But—" Georges started to say.

"Georges, Aniya will open them at home on Christmas morning," Violine said.

"You're right," Hope said. She took the bags from Dylan and put them in Georges's hands. "Take them now. We don't want her asking a million questions about them."

Georges nodded. "She will do that."

Aniya's eyes were open when Hope and Dylan walked into her room, but just barely. Dylan took a seat near her bed as Hope approached the plastic tent around her.

"Hope," Aniya whispered.

Don't cry, don't cry! There are too many lines and tubes around such a small child! She's getting better, she's getting better . . .

"*Bonjour, Aniya,*" Hope said. "*Comment allez-vous?*"

"I'm okay," Aniya whispered. "I missed you."

Hope saw tears in Dylan's eyes. *He's not seeing Aniya right now. He's seeing Shayna. Be strong, be strong.*

She touched Aniya's hand through the plastic. "We've been out shopping all day for you."

"What'd you get me?" Aniya whispered.

"Surprises," Hope said. "Good ones."

"Like what?" Aniya asked.

"You'll find out Christmas morning," Hope said. "When you get home."

Aniya shifted her head. "Hi, Dylan."

Dylan nodded. "Hi." His body shook. "I'm ... I'm sorry." He stood and stumbled toward the door.

Hope grabbed his hand. "Dylan, maybe we can tell her one thing we got her."

Dylan turned, tears pouring down his face. "It's too ... I've been here before, Hope," he whispered.

Hope put her lips on his ear. "And *this* one is coming home," she whispered. "Tell her one thing we got her."

Dylan closed his eyes. "You have to guess, Aniya."

"A baseball," Aniya whispered.

Dylan squeezed Hope's hand, went to the chair, and pulled it closer to Aniya. "Close." He sat, leaning forward.

He's still crying. He's not afraid to cry in front of a child. He's not ashamed, and here come my tears to join his. Hope backed to the shadow of the door.

"Why are you crying, Dylan?" Aniya whispered.

"I want you to come home," Dylan said. "I've missed you. I've burned all of Miss Hope's toast."

"You don't know the trick," Aniya said. "I'll teach it to you."

Dylan nodded, wiping his eyes. "We didn't get you a baseball, but you were close. You get three guesses. That was your first one."

"A hat?" Aniya whispered.

"No," Dylan said. "You're going to have so much hair you won't want to wear a hat anymore."

He's smiling again. He's seeing Aniya now.

"Why are you way over there, Hope?" Aniya whispered.

Just feeling what Dylan felt with Shayna. "You two talk. I'll be outside, and I'll be seeing you on my lunch breaks as often as I can, okay?"

"Okay," Aniya whispered. "I like your ring."

"Dylan has good taste," Hope said. *He also has the best heart.*

Hope returned to the waiting area, wiping her eyes.

"She will be fine," Violine said.

"I know," Hope said.

"*Bondye bon,*" Violine said. "God is good. *Dèyè mon gen mon.* Behind the mountains, there are mountains, but *nanpwen mòn Jezi pa deplase.* There is no mountain that Jesus cannot move." She smiled. "*Lespwa fè viv.* Hope makes one live, *oui?*"

"*Oui,*" Hope said.

Violine sighed. "Georges has gone home with your gifts. He does not like being here. He must stay busy." Violine laughed. "And Aniya wants *your* hair. I had no idea it was so long. She will trip all over herself playing baseball."

So strong. Violine could lose her daughter, and she finds time to laugh.

"Does it not get in the way?" Violine asked.

"Sometimes," Hope said.

Violine sat back, folding her hands in front of her. "They have been talking a long time."

"Dylan is probably telling her everything we got her," Hope said.

"Or he is telling Aniya everything *he* is getting *you,*" Violine said.

Hope stood. "He might be doing just that."

She reentered Aniya's room quietly and saw Dylan watching Aniya sleep.

He saw Hope and reached out his hand.

Hope took his hand and sat on his lap.

They watched Aniya sleep for several minutes.

She's dreaming, and with her big eyes, I hope she's having big dreams.

"What were you two talking about?" Hope whispered.

"Secrets," Dylan whispered. He lifted Hope off his lap and stood. "Lots of secrets."

They returned to the waiting area. "She's sleeping," Dylan said.

Violine hugged him. "Good." She hugged Hope. "What should Aniya wear to the ballet?"

"For most five-year-old girls, I'd say a dress," Hope said. "Tell her that I plan to wear nice slacks, a fancy blouse, flats, and a long coat."

Violine smiled. "So she can wear her normal church clothes. We stopped fighting her about dresses a year ago. She is small, but she is strong. We will be ready."

Dylan took an envelope from his coat and handed it to Violine. "As I told you, Aniya's cards have been selling very well. This is money she has earned so far. I'm sure she'll earn even more."

"Thank you," Violine said. "Thank you both."

As they rode a cab back to her apartment, Dylan twisted Hope's ring. "I hope you're right."

"About what?" Hope said.

"Aniya being home in time for the ballet," Dylan said. "That's two weeks from tonight."

"Wow," Hope said. "We'll have to get you ready."

"What?"

"What are you wearing to the ballet?" Hope asked. "I can't go to the ballet with you dressed any old way." She fluttered her eyelashes. "No hoodies allowed."

"I will wear a suit and tie, Miss Warren," Dylan said, "and shiny black shoes."

"Ooh, I cannot wait to see you," Hope said. "How much did little Aniya earn?"

"She's up to around fourteen thousand cards," Dylan said, "so the check was for a little over twenty-five thousand."

"That's wonderful," Hope said. *That's amazing!*

Dylan sighed. "It won't make much of a dent in their expenses, though, but it's a start."

"It is," Hope said. "So, what are we doing tomorrow?"

"Sleeping in until dark," Dylan said, "and then I will show you the lights."

"I like the sound of the that," Hope whispered. "I could sleep for days."

* * *

The next evening, they rode the Lexington Avenue Express to Union Square in Manhattan to take a bus tour of an Italian-American neighborhood bursting with Christmas lights in Dyker Heights. Hope had never seen anything like it. Lifesize nativity scenes glowed, giant toy soldiers marched, Santas waved, choirs of angels filled yards, and houses became beacons of the holiday spirit.

Their poor electric bills, but wow! Astronauts could see this neighborhood from space! The people around us taking pictures don't need to use their flashes.

"Puts my apartment to shame, doesn't it?" Dylan asked.

"It's beautiful," Hope said. "You turned your apartment into a holiday wonderland just for me to see. These people"—she pointed out the bus window—"they did it for the entire world to see. I'm seeing spots."

The following weekend, after a quiet week at Thrifty and five quiet but inquisitive ("What'd you get me for Christmas, Hope?") peanut-butter-and-jelly lunches with Aniya, Hope and Dylan survived the Brooklyn Flea's holiday market at Fort Greene without buying a single item. Dylan said it had to be some sort of record.

"No one ever leaves here without buying *something*," he said.

Hope did linger a while looking at baby clothes.

Dylan allowed her to do so, smiling the entire time.

After an hour, however, Dylan considered her searching to be a bit excessive.

"You're not cooperating, Mr. Healy," Hope said. "I am preparing to nest, and I need feathers for our child."

"We'll just wrap her in a quilt until she's five," Dylan said.

For that remark, Hope went through the mounds of baby clothes for another twenty minutes.

While she looked, Dylan's phone rang. "Hello, Mrs. Pierre-Louis." As he listened, he closed his eyes. "That's . . . that's too bad."

Hope tried not to eavesdrop, but she couldn't help it.

Aniya's body isn't cooperating. It's not rejecting, but it's not accepting her transplant. She won't be able to go to the ballet, and she has little chance of coming home for Christmas.

Dylan closed his phone and put it into his pocket. "Aniya's new bone marrow isn't producing enough normal blood cells. Dr.

384 • J. J. Murray

Mishra is keeping her on antibiotics. Aniya had another blood and platelet transfusion this morning."

That's three this week!

He sighed. "Once her bone marrow is producing enough healthy red and white blood cells and platelets, she can go home, but right now, she's not ready."

"We're still going to see *The Nutcracker* together," Hope said.

"I wouldn't feel right going," Dylan said. "Not without Aniya."

"We're not going to the ballet, Dylan," Hope said. "We'll take *The Nutcracker* to Aniya on Monday night."

"How?"

"I know a guy," Hope said. *Gently used. I will enjoy. No disappointments. I hope he still has the DVD. I may even find some "new" used jeans in my new size.* "And there's something I'll need you to do, too."

After she told him, Dylan kissed her. "You're going to make Aniya so happy."

"And Kiki, Angie, and Justin will help, too," Hope said. "They just don't know it yet. Give me your phone . . ."

Mr. Al-Hamsi was very happy to take Hope's money on Monday for the *Nutcracker* DVD and two pairs of men's 34-32 jeans. He even had mounds of red-and-white Santa hats and stockings.

"I found *just* for you," he said, pointing at the jeans.

"I told you to find thirty thirty-two's," Hope said.

Mr. Al-Hamsi smiled. "You have filled out. I see you from here. I say, she is getting, um, back."

He did not just say "back"! Though I am getting a little shelf back there. My weigh-ins are turning into church services filled with hallelujahs.

"I get these *just* for you," he said.

The man's been checking out my sexy derriere, yet another man measuring women with his eyes in Brooklyn. "I'm glad you have this DVD, Mr. Al-Hamsi. You're going to make a little girl in the hospital very happy."

After Hope told him about Aniya, Mr. Al-Hamsi handed back five dollars. "*Milad Majid,*" he said. "Means 'Merry Christmas.' Tell the child *Milad Majid* for me."

"*Milad Majid,* Mr. Al-Hamsi," Hope said. "*La paix être à vous.*"

"*Salaam alaikum,*" he said. "*Et bonne année.*"

He understood me and *he speaks French. A trilingual man is selling DVDs and used jeans and checking out "backs" on Flatbush Avenue in Brooklyn.* "A happy new year to you, too," Hope said. "Where did you learn French?"

"*Grand-père,*" Mr. Al-Hamsi said. "He learn from French in Syria. Then French leave after war. French good at leaving mess behind. *Grand-père* teach me."

Hope smiled. "We will talk more so we can improve your French."

Mr. Al-Hamsi smiled and nodded. "And I will teach you Arabic."

"*L'assez foire, monsieur,*" Hope said.

"*L'assez foire?*" Mr. Al-Hamsi shook his head. "Is not fair enough. French easy. Arabic difficult. Not as difficult as Japanese, I tell you."

"You speak Japanese, too?" Hope asked.

"Enough to order sushi," he said with a shrug. "They appreciate when you try. Sometimes give you bigger piece of fish."

Hope laughed. "I'll try to remember that." *Look at all these props.* She handed back the five.

"What is this?" he asked.

"How many hats can I get for five?" she asked.

"With bell, two, without bell, four, one size fits all."

Some of them have bells? "I'll take four." She selected four.

Mr. Al-Hamsi nodded. "You come back after Christmas. Half-off sale. No disappointments."

"I will."

Hope took the rest of the day off to prepare for the ballet, pediatric ICU style. She had already called the ICU nurses Sunday and told them her plan, and they were more than willing to participate. Dr. Mishra thought it was a fantastic idea.

"I have always wanted to be in the ballet," she said, "but I was too short."

Then Hope made popcorn.

Fifty microwave bags' worth.

It kind of looks like snow.

She filled a thirty-gallon kitchen trash bag with the popcorn, and then she called Dylan at Kinderstuff. "How's it going?"

"The red jacket is done and the mouse ears are ready, but the head will still be a little wet," he said. "I've already burned out one hair dryer trying to dry the thing."

"How does it look?" Hope asked.

"Like the real thing," Dylan said.

"Not too scary," Hope asked.

"No," Dylan said. "He's smiling. I don't much like the whole white-tights-and-black-boots thing, though. How's your costume coming?"

What costume? I'm wearing gray sweats, some papier-mâché *mouse ears, and some painted whiskers to be the Mouse King. Only Dylan will be in tights. I'm not crazy. Who wears tights in Brooklyn in December?*

"What about my tail?" Hope asked.

There was silence.

He forgot about my tail. "I can't believe you aren't thinking about my tail."

"I am, *cailín*," Dylan said, "and that's why I forgot about the mouse tails."

Do I believe him? Maybe it's true. I have a nice tail now. "It's getting late, Dylan," Hope said. "You're not going to be able to swing by here, are you?"

"No."

Hope munched some popcorn. "It's okay. I'll get a cab and pick *you* up for a change."

"Gotta go," Dylan said. "I left Ramón in charge of the hair dryer. You know how he likes to burn things. Bye, and thank you."

Don't thank me yet, Mr. Healy. She called Thrifty. "Kiki, it's Hope."

"I am not talking to you," Kiki said. "You think of me only as a mouse. Why is On-Gee a toy soldier? I should be the soldier and she should be the mouse."

"How do your costumes look?" Hope asked.

"On-Gee looks fantastic, of course," Kiki said, "but I do not look good in gray. You will owe me."

"Be there by six-thirty, okay? I want to have a dress rehearsal."

"What is to rehearse?" Kiki said. "The mice fight the soldiers, and the mice lose. You are having me fight the woman I love, another reason I hate you."

"Dylan gets to *kill* me," Hope said. "Put Justin on."

"What?" Kiki cried. "No, Hope. Please. No pictures."

"Put . . . Justin . . . on," Hope said, "or me cuff yuh severely."

"Here he is," Kiki said.

"Hi, Hope," Justin said. "I got the appointment changed. I'll be there the entire time."

"Make sure you get lots of tight shots of Kiki and Dylan, okay?" Hope asked.

"Will do," Justin said.

It's not every day you get to see the love of your life wearing tights and a Jamaican woman wearing unflattering, baggy gray sweats.

Hope rode in the cab to Kinderstuff in her sweats, boots, and new coat, the bag containing the popcorn and the DVD beside her. As soon as the driver pulled to the curb, Dylan rushed out carrying the nutcracker's huge papier-mâché head.

He's wearing some sensationally tight tights. You go, Mr. Healy! Yuh me champion! Dat me grindsman!

"Could I put this up here with you?" Dylan asked the driver.

The driver blinked. "He's kidding, right?"

"He never kids," Hope said. "He's Irish."

The driver squinted. "The Irish kid *all* the time."

"I'm being ironic," Hope said. "Would it fit in the trunk?"

The driver shook his head and opened the front passenger door. The head barely fit.

Dylan slid into the back seat and shut the door. "Brooklyn Hospital Center."

The cab pulled into traffic.

Hope put her hand on Dylan's thigh. "Are you cold, or are you just glad to see me?" she whispered.

"Both," Dylan said with a grin. "Where are your . . ." His mouth dropped open. "You're not wearing tights, Miss Warren."

"Right," Hope said. "We're going to be elephant mice tonight."

"So I'm . . . the only one," Dylan said, smiling and shaking his head. "I suppose Justin will be there to record the event."

"Yes," Hope said. "He's bringing his zoom lens, too."

Dylan pulled up his red coat. "Do I look as if I need a zoom lens?" he whispered.

"Nope," Hope said. "A wide angle lens."

He straightened his jacket. "Thank you."

"Are the ears inside the head?" Hope asked. *That has to be the strangest question I have ever asked!*

"Yes," Dylan said. "Five pairs of mouse ears are in a bag."

Hope grazed his leg with her nails. "You look cute."

"Give me some popcorn," Dylan said.

Hope hugged the bag of popcorn. "You're not stealing my snow."

"You know you can't throw that around the ICU," Dylan said.

She pushed the bag against her door. "They're putting down some plastic to catch it." She walked her fingers across Dylan's thigh.

Dylan grabbed Hope's hand. "Let's not give them a real show, okay?"

Dylan gave Hope the bag of mouse ears and promptly put on the nutcracker's head before entering the hospital. After Dylan had to duck to get into the elevator, Hope held the elevator door so several people could take pictures of him with their cell phones.

"Hope, please," Dylan said.

"I can't hear you," Hope said as more flashes lit up the elevator car. "I might be able to hear you if you take off the head."

"Not a chance," Dylan said. "I am a professional nutcracker. It would ruin the mystery if I revealed my true identity."

When Hope and Dylan entered the pediatric ICU waiting room, Hope couldn't stop smiling as Justin filled the room with flashes. Two ICU nurses wore gray scrubs and black boots, whiskers and button-black noses already painted on their faces. Angie had somehow stuffed all her hair inside a fuzzy black Beefeater's hat and stood at attention in a sharp toy soldier's costume complete with shiny black knee-high boots. Violine was putting the last whiskers on Dr. Mishra while Kiki put on her ears.

"Good evening, ladies," Dylan said, his hands on his hips. "Angie, it seems the mice outnumber us."

"This is a different version of *The Nutcracker*," Hope said. "The mice win because someone didn't make us any tails."

Dylan's huge head nodded. "My mistake."

"Violine," Hope said, "could you make me into the King Mouse, please?"

After Kiki secured all the mouse ears with bobby pins, Angie handed out gray plastic swords, and Hope gave a few instructions, the group tiptoed to Aniya's door.

"Is she awake?" Hope whispered.

"Yes," Violine said. "I will go get a front row seat." Violine entered the room and sat.

Dr. Mishra paced in front of Hope. "I am so nervous," she whispered.

"You'll do fine, doc," Hope said. "Break a leg."

Dr. Mishra shrugged. "And if I really do, I'm in the right place."

Dr. Mishra entered Aniya's room, the plastic tarp crinkling under her feet. "Good evening, Miss Aniya," she said. "Are you ready to go to the ballet now?"

"I can go?" Aniya said.

Hey, Aniya sounds a lot better today. She isn't whispering anymore.

"Why go *to* the ballet," Dr. Mishra said, "when the ballet can come to you?"

Hope pushed Kiki into the room and the two nurses followed, their swords slicing through the air, Justin trailing behind and snapping away.

I wish I could see Aniya's face! I hope Justin gets some good shots.

"Princess Aniya," Kiki said, bowing, "we are mouse soldiers at your service."

"Wow," Aniya said.

And that, *ladies and gentlemen, is why we did this.*

"But like any mouse soldier, we serve a queen," one of the nurses said.

A change in the script. I am now the Mouse Queen. Hey, it's a new millennium.

"And here," Kiki said, "is our bay-it of a queen."

Thanks, Kiki. I'm sure Aniya knows what bay-it is.

Hope slid in throwing popcorn in the air and pelting Kiki several times for effect.

"Hope!" Aniya cried.

Hope smiled and bowed. "I am at your service, Princess Aniya." *It is seriously crowded in here. We are going to have some interesting fight scenes.* She handed the bag to Kiki and soon felt popcorn hitting her back. "These are desperate times, Princess Aniya. It is snowing heavily and suddenly sleeting"—*Ow, Kiki!*—"and our enemies are marching right this minute to fight us." *Look at Aniya's eyes! I didn't think they could get any wider.* Hope looked behind her. "I *said,* our *enemies* are *marching* right this *second* to *fight* us."

Angie marched into the room, her face blank.

"She's a giant," Aniya whispered.

Because she's wearing heeled boots to make her seven feet tall, Hope thought as she moved to the right side of Aniya's bed. *I feel short. Kiki must feel like an ant.*

"You mangy mice," Angie said in a deep voice. "You must surrender." Angie pulled out her sword, which was at least twice as long as Hope's sword. "Or I will cut off your tails."

Oops.

"You already did, you forgetful giant toy soldier, you," Hope said.

Angie broke her blank face and smiled. "Oh, yeah. I forgot."

Aniya giggled.

Hope stood in front of her mice. "Make it last," she whispered, "and don't break anything." She turned to Aniya. "Princess Aniya, we will do our best to fight for your honor, but you must give us the command to attack."

Aniya raised her fists. "Attack the toy soldier!"

Hope watched Aniya's eyes dance as the mice surrounded Angie and sliced her to ribbons in slow motion. When Angie fell, she took up half the tarp.

"Sip sip mouse soldier," Hope said, "take that toy soldier out of here."

Kiki's shoulders slumped. "Yes, Queen Bay-it." She picked up Angie's legs and pulled, the entire tarp flowing with them out of the room and into the hallway.

I guess it has to stop snowing now. Hope kicked a few kernels toward the door.

The second nurse turned to Aniya. "Oh great princess, we have defeated the toy soldier, but the evil nutcracker is going to be so angry with us."

"Where's Dylan?" Aniya asked. "Is he the nutcracker?" She sat up taller in her bed. "Is he, Hope?"

We may have to change the script again. We can't kill her hero.

Hope nodded. "Yes, the nutcracker's name is Dylan, and he has sailed all the way from Ireland to harm us. Oh, what will we do?"

Aniya smiled. "You will *smash* him!"

Okay, we stick to the script.

Kiki ran in waving her hands. "He is coming! Hide, everybody, hide!"

Where?

"Turn and fight, brave mice," Hope said. "Get ready, because here he comes!"

Dylan bounced off the little hallway's walls before straightening his head and arriving at the foot of Aniya's bed.

"Dylan?" Aniya said. "Is that you?"

"It is I, Princess Aniya," Dylan said. "I am nutcracker Dylan at your service."

Oh, Dylan, don't . . . bow.

Dylan bowed.

After Dylan returned his nutcracker head to his own head, he pulled out his sword, which was even longer than Angie's sword. "Princess Aniya, the kingdom has been overrun with mice, and I must exterminate them!" He sliced the air. "En garde, evil mousies!"

In the original script, Dylan was supposed to dispatch Kiki and the two nurses with ease before facing off with Hope.

He didn't.

He couldn't *see* them.

Though his sword sliced and diced, the mice were too quick, ducking under and whacking him in the tights with their swords. Kiki delighted in hitting him squarely on his sexy derriere.

"Run into his sword," Hope whispered tersely to Kiki.

Kiki rolled her eyes and walked into Dylan's sword, falling over. The two nurses soon followed.

Too many bodies in the way.

"Will the nutcracker allow his enemy to clear the battlefield before the final battle?" Hope asked.

"What?" Dylan asked.

He's deaf and blind in that head. He must have used four layers of papier-mâché.

Hope dragged the nurses out carefully. She smiled at Kiki. *You hit my man in the derriere. Yuh goin' out hard.*

Dylan chose this moment to swing his sword, narrowly missing Hope's forehead.

"Get out of here," Hope whispered to Kiki.

Kiki crawled away.

Hope drew her sword and tapped Dylan on the shoulder. "Turn and fight, you vile piece of wood!"

Dylan turned, but his head did not.

Aniya giggled.

I'll bet he did that on purpose. That was funny.

He righted his head and took up a fighting stance. "No more will you . . ."

Hope heard paper rustling. *He has the script inside the head.*

"Here it is," Dylan said. "No more will you devastate the land, King Mouse."

"She's a queen, Dylan!" Aniya cried.

"That she is," Dylan said. "No more will you devastate the land, Queen Mouse. My princess, you may not want to watch this. It is not going to be pretty."

It wasn't.

Hope treated the nutcracker's head like a piñata, cracking it so hard that paint and papier-mâché flaked and flew off in huge chunks around the room.

"Get him!" Aniya yelled. "Knock his head off!"

Before Hope could reach up and tip the now hideous nut-cracker's head from Dylan's shoulders, Dylan threw it off, his face as white as plaster. "Not so fast, Queen Mouse." He tossed the sword back and forth between his hands. "You may have taken my head, but you'll never take my heart!"

Hope pouted.

"You know what I mean," Dylan said.

Hope smiled.

"En garde!" Dylan cried, circling to his right and lunging forward.

Hope grabbed the plastic blade and bent it back toward him.

"No fair," Dylan said, staring at his sword point staring at him. "Princess Aniya, I am in trouble!"

"Off with his head!" Aniya said, giggling.

"No fair," Dylan said.

"As you wish, my princess," Hope said. "May I kiss him before I take off his head?"

Aniya nodded. "Yes, but only once."

Hope stuck her sword under Dylan's chin. "Do you yield, vile king?"

Dylan smiled. "No."

Hope kissed him. "Do you yield now?"

"I surrender," he said, falling to his knees. "Please don't cut off my head."

Hope looked at Aniya. "It's not a bad head as heads go."

"Yeah," Aniya said. "Let him keep it."

"Thank you, oh great and wise princess," Hope said. "You have saved your kingdom." She bowed. "The end."

The nurses, Kiki, Angie, and Dr. Mishra crowded in for their bows, and Aniya and Violine clapped. Kiki dug the present out of the popcorn bag and handed it to Hope.

"Aniya," Hope said as Dylan collected what was left of the nutcracker's head, "what you just saw is *nothing* like the real story of the nutcracker. When you have time, watch this." She handed Aniya the DVD, and Aniya tore it open.

"Thank you," Aniya said.

Dylan sat on the edge of Aniya's bed. "So how did we do?"

"You were funny," Aniya said, "and I don't want you to go."

I don't know how Violine handles all this. I'd probably cry every time that child spoke.

"Go?" Dylan said. "The night is young. Hey, let's get you in a cast picture." He turned to Justin. "Can you get us all in a shot with Aniya?"

Justin nodded. "Mice to the left, soldiers to the right." He took a dozen pictures. "I'll make sure you get a poster of this, Aniya."

"Cool," Aniya said. She held up her DVD. "Can we watch this now?"

Hope looked at Dr. Mishra. "Can we? We'll be as quiet as mice."

Dr. Mishra checked her watch. "You'll need to clear the room for about half an hour."

Aniya slumped into her pillow. "No more tests."

They're for you own good, little one. "We'll be right outside, Aniya," Hope said. "You'll probably be able to hear us giggling."

Aniya nodded.

Angie led Kiki out of the room.

Hope winked. "See you in a few." She took Dylan's hand. "Come on, King Klutz."

"See you in a few minutes," Dylan said as they left.

Violine followed them to the waiting room. "She will be asleep in a few minutes," she said. "I am surprised she was awake so long. The medications are so strong. She was not sick once this evening, and I know she was excited. It is a good sign." She hugged Kiki. "You are a funny mouse." She hugged Angie. "You are too tall." She hugged Dylan. "You were a good and funny king." She hugged Hope. "You are just good."

"Thank you," Hope said. "Are you sure she's going to fall asleep? She seemed pretty alert."

"She is having her sleep medications now," Violine said. "She heals best when she's asleep." She turned and hugged Justin. "I want as many pictures as you can spare. I want to show Georges what he missed."

"Sure," Justin said. "Gotta run. See you all tomorrow."

Justin started for the elevators, turning and flashing one more picture.

"God bless you all," Violine said.

On the elevator ride down to the lobby, Hope rested her head on Dylan's shoulder while he picked popcorn from her locks. "You were a pretty wooden actor, Mr. Healy," Hope said. "I think your tights were cutting off your oxygen supply."

"And you were kind of mousy," Dylan said.

Kiki shook her head. "Do you never stop with the puns?"

"No," Dylan said. "We like to *pun*ish people."

Hope smiled at Angie and Kiki. "That's about the tall and short of it."

Angie laughed.

Kiki sighed. "Please stop. You are infecting Angie."

"It was funny, Kiki," Angie said. "Lighten up or I'll give you the boot."

Hope laughed. "Which one?"

"*Both*," Angie said. "Then it will be the tall and *shorter* of it."

The elevator doors opened, and Kiki pushed Angie out.

"Quit being so *pushy*, Kiki," Angie said.

Kiki stopped and turned to Hope and Dylan. "I blame you both for this. She used to be so shy, and now look!"

Hope hugged Kiki. "Thank you for being such a mean little mouse, Kiki. Next time I will make you a sip sip soldier."

Kiki looked at the ground. "I hope there is no need for a next time. Will she get better?"

"I hope so," Hope said. "No one knows for sure."

Kiki nodded. "I think I will visit her tomorrow at lunch with you. We will bring her the poster and the pictures."

"Okay," Hope said.

Dylan and Hope watched Kiki and Angie walk into the night, a tall toy soldier and a buxom mouse.

Only in Brooklyn.

"Where to?" Dylan asked.

Hope pulled her coat around her. "It's cold."

"How do you think I feel?" Dylan asked. "The wind is quite unkind to a man in tights."

They took a cab to Hope's apartment, and once inside, Hope relieved him of his tights. As soon as they hit the floor, Whack dove on them and started shredding them.

"She doesn't like tights," Dylan said.

Or dresses. Hope blinked. "I guess not."

Dylan looked down at his boxers. "How am I going to get home now?"

Hope went to her wardrobe and returned with a pair of jeans. "These are the ones I borrowed from you. They don't fit me anymore."

Dylan smiled as he put on his old jeans. "I've noticed the tightness of your clothes, Miss Warren. Even those sweats are crying a little to be released." He pulled her to him and rubbed his hands on her sexy derriere.

I want him so bad, but my friend is still here, and it's going on two weeks. "Dylan, I'm still on my period. My body is still figuring itself out down there."

"How long does your period usually last?" Dylan asked.

This is the first time any man's ever cared to ask me. "At most six days, and that was usually when I was fighting a cold. I thought I was winding down a few days ago, but it came back with a vengeance." She put her hands into his back pockets. "I want you so badly."

"Maybe we can hold each other all night instead," Dylan said.

"On a Monday night?" Hope asked.

"I will have to set your alarm for five," Dylan said, "and I will have to borrow my hoodie from you."

Hope led him to the bed. "Sneaky man," she whispered. "You're only staying so you can get your clothes back."

"I'm staying so I can rub on your back," he whispered.

Hope flattened herself on the bed. "Rub away, my noble nut-cracker, rub away, and please don't spin your head around at any time during the night . . ."

Hope did not appreciate what five AM looked like. *Too dark, too cold.*

She did appreciate the kiss Dylan gave her at 5:15 AM.

"You smell so nice," she whispered dreamily. "Come back to bed."

"I want to," Dylan whispered, "but I have to be there by six, and I have to make your breakfast. Aniya explained the trick to me."

"What's the trick?"

"Never leave the toaster," he whispered. He kissed her lower back. "Get better soon. See you in a few hours."

Hope woke the same way for the rest of the week, and she began to appreciate five AM. She tried to keep Dylan from leaving the bed, grabbing on his hips, but he easily pinned her to the bed and kissed her neck before leaving for the shower. She waited until she heard the water before opening the washroom door and racing back to bed. She enjoyed watching him brush his teeth, shower, towel off, shave, and get dressed. She most enjoyed the kiss before he left.

This could be the start of my everyday life in less than three weeks. Up early with my man, bathing together—I hope that basement apartment has a big tub!—and then going upstairs to wait on the first arrivals at Art for Kids' Sake while eating toast and jam and drinking our coffee. We have to get a decent coffeemaker and a toaster we don't have to watch. And at least for the time being, I can hang out until 8:30 every morning before going on to Thrifty.

Hope visited Aniya with Kiki during lunch and with Dylan after dinner, and though Aniya seemed to be improving—and staying up later and later to watch the *Nutcracker* DVD with them several times—she was still no nearer to going home.

"I am as frustrated as Aniya is," Dr. Mishra said once Aniya had fallen asleep Friday night, only a week before Christmas. "Her counts are going up, but not as quickly as I'd like them to. Her white blood cells, the ones that help fight infection, are not half what they should be. She has been fighting this disease for so long, and her little body is exhausted from the fight."

"Could she go home for Christmas, even for a few hours?" Dylan asked. "She only lives a few minutes away on Nostrand. What's an hour?"

"I am afraid that would be unwise," Dr. Mishra said.

"At least let her open her presents at home." Dylan pointed at the poster Justin made and what was left of the nutcracker's head staring out of a corner. "This room isn't very festive, not for a child at Christmas."

"There would be too great a risk for infection," Dr. Mishra said. "She cannot fight off any infection now. She's safest here."

"Christmas is only a week away," Dylan said. "What has to happen before she can go home?"

"Her CBC, her complete blood count—and that includes white and red blood cells and platelets—has to *double*," Dr. Mishra said. "At present rate, that will not happen."

"Aniya will do it," Dylan said later that night as he and Hope watched *Frosty the Snowman.* "She has to. I've been sneaking her candy canes."

"What?" Hope said.

"They're red and white, right? Christmas colors. Her red and white blood cell counts have to go up."

"Dylan, you shouldn't be feeding her sweets."

"I'm not feeding her," Dylan said. "I'm sneaking them to her. What she does with them on her own time is her business." He rolled on top of her, placing her legs on his hips. "Is it possible for me to feed you sweets tonight?"

Hope poked out her lip. "Is your candy cane lonely?"

Dylan nodded.

"I am lonely for your candy cane," Hope said, "but my friend is threatening to stay through the holidays. Let's give it more time, okay?"

Dylan nodded.

"What are we doing tomorrow?" Hope asked.

"Tomorrow, you will see me fall fifty times," Dylan said.

Hope smiled. "I was wondering when we'd go ice-skating."

They spent the day at the Wollman Rink in Prospect Park, and Dylan only fell a few times while Hope skated like a champion.

"How did you learn to skate so well?" he asked as they shared hot chocolate and hot pretzels.

"I am from Canada," Hope said.

Dylan blinked. "There is no skating gene, Hope. There has to be a story behind it."

"Are you saying black people aren't predisposed to ice-skating?" Hope asked.

Dylan wisely did not answer.

"Most Canadian children learn from their parents in backyard rinks and on lakes," Hope said. "Since I was the child of Bahamian immigrants, my parents forced me to take skating lessons for four years."

"You skate very well," Dylan said. "You kept me from falling numerous times, and my derriere thanks you very much." He looked out at the mass of skaters. "Explain something to me. Why is it that the young ladies can wear so little while they skate?"

Hope saw several "ballerinas" wearing high skirts, tights, and leggings as they spun in the center of the rink. "Those outfits are ridiculous. Normal girls wear jeans and sweaters." She pushed his arm. "But why are you staring at them, Mr. Healy?"

"Oh, just imagining what you would look like in those skirts," Dylan said. He stood. "You will teach me how to skate backwards now."

The man has trouble going forward. "Maybe another day. I don't want your *boomsie* to be too sore for later."

"What's later?" Dylan whispered.

"I'm a ready *vooman*," Hope said. "That means I'm really horny and I'm almost positive my friend has finally left for the holidays."

Dylan dropped to the bench and began unlacing his skates. "While I would like nothing more than to skate and fall some more and then later hear the Brooklyn Philharmonia Chorus singing carols at the Lefferts House over there"—he pointed—"because I have never missed the chance to sing Handel's *Messiah* here in Prospect Park for the last fifteen years, I would much rather spend the rest of this weekend with a ready *vooman* doing interesting things with my candy cane."

Hope loved having a ready man.

Hope stripped completely as she entered her apartment and went straight to the scale in the washroom, Dylan looking over her shoulder as he wiggled out of his boxers.

"One thirty-four," he said. "That's good, isn't it?"

Thirty-five pounds in twelve weeks! "That's fantastic, not good! Go warm up the bed."

With Dylan gone, Hope closed the washroom door and opened the closet, pulling out the Santa hats she'd bought from Mr. Al-Hamsi. She put the first on her head. The second and third she secured to her breasts by rolling up the bottoms. *I'm wearing B cup Santa hats.* She tore the stitching out of the fourth and secured it to her waist with dental floss. *This won't stay on long.* She smiled. *But that's the point, isn't it?*

Now look who has props.

She opened the washroom door and closed it behind her, her left foot inching up the door. "Will you fill my stocking and eat my cookies, Santa?"

Dylan threw back the covers and sat on the edge of the bed. "Only if you jingle my bells, Mrs. Claus."

Whoa. Look at all that man candy. Hope took a step forward, the movement causing her "flap" to rise and fall. *That was chilly.* "I need you to slide down my chimney, Santa. I am feeling like a ho ho ho."

Dylan stood. "My pole is definitely pointing north, Mrs. Claus."

Oh, yes. "You sleigh me, Santa." She took another step, and her "breast hats" fell off.

Whack shot out of the kitchen, snatched one, and ran off with it.

"Your hats fell like rain . . . dear," Dylan said.

That was horrible! She moved closer. "It's beginning to look a *lot* like Christmas."

Dylan breathed deeply. "Let me unwrap your package . . ."

It was definitely no silent afternoon or silent night in Hope's apartment after that. Hope's neighbors told them to be quiet in four languages as Hope shouted *"Allez plus profonds!"* (Go deeper!), *"Plus vite!"* (Faster!), and *"Serrez mon derrière sexy!"*

Hope liked to have her sexy derriere squeezed now that she had one, and Dylan did his best to separate it from her body.

During a rare lull in the action, Dylan cradled her face as she lay beside him. *"Ta tu go halainn, mo anam cara.* You are beautiful, my soul mate."

"And I finally feel beautiful, too." She kissed his hands. *"Merci."*

"I want you to teach me some more French," Dylan said. "How do you say, 'I could do this all night long'?"

"Je pourrais le faire pendant toute la nuit," Hope said.

"You could? Good. I intend to." Dylan kissed her and slid his hot hand down her side to her hip. "How do you say, 'You are the best lover I will ever have'?"

"Vous êtes le meilleur amant que j'aurai jamais," Hope whispered.

"Merci," Dylan whispered. "You make me feel like the best lover who ever lived. You weren't kidding about your *orgasmes.*"

"I've already lost count," Hope whispered. "You need to catch up."

He caressed her thigh. "I don't want to. How do you say, 'I have waited for you all my life'?"

"J'ai attendu vous tout ma vie," Hope whispered.

Dylan sighed. "Sorry I kept you waiting. How do you say, 'I want to spend the rest of my life with you'?"

Hope's heart raced. "*Je veux passer le reste de ma vie avec vous.* You do?"

He kissed her. "I can't imagine living another moment without you. I want to be with you all the time. How do you say, 'Let's make a baby'?"

Hope began to cry. "*Je t'aime.*"

"No, that means 'I love you,' and while it's nice to hear, that doesn't answer my question," Dylan said. "How do you say, 'Let's make a baby'?"

"*Permettez-nous de faire un bébé,*" Hope said, hugging him close to her. "*Je t'aime.*" She reached down and found him ready again. "*Le faisons de nouveau,*" she whispered, turning onto her back.

"I hope that means let's do it again," Dylan whispered.

Hope nodded. "*Quintuplés,*" Hope whispered. "*Je veux des quintuplés.*" She raised her hips to meet him and felt him plunge deep inside her. "*Je t'aime, Dylan.*"

"I love you, Hope." He smiled as he began to move. "Five?" he whispered. "Really?"

"Or eight or nine . . ."

This is what it's all about! She gripped his sexy derriere.

"Or ten . . ."

CHRISTMAS EVE

Last day to shop before Christmas . . .

Chapter 25

With Thrifty closed for the day, Hope woke up smiling in the darkness on Christmas Eve morning while Dylan showered and Whack finished shredding the Santa hats somewhere in the kitchen.

Big day. Huge day.

She sighed as Dylan came out of the tub. *The man makes me tingle just looking at him. If I weren't being sneaky today, I would do him right there in the washroom.* She wandered her fingers down her stomach. *So glad this works again. Damn. Turn this way, turn this . . . way . . . Oh, yes . . .*

Already? Yes!

I don't want to leave this bed now.

"Will you come to breakfast?" Dylan asked.

I came before *breakfast. It's time to start the charade.* "I'm sleeping in."

Dylan pulled on his pants. "Good."

"Maybe we can do lunch," Hope said, working a leg out from under the covers.

Dylan sat on the bed and caressed her leg. "I'll be working through lunch today," Dylan whispered. "I have to batten down the hatches since we'll be closed for four days. Though the softness and heat your leg is giving off is giving me second thoughts."

Hope pulled his hand up to her breasts. "Only second thoughts? Why not thirds?"

He kissed each nipple. "Later, I will have fourths," he said.

"I could bring you lunch," Hope whispered.

"We'll do dinner instead," Dylan said.

We'll see about that. "Is your apartment ready, Santa?"

Dylan pulled on a T-shirt. "I haven't been there in so long. I guess. I hope the tree hasn't dried out."

"When will you be available to come get me?" Hope asked.

"I don't know," Dylan said. "I'll call you later."

She slipped out of bed and wrapped her arms around him.

"You are completely naked, Hope," Dylan whispered. "Will you kiss me good-bye this way always? Please say you will."

"I will." She kissed him and led him to the door, opening it.

Dylan jumped into the doorway and shielded her. "*Cailín*, what are you doing?"

Exorcising a goblin from my past for the last time. She kissed him tenderly. "Turn around."

Dylan turned.

Hope cuffed him sharply on his *boomsie*.

"Ow," Dylan said.

"There's more where that came from," Hope said.

Dylan smiled. "As long as I can reciprocate."

"You better," Hope said. "Have a great day." She kissed the back of his neck.

"You, too."

As soon as Hope closed the door, she checked the clock.

Five-thirty.

Time to get to work on my day off.

I have a lot of work to do and barely enough time to do it.

While she ran hot water in the bathtub, she assembled all the shampoo and conditioner she owned near the lip of the tub.

I hope I have enough conditioner.

She shut off the water, disrobed, and lay in the bathtub, soaking her dreadlocks for ten minutes while trying to keep her body from contacting the hot water for too long. Once her hair was sufficiently soaked, she shampooed and rinsed her dreadlocks with hot water for the next half hour, her fingers cramping, her arms aching, her scalp burning. Confident that no wax or grease remained in her hair, Hope stepped out of the bathtub and immediately worked co-pious amounts of conditioner into each dreadlock.

And now for the not-so-fun part.

Removing the only metal comb she had from her medicine cab-inet, she began picking out each dread, beginning at the bottom and working her way to the scalp.

She did this for the next two hours until her dreads were no longer locked, her scalp was on fire, and her fingers were nearly numb.

She returned to the shower and washed her hair rigorously de-spite the pain, drying it thoroughly with a hair dryer that dimmed the washroom light. She looked in the mirror, pulling her hair away from her face.

I'll look all right.

She wrapped her face with her hair one last time. *This isn't my hair anymore. It belongs to a child. Yes. A princess out there is wait-ing for this queen's hair.*

She watched a few tears fall into the sink.

It'll grow back. Aniya's will grow back, too. Right. We'll grow our hair out again together. I just hope Dylan—

Hope tried to part her hair in the center of her head, but the going was painfully slow. She felt her depression creeping up on her again. *Doh ge' meh vex, nuh. Not today. I don't need to be de-pressed today. I am deeply in love, we're working on a baby, and I'm happy. Go away. I'm confident Dylan will like my hair. I hope he likes it, but even if he doesn't, a child will like it, and that's what re-ally matters.*

After combing her hair to each side, Hope separated her hair into what she hoped were six equal sections, twisting and flopping them over her ears. She laughed at the woman in the mirror. *I look like Aniya's Medusa masks.* She slid rubber bands up the length of each thick ponytail, leaving herself two inches of hair. *Now I look like Dread Woman. No more stick figure girl for me.* She shook her head one last time. *I'm about to lose two pounds!*

She sighed and picked up the scissors.

Make him still love me.

She cut above the last rubber band until the ponytail was in her hand. *Look at that. Eight years of hair.* She cut the other five, wrapped them in tissue paper, and put them in a Ziploc bag. *They might get two wigs out of all this hair.* She slid the bag into a large envelope and addressed it:

Wigs for Kids
24231 Center Ridge Road
Westlake, Ohio 44145

She showered again, watching hair clog the drain, and then she inspected the damage in the mirror.
Dear God, what a mess.
More tears fell into the sink.
She tried to comb it out, but it wouldn't cooperate.
I need some help.
I need a lot of help.
On the day before Christmas when most salons are filled to capacity.
She dressed hurriedly and put on a toque, dropping the envelope in outgoing mail downstairs and rushing outside to the nearest ATM, a Capital One Bank ATM that charged her a fee.
I did not think this through at all.
She threw back her shoulders, collected her thoughts, and entered Divine Connection Hair Spa, the salon already packed and noisy at 9:30 AM.
Hope approached a woman at a counter. "Is there any chance I could get an appointment this morning?" she whispered.
The woman, wearing a brown smock with a "Samantha" name tag on the strap, shook her head. "We can't possibly get to you today. I'm sorry."
Hope removed her hat. "Please."
All noise in the Divine Connection Hair Spa ceased.
Hope felt tears.
"Child," Samantha said, "what did you *do*?"
Hope looked around at the eyes looking at her. "I cut off my

hair for Wigs for Kids. For children who lose their hair because of illness." Tears hit the counter. "I just mailed my hair to Ohio."

Samantha moved around the counter. "Oh, I remember you. Your hair was so long. You walk by here every day, don't you?"

Hope nodded. *There are too many mirrors in here.* "My . . . my boyfriend hasn't seen me yet. It's going to be a surprise."

"She can go in front of me," an older woman said.

Hope put both her hands on her head. "Do I look that bad?"

"You could look a *lot* better, honey," the woman said. "Some surprises need some extra help. Your hair needs some divine intervention, child."

Hope turned to the woman. "Thank you. I'm, um, I'm Hope."

"Good name," the woman said. "I'm Joy. Nicole will take good care of you, child."

"Thank you, Joy."

Nicole led Hope to her chair as the noise increased. "Don't worry about a thing," she said. "You ain't hopeless." She pulled up some of Hope's hair. "How long was it?"

"Sixteen inches," Hope said. "More or less."

"Least you left me something to work with," Nicole said. "Anything in particular you want done?"

"I just want to be . . . acceptable."

Nicole smiled. "I don't do acceptable. I'm gonna make you beautiful."

"Thank you."

Nicole handed Hope a tissue. "It won't be hard," she whispered. "You already are." She squeezed Hope's shoulders. "Leave everything to me."

In a matter of hours, Nicole transformed Hope into an angel with tight ringlet curls that fully showed off Hope's eyes, forehead, and ears.

"What do you think?" Nicole asked.

"I look like a little boy," Hope whispered. "I want him to like me."

"Girl, with that body, you do *not* look like a boy," Nicole said. "God has been good to you."

Hope turned her head side to side. "Yes. He has." *Three months ago I was an anorexic stick figure dread girl, but now there's a curvy, sexy, short-haired woman staring at me.*

Hope stepped out of the chair. "How much do I owe you? I haven't had my hair done in over eight years."

Divine Connection Hair Spa again became silent.

I must learn not to speak in this place. "So I don't know what things cost," Hope whispered.

It was still quiet.

They're curious, too. I don't blame them.

Nicole looked around the salon, and then she shrugged. "Normally, I charge extra for a rescue."

Hope took out a roll of twenties. "A hundred sixty? Two hundred?"

Nicole hugged her. "Child, I was going to say eighty."

Hope handed her ten twenties. "You saved me. Take it."

Nicole took the money. "God bless you."

Hope smiled at Joy. "When should I come back?"

"Soon?" Joy said.

Divine Connection Hair Spa filled with laughter.

"I'll be back," Hope said. "Merry Christmas, everybody." She took out her toque and started to put it on her head.

"No!" sounded out from all over the salon.

Hope pulled the toque off, holding it in front of her. "But it's cold outside."

"Let it *breathe*, girl," Joy said. "Let the world see you."

Hope stuffed the toque into her pocket. "Okay. Thank you for giving up your spot."

"I have nowhere else to be today," Joy said. "It's one of the perks of being a granny. *They* come to *you*. I imagine you have plenty of errands to run today."

Hope nodded. "Yes."

"He'll love it," Joy said. "When you do something for love, love always comes back to you."

Hope nodded. "Thanks again. Merry Christmas."

Though the wind stung her ears, Hope walked briskly down Washington Avenue to the Brooklyn Museum, where she caught a cab with a single wave.

"Where to, miss?" the driver asked.

A chivalrous driver? "Macy's on Fulton," Hope said.

"You sure?" the driver said. "The one in Manhattan is much nicer."

"I'm a Brooklyn girl," she said, "and isn't the one on Thirty-fourth Street packed with tourists today?"

"You're right," the driver said. "Macy's on Fulton it is."

Ten minutes later, Hope was inside arguably the dingiest, darkest, draftiest Macy's on earth, but despite the holiday, it wasn't very crowded. As she navigated the cosmetics section, she heard sales staff calling out to women rushing by and then talking badly about them when they wouldn't stop at their counter.

"You see her turkey neck? Oh my *Gaw*-ud, she couldn't hide that nose unless she had it cut off and buried!"

This should not be allowed to happen at any time, especially on Christmas Eve.

Hope stopped and stared at one saleswoman who had called out to her. "Do I look as if I need your product?" Hope asked.

The saleswoman shook her head.

"Then why are you yelling at me?" Hope asked.

The saleswoman took a step back from the glass counter. "It's, uh, my job, to, um, to—"

"To be mean and rude?" Hope interrupted. "I heard what you said about that woman. She was Italian, or didn't you notice?"

"I, uh . . ."

"She was born with that nose, and she wears it with pride," Hope said. "What are you going to say about me when I walk on?"

The other saleswomen had quieted.

"Um, nothing, actually," the saleswoman said. "You have flawless skin."

"*Merci,*" Hope said. "But you're missing the point. What if I didn't?" She whirled and gave the other saleswomen the cut-eye. "Yuh bes' nuh talk 'bout me when me leave, nuh."

Hope walked on.

In silence.

I am Island woman, hear me roar.

She found a silver-and-gold stainless steel watchband for

Dylan's watch easily, and it was on sale, but she could find no one to ring her up. Three saleswomen lounged and chatted near a display for some gaudy, overpriced handbag obviously no one was buying this year.

Before Hope could even speak, two of the three saleswomen held up fingers. The third seemed to smirk.

You want me to wait? You're not busy. Do I go Island on them, or do I embarrass them? I need this purchase. I'm on a tight schedule and I have a man to surprise soon. If I go Island, I may end up cuffing them all.

Hope smiled. "*Je voudrais acheter ce bracelet de montre,*" she said sweetly.

The smirking woman blinked. "Do you speak any English?"

I'm speaking American just fine. "Yes," Hope said without a trace of an accent. "Will one of you please ring me up?"

The smirking woman stopped smirking, scowling instead. "Come on," she said.

Hope followed the woman to the register and handed the woman the watchband and her debit card. "*Merci de faire votre travail,*" she said.

The woman looked up. "What did you say?"

"I thanked you for doing your job," Hope said.

The woman scanned her card and bagged the watchband. "What are you, some kind of an interpreter?"

Hope took her card and the bag. "*Non, je suis un américain.*"

"What?" she said.

Hope shook her head. "I'm an American."

"Did you ever think you might be confusing people a little by switching back and forth like that?" she asked.

"It's about as confusing as watching three workers *not* work on Christmas Eve, don't you think?" Hope smiled. "*Joyeux Noël.*"

After spending ten minutes getting the watchband wrapped in a small box, Hope took another cab, this time to 1001 Flatbush.

I have the sign in my pocket, but I have no tape.

She went around the corner to Staples, but when she went inside, she walked back out immediately.

One cashier on Christmas Eve? One? Are they insane? I'd be waiting an hour to get a roll of tape! Whatever happened to good old-fashioned customer service? No wonder people hate the holidays.

She opened the door to Dylan's dream, closing it behind her. *Brr. Mr. Vacca was right about the furnace. I wonder where the controls are.* She took out the present and borrowed a few slivers of tape from the wrapping paper, centering the "Art for Kids' Sake" sign in the window.

Now all I have to do is get him here.

Without a phone.

I need to get a cell phone. I now have people to call!

This surprise is turning into a surprise to me, too.

She left the building, locking the door behind her. She looked up and down the street for a pay phone. *I know I've seen one today. Wasn't there one in front of Staples?*

She rushed around the corner at Tilden and picked up the receiver carefully, holding it away from her ear.

I have no change.

She hung up the phone and crossed the street to Rainbow, a clothing shop, and stood in line to ask the cashier for change. As she waited, she looked at the outfits around her. *This store is perfect for women like me. These are some nice clothes! Look at all the colors! I would look so good in that top, and the prices are incredible! Oh, I love that—*

"Ma'am?"

This line moved fast. Dylan will bring me here. There is a whole new wardrobe waiting here for me. "May I have some change? For the pay phone."

"Local call?" the girl asked.

"Yes."

She pointed to a phone at the end of the counter. "Go ahead."

Hope squinted. "Really?"

The girl nodded. "You calling to ask him if you can spend more of his money?"

What a great idea! "Yes. Thank you."

She dialed the Kinderstuff number, which rang and rang before she heard a message: "This Kinderstuff location will be closed until Monday . . ." She dialed Dylan's cell number.

"Hello, sexy," Dylan said.

Hope looked at the lingerie section. Those bras are so sexy. "Where are you?"

"Working," Dylan said. "What's up?"

"I need you to meet me at Rainbow on the corner of Tilden and Flatbush as soon as you get off," Hope said.

"I know where it is," Dylan said. "Are you going to let me buy you new clothes? I've already looked around that store a couple of times for you, but when you said you didn't need anything . . ."

He's already been here shopping for me? There is a God! "I'll let you." *Just not today.* "Get here quick." She looked at the front window. "They close at three today."

"I'll be there as soon as I can," Dylan said. "I have some major cleaning up to do around here."

"Please hurry!"

"I'll try. Bye."

Hope hung up. "Thank you," she said to the cashier, and then she browsed the store.

Or, maybe, the store browsed Hope Warren.

Everything she looked at, felt, and held up to her body thrilled her. Tie-dyed surplices, floral tube dresses, rugby racer-back stripe dresses, skinny jeans, belted chiffon dresses, lacy tank tops, *hachi* sweaters, suede boots, ballet flats, kitten heeled slings, belts, bags, and even a simple straw fedora talked to her, beckoned to her.

She checked a clock. *It's two o'clock already? He should be here by now.*

She left Rainbow and walked up Flatbush to McDonald's, hoping to run into him along the way. Not wanting to wait twenty minutes for a large fry and a Coke, Hope continued up Flatbush looking for Dylan. She stopped in front of Bella Jewelry, staring at the diamond rings in the window.

A woman poked her head out the door. "You want to come inside and look? It's cold out."

Hope smiled. "Just window-shopping. Dreaming."

"We're having a sale," she said.

"I don't want to buy," Hope said. "I want *him* to buy." *But mostly I want him to get here!*

"What about earrings?" the woman asked.

Hope touched her earlobes. "They're not pierced."

"I have just the thing," she said. "Come in."

Hope looked up Flatbush past Linden Boulevard. "I'm waiting for someone. I don't want to miss him."

"I'll come out to you then," the woman said. A few minutes later, she reappeared in a heavy sweater holding some tiny gold bands. "They're called ear cuffs." She attached one to the cartilage of her own ear. "Fourteen-karat gold."

"It won't fall off?" Hope asked.

The woman handed her one. "Just pinch."

Hope put one on, the cold metal giving her goose bumps.

"It almost matches your ring," she said. "You might even consider two ear cuffs for each ear. Half off everything today."

Hope looked at her reflection in the window. "How much?"

"Today, thirty for four."

Hope sighed. "I can't remember the last time I bought myself jewelry." *These ear cuffs make my exposed ears look very sexy, though.* She handed the woman two twenties. "I'll get four."

"I'll get them and your change," the woman said.

Hope looked up Flatbush.

No Dylan.

Where is he?

The woman returned with a ten and helped Hope put the other three on her ears. "They really look good on you. I'm sure he'll like them."

Hope blinked.

"The man you're looking for," the woman said. "He's running late, huh?"

Hope nodded.

"This is the best day for running late," she said. "It might mean he's planning a surprise for you."

I'm the one who's supposed to do the surprising today. "I hope so."

"He'll like them," she said. "Just make sure he doesn't accidentally swallow one. Merry Christmas."

"Merry Christmas to you, too," Hope said.

She drifted down Flatbush, twisting her promise ring. *I hope this ring isn't another empty promise. I hope he isn't getting cold feet. Only my feet are cold today. He had my feet burning up Saturday night. But maybe I scared him away. He saw how powerful I was. Maybe he liked the shy, skinny, hairy blind girl better. He could take care of her. This new short-haired Island girl is much too formidable for him.*

No! Dylan can still take care of me. He loves me.

Hope returned to Rainbow and again asked to use the phone. She dialed Dylan's cell, and it went straight to voice mail. "Dylan, hi. Where are you? I'm still here waiting at Rainbow, and they're getting ready to close up. I hope everything's okay. Please hurry."

Hope watched the clock and Flatbush at the same time. "Come on, Dylan. Come on."

Perhaps he found a better way to spend his holiday, Hope thought. *Perhaps Marie surprised him with a visit. Old lovers do that. They like to drop in for the holidays. Old flames are still flames. They still burn hot. Dylan was probably Marie's first love. It's so hard to forget a first love, and—*

"We're closing, ma'am."

Hope nodded at the cashier. "I guess he got lost." She left Rainbow and stood under the Rainbow sign, staring across the street at Staples. *Dylan is never lost. He knows every street in Brooklyn. Where is he?*

She watched people trickling into and out Staples for the next half hour.

Maybe he saw what I look like and kept walking!

"No," Hope whispered. "No. He would never do that."

There he is!

Finally!

But why is he on Tilden instead of Flatbush? Where is he coming to me from?

Dylan dodged traffic across Tilden and stood in front of her, his hands in his pockets. "Sorry I'm late, Hope. Traffic was a nightmare. Hey, what happened—"

"Traffic?" Hope interrupted. "What traffic? Most people are inside getting ready for Santa. You see anyone out here on the street? Your watch stop or what?" *Where is his watch?* "Where is your watch? Did it fall off?"

Dylan wisely stepped back. "No, I, um . . . but what have you done—"

"Where is your watch?" Hope interrupted, her hand pointing at his wrist. "Did you lose it?"

Dylan wisely stepped to his left. "Sort of. Hope, I really like—"

"I knew that duct tape would die one day," Hope interrupted, "and here I got you something for it." She took the box from her coat pocket and tossed it to Dylan. "It's an unbreakable watchband. What good it will do."

Dylan took several quick breaths. "I gave my watch to Aniya. It's wrapped and under her tree. She'll get to open it tomorrow."

"What?" Hope shouted.

"Dr. Mishra is letting her go home for a few hours tomorrow," Dylan said. "Aniya's counts are great. Hope, I have to tell you that you look—"

"Why'd you give her your watch?" Hope interrupted. "After all we already gave that child. Why'd you give her *that* watch?"

"I wanted to give it to Shayna, but I never got the chance," Dylan said. "Those, um, clips in your ear are—"

"So I should give your watchband to Aniya then," Hope interrupted.

"If you want to," Dylan said. "We can drop it by her house right now. Are you all right?"

"Oh, *now* he asks!" Hope shouted.

"I've been trying to talk to you, but you keep—"

"No, I'm *not* all right," Hope interrupted. "You're three hours late, you don't have the watch for the Christmas present I got you, and you haven't said a thing about my hair!"

Dylan wisely counted to ten. "May I speak now?"

Hope turned away. "I don't want to hear anything you have to say."

"Okay, don't listen then," Dylan said. "I've been trying to compliment you, but you keep interrupting me. I *really* like your hair."

Hope snapped her head to him. "Like it? You only *like* it?"

Dylan blinked. "It will take some getting used to, but it's sexy. It makes your eyes even bigger and sexier. Even your head has a sexy shape, and those gold hoop-things in your ears are nice. Do *you* like your hair?"

"Yes, but it doesn't matter now," Hope said. "Where were you?"

Dylan stepped closer and reached for her hand.

Hope moved her hand out of reach.

"I love the sacrifice you made, Hope," Dylan said softly, "and I hope to meet the little girl who wears your hair someday. I know I'll recognize it."

"How'd you know I didn't cut it just to cut it? Eh? Eh? I could have just cut it to cut it. I could have had it cut because I was sick of it. I could have cut it just to please you, and you only *like* it."

Dylan smiled. "I love it, Hope. *Très sexy.* I will run my fingers through it often. When you're not as angry. Or even if you are."

"Why were you late?" Hope asked, her lips quivering. "I didn't know where you were, and I was so worried that . . ."

Dylan grabbed her hands. "That I wouldn't show up? Hope Warren, I have *far* too much invested in you to *ever* walk away from you."

"So where have you been?" Hope asked.

"It's not easy to explain," Dylan said, smiling. "In fact, it's kind of funny."

"What's so funny?" Hope asked.

Dylan bit his lip. "Do you want your new hat now?"

"What?" Hope blinked. "What? You got me . . . a hat?"

Dylan winced. "Yeah." He pulled a green, yellow, red, and black tam from his coat pocket. "Kiki helped me pick it out for you."

Oh my goodness! He got me a tam to hold my dreads! It would have looked so good, too! She took the tam and tried not to smile. *This is so ridiculous.* "Do you really like my hair?"

"I will miss washing your locks, but it will be easier getting to your ears." He leaned in and kissed her lips. "Aren't we a pair? We're the new Magi."

She rested her head on his shoulder. "The what?"

"It's an old Christmas story I read as a kid," Dylan said. "It was called 'The Gift of the Magi.' I always thought it was a silly story, but now life is imitating art."

"Please explain," Hope said.

Dylan looked around. "Can we walk somewhere? We've been drawing a crowd."

Hope looked across at Staples, where several people stood and stared.

"I wasn't that loud, was I?" Hope asked.

"The acoustics against this wall are excellent," Dylan said.

I was loud. "Sure. Let's walk up Flatbush." *To your dream.*

They crossed Tilden.

"In the story," Dylan said, "a woman cut her hair to buy a silver watch chain for her husband, but he had sold his silver watch, a family heirloom, to buy her some special combs to put in her hair. They were the Magi. They gave sacrificial gifts to each other."

We are the Magi, and I haven't even given him his dream yet!

"I'm sorry Rainbow was closed," Dylan said. "We can come back after Christmas."

"That's okay." *There's our oak tree.* "Dylan, I have something to show you." She stopped him at the tree. "Look around."

Dylan looked around the tree. "What am I supposed to be looking for?"

I see the sign in the window perfectly from here. "And I used to be blind. Look!"

Dylan looked at the window and froze. "Is that . . ." His voice broke. He took a step. "Is this . . ." He took a few shaky steps to the window. "Hope." He turned to her with tears in his eyes. "Did you . . ."

Oh, these are good tears I'm crying today! She took the key from her pocket. "I would have put it in a little box."

"But . . ."

She put the key in his hand. "Take a look at your dream, Dylan Healy."

He closed his hand on it. "But what about your beach house?"

She pushed him toward the door. "I don't really need it. It was just a dream."

Dylan wiped his eyes.

He nodded.

He smiled.

Then Dylan Healy laughed so loudly that Hope shrank back and several people moving by walked faster. "Merry Christmas, Brooklyn!" he shouted.

The man has lost it! "Quick! Go inside!" *You're scaring the neighborhood!*

Dylan took the key and opened the door. "And it opened without a fight." He held the door for Hope. "I can't believe you did this."

Hope stepped inside. "Merry Christmas, Dylan."

He kissed her, locking the door behind them. He laughed again. *I hear an echo!*

He turned to his left. "I see another card shop lurking over there." He stomped on the floor. "Hardwood floors." He looked up. "Where's all that light coming from?" He grabbed Hope's hand. "Let's go look!"

They tore up the stairs, two stairs at a time, pausing briefly on the second floor. "Look at those windows!" Dylan shouted. "They'll catch the sunset every day!" He hugged Hope. "They used to be bricked up."

"I worked something out with Mr. Vacca," Hope said, "and, oh, there's a basement apartment."

"Yeah?" Dylan said. "Is it nice?"

"I don't know," Hope said, holding him tightly. "My lease is up at the end of this month and I intend to live there."

Dylan stepped back and laughed. "You do? So do I! What's it look like?"

"I don't know," Hope said. "This is my first visit, too."

Dylan blinked rapidly. "You leased this place without looking at it."

Hope nodded.

"You leased this place . . . blind?"

That's one way to look at it. "Yes."

Dylan hugged her. "I didn't get your eyes fixed to lease strange buildings blind."

"I saw it with my heart," Hope said. "My heart has never been blind." *Okay, once.*

Dylan nodded. "You're right about that, *cailín*. Let's go visit our apartment!"

Hope held his hands. "Does this mean we're moving in together?"

Dylan grinned. "Yes, it does."

They returned to the first floor and tried several doors—a washroom and two storage closets—before finding a set of stairs down to the basement. Dylan found a light switch.

Wow. It's huge, paneled, and spotless, with built-in shelves, thick carpet, and—

"Think all our stuff will fit?" Dylan asked. He opened a small washroom. "We may not fit in here. We'll have to use lots of soap to squeeze in." He walked into the kitchen. "This kitchen is fantastic!"

It's even bigger than mine is. This is . . . perfect.

"I know I shouldn't ask," Dylan said, "but . . . how much? No more than eleven a month, right?"

Hope ran her fingers over a bookshelf. *No dust.* "Nine a month, one year lease, all utilities paid."

Hope felt strong arms around her. "You made him practically *give* this space away," Dylan said, spinning her to face him. "So you put eighteen grand down?"

"No," Hope said. "I paid for five months plus the security deposit."

Dylan looked at the ceiling. "You put . . . Oh, Hope!" He laughed. "This is crazy! Have I said I love you today?"

Hope smiled. "No."

"I love you! Oh, listen to that echo."

"It won't echo for long," Hope said. "I got you your first student, Mr. Vacca's grandson Joey. He'll start as soon as we open in January."

"January is in a week!" He lifted her into the air. "You are amazing!" He set her down gently. "And I don't deserve you. I've completely lost my mind. What time is it? Oh, I don't have a watch."

He checked his phone. "It's almost five. We've got to go." He pulled her to the stairs.

"Go where?" Hope asked as they ascended.

"We have to go out to eat now," Dylan said.

Hope pulled him to a stop at the front entrance. "I thought we were having a quiet little dinner at your place, you know, snuggle all night, roast some chestnuts by the open fire."

Dylan shook his head. "I'm too hungry and excited to do that right now." He kissed her.

"We could go to The Islands," Hope said, "but we have to get there soon. They're closing early."

Dylan shook his head, opened the door, put his hand on Hope's sexy derriere, and gave her a firm push outside. "No time for that either. There's a new place I want to try." He turned and locked the door.

"What's the rush?" Hope asked.

"We'll need a cab," Dylan said. "Come on."

He took her hand and dragged her around Staples to a parking lot, stopping in front of an old cab. "Get in."

Hope looked at the cab. "Where's the driver?"

Dylan took a set of keys from his pocket. "I am. It's *our* cab. It's a seventy-four Checker Cab with the original yellow paint." He tapped his hand on the hood. "Yeah, the Checker decals and trim are missing, but it's ours."

The man has *lost his mind.* "We now own a cab."

"Yes," Dylan said. "Isn't she beautiful?"

"People will flag us down," Hope said, "and they'll flip us off when we don't stop."

"Got it cheap, too," Dylan said. "Runs great. Only ninety thousand brutally hard, Brooklyn miles on it."

He's not hearing me. "Dylan, why did you buy a cab?"

"And we'll paint it every color of the rainbow," Dylan said. "Yeah, and we'll paint 'Art for Kids' Sake' on it. People always look at the ads on cabs, right? It'll be a rolling advertisement wherever we go."

Hope shook his arms. "Dylan, *honey*, why did you buy this cab?"

"Oh. This is the same kind of cab I *took* when I was a kid. It's a reminder of how far I've come." He opened the door. "And look! It has bench seats so you can snuggle up to me while we drive. We'll never have to walk or take the subway or ride the bus again. So do you like it?"

Hope peered inside. *It looks . . . like a cab.* "It'll take some getting used to."

"Like your hair," Dylan said.

"It'll grow back," Hope said.

"And this cab will grow on you," Dylan said. "Look at those original vinyl seats!"

"Is it paid for?" Hope asked.

Dylan nodded.

No rent payments, no car payment, and it's not as if he'll ever have to drive to work. I can take it to work. Oh, I'll need a license first. "I like this cab very much. Where is this restaurant?"

"Kismet!" Dylan shouted.

"What? That little town on Fire Island?"

Dylan nodded. "Let's go! We have a water taxi waiting."

They sped east to Fire Island, their cab purring along on six cylinders and nearly bald tires, past a million Christmas lights, the traffic lights mostly green, and arrived in Bay Shore in less than an hour thanks to sparse traffic and Dylan's lead foot.

On the chilly water taxi ride, Hope and Dylan rode inside with the pilot.

"Are we going to the Kismet Inn?" Hope asked.

"The other one," Dylan said. "Surf's Out. I've already called ahead with our order. You see, Hope, I wanted to establish our own Christmas Eve tradition. We will always eat Christmas Eve dinner on a beach for as long as we live, okay?"

"I like it," Hope said.

"You only like it?" Dylan asked.

"I love it," Hope said, "and I love you."

They jumped off the boat and ran to Surf's Out, which was minutes from closing.

"Sorry we're so late," Dylan said. "I placed a carryout order. For Healy."

The cashier smiled. "I was beginning to think it was a prank."
She went into the kitchen and returned with five large bags and a
two-liter of Pepsi.

"What did you order?" Hope asked.

"Lobster egg rolls, fish and chips, that sort of thing," Dylan said
as he paid. "Oh, and a couple Grass Skirt sandwiches."

"What are they?" Hope whispered.

"I don't know," Dylan said. "They sounded good." He picked
up the bags. "Let's go."

"Where?" Hope asked, grabbing the Pepsi.

"To the beach," Dylan said. "We're going to have a picnic."

"It's freezing, Dylan," Hope said.

Dylan backed out the front door, holding it until Hope passed
him. "I'll keep you warm. Come on! Let's go look at the ocean. I
don't want to miss what's left of the sunset. That will have to be a
Christmas Eve tradition, too."

They trotted down East Lighthouse Walk toward the beach.

"We won't be able to see to eat much longer," Hope said, breathing hard.

Dylan cut up a sand dune. "Follow me."

Hope trudged up the dune. "Where are we going?" She reached
the top of the dune and saw a weather-beaten blue beach house.
"Hey, there's that lonely little cottage."

"And it has a deck with a picnic table on it," Dylan said. "It
doesn't look as if anyone's home. Come on."

Hope didn't move. "Dylan, what are you thinking? This is pri-
vate property."

"No one's here, Hope," Dylan said. "It's Christmas Eve. Who
goes to a beach house for a picnic on Christmas Eve? Besides us."

"It's called trespassing."

Dylan sighed. "They'll never know." He continued to the little
beach house, walking up onto the deck and setting the bags on the
picnic table.

Hope looked around. *This is how horror movies begin.*

"Come on," Dylan said. "You're missing this view."

Hope stepped onto the deck. *Springy thing.* She set down the
two-liter and slid carefully next to Dylan.

"Look," Dylan whispered.

Hope looked out over the dune at a gorgeous purple-orange sunset sinking into the dark water. "It's beautiful." *It's more than beautiful. It is beauty.*

Dylan handed her a sandwich. "I think this is the Grass Skirt. Smells like steak."

Hope took a bite. "Delicious."

Dylan pulled out a bag of fries. "I wonder how much it would cost to live here."

Hope nudged his leg with hers. "All our arms and legs."

Dylan looked back at the beach house. "I don't know. It's a shack, right? It's a fixer-upper. Paint's peeling. Siding droops here and there. Not very big, what, maybe two bedrooms? This deck is spongy, and that roof has seen better days."

Hope looked out over the water, smelling the salt and feeling her ears turn to ice. "Bet it still costs at least a million."

"At least it has lots of windows," Dylan said, opening the Pepsi. "No cups. We'll have to share." He took a long swig. "Oh, that window's boarded up. That one has a crack. The whole exterior could use some paint."

Hope nodded. "I'll bet it smells like mildew inside."

"And it doesn't even have a house sign," Dylan said. "I have noticed that people always name their beach houses. I'd name this one 'Fix Me.' "

Hope laughed. "That's a rotten name for a beach house."

"It fits," Dylan said. "I wouldn't pay more than . . . four hundred thousand for this fixer-upper."

"Right," Hope said. "Not for this view."

Dylan ripped a hunk out of his sandwich and wiped his lips. "Oh. Almost forgot." He pulled a small wrapped box from his coat pocket. "One more present."

Hope dropped her sandwich and gripped Dylan's leg fiercely. *Oh my God! This is why he brought me here! He's going to propose to me on a beach at sunset on Christmas Eve!* "Dylan, you didn't."

"I obviously did," Dylan said. "Open it."

Hope removed the paper and held a fuzzy black box from Tiffany jewelers. "Oh my goodness, Dylan." Her hands shook.

"Open it," Dylan said.

Hope opened it slowly and saw ... a beat-up, dingy brown key. *This isn't a ring! Where's the ring?* "Is this the spare key to the cab?"

"Oh yeah," Dylan said, munching more fries. "I need to get you one. I want to see you drive. I will enjoy giving you lessons, but no, that's not a car key."

"Well, what's it for?" *Oh no! This was his way of asking me to move in with him!* "Is this a spare key to your apartment? You were going to ask me to move in with you, weren't you, only now we'll be living—"

"Nope," Dylan interrupted.

Oh no! "Dylan, you didn't already lease another space, did you? And this is the key to—"

"Nope," Dylan interrupted again.

Hope stared at the key. "Dylan, what's this key to?"

Dylan turned to her and smiled. He pointed behind him. "*That* door."

No ... way ... What? "That ... door."

Dylan nodded. "*That* door. Go open it."

I can't feel my body, and these goose bumps aren't from the cold!

Legs loose as jelly, nose tingling, and with no feeling in her hands, Hope stood and nearly dropped the key as tears formed in her eyes.

"Open your door, Hope," Dylan said.

Tears flowed from her eyes. "I can't believe it ..."

Dylan stood. "Believe it."

She held out her hand. "Help me."

Dylan guided her to the door.

Hope slid the key into the lock and turned.

She heard a click.

This is my beach house.

This ... this is my dream.

She turned the knob and pushed the door away from her.

Dylan reached in and flipped several switches, instantly bathing the deck and interior in amber light.

"This is ours?" Hope asked.

"Yes," Dylan said, "*and* the bank's. Go in. I had a lot to do today to get everything ready for you. See all the sand outside? It was once *inside*. I will be sealing and resealing this house for years. Come on, Mrs. Claus. It's getting cold out here. Come into your house."

Hope stepped inside, shutting the door behind her and seeing another Christmas card tree on the back of the door. In a corner sat a small, undecorated Christmas tree, above her a sprig of mistletoe. The large windows forming the front of the house were all streaked green with salt.

"How many bedrooms?" Hope asked.

"Two bedrooms, one bath," Dylan said, "and the bathtub is huge, almost a two-seater."

She looked down at the threadbare blue indoor/outdoor carpet. "How did you . . . Dylan, what did you pay?"

Dylan laughed. "I already told you. Four hundred thousand. I put eighty grand down." He hugged her. "And I am flat broke! We will own it in about thirty years if we're extremely thrifty, and you *may* have to keep working there. At Thrifty. Until you're sixty. You're really nifty. Merry Christmas!"

Hope shivered. "It does have heat, doesn't it?"

"Not yet," Dylan said. "We'll have to use body heat tonight, but we'll get some space heaters to take the chill out of the air."

Hope drifted through the beach house, peeking in the washroom (*that tub is huge!*), checking out the kitchen, and going upstairs to look at two small bedrooms. "Dylan, why did you buy me this house?"

He held her close. "I liked your dream better than mine, and this dream will last us forever provided we fix it up."

Hope shook her head. "Your dream is much more practical than mine is."

Dylan pulled a board from a window, the remains of the sunset glowing into the room. "They're both practical, and necessary. One dream will pay for the other."

One dream will pay for the other. "Can we afford it?"

He removed another board. "Can we afford to have one dream pay for another? Of course!"

"No, I mean can we really afford this house."

"Sure," Dylan said. "The payment on this house is only sixteen hundred a month."

No way! "Really?"

Dylan nodded. "If you put twenty percent down, you get the best interest rates. For the price of rent in Brooklyn, you can afford a beach house fixer-upper on Fire Island. Now all we need to do is bring in eleven grand a month and we'll have two places to live."

Hope stood beside him watching the sunset. "And how are we going to do that?"

Dylan pulled her in front of him, nibbling on an ear. "I think I heard someone say that Odd Ducks was going to take off."

Hope sighed. "I was saying that to impress Mr. Yarmouth."

"You sold me," Dylan said. "We're already selling Valentine's Day cards, aren't we? That will pick up like crazy in January, and then there's St. Patrick's Day. Oh, the dill pickles we can draw. And then Easter. Think of all the people showing up for family pictures for *those* cards! All in their matching outfits. And we'll have another card shop at Art for Kids' Sake. Right there in the front window. That will give us two card shops like bookends on Flatbush Avenue. Won't that be—"

"Dylan, slow down," Hope interrupted. She grabbed his face.

"I can't, *cailín*," Dylan said. "There are so many possibilities!"

"Dylan, please," Hope said. "This is all so overwhelming. You know I don't want to go back to Thrifty, but we'll need all the money I can make until we get some children to instruct. How are we going to get fifty children in a week?"

"That was for the other building," Dylan said. "Twenty, heck, fifteen artists—and that's what we'll call them—fifteen artists ought to be enough, especially if you taught alongside me. I wouldn't have to pay you a salary, would I? I could just give you lots of bonuses."

"I really like those bonuses, too, but . . ." Hope sighed. "Aren't you worried?"

"Nope," Dylan said. "It's Christmas Eve, Hope, and we are about to live our dreams."

"I know that, but . . ."

"We will live in the basement apartment during the week and live here on the weekends," Dylan said.

"That sounds . . . I like that idea." *I love that idea.* "Okay, but what about . . ."

"When we're at the art center, we'll work on it," Dylan said. "When we're here, we'll work on this. Both places are works-in-progress, aren't they? Just as we are. We are a work-in-progress, and I am so glad we are progressing." He kissed her nose. "And whatever we do, whether here or in Brooklyn, we will do it together."

"I just don't see how we can—"

Dylan kissed her lips. "Shh, Hope. We'll figure it out. We've figured out so much already, haven't we?"

"Yes." She took his hands and held them to her face. "Yes, we have, but like you said, we're flat broke."

Dylan smiled. "Isn't it enough that we have each other? I have been wanting to say that to you for the *longest* time."

Hope shook her head. "That was my line."

"It's not a line, Hope," Dylan said. "It's a reality. You saved my dream, Hope, and I will forever love you for that, and I will spend the rest of my life trying to repay you."

"You saved my dream and my *life*, Dylan. I can never repay you." She kissed his chin. "But I'm going to try."

Dylan ran his fingers lightly over her hair. "So sexy." He smiled. "I guess there's only one more thing you need to do."

"Besides worry?" Hope said.

"No more worrying," Dylan said. "We're exactly where we're supposed to be."

"In a freezing-cold beach house on Christmas Eve?" Hope said.

"In each other's arms," Dylan said.

Hope nodded. "What do I have to do?"

"There's one more present hidden somewhere in this house," Dylan said, "and you'll have to find it."

"You could just give it to me," Hope said.

"And ruin the surprise? Never!" He rubbed her back. "Go find it."

Hope looked in both bedrooms.

"Very cold," Dylan said.

She went downstairs to the kitchen.

"Warmer," Dylan said.

She opened cupboards, the ancient refrigerator, and several drawers and found nothing but crystals of sand. "Is it outside? You didn't bury it in the sand, did you?"

Dylan shook his head.

"It's not on you, is it?" Hope asked.

"You'll get *that* present later. At least twice if you've been nice, and three times if you've been naughty."

"I have been so naughty," Hope whispered. She squinted at the tree. *That's where it is.* She walked toward it and looked among the branches, finding a bird's nest. She showed it to Dylan. "Look. A nest-warming gift."

"Boo," Dylan said. "But you are getting colder."

He isn't kidding. "Please tell me where it is."

"You walked right . . . under it."

What did I walk under? She looked above the front door. *That's something . . . golden up there in the mistletoe.* She pointed. "Is that it?"

Dylan nodded.

It was in the last place I looked.

Dylan pulled down the entire piece of mistletoe, holding it over Hope's head and kissing her. He slid the ring off a thin branch. "Let's go down to the shore. It's probably warmer down there anyway."

The sunset fading from purple to gray, heavy dark clouds floating just offshore, Dylan led Hope through a few dancing snowflakes to the water's edge.

It's snowing! It's snowing at the beach!

He knelt on the sand and looked up at her. "This may be the last time I ever ask you to do something."

Hope's heart pounded. "You can ask me to do anything."

"I don't think so," Dylan said, smiling. "You're going to be asking me for a new kitchen, roof, deck, appliances, furniture, driving lessons . . . I won't have time to ask you anything, so I better make this count. I love you, Hope. *Je t'aime.* And my knee is soaked because I am kneeling on wet sand, but I'm not moving. You have given me life again, and joy again, and peace again, and no matter how much you claimed to hate Christmas, you kept Christmas all along, and you sacrificed your dream for mine. I give you this gift, this eternal gift, because I want to spend an eternity of sunrises and sunsets with you. We love what we do, and love found us. *Vous marierez-vous avec moi?* Please marry me. I don't want to live another day without you."

I should be crying. Why am I not crying? I'm too happy to cry!
"Dylan, you're the only one I could *ever* marry. You saved my life, and I give it back to you. I love you."

Dylan slid on the ring, and it glowed brightly as stars poked through the gloom while larger snowflakes drifted down.

They stood at the shoreline, looking at their ocean, their stars, and their waves. Hope thought of a lifetime of mortgage, debt, leases, uncertain finances, one child . . . or eight or nine . . . maybe ten—and a lifetime of dreams, dreams that had come true and would continue to come true as long as the ocean rolled with this man by her side, this Island man, this gentle man who taught her to live again.

"Let's go inside and warm up," Dylan said. "I filled the closet with quilts."

Hope kissed him. "I'll be there in a minute."

Dylan squeezed her hand and nodded. "Take your time, *cailín.*"

As Dylan walked up the dune behind her, Hope took a deep breath and closed her eyes.
Are you still there?
Hope heard nothing but the waves kissing the shore.
That's what I thought.
Yuh vex meh nuh more, Depression. Yuh vex meh nuh more.

She opened her eyes and looked up, snowflakes landing and melting on her face. *Snowflakes dissolving on my face. This is the only way I am going to "cry" for the rest of my life.*

She climbed the dune, bounced across the deck, and opened her door. "Dylan, I know what we can name this place."

Dylan sat under several quilts in front of the tree. "What?"

"We're going to call his place Hope's Landing."
He held out his hand. "It is a good name."
She joined him and wormed under the quilt, feeling his warmth.
"Merry Christmas, Hope."
"Joyeux Noël, Dylan."
Bonjour, amour.